PRAISE FOR
THE CONNECTIONS SERIES

Torn

"I was riveted from the first line and couldn't put it down until the last word was read." —*New York Times* bestselling author A. L. Jackson

"After an edge-of-your-seat cliff-hanger, Kim Karr returns to beloved characters Dahlia and River. . . . Their passion is intense." —Fresh Fiction

"The story is fabulous, the characters are rich and full of emotion, and the romance, passion, and sexy are wonderfully balanced with the angst and heartbreak." —Bookish Temptations

Connected

"I was pulled in from the first word and felt every emotion . . . an incredibly emotional, romantic, sexy, and addictive read."
—Samantha Young, *New York Times* bestselling author of *Before Jamaica Lane*

"Emotional, unpredictable, and downright hot."
—K. A. Tucker, author of *Ten Tiny Breaths*

"This book had all my favorite things. Sweet, all-consuming romance, smart and real characters, and just enough of every emotion to keep me unable to put the book down. This was one of those holy-smokes kind of books!" —Shelly Crane, *New York Times* bestselling author of *Significance*

"It's been two weeks since I finished *Connected* and Dahlia and River are still in my head." —The 2 Bookaholics!! (5 stars)

"I am now in awe of Kim Karr." —Shh Mom's Reading

continued . . .

ALSO BY KIM KARR

The Connections Series

Connected

Dazed (digital novella)

TORN

The Connections Series

KIM KARR

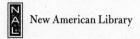 New American Library

NEW AMERICAN LIBRARY
Published by the Penguin Group
Penguin Group (USA) LLC, 375 Hudson Street,
New York, New York 10014

USA | Canada | UK | Ireland | Australia | New Zealand | India | South Africa | China
penguin.com
A Penguin Random House Company

Published by New American Library, a division of Penguin Group (USA) LLC. Previously
published in an InterMix edition.

First New American Library Printing, April 2014

NEW AMERICAN LIBRARY TRADE PAPERBACK ISBN: 978-0-451-46828-4

Printed in the United States of America
10 9 8 7 6 5 4 3 2 1

Set in Bulmer MT
Designed by Spring Hoteling

PUBLISHER'S NOTE
This is a work of fiction. Names, characters, places, and incidents either are the product of
the author's imagination or are used fictitiously, and any resemblance to actual persons, living or dead, business establishments, events, or locales is entirely coincidental.

For my daughter . . .
My hopes for you are that you grow up to be a
strong and independent woman
who finds her HEA

AUTHOR'S NOTE

Music means a great deal to me so I spent many hours searching for songs that reflect the content of this book. I hope that listening to these songs before you read each chapter will enhance your experience. Please visit my Web site at www.authorkimkarr.com for song links to Spotify.

Torn Playlist

Chapter 13

♪ My Darkest Days—"Come Undone"

Chapter 14

♪ Muse—"Madness"

♪ Breaking Benjamin—"Into the Nothing"

♪ Imagine Dragons—"Radioactive"

♪ Pitbull ft. Christina Aguilera—"Feel This Moment"

Chapter 15

♪ Gavin Rossdale—"Love Remains the Same"

Chapter 16

♪ The Fray—"Never Say Never"

♪ Adam Lambert—"For Your Entertainment"

♪ David Guetta—"Little Bad Girl"

♪ fun.—"Some Nights"

♪ Ke$ha—"TiK ToK"

Chapter 17

♪ Michelle Branch—"Everywhere"

Chapter 18

♪ Linkin Park—"What I've Done"

Chapter 19

♪ Sum 41—"Pieces"

♪ The Wanted—"I Found You"

Chapter 20

♪ Foo Fighters—"Everlong"

♪ Billy Joel—"Lullabye (Goodnight, My Angel)"

Chapter 21

♪ Lifehouse—"All In"

Chapter 22

♪ The Script—"Six Degrees of Separation"

Chapter 23

♪ Evanescence—"The Change"

Chapter 24

♪ Labrinth—"Beneath Your Beautiful"

♪ Zedd—"Clarity"

♪ Seether ft. Amy Lee—"Broken"

♪ Justin Timberlake—"Sexy Back"

Chapter 25

♪ Theory of a Deadman—"All or Nothing"

Chapter 26

♪ Keane—"Everybody's Changing"

♪ Elton John—"Believe," "Crocodile Rock," "Bennie and the Jets"

Chapter 27

♪ Kodaline—"All I Want"

Chapter 28

♪ Eric Clapton—"Tears in Heaven"

Chapter 29

♪ Matt Nathanson ft. Sugarland—"Run"

♪ Rihanna ft. Jay-Z—"Umbrella"

♪ Maroon 5—"Moves Like Jagger"

♪ Bon Jovi—"Wanted Dead or Alive"

♪ The Beatles—"Come Together"

♪ The Fray—"Never Say Never"

Chapter 30

♪ Lenny Kravitz—"I Belong to You"

TORN

PROLOGUE
Color-Blind

River

Close your eyes, and you can imagine what it was like. Hot, sticky, crowded. Smoke, flashing screens, and lighters flickering. Fans screaming, laughing, clapping, and crying. Bodies pushing, shoving, trying to catch a glimpse. Everyone wanting to see the stage—the lights, the equipment, the musician himself.

He was running back and forth singing, headbanging, and playing his guitar. The lyrics were jumbled, his movements out of sync. The sound of the bass thumped through the crowd so loud my body vibrated with every wrong note played. I just wanted it to end.

Nick Wilde was opening for the Counting Crows at the Holly-wood Bowl. It was his second chance—and he blew it. The crowd was exhilarated at the start of his first song, and he had owned the stage, but it didn't last long. By the third song he was improvising, pulling notes, and forgetting words. He was lost in his own trance, soaked in alcohol, and no one could help him . . . not Xander, not my mother, and definitely not me. The Counting Crows' "Mr. Jones" started playing before he even finished his fourth song. Nick Wilde never played onstage again.

Music was his soul; it was all of our souls. When we were younger he taught us everything he could . . . how to play, to sing, the right way to command a stage. We knew every song by every artist. We traveled to concert after concert. Music was his life, and it became ours.

But he wasn't happy just playing. He had a dream—he wanted to be famous. And somewhere along the way his dream became an obsession. I'll give it to him, he got further than most do. By the age of nineteen he had been signed by a label and cut his first album. But after disappointing sales numbers, the label released him. He spent the next fifteen years working the circuit—clubs, churches, weddings, birthday parties—as he waited for another big break. And then, just like that, he blew his golden opportunity.

Everything in our life changed after that. The drinking got worse, Grandpa came around more to check on us, and Mom went back to work. Every day left another kink in his chain as he lived in his own world. I was sixteen when his plan A became my plan B and, just like him, at a young age, I cut my first album. But unlike him I had Xander. He wasn't going to let me fail. The band's album had a slow start, but after a year of touring it started to gain popularity.

I remember the first time the Wilde Ones graced a real stage. We were restless. We had been sitting around for hours waiting. When we were finally up we strutted confidently across the stage like we had in rehearsal, but we were nervous as hell. The lights were much brighter and the audience so much bigger than we were used to. When the guys started to play, soft, barely audible words flew out of my mouth so fast I forgot to breathe. The band was drowning me out and I knew it. Looking around, I adjusted the microphone height and took in the crowd. They were cheering me on with such enthusiasm that my voice finally soared over them. It was the same voice I'd grown up with, the one my dad had fostered. It was raw and present and soulful, and, in that moment, my music came alive. The crowd went crazy, and just like that my life changed again.

Xander struck while the iron was hot. He arranged to go on tour. That was the beginning of the end for me. We started out small: tiny venues, shitty hotels, crappy food, and a lot of drinking. We opened for band after band, and the relationships I made kept me going—that and being up on that stage doing what I loved . . . It kept me going, wanting to make my dad proud—yeah, that, too.

But touring was a constant infringement on my personal space. I hated the cramped quarters, lack of privacy, constant strict schedule, never being in the same city for more than two nights, people following me everywhere, people always wanting something from me. Even the girls throwing themselves at us got old. It was the longest year of my life, but I did it for *him* because somewhere along the way his dream morphed into mine. What I came to realize was that his dream wasn't mine; his dream was about fame, while mine is about music.

As the venues got bigger so did the crowds, the fanfare, and I could see how you could get lost in it, caught up in it—but I was determined not to end up like my father. He was addicted to the fame. I'm addicted to the creative process. I hope that difference between us is enough.

The tour ended, and we wrote and played around LA. Life was good, but I had put off releasing another album long enough. This time I was doing it for the band and for my brother and for me—because I love the music. Cutting the album—that's the fun part. It's the promoting I dreaded, at least until the day I saw her through the glass. The girl who inspired our song "Once in a Lifetime," the girl Xander always referred to as my muse, the girl who stole my heart one night and then crushed it at the very same time.

She was as beautiful as I remembered and with one glance she took my breath away. She walked my way, pulling a suitcase behind her, and my heart skipped a beat. I knew immediately she was the one sent to interview me and suddenly any negativity I had about doing press was gone. I couldn't help but watch her. I wanted her unlike anyone I had ever wanted before. I had to stifle a laugh when her briefcase fell off the top of her suitcase and she glanced around to see who saw. I wanted to yell, "Only me and don't worry because everything about you is sexy as fuck."

I rushed to grab the door for her, but she pushed it forward and fell into me—not that I minded in the least. I'd catch her over and over. There wasn't a thing about her that I didn't remember from the first time we met and even the awkwardness of the moment brought me to full attention. When her body pressed against mine, I knew in that instant . . . *this* time I wasn't letting her get away so easily. I'd go on a thousand tours to have her in my life—there was just something about her, a light in her eyes that made everything wrong feel right. And just like my dad, I got a second chance—it was her. But unlike him, I wasn't going to blow it.

When she extended her hand and said, "Hello, I'm Dahlia London from Sound Music. I'm so sorry I'm late," I knew she had to be mine.

CHAPTER 1

A Thousand Years

A glimmer of light catches my eye through the partially open curtains across the room as I wake. It must be dawn because the sky is turning various shades of pink, red, and orange. Before I know it, the sky blazes with color; it's as if it's on fire—just like my body, but I push my pain aside. It's a glorious new day. And I'm here to share it with him. I look at the gorgeous lines of his body slumped over in the chair next to my hospital bed. He's asleep, but not very soundly. I study him, taking in his strong jaw, sculpted nose, and toned body. But it's his soul, his playfulness, and his amazing personality that made me fall in love with him. He's so much more than I could ever have asked for—he's my soul mate in every sense of the word.

Carefully removing my hand from his, I try hard not to wake him. Then I slowly ease myself up from the bed and make my way to the bathroom. When I return, the sun has fully risen and so has he. He's staring out the window with the curtains now completely open. I sweep him with my eyes so that I can appreciate every little thing—at just over six feet he's glorious. Strong shoulders, a lean waist, abs that seem to flex with his every movement. Arms crossed, his head cocked just so, his T-shirt tucked into his jeans haphazardly, and his stance so straight and sure. The soft bluish-gray sky of the early morning is almost as breathtaking as the sight of him.

Trying to see what he's looking at, I only notice the fluffy clouds drifting by. They appear so white against the morning sky; they make me start to smile. But I know that's not what he's seeing right now and when a bluejay flies by and he turns around I want to erase the pain I see in his sorrowful expression and sad green eyes.

I don't want to dwell on the events of yesterday's incident, but he seems to be preoccupied with it. His mood has been somber ever since it happened. He calls it an *attack*—I prefer *incident*. After all, I'm here alive and merely bruised. I'm not going to waste my time thinking about one bad day—I'd rather celebrate the good things in each new day. But he blames himself. I haven't been able to convince him that if anyone was to blame it's me. Then again, a random act of violence couldn't have been prevented and, thankfully, I'm all right. I just want to leave the hospital and go home.

Grabbing my clothes from the chair, I throw them on the bed. I'm standing in front of him on the cold linoleum floor in nothing but a hospital gown. I make a twirling motion with my finger impatiently. "Do you mind turning around?"

Sighing, he runs his hands through his already-messy hair. "I'm not turning around. I want to help you. Seeing what he did to you can't make me feel any worse. Believe me."

I swallow the lump in my throat and try to gather the right words to respond, and help put his mind at ease. "River, it was *not* your fault. Some perverted animal, looking to get his kicks by attacking women—that isn't your fault."

He can't hide his shudder from my eyes. "Dahlia, it wasn't a fucking *incident*. You were attacked. If I had been with you it wouldn't have happened. I shouldn't have been sleeping. It's really just that simple."

I stand there shocked by his tone, even though I know he doesn't mean to be so harsh. "No, it's not just that simple—" I start to argue, but he cuts me off.

"Dahlia!" His shoulders sag. He promptly diverts his eyes to the ground and shoves his hands in his jeans pockets. "I'm sorry, Dahlia. I don't mean to yell. I just can't stand that you got hurt. It kills me to see you like this, to know what could have happened to you. It just kills me."

We've had this conversation twice already. I know my reassurances will go nowhere. So I repeat myself and contemplate making my way to the duffel bag lying next to the chair to get my socks and shoes and then going into the bathroom to change. But I plead one more time, "River, please turn around."

He's standing in front of me with only the bed between us, but for some reason it feels like we're miles apart. He doesn't move toward me, but I can see the overwhelming emotion in his face and in his eyes. He's hurting. I can also hear it in his voice, and his sorrow not only makes me sad, it tears at my heart.

I've never been shy around him. I just know that I'm covered in bruises and I want so badly to spare him the heartache of seeing me this way.

"No, let me help you," he whispers. His tone is barely audible.

With a deep sigh I resign myself to his plea. Pointing near the chair I ask, "Can you please hand me that?"

Grabbing my bag, he sets it on the bed.

As I untie the ugly green gown and slide it down my arms, he watches me. But not in an *Oh, I want to see you naked* kind of way, more like an *Oh God, I might be sick* way.

The gown puddles on the floor and I stand there completely naked in front of him. I watch as he looks at me. He scans my body from head to toe before his eyes drift back up to meet mine and he swallows.

In an attempt to lighten the mood, I pick up the hospital gown and playfully toss it at him. "Your turn to play dress-up."

His lips finally turn up in a semblance of a smile, but his eyes are still filled with sadness. "I think I'll pass this time, if you don't mind," he says, holding the gown up to him. "Green isn't my color."

Both of us smiling, I know he's looking beyond my bruises. At last. And all his love for me is now reflected in his eyes—it means everything to me.

He strides around the bed and insists on helping me put on my panties and jeans. I want to comment on how easy it would be for him to get in my pants right now, but I refrain. But when he ever so carefully starts to pull my sweater over my head, I can't hold back. Grabbing his hand, I press it over my heart and look at him. "See, you can touch me. I won't break. I'll even let you get to second base," I say, sliding his hand down to cup my breast.

He resists at first, but eventually sighs and brushes his thumb over my nipple. A slow grin crosses his lips. "Second base, that's it? I think I had a better chance with the pants."

We both laugh a little and I continue to hold his hand in place. His eyes burn into mine as he moves his hand to cup my cheek. Leaning into my ear he whispers, "You better stop it. You're going to get me all worked up and when Nurse Smiley Face comes in here she's going to kick me out."

He pulls back and I roll my eyes as he tugs my sweater down the rest of the way. I silently wince a little in pain. My shoulder is sore, my wrist is sprained, and my body is bruised. The doctor wanted to cut off my bracelet, the only jewelry I was wearing, because of the swelling, but I begged him not to. It's the one thing of Ben's I have left and I need it to always remind me to live my life with no regrets.

Once I'm dressed, he gently places his arms around my waist and pulls me to him. "I'm sorry. Did I hurt you?"

"You could never hurt me," I respond in a low, comforting voice.

Leaning back, he crosses his finger over his heart. "I promise I will never let anything happen to you again." The ache in his voice cuts through me and I have to take a deep breath to prevent tears. I just want to throw my arms around his neck but my aching body won't let me, so I settle for circling my arms around his waist instead. He, in turn, slips his back around mine and we just hold each other. Then he kisses each of my eyelids and rests his forehead against mine. And with each passing second I can feel our love growing stronger, if that's even possible. We stay like this in silence until the nurse enters the room.

When she clears her throat, he whispers, "Nurse Smiley Face caught us again. I'm in trouble now."

I giggle and we pull apart. She's nice, but she didn't like that River stayed the night. And once last night when I asked him to lie next to me, she came in to check my vitals and made him get off the bed.

She takes my blood pressure one last time and goes over the discharge instructions left by the doctor—basically rest, no strenuous activities, and if I experience headaches of any kind I am to see my doctor immediately.

Once I've signed all the paperwork, the nurse calls for an orderly and when he arrives he wheels me to the door. River gets his car and we are finally allowed to leave the hospital. He decided earlier that we should spend the night in Tahoe and head home in the morning. On the way to the hotel, he looks over at me. "Did I tell you Xander and Caleb are here?"

I look at him questioningly. "No, you didn't. Why are they here?"

He laughs a little and says, "What do you mean 'why'? They're here to make sure you're okay."

"But we're going home tomorrow. They could have just checked on me then."

Shrugging his shoulders, he answers, "I know, but I want Xander to drive us back so I can sit with you."

"Oh, that's really sweet of you but not necessary. I'm fine."

"Well even if you're fine, it's not a short ride. I want you to be able to stretch out in a backseat. I want to be able to be close to you, to take care of you if you need anything."

I look at him lovingly; he really does always say the sweetest things. "Thank you. But why did Caleb come? Do your brother and Caleb even really know each other?" I have to ask because it wasn't so long ago that the tension between River and Caleb was palpable and I believed he didn't care for him. Now Xander was riding up to Lake Tahoe with him.

"Yeah, of course they know each other. They've met a few times, actually. And since I decided yesterday to hire Caleb to install additional security in our house, I thought it would be a good idea to discuss the upgrade with him before we get home. That way he can start on it as soon as possible."

"We don't need additional security at home because of what happened. River, I think that's a bit much."

"Dahlia, I never had the security system upgraded when I moved in, so I'm just taking a precautionary measure, that's all. You'll be coming back to LA alone during the tour, so I want to make sure you're safe."

Shaking my head, I throw in, "I didn't even think you liked Caleb."

"I never said I didn't like him."

"No, you didn't say it, but I felt it every time you talked to him."

"Hmm. Well, regardless of how I feel about him I know he's good at what he does—and when I called him he said he had time. Oh, and one more thing—Caleb or someone who works for him will be escorting us places."

I narrow my eyes at him. "You mean like bodyguards?"

"Well, I wouldn't call them bodyguards, just additional security."

"That sounds really awkward."

"Dahlia, I promise you won't even know they're around."

"I doubt that." I rest my head against the window and close my eyes. I find the whole amp-up-the-security thing a little absurd, but since it makes him feel better, I won't protest.

When we get to the hotel, we learn that Caleb had our room changed and that he and Xander now occupy the adjoining room next door. I want to tease River—"we won't even know they're around" —but I don't.

The doctor gave me some pain pills at the hospital and they've made me so tired that I spend the rest of the day in bed, snuggled in River's arms. I must have fallen into a deep sleep because when I wake, it's well after midnight. The first thing I do is reach for River, only to find that he isn't next to me. Looking around the room, I'm a little disoriented at first. But I see River huddled in the corner with Caleb and Xander, discussing something in hushed whispers that I can't hear. When he sees me try to sit up and move to get off the bed, he hastily rushes over.

"What do you need, baby?" he asks in almost a whisper. His face looks worn, tired, and worried.

"I need to go to the bathroom and get some water." I try to smile at him, but my mouth tastes like it has a wad of cotton balls in it and my body feels completely detached from my mind. I'm not sure I can actually walk to the bathroom without falling. I also feel light-headed.

"Let me help you," he says as he moves my legs to the floor and carefully helps me stand up. But when I start to wobble a little, I grab his shoulder for support. I think the pain medication has not only made me light-headed, but also unstable.

He's already wrapping my arm around him as he picks me up. "Dahlia, let me help you."

Xander and Caleb look over at me, appearing worried. They stand and both say good night, disappearing through the adjoining door.

Once we reach the bathroom, River gently sets me down and removes my pants. I grip the counter and begin to regain my stability.

"Can you grab me a T-shirt?" I ask him quietly.

"Sure, beautiful girl, whatever you need," he replies with a smile.

When he leaves the bathroom I push the door slightly closed and frown as I take the first real glimpse of myself in the mirror since the incident. I look much worse than I did earlier this morning. The bruises have turned purple, my wrist is still swollen, the scrapes on my cheek from where my attacker held my face to the ground are crusted over, and my shoulder aches from where he shoved his knee to hold me down.

I carefully pull off my sweater and hastily wrap a towel around me. I consider a shower, but decide against it. It seems like it would require too much energy right now. I do manage to brush my teeth. Once I finish, I look back into the mirror and see that he's standing behind me in the doorway with such sadness in his eyes. He walks over to me as I wipe my mouth with a towel.

"Let's put this on you," he says while pulling his long-sleeved 30 Seconds to Mars T-shirt over my head. "It will be easier to get on and off than one of yours, and it will keep you warm."

I let him dress me like I'm a small child. Happy memories of my father getting me ready for school pop into my head. My dad would help me get dressed and drop me off at school when my mother had to leave early for work. I loved those days. I loved every day my parents were alive.

"You all right, Dahlia?" he asks with concern.

"Yeah, yeah, I'm fine."

Then, smiling, I tell him, "You dressing me now just reminded me of happy times when my dad would let me pick out whatever I wanted to wear to school whether it matched or not. Since my mom wasn't home to make me change, I usually wore his concert T-shirts."

He smirks. "You mean your mom, the fashion designer, didn't like it when you wore your dad's grungy T-shirts to school?"

"How did you guess?"

"Intuition," he tells me. "Personally, I think you make everything you wear look incredible, but I could see where your mom might have a different opinion."

I lean into him just to feel his warmth and nuzzle his neck. "I wish you could have met my parents."

"I may never be able to meet them, but I know them through you."

Pulling away, I smile at him and press my palms against his chest. "That means everything to me," is all I can say, because it does.

He nods and we stay silent for a few moments.

"I think you should lie back down." Carrying me back to the bed, he sets me down on the opposite side from the one I woke up on. But I don't care which side I sleep on as long as he's next to me. I take his hand and squeeze it. "Thank you."

"You don't have to thank me," he says, kissing the top of my head. "I ordered you something to eat while you were in the bathroom."

"I'm not really hungry. I'm just really thirsty."

Pulling the covers up over my legs, he sits beside me. "You have to eat something when you take these pills." He opens the medicine bottle on the night table and pours two oblong, white, horse-sized pills into his palm then sets them down next to the open bottle.

"There's no way I can swallow those."

He laughs quickly and then stands up and walks toward the TV. "I ordered you grilled cheese and French fries to eat and a milkshake to swallow the pills with." He opens the adjoining room door and says, "Hey, Xander, just bring the food over here when it comes."

I'm staring at his backside when he turns his head over his shoulder and catches me. He throws me a wink and I smile back. We don't exchange words but we both start laughing. That is my all-time favorite sound. God, I love it when he laughs; it's soft but husky and oh so sexy.

I hold my bruised ribs in pain, and he apologizes for making me laugh.

"River, it's okay. I want to laugh. And, really, I just couldn't resist the view."

He stifles more laughter and I ask, "Why did you order food and have it delivered to Xander's room?" I pause a moment before adding, "And why are we sharing a room with Xander and Caleb anyway?"

His laughter stops and he becomes more serious. "We aren't sharing a room with them. The door closes between us, silly girl." As if to prove his point, he opens and closes the door in a swinging motion. Leaving it open, he walks back over to the bed and sits next to me. He cups my unbruised cheek before leaning in to kiss my forehead. "And I ordered food to be delivered to their room in case you fell back asleep. I didn't want the knocking to disturb you."

"Oh, that makes sense. Well now that you mentioned my favorite— grilled cheese dipped in a chocolate milkshake—I might be feeling a little hungry."

"Have I told you how gross I think that is, by the way?" he asks, raising his eyebrows.

"Only a thousand times, and yet every time I order it you manage to steal a bite. And don't think I haven't noticed you dip it in your shake first."

Chuckling, he pinches his thumb and index finger together and says, "Well, I might like it just a tiny little bit."

I smile at him and lay my head down on the pillow just as Xander brings in the tray of food. River points to the empty spot next to me on the bed. "Thanks, man, just put it down right there."

"Dahlia, do you want anything else?" Xander asks.

"Just a gallon of water," I say jokingly. "My mouth feels like a desert in the middle of July."

He grins at me and starts to pour the liter of bottled water into a glass as River takes my giant pills, along with a knife from the tray, and goes over to the table.

"I'll take the whole bottle, please. No need for a glass."

Xander hands me the water as River cuts the pills in half.

"Stop looking like you're going to someone's funeral, Xander. I'm fine. You and Caleb really didn't have to drop everything to come up here when we're just going home tomorrow anyway."

"Will it make you feel better if I tell you I came for my brother?"

I take a huge sip of water and eye him before giving him a full smile. "Since I know you'd never admit you came for me, then yes it will."

He kisses me on the forehead. "Good night, Muse. If you weren't such a pain in my ass I might find you funny. I might even like you." I don't mind him calling me Muse since he repeatedly tells me the Wilde Ones' claim to fame is the song "Once in a Lifetime," which River wrote after meeting me that first time.

"I'll keep hoping and wishing for the day you say you love me."

He looks at me with all trace of humor gone. "I'm really glad you're okay, Dahlia. Good night. See you in a few hours."

Glancing over at River, he gives him a nod before closing the door. Our plan is to leave in the middle of the night to get home early enough for Xander to get to work. River comes to sit next to me and once I swallow the disgusting horse pills we share the tray of food and then fall asleep in each other's arms.

Moonlight cascades through the windows and the stars shine bright above us as Xander drives us home. Lying on River's lap, I am listening intently to him. He's strumming his fingers through my hair and singing along to "Losing My Religion," but his voice sounds sad, reminiscent of something almost. When the song finishes I reach my hand up to caress his cheek. "I love that song. I saw R.E.M. perform it at the Greek the year it came out."

He takes my hand and kisses my knuckles. "I have a love/hate relationship with it myself."

Xander snickers from the front seat. "Yeah, more like it had a love/hate relationship with you."

Combing my fingers through his hair, I tug on a strand and he grins. "Why?" I ask.

He slouches a little more so I can rest my head on the tautness of his abs. His fingers tap my arm and he laughs. "When it hit the top five my dad decided I should learn to play the mandolin. He studied hit songs all the time, trying to dissect them for what drove them to the top. He took note of anything different used in its production, and 'Losing My Religion' was only the second hit song ever to feature a mandolin prominently."

Xander starts laughing so loud it surprises me. I don't think I've ever heard him laugh like that. River shakes his head. "Shut up, Xander."

River's eyes seem to dance in the moonlight at the memory and it thrills me to see him laugh when he mentions his father. He doesn't mention him often but on the rare occasion he does it's never with any sign of emotion. I'm glad he has happy memories of his dad, like I do. I have a sudden urge to kiss him and pull his head down closer to mine so I can press my lips against his. "Tell me," I whisper, tracing the outline of one of his perfectly defined pectorals.

"Don't laugh but you know the saying 'It's all in the wrist'?"

I nod.

"It's absolutely true. Subtle, nimble wrist movements are the key to playing the correct note on the mandolin, and no matter how many times I tried, I just couldn't get it down."

"Tell her the rest," Xander interjects.

River rolls his eyes. "Okay, so my dad knew I was getting frustrated and tried teaching me by using the only other hit song featuring a mandolin."

Xander laughs loudly again. "Man, I can still picture it," he manages between snorts.

I move to sit up but River reaches out to stop me and continues, ignoring Xander. "My dad was teaching me how to play 'Maggie May,' so I watched some of Rod Stewart's music videos and Xander walked in when I was practicing Rod's walk from the 'Hot Legs' video. I had decided to give up my attempts at the mandolin and decided I'd rather move like Rod."

All three of us burst out in a chorus of laughter and the vision in my head is priceless. God, sometimes it feels like my heart will burst with love for River. Everything about him drives me wild but especially his sense of humor.

His gaze captures mine and although we're having a conversation with his brother, we've somehow moved from playful touches to sensual caresses. His hand rests on my stomach and his fingers are under the hem of my shirt, resting on my bare skin. I'm drawing lines back and forth across each muscle of his washboard abs. The lower I get, the heavier he breathes. Leaning down, his soft lips meet mine and I wrap my arms around his neck and press harder. We get lost in each other for a moment and a small moan escapes my throat.

Xander clears his throat. "The windows are steaming up. Could you stop acting like a couple of teenagers?" Then he turns the radio up.

It's shortly before dawn when Xander drops us off at home. With coffees in hand we sit outside and watch the sunrise. I'm content to sit near him quietly and appreciate the company, but in the calm of the bright crisp morning River asks me, "Why are we waiting to get married?"

He kisses my hair and continues, "It seems like all I was really doing was waiting for you my whole life anyway, and I don't want to wait anymore."

I shift so I'm lying on my side and can look up at him. "I'm not really sure. But, when you put it that way, I don't want to wait, either."

"How would you feel if we charter a plane to Las Vegas and get married today? I can have it arranged in a matter of hours. We can fly up there, get married, and be back here by sunset."

"You don't mind if your family's not there?"

He hesitates only a moment before pulling me closer. His arms tighten around me as the green depths of his eyes stare into mine. "I won't be satisfied until I wake up next to my wife every morning. Dahlia, all I want is you and me forever. We can celebrate later once you're feeling better. We can even have another ceremony here, but what happened in the hospital I never want to happen again. So will you marry me today?"

He's romantic, fearless, and full of life, and I love every inch of him. I loop my arms around his neck and my lips find his. Smiling at him as the sun rises and with the Hollywood sign as our backdrop, I say, "River Wilde, I would love to marry you today."

He groans against my mouth and the sound echoes through my skin, making me smile even more. He kisses me. Then he kisses me again. Then some more. Once we're both breathless he moves me enough to stand up. His smile, the real one, breaks across his face. "Stay here. I'll be right back."

I have no intention of going anywhere, so he's safe. When he comes back he has Stella firmly in his clutch. Joy radiates from him and there's a familiar gleam in his eyes as he sits down at the end of the lounge chair with the guitar. The slight breeze in the air blows his hair. I move toward him and rest my chin on his shoulder, my front to his back. His hot skin awakens all my senses.

I peer down and watch as his hand dances over the strings and he starts singing "You and Me." As he plays I can feel every motion of his body as if I'm the one playing. Curling my hand around his hip I feel him shudder as heat travels through my arm. My eyes shift to his face and it's a picture of what is real, what is right in my life, and what we have . . . true love everlasting.

He sings the final verse, "The clock never seemed so alive," into my ear and I shiver as his warm breath grazes the skin of my neck. I could watch him play and listen to him sing a thousand times over and never grow tired of it. Not ever. He cocks his head to mine and picks the last notes on his strings as the sound of his music fills the air. I can't help but think how lucky I am to get to spend the rest of my life with him.

A few hours later I'm sitting at the breakfast bar, having just finished up a security system lesson with Caleb, when the doorbell rings. I know who it is before River answers it. Aerie screams, "There you are! How are you?"

It's only been sixty minutes since I called to tell her we were home and she's already here. She runs over as I stand up slowly. My body aches much more today than it has since the incident, probably from sitting in the car on the ride home. "I'm okay—really! I look much worse than I actually feel."

"I'm so sorry I didn't come to see you in the hospital. Work has been crazy," she says before throwing her arms around me in a tight embrace. I wince a little and she pulls away. "Oh my God, I'm so sorry! I didn't mean to hurt you!" Her face is full of concern—this woman who has helped me in more ways than I could ever count. Of course she's here now. And she's a vision of perfection in her red shift dress and black high heels, with a matching headband.

"I'm fine," I lie so she doesn't feel bad. I've talked to her on the phone so many times since I was hospitalized I think she knows more about the incident than River does.

"What's going on at work?"

Rolling her eyes she says, "The owner's son decided he wants to be more invol—" But before she can finish, she's giving me a speculative glance. "Why are you dressed like that?"

"Dressed like what?" I coyly ask, trying to keep my smile from exploding.

"You're wearing a dress! In fact, you're dressed like you're going somewhere when you should be in sweats and lying in bed. You even have heels on. You never wear heels unless I make you."

I glance over my shoulder to see River standing in the kitchen with Caleb. He nods his head. I'm so excited I just blurt it out, "We're leaving this afternoon for Las Vegas to get married!"

She claps and jumps up and down with excitement, then suddenly stops. "Wait a minute! You are not eloping, Dahlia London. You can't. I want to see you get married." She hugs me tightly again before pulling away. "Sorry, sorry," she says, wiping the tears from her cheeks and trying to gain her composure.

I start to feel a little guilty, but rapidly try to push those feelings aside. "We'll have a party after the band's tour and all of us can celebrate then, okay?"

River comes around the counter and hugs Aerie before whispering something in her ear. Pulling me into his side, he says, "We'll celebrate later, but we want to get married now."

"Is it safe for you to travel?" Aerie says with concern.

Nodding my head, I try to convince her not to worry. "Really, Aerie, I feel fine. I promise."

River kisses my hair softly. "Coffee?" he asks Aerie.

"No, you know I don't drink that stuff. It's pure octane and tastes like it, too."

Laughing, he walks back into the kitchen, mumbling, "I don't know how anyone survives without caffeine."

River's phone rings and I hear him say, "Xander, I told you I'm

not meeting her today or tomorrow. I don't give a shit what she wants."
I give River a concerned glance and he nods at me, flashing me what I
know to be his make-believe smile. Once he ends the call, he turns to
me. "Dahlia, I have a few things to take care of. Will you be okay?"

Aerie shoos him away. "She'll be fine," she says and pulls me over
to the sofa.

River comes over and kisses me again. "You sure?"

"I'm fine. Go already," I tell him, kissing him back.

"Okay. Caleb is in the music room if you need anything. He set up
his computer in there for now. I won't be long."

Aerie and I talk for a while. Once she feels she has wrung every
ounce of information from me, she stands and says, "I'll be back in an
hour. Don't leave until I get back. I mean it!"

"Where are you going?" I glance at the clock.

"It's a surprise. Wait for me. Please?"

"Okay, you have an hour, that's it."

She waves at me as she rushes out the door.

With minutes to spare she returns, holding a gray suit bag in one
hand and a shopping bag in the other. She leads me to my bedroom.

"Every princess has to have a wedding dress to get married in,"
she says as she unzips the bag and pulls out the most beautiful white
silk dress. It's simple, yet elegant. It's a sleeveless cocktail-length dress
with a deep V-neck and an A-line skirt adorned with tiny pearls.
There's also gorgeous, yet subtly patterned silk embroidery on the
bodice, making it special enough for the occasion but not overwhelm-
ingly fancy. It's perfect.

She sits me on the bed and pulls out a simple pair of silver high
heels and slips them on my feet. "Just like Cinderella, Dahlia, you got
your Prince Charming," she says as a tear slides down her cheek. She
pulls one more item out of the bag for me. I look at the beautiful white
band of fabric with small blue jewels all around it as I take it out of the
box. "The dress is your something new—here is your something

blue." It's a garter, and as she takes it from my hand, she slips it on my leg and up to my thigh; I laugh at her need to make sure I follow the typical bridal wedding traditions.

Once she has powdered and primped me, covering my bruises as best she can with makeup, she stands up and removes the pearl earrings from her ears. "And these are your something borrowed." They are her great-grandmother's pearl earrings, the ones I've always loved. I remove my earrings and insert hers, then stand to look in the mirror. Now I really look like a bride. I throw my arms around her despite the pain shooting through me. "I love you, Aerie Daniels, forever and always. Thank you so much!"

"You don't have to thank me. I can't have my best friend getting married in just anything. And to be honest I was afraid you might end up in your Converse sneakers." I puff out a laugh and grab my camera. I hold it out in front of us and snap a picture. She's been my best friend for so long; I want to remember this time with her forever.

Aerie and I say our goodbyes—she has to get back to work—and I find myself alone, thinking about how drastically my life has changed over the past year. When I catch sight of my Grammy's pearls hanging on the mirror, I walk over to the dresser and pull down my something old. As I slip them around my neck, I have an odd déjà vu feeling. Today I'm going to marry the man who turned my life around, the man who taught me to love again. I thought Ben was my once-in-a-lifetime, but who knew a once-in-a-lifetime love could happen twice?

I feel so incredibly happy, but a sudden sadness washes through me for those I've lost and I shift my eyes to the ceiling to say a silent prayer for each of them. I tell my mother and father I wish they could be here with me today. I thank my uncle for looking after me and keeping me on the right path. I think of my aunt and her mother and how they taught me that life is full of magic. Then I whisper to Ben, the man I intended to marry who was taken too soon, that I will always love him and he will forever hold a special place in my heart as my first true love. I finish looking in the mirror and take a deep breath. I'm ready.

The battery in my cell phone is almost dead, and I hope I have time to charge it. I walk into the empty living room and head over to the kitchen to get my charger. Once I've plugged it in, I turn around and see his gorgeous silhouette framed in the doorway. He walks toward me, looking irresistible.

All I can do is stare at him, because today I get to marry this man. River's mouth slowly curves into a smile. "You look amazing."

I return his smile and walk toward him. We meet in the middle and he gathers me close, whispering in my ear, "Come on, beautiful, you don't need your cell today."

We break apart, both of us ready to take the next step. His phone rings and he pulls it from his pocket. I glance at the screen and see it's his brother. He ignores it. I'm looking up at him while I ask, "Hey, what's going on with Xander? What was with him on the phone earlier?"

He looks back at me and shakes his head. "You know Xander. He always wants what he wants *now*."

"And he wants what right now?"

"He wants me to meet with Ellie."

"Who's Ellie?"

"She's his contact for the label. Nothing to worry about now, though."

He places soft kisses on my forehead. He pulls back and gazes into my eyes with a look of adoration that I love. "Are you ready to become my wife?"

My legs start to quiver as I pull back to look at his handsome face. "Only if you promise to love me forever."

He cups my cheeks and says, "Beautiful, I made that promise to myself the first time I kissed you. I promised to love you always. How could I not?"

My tears spill over at his heartfelt words. I love him so much. He's hugging me, not too tightly, but enough that I feel his love and I know he will always be mine. He kisses me again and says, "The instant you become Mrs. River Wilde I'm going to show you just how much."

He grabs my hand and we head toward the door. "Amazing Grace" starts playing from my phone in the kitchen just as we're about to leave, and I turn back. "River, let me quickly grab that. I don't want Grace to worry about me any more than she already has."

I drop his hand and walk to the kitchen counter to answer my phone. "Hello?"

CHAPTER 2
Home

Ben's Journal

I'm finally home and out of that conference room. I never expected to be back so I can't say it's been a long road, but I can say I'm sure as shit glad to be here. I can't believe I'm in Laguna, the place that I love, with all the people I love.

The suits reassured me before leaving the office on Wilshire Boulevard that my reappearance wouldn't be made public until the trial. So I won't have to deal with all the questions right now, except from my family and my girl. Seeing my mother was way more emotional than I expected. When one of the suits came in and told me she was talking to Special Agent Bass in the waiting room I tried not to lose my shit as I tore out of the room. I wanted to be there when they told her. I knew it would be a shock that I was really alive. That I wasn't actually gunned down that night almost three years ago on my way to an awards ceremony while my girl watched it all go down from the car.

I ran through the hall and past the round gold seal of the Federal Bureau of Investigation, the framed picture of the President, and the various most-wanted posters. The special agent talking to my mother was a woman, and they were sitting in the corner of the room. Mom was crying so I knew she had been told and her tears made me instantly regret ever agreeing to leave. Her face was an emotional wreck and my remorse for the choice I made to leave, to not stay and turn this over to the FBI, weighed heavier than it ever had on my mind. But Caleb had taken things into his own hands and contacted them shortly after I left. So even though I hadn't known it, they had been involved for some time.

When she looked up her mouth fell open, and I could see she was shaky, unsure. She stood up and I walked over to her to assure her I was real. When I was standing in front of her, she blinked and then sighed before throwing her arms around me. I was overwhelmed. I hugged her for the longest time. She was always my biggest supporter. To her I could do no wrong—I was her golden boy, the son that looked just like his father, the man she had also loved unconditionally. When I pulled back I kept my voice soft and answered as many of her questions as I could.

Our brief but emotional reunion was interrupted when the suit ushered us forward. We were escorted back down the drab hallway and into the same conference room I had sat in for hours, but this time they left us alone. Looking at me, my mother broke down and I broke down along with her. I had missed her. She, like Dahl, was always there for me, always believed in me, and always loved me, no matter what. When she was finally able to compose herself enough to hear where I'd been for the past three years, I explained everything to her, including the events that brought me back home.

I tried not to give her too many details—just enough so she

could understand, but not too many that she'd grow more concerned.

Once we got home, she called Serena and Trent and they came right over. Serena was actually pissed at me at first—she yelled and screamed and then finally cried. Trent, on the other hand, wasn't just happy; it was more like he was relieved. He looked jittery, and I thought he might be on something. My mom looked really upset when I asked about it, and I felt like she knew more than she was telling me. But all she said was that Serena was going through some stuff with him and had been having a hard time getting him to listen to her. We spent the rest of the day just talking, and she told me how much she missed me.

I thought seeing Dahl would be the most important thing but after talking to Mom I knew right then that she needed me more. It wasn't until later in the day that I got a chance to call Dahl, but Mom insisted we wait until tomorrow and that she be the one to do it. I really didn't want to push, so I didn't argue. She already seemed so stressed.

But I did ask her if Dahl was seeing anyone. She was hesitant to tell me anything at first, but she said there was a guy and Dahl had been seeing him for a while. I guess I can assume he's the same guy Caleb told me about. It's not that I didn't want her to move on—I never thought I'd be back. But I just never thought I'd have to see it.

I also asked if Dahl had dated many guys and she told me no, just the one. I had hoped there were more because that would make her more like me. She would have been doing what I had been doing—trying to find a substitute for her. When I first got to New York I was lost. I had no one. For months I didn't go out or talk to anyone. Then after a while I tried to date someone, but everything we did just brought me back to the life I left, the life I missed, and it wasn't fair to that girl.

I started teaching that fall, but it didn't help me forget Dahl. That Halloween I knew she needed me and I wasn't there. I went out and got shitfaced and fucked a girl that looked like her. That started me down a road I can't even remember. Work, eat, drink, fuck. I never thought I'd see her again, so I fucked just about every tall blonde I ran into. And New York was loaded with them. But I never stuck around . . . they weren't her, and I didn't want to get that close.

Over time I stopped trying to replace her because no matter how much I wanted it, there was no substitute for her. As time went on it didn't matter if the girl I fucked was tall, short, blond, or brunette—they were just there to fill a need. My need to have Dahl in my life never went away, but I met Kimberly shortly after Caleb told me he had seen Dahl with some guy in the Hills. For some reason, although I hated that she had moved on, it brought me closure and I stopped fucking around. Kimberly and I started dating and after a few months, I found a happy medium. I was able to have a relationship and function almost like I used to. I didn't screw around on her. I liked her enough. So yeah, maybe she looked a lot like Dahlia, but she didn't act like her. She never called me on my shit and never put me in my place. We had a good sex life and a decent time together. She wasn't needy and didn't pressure me for more than I was willing to give. We had a good thing going.

Hopefully Dahl's commitment to this guy is like my commitment to Kimberly—committed until something else came around. I was committed to Kimberly until I was told I could go back. I did call her and tell her I had an emergency back home and I'd be in touch soon. She didn't know anything about where home was . . . I was always vague. She knew I was from California and she knew me as "Alex." I didn't want to explain anything different. So I haven't talked to her since I left. I am going to call her—I owe her that. I just haven't figured out what I am going to say.

I remember the hardest part of thinking about Dahl moving on was accepting that at one time I was the only one Dahl had ever been with. I had thought I would not only be her first, but also her last. Now I've lost that. And thinking back I wonder why I didn't try harder to make our life together perfect. Is that why she has stayed with that new guy? It drives me crazy trying to figure out what she could see in him. There has to be something because of all the things that have happened in the last three days. What my mom told me about Dahl shocked the shit out of me most of all—she told me Dahl's engaged. As if knowing someone else has touched her isn't bad enough, hearing she's going to marry another guy has torn my heart apart.

CHAPTER 3
Here and Now

We head to Grace's house once I've changed into one of River's shirts, a pair of jeans, and my Converses. I'm worried about what made Grace call and say she wants to talk to me in person. I hope she's all right. She sounded like she had been crying when I spoke to her and the sense of urgency in her voice was clear.

My unease must be evident because River looks over and gives me a concerned look as he squeezes my hand tight. Then he gives me what I know is his fake smile, hoping to reassure me. I want to ask him what he thinks she wants to talk about but I'm afraid of what he will say. What if Grace or Serena or Trent isn't well? My throat tightens and I pick up the bottle of water I brought with me, slowly twisting the cap and taking a big gulp.

His phone sits in the pseudo-ashtray, charging, and I jump when it rings. "Charlotte Tyler" flashes across the screen. As I reach to grab it, he covers my hand. "Let's not answer my mom's calls right now. I think Xander suspected something when I talked to him earlier. He probably mentioned it to Mom and now she's calling to find out what's going on."

I nod my head as the phone stops ringing; he picks it up and holds down the top button, turning it off. I turn the radio on and stare out the window, but when Gavin DeGraw's "In Love with a Girl" comes on, I quickly reach to turn it off. I can't listen to that song. It always reminds me of the last time I saw Ben.

I've never been so grateful to see the stone driveway leading to Grace's beach house as I am right this minute. As soon as the car is parked, River brings my hand to his mouth and kisses it before turning the ignition off. I can't take my eyes off him, and I know I'm probably squeezing his hand too tight. "I'm sorry we had to postpone leaving for Las Vegas, but Grace sounded like she really needs me."

He returns my quick smile. "Beautiful girl, we are going to be together for the rest of our lives. Another few hours or another few days doesn't change anything. Let's see what Grace wants. And who knows, we might still make it to the airport later tonight."

He opens my door for me and we walk down the path to the front porch. Looking behind me, I catch sight of Caleb parking in the large U-shaped driveway. It's a little ridiculous that he followed us all the way here, but now is not the time to discuss it. I also see Serena's car in the driveway near the garage, and my concern turns to full-out worry. I take a deep calming breath as I open the front door. "Grace? We're here. Sorry it took so long, there was a lot of traffic," I call out as I lead River into the house I've always considered a home.

The large family room is dimly lit, and Grace stands on the other side in the kitchen doorway. I look around but don't see Serena or Trent anywhere. I notice the room seems to be in a bit of disarray. Shopping bags on the floor, a duffel bag thrown at the bottom of the stairs, and a stack of newspapers on the desk. Seeing us, she swiftly turns and walks back in the room. She wipes tears away as she approaches and I know for sure something is terribly wrong. The feeling grows when she pulls me in for a long embrace. "Dahlia," she sobs as she hugs me for what seems like hours. When she steps back she cups both my cheeks. "Oh, my darling girl, I'm just not sure how to do this." She drops her hands and gives River an odd look, quickly hugging him as well.

Serena enters the room with a tray holding a pot of coffee and mugs. She sets it down on the table and says, "Dahlia, River, you're here." Then she furrows her brow at Grace and says, "Mom, come on and sit down. Give Dahlia some room to breathe." I can tell Serena has been crying, too, and my worry becomes full-out panic. I turn to River for reassurance and he grabs my hand and follows Grace, leading me to the large overstuffed sofa in the middle of the room.

I sit down next to Grace with River on the other side of me. "Grace, what's the matter? You're freaking me out."

Tears are streaming down her face and they're soon mimicked by my own. I look to Serena for comfort, but she, too, is crying. "What's going on?" My heart has started pounding quicker and quicker with every passing second. When no one answers, I squeeze River's hand so tightly it actually pulses in mine.

Finally, Serena clears her throat and speaks. "Dahlia, River, we have something to tell you. I know it's going to be a . . ." I try to listen but can't help but tune her out as I see a shadow walking toward us from the kitchen. When I look up I see an image of Ben. I gasp and my stomach clenches. Am I dreaming? This can't be real. He's dead. I know he is. What's wrong with me? I clench River's hand even harder and start to worry that maybe I'm suffering from a head injury. I close my eyes, hoping my hallucination will be gone when I reopen them, but it's not. I am so confused. I'm also really scared.

He stops moving and stands on the other side of the table. I hear voices, but no words. I hear River's voice. I hear Ben's voice. I hear someone crying. Wait—this can't be Ben. I remember crying when he died. I remember sitting in the pew between Grace and Serena, gripping both their hands while listening to Father John recite the Final Commendation and Farewell. Grace leaned against me and I leaned against Serena. I remember the tears they cried, the tears I cried. They were all cried for him—because he was dead.

I remember the painful final chorus of amens before the pallbearers loaded his ivory casket into the hearse that brought him to his final resting place. I remember saying goodbye to him as they lowered him into the ground. I said goodbye a million times after that.

Yet for some reason, despite knowing that he's gone, I can still see him. He's standing in front of me. I stare at the figure that looks so much like Ben. No, not just looks like Ben—it is Ben. I see a face that's completely unreadable to me. Eyes that are as blue as I remember them. Hair that's shorter than I remember, but still wavy and dirty blond. Clothes that look like his—lightweight hoody and cargo shorts. Soft tears are falling down his cheeks. This figure looks the same as Ben, but somehow different at the same time. Older, maybe? Still beautiful, though. Still Ben in every way. He sniffs a little, which makes the figure seem even more real, and I have to go see for myself that it isn't. I stand up, drop River's hand and slowly, cautiously, walk toward it. My fists clench, my heart pounds, and fear wrenches through my entire body. I feel the prickle of stares from everyone in the room. I know River is talking to me but I'm not listening. I have to figure out what this is that I see.

I'm barely breathing, nervous and petrified as I study his shape. I approach his image with uncertainty. And as I stand in front of him, I can't help but think, *this really* is *him*. I cautiously cup his cheek with my hand. His skin is smoother than I remember, and it feels so real. His hands trap mine and his eyes search me, search through me, looking for something I'm not sure he can find.

When I don't respond, he drops his hands. His body trembles as he fingers the pearls around my neck. He pulls me to him. "Dahl, I've missed you so much."

Struggling to break free of his hold, I feel like I'm suffocating. All the air has left my lungs and my head spins. Why am I dreaming about Ben in the middle of the day? I've put Ben to rest. Why does his touch feel so real? Why does his voice reverberate through me in such a familiar way? This makes no sense. The room seems to disappear.

"Benjamin," Grace says softly, "I think we should all sit down and explain what's going on. This has to be an enormous shock to Dahlia."

With widened eyes I snap my attention over to her and point my finger. "Did you say 'Ben'? Do you see him, too?"

"Dahlia, please come sit down," she says in the same calm, soothing tone she always uses when she knows I'm on the verge of hysteria. Her hands are on my shoulders as she attempts to turn me back to face her. River approaches me with a blank stare, complete shock evident on his face. I turn back to the figure I thought was just a figment of my imagination.

When he says, "Dahl, it's me. It's really me. I wasn't really shot. I didn't actually die. I did it for you. I did it all for you," I have to blink over and over to focus my eyes and try to hear what he's saying.

As I process the words, I begin to think I might be in some alternate universe. My body trembles and my knees are weak as I look at him and scream, "Did what? Oh my God! You did what for me? Who the hell are you?"

River's arms are instantly at my side, trying to pull me away, but I am frozen in this spot. I can't move. I am entranced by this man who looks so much like my Ben. Then I look into this man's forget-me-not blue eyes and suddenly I know he's real, this is my Ben. I can see him; the boy I grew up with, the guy I knew so well. The man I was going to marry.

River yells, Grace cries, and Serena whispers, but I don't hear their words as I continue to stare at the man I spent most of my life with, the man I believed was dead. His eyes are still glued to mine.

Tears stream down his face and I know my tears are now out of control. "Dahl, do you understand what I'm saying? Do you hear me?"

I don't let him finish; instead my fists pound into his chest with the force of my whole body. "What the hell are you talking about? You're dead! I saw you die!" His face collapses and my lungs seem to stop expanding.

River practically sprints forward, pulling me away. Ben's hands are at my waist, grabbing for me. My legs aren't there to support me any longer. The room starts spinning and I lose all sense of what is real. As I feel myself start to fall, I reach for River but his strong arms are already clutching me tightly. I see shapes but no faces. I hear yelling, screaming.

"Nothing has changed. She belongs with me."

"She belongs with me!" River yells, and his voice sounds like it could cut through steel.

"Fuck you," Ben responds.

And I don't hear anything else as everything around me goes black . . . until the fresh air outside hits my senses and I begin to regain consciousness. River cradles me in his arms on the way to the car. Grace is behind him. She's pleading with him to stay and bring me to her room. I don't hear his answer. He sets me in the front seat and I'm at least able to sit up. Leaning into the car he asks if I'm okay, but I can't even nod my head. He whispers in my ear that he just wants to get me home.

At the edge of my vision I see Caleb getting out of his car and taking in the scene. River hurries across the car to the driver's side. At the front door of the house, Serena is grabbing Ben's arm as he moves toward us, screaming at River. My throat tightens with an unfamiliar feeling. River's yelling as he storms toward Ben, but Caleb gets to Ben first and pushes him toward the house. Needing some air, I roll down the window and hear Ben yell, "You filled a void when I wasn't here, but you're no substitute for the real thing." Not wanting to hear his voice anymore, I close the window.

When I see Ben lunge for River, I'm relieved that Caleb stops him as River heads back to the car. As the door opens I hear Ben yelling, "Dahl, don't leave!" My trembling intensifies at hearing his voice again and the tears are flowing from my eyes like a heavy rainstorm. I try to blink back the confusion.

The door slamming startles me from my emotional turmoil. He's angry. His body is tense and he pounds his hands against the steering wheel. "Fuck, fuck, fuck." The sound echoes between us. Keeping his head bowed for a few seconds, he looks up at the ceiling before looking at me. "Are you okay?" His tone fails in its attempt at normalcy.

Nodding is all I can do. My limbs are limp and a broken sound escapes my lips. Studying me, he reaches over and moves the strand of hair that has fallen into my face away from my eyes. Pulling my chin up, he wipes my tears away but says nothing, and neither do I. I don't even know what I would say . . . I don't even know how I feel, other than that I might explode—cry, scream, might even laugh.

I can't imagine how he feels right now. I hear the rhythm of his breathing and feel his hands trembling. The tips of fingers on my face are warm and loving, and I lean into them.

My eyes are focused on him and I jump when there's a rap on my window. It's Grace checking on me. River lowers the window, but I keep my eyes on him. Her words fade in and out as I focus on his face—the one constant in my life right now. Telling her he'll call her in the morning, he closes the window even though she's still talking. No more words are spoken as he starts the car. When the car accelerates with a quick jerk, I rest my head against the glass window and allow myself to fade back into unconsciousness.

When I wake up groggy at home on the sofa, River says in the most somber tone I've ever heard him use, "Let me get you some water." He stops to turn the gas fireplace on and then heads for the kitchen. From where I'm sitting, I can see him standing at the sink. He puts both palms over his eyes and holds them there for a short while. Then he fills a glass with water and gulps it down before refilling it and bringing it to me. I rub the glass against my forehead, but it's not cold enough to numb the turmoil swelling in my soul. I watch him as he sits next to me on the couch. He takes my ringing phone from his pocket and turns it off. Then he takes out his own phone, turns it on, and moves his finger around on the screen before speaking to me.

The pain of my sore body is a welcome distraction from the pain of seeing Ben alive. I wish it would overcome me and mask the emotion I'm not sure I should be feeling. *Is Ben really alive? How? Why?* I have so many questions, but I'm not sure I'm prepared to learn the answers.

"Do you want to talk about it?" he says calmly. Almost too calmly . . . he sounds detached, like he's talking but not listening to his own words.

"No! No, I don't. Not now! And stop talking to me that way."

He flinches. "I'm not talking to you in any way."

"River, I'm sorry. I'm just so confused right now."

My tears turn into near-hysterics and he pulls me to him. "You don't have to apologize. I'm here to talk whenever you're ready." Then he kisses my head and just holds me.

After what seems like hours, my crying wanes. I'm drained, depleted of all emotion. I don't even have enough energy to cry anymore; I don't have any more tears left to shed. Looking up into his conflicted face, I know it's a reflection of my own. "I love you. This doesn't change anything," I whisper, feeling strongly that he needs to know this.

"It changes everything, Dahlia."

I can tell he's trying to keep his voice neutral but contempt flares at the edges of his words. His tone is despondent, disconnected, and I can't even fathom what he thinks about Ben being alive. He needs time to process this, just like me. But right now I think we both need to push it aside. Neither one of us is in the right frame of mind to discuss the impact Ben will have on our lives.

Just wanting to feel something other than pain or despair, I crush my lips to his, needing to let him know, to feel, how much I love him. He returns my kiss, but when I move to straddle him and start to lift his shirt, he gently pushes me back. He stares at me.

"No, Dahlia, not now. I can't right now," he whispers in a broken tone.

"River, it's okay. *I'm* okay."

He shakes his head and pulls me to him. He turns the TV on and lays us down on the couch, tucking my head under his chin. He starts to watch a boxing match and rubs my back. I eventually nod off.

But it's all waiting for me when I wake up a little while later. I'm lying against the back of the sofa and River is facing me with his arms and legs bracketing my body. While looking at him, everything comes rushing back. Why we fell asleep out here. What happened wasn't a dream or a hallucination. *Ben.* He's alive. He really was at Grace's, touching me, speaking to me.

With all of the questions pounding through my mind, I really can't even understand how any of this is possible. What was he talking about—he did it for me? Did what? One minute I'm running off to Las Vegas to marry the man of my dreams . . . the next minute the man I spent most of my life with, the man whom I thought was dead—is back.

The flickering blue light from the TV and the flame from the fireplace are the only lights in the room. I look at River and wonder how this will affect us. He's twitching in his sleep and I rest my hand over his heart to feel the steady beat. I can feel the warmth of his skin under his thin T-shirt and I want him—I want to touch him, to connect with him.

Leaning into him, I softly kiss his jaw as I run my hand up his chest. He instantly responds as his arms, already wrapped around me, tighten.

In his ear I whisper, "River."

He shifts slightly so that I am lying on top of him and his eyes open. "You okay, beautiful?" he asks as his green eyes flicker and then meet mine.

I nod and trace my tongue around the seam of his lips. He places his hand on my head and pulls it down to his chest, clutching me close to him, like he wants to hold me forever.

Lifting my head, I kiss his neck. I hear his breathing pick up, but once again he pulls me close and hugs me. I push myself back up so we're face-to-face. "River, I want you."

He closes his eyes and when he reopens them, he combs his fingers through my hair, then pauses to cradle my head with both hands. He sighs as his forehead meets mine. I kiss the very corner of his lips and his mouth opens to welcome me. Our tongues entwine and I close my eyes as I slide my hands down his sides. I want to mold my body against his, showing him how much I truly love him. I need to show him for him and for me.

He tears his lips from mine as he places his hands on my shoulders and lifts me off of him slightly. "Dahlia, we should probably talk . . ."

But I cut off his words. I don't want to talk. I just want to feel his love. I suck on his bottom lip for a long moment and then run my tongue down his neck. Pressing my lips against his smooth skin, I wedge my knees between his legs and a small moan escapes his throat. I kneel and he spreads his legs wider. I study his long lean body that I have come to know so well and feel myself shiver in anticipation. My eyes lock on the elastic of his boxers peeking under the waistband of his jeans. A hint of his toned abs shows from where his shirt has lifted and I want to lick what's under that black band.

I pull my shirt off and toss it to the ground, keeping my eyes in line with his. Biting down on my bottom lip, I let my fingers slide over the lace of my bra and I feel my nipples harden. He's watching me in a way that makes me want to keep doing what I've started. My hands travel down my body and instead of unbuttoning my jeans, I slide my palms down the front of them. Stopping, I push against the spot at the bottom of my zipper. His lips part and his breath hitches. I bite down harder on my bottom lip and take this to the next level.

Unbuttoning my jeans, I pull them down. Leaning back so my head rests on the sofa arm, I shimmy out of them. I lie there in my underwear and his scrutiny overcomes me. The look on his face is enough for me to see this through.

I push my feet under his thighs and he strokes his hands up my calves. His chest rises and falls rapidly. Every one of my senses comes alive as I watch him watch me through heavily lidded eyes. When my fingers find their way inside the lace of my panties, he rises to his elbows. He surprises me when he says, "Take them off." His voice is commanding, edged with need.

Sliding the lace down, I pull my feet together and he grabs my panties, throwing them to the floor. I tuck my feet back under his thighs and this time move them a little further up and he groans again. With my hands dangling between my legs, my fingers make contact with my slick flesh and I imagine they are his fingers touching me. A small moan escapes my lips and I throw my head back.

Before I do what I've never done in front of another person, he unzips his jeans and sits up. Moving swiftly, his lean, hard body is on top of mine, his elbows on either side of my arms. A low deep growl vibrates against my lips. "That's only for me. I'm the only one who gets to make you moan."

The press of our bodies together sends me into a state of desperation. My breath comes in short, harsh pants and I reach out to tangle my hands in his already-messy hair. His hips grind into mine and I can feel what I can't wait to have. His breathing is labored and his heart beats fast with desire. He nips my lower lip and then pulls back to look at me. The flames of the fire are still glowing, making his slight smile light up. Wanting his mouth back on me, I pull his lips to mine. When he jets his tongue in and out of my mouth, I want to drink him in—savor the feel and taste of his mouth on mine to have for always.

"I need you," he says as he positions himself between my legs.

"I need you, too," I manage, rubbing myself against him.

Gripping his hips I urge him to take me and he does. He enters me, fills me, and as he slides deeper it is the most wonderful feeling in the world. With it my confusion melts away and we both get lost in the moment. He pulls back, almost withdrawing completely, and I tremble with need all the way to my core. He pushes back inside me and as he moves faster, I clamp my legs around his and grind my hips into him. His eyes close as he maintains the fast rhythm.

I can feel my own pleasure building and I'm craving the release. I close my eyes and rock upward. Our mouths connect hungrily as our pace quickens. My muscles begin to tighten and I know it won't be long. I am so close.

His tongue circles the shell of my ear. "Say you're mine," he breathes. The vibration of his voice and the sound of his words send a shudder through my body and I swear it makes my cheeks and lips quiver.

"I am. You know I am," I tell him and I roll my hips to mimic his movement.

His breath is warm against my cheek. "Say it."

"I'm yours, River."

Within seconds his hands slide down to my hips and he takes complete control. I throw my arms over my head and clutch the sofa, trying to block out everything but this, the here and now.

"Dahlia, let go." His voice shakes as he speaks.

Taking a deep breath I do just that—I finally feel what I have needed to feel since we got home. A muffled sound lodges in my throat and then I call out his name as he pushes me over the edge into pure bliss. "Oh God, River!" I shout as I come hard, waves of pleasure rippling through me.

As if that was the signal he was waiting for, River groans and thrusts deeply one final time before I feel the warmth of him filling me deep inside. He collapses on me and lays his head on my chest, whispering, "I love you. You're . . ."

His words trail off as he rolls against the back of the couch and tightens his hold on me. After a few minutes, he stands and takes my hand, leading me to our bedroom, where we crawl into bed and find each other immediately. I'm completely wrapped in his body, our arms and legs entangled as tight as they can be, my face buried in his chest. I'm so warm, so comfortable; it's where I always want to be.

"I love you. So much," I say one last time because I hope that with those reassuring words everything will be okay. But a small amount of doubt can't help but weigh on me, and I feel like it's hanging over us.

As I start to drift off to sleep I keep hearing Ben's strained voice and seeing his distraught face. Why the hell would he pretend to be dead when he wasn't? Why would he put us all through the grief and sorrow that irrevocably changed our lives? I know I have to see him to understand what's going on.

CHAPTER 4
Like We Used To

Ben's Journal

I never thought I'd see her again and when I finally did—my heart stopped. Mom wanted me to stay in the kitchen so she could explain everything to her. I tried to wait until she was done, but when Serena called her by name, I couldn't wait any longer to get my Dahl back.

When I saw her beautiful face bruised and battered, my gut instinct was that that son of a bitch sitting next to her had hit her. It wasn't until she left and Caleb sat me down that I knew her injuries were a direct result of my actions. Fuck me—what had I done? How can I ever make this up to her? I don't know how I'll do it, but I need her to give me the chance . . . because if she does I'll spend my whole life making it right. I swear I will.

Seeing her bruised and battered enraged me, but her reaction to seeing me—that just wrecked me. I knew she'd be shocked, even pissed, but fuck, I didn't expect apathy. She approached me like a zombie and the jackass she brought with her wouldn't shut the hell up. But then the sign came. The sign that she cared for me.

She touched me. Her hand tenderly brushed my cheek. A simple reminder that we had loved each other our whole lives, that we had known each other since we were five years old, that we were always there for each other. I didn't need the physical reminder to recall those feelings . . . but maybe she did.

It had been so long since I felt her soft skin against mine. Sure, I'd written to her in the journal, the one I kept just for her when I thought I'd never see her again—I'd written to her about how much I missed her and tried to explain the choice I'd made. But then she was standing in front of me and I couldn't believe it. I had dreamed of her touch so many times but never thought I'd feel it again. A simple reflex action—to reach out and touch someone—and she did it, almost intuitively. I thought that meant she had missed me, but now I'm not so sure what it meant.

Nothing up to that point had gone as I thought it would. But there she was, wearing her Grammy's pearls, and all of the times she had worn them before flashed in front of my eyes. It was more than I could take. It broke me. I tried to pull her to me, to hold her but she resisted. I saw the look of confusion on her face, that same look I've seen before. If I could just hold her, she'd be mine, but that pretty boy stood up and I knew I didn't have much time. I spewed out what I could, as fast as I could, but it wasn't enough.

She stared at me and I knew at last she finally saw me. Relieved, I tried to tune out all the chaos surrounding us but she suddenly went apeshit on me. When he tried to take her from me, I pulled her back; I wasn't done talking to her. How dare he threaten me, she's my girl.

She collapsed, but he got to her first. When the dick picked her up, he looked at my mother and said, "This is bullshit. We're done," and headed for the door. I'd had enough. I had to stop myself from pounding the shit out of him. I told him to put her down and get the fuck out. That fucking asshole was not taking her.

Mom ran after them and I tried to but Serena held me back. I couldn't let her just leave so I shrugged off my sister and went to get my girl. When I saw him putting her in his car, I yelled at him to bring my Dahl back. When the prick told me, "She's mine. You don't deserve her, you never did," I let him know how it really was—that he was just a substitute, not my replacement. And I wanted to beat the shit out of him, I really did, when he said, "Then I've been your substitute for way longer than you've been dead." But Caleb appeared out of nowhere and stopped me. He tried to calm him down. I still can't believe Caleb even talks to that fucker. I was literally blown away to learn that he had worked for him! I only found this out because he actually fired Caleb once he heard that Josh Hart, Dahl's attacker, had been caught.

I couldn't free myself from Caleb to go after him, so I yelled my last plea. But I couldn't tell whether Dahlia heard anything I shouted to her. So much for a happy reunion. What the fuck?

I had to watch as he acted like the hero for her. But she was my girl, _is_ my girl, not his. That should have been me trying to get her to stop crying and wiping away her tears. They drove away and his last words—_I've been your substitute for way longer than you've been dead_—echoed in my mind. Fuck! I don't want to even think about it, but what did he mean?

CHAPTER 5
Torn

I'm tangled in River's arms and legs as I wake up and try to slide out from under him. He instinctively reaches for me without waking, as he usually does regardless of which side I sleep on. I remain still until he settles back into sleep. One look at him and everything comes rushing back. What happened yesterday wasn't a dream or a hallucination. Ben. He's alive. He really was at Grace's. . . .

Yesterday I didn't want to believe it. Today I know I have to. But what was he talking about? He did *what* for me? With so many questions, I can't even think straight. I really can't even understand how any of this is possible.

It's just after four in the morning as I quietly make my way to the bathroom, then out to the living room. I slip on the same clothes I wore yesterday, grab a sweater, turn off the alarm, and leave him a note.

River,

I'm sorry, but I have to talk to him. I need to understand how he's here and what he was talking about. Don't worry about me.

I love you. I love you more!

I leave the house, feeling lost and unsure. But I know this is something I have to do. The drive to Laguna Beach is long and quiet. I have the radio turned on, and even though I'm not really listening to what's playing, every song brings a memory. When I exit the freeway and pass through town, the traffic is almost nonexistent. I drive down the narrow streets lined with delivery trucks, boutiques, bars, and restaurants, and my mind wanders to the life I had here.

This entire town is filled with memories of Ben. The beach where we spent endless summer days, the corner coffee shop where we would sit and read the paper together, and downtown where we hung out and people-watched. I have to open my window to catch my breath as the memories of my happy life before his death flood my mind. But when I pass the cemetery where I laid him to rest, those memories turn dark—the shooting, the funeral, the lowering of his casket, and how completely lost I felt. How alone I was.

Then I remember it wasn't until the day I walked down that hallway in Vegas, looked through the glass wall of the meeting room, and saw River that the veil was lifted. It was River's unwavering love that showed me how to live again. He made me whole and I can't help but think about how much I love everything about him.

Images of Ben, images of River, memories of both men—it all fills my head. Ben's back—what happens next? I don't know the answer to that, but I do know that my intense connection with River is undeniable. The love I have for him is like nothing I've ever felt before; but Ben was my first love and that kind of love never leaves you—does it?

All of these thoughts tumble through my mind and I suddenly feel sick. I have to pull over as my stomach clenches with apprehension. I park illegally, turn off the car, open the door, and hang my head between my knees. When the wave of nausea finally passes I look at my reflection in the rearview mirror. Oh God, what am I doing going to see him?

I grab my purse and fumble inside for my phone. I can't do this. I need to call River. I want to go home. He needs to come get me. I don't think I can drive. I shouldn't have come. I dump my purse out on the passenger seat in search of my fucking phone, but it's not there. Shit! River has it.

I sit back and take a few calming breaths. After finally pulling myself together, I decide it has to be now. There's no sense in putting this off, and I know never isn't an option. I'm almost there, so I might as well see this through. With wavering resolve, I start the ignition and head toward the beach to find out from Ben what happened.

I drive the rest of the way in silence, afraid to turn the radio on for fear of hearing familiar songs that might awaken even more memories. As I turn into Grace's driveway, I once again start doubting this course of action and wonder if I should be doing this now. I mean . . . what am I even looking for? But I know the answer to that—I need some answers. Answers to two questions—why did Ben leave; and what brought him back?

Putting the car in park, I lean my head back. I sit there for a moment staring at the house, trying to figure out what I'm going to say to him. From the outside, the house still looks like the same tranquil place it has always been, a home—Grace's, Ben's, mine. But I'm uncertain of what lies in wait on the inside—what if tranquility is not what I'm about to walk into? I draw deep steady breaths and turn off the engine, preparing myself to see him, all the while wondering if we would even still be together if he never "died." I want to believe that in the end, River and I would still have found our way to each other.

As I glance toward the moonlit path, there stands Ben on the old weathered planks, staring at my car, at me. My breath catches at the sight of him. I stay where I am, frozen in place for the longest time. I didn't expect to see him outside. He looks mostly the same: ruggedly handsome chiseled face, tall figure, khaki cargo shorts, messy blond hair peeking through the hood of his sweatshirt. He looks thinner than he was, not as tan as he used to be, but he's still Ben, still all surfer. He's not a figment of my imagination and, for a moment, time stops and I'm transported back to the days when he'd stand there like that, waiting for me to follow. I can't believe it's really him . . . my friend, my rock, he's not really dead. What I'm afraid of I'm not even sure. But the longer I sit here, the longer he stares, and I finally open the door.

As I walk toward the bridge, my feelings are so undefined. I'm not sure how to handle this conversation. But my uncertainty quickly fades when the slightly cocky grin I know so well appears on his face, and the apprehension I felt earlier wells within me. I'm no longer questioning if I should be here because I know I should—I need to know what happened to him.

When I stop a safe distance from him our eyes meet and his grin immediately disappears. He pulls his hood off and lowers his head but never once takes his gaze off me. With his hands shoved in his pockets he leans back against the unstable railing, looking almost stoic. I can't stop staring at him. My heart beats faster with every passing second and I feel like I'm sinking in quicksand. I have the urge to run and escape whatever it is pulsing through my body but I don't. I can't. I'm glued to this spot, held captive by his gaze.

Biting my lip, I stop and stand in front of him, motionless—we are former lovers turned strangers. Neither one of us speaks a word for the longest time. When an owl hoots in the distance, Ben lifts his head and a warm smile appears. "Dahl, Hoot is back. She must have known we'd need someone to break the silence." Every time we used to hear an owl, he would tell me that its name was Hoot, as if there was only one.

"Can we talk?" he asks, and the sound of his voice scares the living shit out of me. It's the voice I missed for so long and up until nine months ago would have given anything to hear.

I nod my head. We do need to talk. That's why I'm here. It's just strange, odd, forced; I can't even open my mouth to speak to him. It's not like we haven't seen each other in a long time and I'm just here to catch up. He was dead.

He, however, seems at ease, comfortable, and just like always he finds the right words for the situation. Standing, he straightens and motions with his shoulder to the beach. He heads toward the water and I can't help but notice that he walks with the same stride he always has—slow and steady. I study him as I follow behind. The muscles in his shoulders are much less pronounced and the span of his back seems narrower. I've never seen him this lean. He must not have been anywhere where he could surf.

Keeping my distance, I don't want to get too close . . . don't want to touch him. This interlude is so strange because this is the one place we always held hands. Every time we walked over this bridge in the past our hands were connected, since we were five years old. But now, those fond memories are all blurred by the fog of utter confusion that his return to my life has brought. My stomach feels uneasy again as I continue down the path that I know can only lead to imbalance—an encounter that may just turn my world upside down.

The beach stretches for miles but he heads toward the water. When he stops near the shore, I can hear him sigh before he turns around to face me. As he twists his familiar features become clearly recognizable—the fine chiseled nose, square chin, and eyes that could talk to me without him ever speaking a word. As they do when I watch them dart to my wrist and narrow in on the Cartier bracelet he gave me the night he died.

"You're still wearing it," he observes.

I promptly cover it with my left hand, as if that could make it disappear. My action only makes his gaze intensify as he now stares directly at River's ring—not his ring—on my finger. A sudden pang of guilt scorches me but he says nothing and neither do I.

The water slushes up over his flip-flops, but he doesn't seem to notice. As the moonlight cascades down upon us, he takes a deep breath and rubs his bloodshot eyes. Scrubbing his hands in his face, he says, "I'm glad you came. I wasn't sure if after yesterday I'd ever see your gorgeous face again and I've missed it so much for so long."

He moves as if to cup my cheeks, but I step back. I put my hands out, signaling for him to keep his distance. I feel conflicted, torn, not sure what to say or what to do, but I don't want him to touch me.

He instantly freezes. "You don't have to be afraid. It will all make sense soon—please just hear me out."

It's the same voice I've always known. The same guy I had spoken to every day for almost twenty years, yet he sounds like a stranger.

Retreating from the water, he drops down and sits in the sand with his knees bent and motions with his head for me to sit next to him. I fall to the sand beside him and escape his steady stare by untying and removing my sneakers. I curl my bare toes in the sand, hoping to find comfort. I bend my knees and wrap my arms around them. Resting my chin on my legs as I stare out at the vast ocean, I can feel his eyes on me. I have yet to speak a word. I'm sure he's interpreting my silence as confusion because he thinks he knows me—does he? Or have I changed?

While I'm trapped in my own thoughts, his voice catches me by surprise. "You don't have to talk if you don't want to, just listen. Okay?"

Again, I nod my head.

"What I had to do wasn't easy, but I did it all for you. To protect you. I just hope you can see it that way."

Twisting to the side, planting my hands in the sand, I finally find my voice. "What are you talking about?"

He rubs his palms over his shorts and I can tell he's nervous. "Fuck, I don't even know where to start."

I level my head to look at him. "The beginning. How about you start at the beginning? Why you made us all think you were dead, when you weren't." I can hear my own voice sounding sad and that scares me.

He takes a deep breath, leans back, and shoves his legs out in front of him. He looks around and then finally at me. "That's just it. I don't even know anymore where it all started. But two weeks before the awards ceremony is probably the beginning. Caleb called me, and I remember the day like it was yesterday. You were at work and I was writing at home. His call was a surprise; I didn't even know he was back from Afghanistan. We met and he told me an FBI task force approached him when he arrived home and he was asked to assist them in taking down a big drug ring. After a few weeks on the job, he couldn't stand it anymore. He didn't like the way the task force was operating and that's when he called me."

Feeling even more confused, I chime in to ask, "What did that have to do with you?"

Ben pulls his knees in, resting his elbows on them, and leans forward. "It had everything to do with me, with us. He asked me to write an article for the *Los Angeles Times*. And of course I said I would—who could say no to a story like that? He told me what he knew and I started researching. And son of a bitch if every time I found one thing, it didn't easily lead to another. Before I knew it I had collected a shitload of incriminating information. What I didn't know was that the investigation and my article were putting both of us in danger."

"I don't understand. Why would writing a story put you in danger? And what does this have to do with you pretending to be killed?"

"I found out things, traced the money, the drugs. I had the operation figured out. Caleb and I thought publishing my article would bring the cartel's drug ring down faster than the FBI could. But we were wrong. The cartel found out and wanted the story stopped, so I said I'd kill it. But Caleb giving the information to them wasn't enough. I was in danger. You were in danger."

My eyes flash to his as the shock of what he's saying hits me. "Ben, you were a journalist. That makes no sense. Journalists investigate stories all the time. Why would your story be any different?"

He rests his hand in the sand and his muscular arm draws my attention until he answers. "Because I had gotten closer to the truth than anyone else before me. I knew the ins and outs of the operation and they didn't like that. How they found out—I'm not sure, but they did. Maybe a tip-off, maybe a data trace. I don't know. But they knew about me, and they knew I had information."

"Okay, Ben, let's pretend I understand. So where does the shooting come in? Why," my voice breaks, "did you have to die?"

"To save you. They threatened me. I had to protect you. It had to look like I died so they'd leave you alone. They had to think I was dead, or eventually you and I would both be killed."

My thoughts are racing as I try to comprehend what he has explained, to determine whether this isn't some wild, fabricated story. I anticipated further imbalance from our conversation, and listening to him only reaffirms it.

He looks at me and continues. "Once I agreed to the plan, Caleb took care of everything. He arranged for someone to take the fall for shooting me, arranged my new location, my new identity—he arranged it all."

Raking my fingers through the sand, I turn to watch a surfer as he rides a wave. "Wait—so Caleb knew this whole time that you weren't really dead? He helped you?"

"Yeah, he did. He also promised me he'd watch out for you."

I have to ask, "Did he also know you were coming back?"

"No, he didn't. I saw him for the first time yesterday. He hasn't been involved with my case for a while."

Shaking my head, I'm still trying to understand everything. Ben is a case? Is he still working with the FBI?

He inches closer to me until he's much too close, it feels too familiar, and I need to put some distance between us. But he captures my attention and I don't move. He hesitates for the slightest moment, stopping inches from me. "So now do you see? I left for you. It was the choice I had to make."

Gasping in disbelief, I move back, and the apprehension I felt earlier turns to anger. "What do you mean 'choice'? You had a fucking choice? Dying was a choice? Leaving me all alone was a choice?"

Talking over me with the same commanding tone he always used when I'd get riled, he says, "Choice wasn't the right word. Just calm down."

I can't take it anymore. "No, I'm not going to calm down!"

He tenses, his shoulders rising. "Dahl."

"Don't call me that! You don't get to call me that anymore!"

"Okay. All right. Just let me finish."

I swivel in the sand to narrow my eyes at him. "No, Ben, it's my turn. Do you have any idea what I've been through? What you put me through? You died in front of me and you weren't even dead? You aren't dead!"

Watching the different emotions pass over his face is too much. I divert my gaze to the water. Staring at the waves, I can feel his eyes on me. He says, "I don't know. I only know what I went through and can only imagine what you had to endure was much worse. I'm so sorry you had to live with my death for so long. But I had to disappear."

I snap my head back up and look right into his deep blue eyes, feeling the anger seep through every pore of my body. "You didn't just disappear, Ben—you fucking died in front of my eyes. I saw him—the asshole that shot you. I saw the coroner take your body away. I went to your goddamn funeral, knowing we had to have a closed casket. And you weren't even in there! While I cried for you, mourned for you, loved you, missed you. At times I just wanted to die without you. Are you kidding me?" Trembling, I scream even louder, "Are you fucking kidding me?"

He takes a deep breath. "I didn't know writing the article would lead where it did. If I had, I never would have stuck my nose into it. I swear I would have just let the FBI deal with it." He leans closer to me, and I stand up. He grabs my hand and forces me to look at him. A strange feeling runs through me, but it isn't love.

I step back, forcing him to drop my arm, but it doesn't stop his words as he stands and says, "I'm so sorry that I didn't share my secret with you before I left. No, actually 'sorry' doesn't even begin to describe how I'm feeling right now. I don't think I will ever find the right way to express the remorse I feel about what I've done."

I shake my head and open my mouth to say something, but he moves forward and touches a shaky finger over my lips. "Through everything, after all this time, you need to know . . . I have never ever stopped loving you, not for one second. And it scares the shit out of me to think that you don't still love me. That you might actually love someone else."

That's when I lose any sense of control. Unable to listen to any more I scream, "'Might love someone else'?" After taking a deep breath I continue, "What did you think would happen? You died three years ago and it took me so long to move on. Getting past the grief, the sorrow, wasn't easy, but I was finally able to move forward. So yes, I'm in love with someone else. You can't come back here thinking"—I motion between us—"that we're going to just pick up where we left off. You can't possibly believe that! Why did you even come back?"

He steps into me. He runs the tips of his fingers over the scrape on my cheek before I can move away and says, "Because I finally could, when I never thought I would be able to. Dahl, the FBI caught the people that were after me. The ones who threatened your life. They fucking caught them. And I was free to come home. Don't you get it?"

"I get it, Ben, but it's crazy—FBI, free to come home. It's just crazy."

"I know it sounds that way, but it's all true. All of it. It's one big clusterfuck. You were never supposed to know any of this. I was dead—you were safe. That's what was supposed to happen. But they suspected there was still information out there and they wanted it. They broke into our house looking for it; how they knew I have no idea. Then when the paid-off shooter was released, they went after him for it. He was scared and told them he didn't have the information, but that I was alive. They wanted to know where I was so they threatened his family if he didn't find me. He went after you, assuming you knew where I was."

I feel my jaw drop. "Wait a minute! Is he the one who attacked me?"

Flinching, he says, "I'm so sorry. I never thought that would happen. I didn't make the right decisions back then. Even when I was planning to leave, I still didn't understand the full scope of the danger. So when Caleb asked me to hand over all the evidence I'd gathered, I stupidly kept some of it."

Not even hesitating, I tell him, "Do you know when he attacked me, I thought I was going to be raped? And now I find out he was looking for you. Looking for information you kept."

Ignoring my questions he doesn't falter in his resolve. "I did it for you . . . I kept it as an insurance policy . . . just in case."

Screaming at him, my whole body shaking, I tell him what I really believe to be the truth. "You didn't do shit for me, Ben. It was for you. You've always done everything for yourself. Don't try to fool yourself into thinking anything different, because I don't. And what you just told me proves it."

In an attempt to redeem himself he says, "You're not hearing me. I didn't do anything for myself. In fact, I wish I was there when that asshole attacked you because I would have fucking killed him. But I'm back now to protect you so it won't happen again."

"I don't need that kind of protection from you. Don't you get it? I have someone who will protect me."

I see his jaw tighten, and he moves to grab my left hand. At the sight of my engagement ring, his eyes narrow. "Then why didn't he protect you?"

I look at him in disbelief. "Protect me from what? The mess that you made? How would River even know?"

With a cocky grin he says, "You don't know—do you? He knew. Caleb chased the shooter out of our house the night before your attack. Then he told that prick you've been playing house with to watch out for you, but obviously he didn't. Luckily, the FBI caught the shooter, the guy that attacked you, that same afternoon. I guess you weren't told that, either. That's how all of this transpired. My shooter was the key. Once they caught him, all the pieces fell into place and the cartel's operation was brought down."

I yank my hand away and yell one final time, "Enough! Just stop!"

"No, Dahl, I won't. You need to hear me out."

I can't hear anymore. Or think anymore. Right now I'm feeling only one thing—betrayed. Any residual pain from my injuries is completely subdued as this new pain courses through my body. Ben left me all alone, left me to mourn him, and he was never really dead. River knew who attacked me. Someone broke into my house again. And River didn't tell me any of this. As this despair courses over my deepest wounds, the word *trust* rings in my ear. I trusted Ben—was I wrong? I trust River—am I wrong? I have an overwhelming urge to escape this madness.

So I gather my socks and shoes, knowing I have to get away from here, that I've heard enough. He pretended to die because of something he was doing to further his career, he kept information that put me in danger, and now he wants to protect me. Is he kidding me? I believed in him. Now I wonder if I ever really even knew him. The Ben I thought I knew would never have left me alone for any reason.

He reaches for me, but I twist away. "Stop! Don't touch me!"

As I leave he calls after me, "Don't walk out of my life. I know I don't deserve you but not having you will . . ."

He doesn't finish or maybe he does and I just don't hear what he says because I've stopped listening. I'm too distracted by my own thoughts. I can't believe what he told me is true. I try to focus on the water crashing against the rocks instead of feeling the heavy burden of betrayal. And as I walk back to the old weathered planks, any confusion I might have had about Ben when I arrived is gone. I have nothing left to say to him. But my confusion has shifted to River. Does he really know everything Ben said he does?

I cross the threshold from the beach to my safe haven and look over at Grace's house. Now is the time to remove any shadow of doubt because River is there, standing in the driveway. He's leaning against my car with his arms folded and head down. He raises it just as I pass his car. I'm a mere ten feet away from him when his eyes graze the length of my body and then snap back up to mine.

His jaw tight, he spits out, "How was your little chat? Did you find out everything you needed to know?"

I'm taken aback by his hostility so I freeze. Before we get into any discussion over my coming here, I need to put Ben's accusations to rest. With my heart racing, I ask, "Do you know the identity of the man who attacked me?"

His body straightens and his eyes are cautious. He swallows before nodding his head. At that moment something inside me erupts as my trust in him starts to erode and an anger fiercer than I have ever felt surfaces. My fists clench without conscious thought as I storm toward him. I slam my hand on the hood of my car and his eyes dart to mine.

I get as close as I can to him and with a craziness I never knew I had in me I scream, "You knew! You knew who attacked me! And you didn't tell me!"

Shock and alarm cross his face, but he immediately composes himself. He grabs me and pulls me to him. Clutching my shoulders tightly, his eyes travel across my face. "Yes I knew, but . . ."

I twist around with all my strength to free myself from his grip. "There is no *but*. I trusted you to always be honest with me."

His face pales, his jaw drops, and his forehead wrinkles. "What I didn't tell you has nothing to do with honesty and trust, but what you did by coming here—that does."

Irritated, I step back into him, now only inches away. "Are you kidding me? You're going to turn this back around on me? I don't think so."

"Dahlia, I think we need to talk about all of this. Let's just leave your car here and go."

"What exactly is 'all of this'?"

"I want to know why you came here to see him without telling me, without bringing me—why you would sneak out when I was sleeping."

I shake my head as his eyes narrow on me.

He grabs my hand. "Come on, we're leaving."

With so much pain and anger welling up inside me, I know I can't have this conversation with him right now. Feeling strangled, out of breath, I take a step back and free my hand from his. I trusted him completely—and he kept this from me. I have to calm down and figure out what that means. At the same time I can't help looking into his mesmerizing green eyes. I can't handle seeing my own fear and anger reflected in his eyes any longer. His stare intensifies and he's looking at me, and I mean really looking at me, as if willing our connection to fix all of this.

I swallow a few times before forcing myself to look away. "No, River, I can't talk to you when we're like this. I know we will both say things we don't mean. We need time to figure our anger out before we sit down and have a conversation."

He tries to yank me flush to his body. His voice shakes with fury. "I don't need time to figure anything out. I get it. You left me a note. You ran here the first chance you got to see him! Was it a happy reunion or were things just getting started?"

I have never heard this kind of furious tone from him before, and, without any control, I pull back and slap him. "I told you I'm not having this conversation right now. Listen to yourself!"

Stomping over to my door, I get in, turn the key, and start to shake uncontrollably. I watch him through the window as he stands there in shock with his hand on his face. I want to get out of the car and say I'm sorry. I want to throw my arms around his neck and kiss him. I want him to hold me forever, but I am stuck in the moment, suspended between right and wrong, what should be and shouldn't be. I know he's questioning things, questioning Ben's reappearance, and how it will affect us.

We just need to calm down. I'm still trying to wrap my head around what's happening. Ben is a stranger to me; he did things I never imagined my Ben would do. And River kept something huge from me. It's not even what he kept secret that bothers me; it's the simple fact that he kept anything from me in the first place.

When "Amazing Grace" suddenly plays on my phone, I look down, startled that my phone is lying on the console, plugged into the charger, but not surprised. River must have put it in here when he got to Grace's. I shut my eyes and exhale a deep breath. I am wishing this day could start over as I listen to the same ringtone that started me on the path to where I am right now. I look toward the house and Grace stands there, her phone in hand. I silence my phone, turn it off, and drive away.

I turn the radio on, hoping to drown out my thoughts with music.

When I hear Bruce Springsteen's "Born to Run," I blast it. I've never been one for confrontation and what just happened felt more like a war. I can't face the truth right now—the truth that the two men I trusted most in my life lied to me. Not knowing where to go, I drive toward the rising sun.

CHAPTER 6
Remember When

Ben's Journal

Yesterday didn't go exactly as I had planned. I can't believe how much I let that prick get under my skin. I have this feeling that I know him, and I can't seem to shake it. Sleep proved impossible so I headed to the beach, still thinking about what he said and what it meant. Just as I was about to walk over the old bridge, Dahlia pulled into the driveway. When I saw her I thought she was coming back to me—that she had missed me as much as I had missed her. I waited for her to get out of the car and come running to me, but instead she approached cautiously. I saw the trepidation in her eyes and I hoped she wasn't scared. I wanted to take her in my arms and assure her it was me, tell her I was back for her, but I didn't. She felt too distant, too far removed.

Even though I was stoked she was still wearing my bracelet, seeing someone else's ring on her finger enraged me. My whole flight back home, all I could think about was putting my ring back

on her finger, marrying her, and finally having a family together.
I figured she must have taken my ring off when I heard from
Caleb that she was with some jackass. My suspicions were con-
firmed when I asked Mom if she knew anything about my ring
and she told me she had tucked it away. Fuck! That hurt. Dahl
didn't even keep it.

I could see she was afraid to let me touch her; maybe afraid
of what she might feel. So maybe there's a chance for us. I think
we just need more time to get things back to how they used to be
between us. I thought when I finally got to talk to her for real, not
just in the journal I was keeping for her, she'd listen and be rea-
sonable, but she went off on me instead. Her rage intensified with
every fucking wrong word I said and she didn't give me a chance
to explain.

She might have left me on the beach, begging her to not walk
out of my life, but I don't care. Yeah, she walked away from me, but
in the end, despite the shitty conversation, I'm glad she came to see
me—and she came alone. Although as soon as I told her the prick
knew about her attack, she not only mentally checked out, she left.

I'll keep trying. I've needed her since the day I left. I wished I'd
have told her that. I actually wish I had taken her with me. Maybe
that was what she needed to hear. I did run after her but stopped
when I reached the end of the bridge. He was there, looking all
kinds of smug and arrogant. Who the fuck wears jeans and boots
to the beach?

But Dahl, she was pissed. She stormed right up to him and,
fuck, did she go off. From the looks of it there are cracks in their
relationship. Things he doesn't know or understand about her like
I do. He didn't tell her what he knew. I know better. She's pissed as
fuck at him and getting her to forgive him isn't going to be easy.
That's exactly what I need—for them to be apart. Time for her to
remember us and forget them.

If she breaks up with him like she did with me that one time, I'll have plenty of time to get her back. Fuck, she may never get back together with him. She broke up with me for what she thought was only the start of something with someone else, and I let her believe that. I had to. I couldn't tell her the truth. I knew if she had found out we'd be over forever. She would never forgive me; fuck, I still can't forgive myself. I made one slip in judgment, but I would never do that to her again. Not even if it's served right in front of me. The one time ate away at me.

Each time I thought about it I hated myself for being weak, but in all honesty I enjoyed every minute while it happened. For some reason that copper-haired girl got my blood pumping. I didn't want to know anything about her. I didn't even know her last name. In fact, every time she came on to me, I ran away. How fucking pathetic. Why couldn't I just tell her to back off? For some reason I couldn't. And I didn't the night I was shitfaced and she cornered me at the after-party. She did her usual come-on and I did my usual and hightailed it away from her but she followed. Trevor hadn't come back to school yet and the room was empty so I headed there. I went into the bathroom and splashed water on my face. When I looked in the mirror—there she was, taking her clothes off. Yeah, her body was amazing and the way she offered it to me was fucking hot, but there was more. It was something in her eyes that drew me in. I felt like she got me. I couldn't stop myself, but I know I should never have fucked her. It could have destroyed my relationship with Dahl. Almost did.

We stayed locked up in Trevor's empty suite and I didn't just screw her once—but over and over again, all night long. She was kinky as fuck and we kept at it until dawn. I knew it was wrong.

Why am I even still thinking about her? Maybe it was her eyes? Maybe it was the way she blew me? Maybe it was the mind-blowing sex? I have no fucking idea . . .

But later when that girl e-mailed me asking to meet, I was determined to stay away. Fuck, I thought maybe she was going to tell Dahl or tell me she had VD. Eventually I agreed when she said it was really important. In the end I never met her because Dahl came home early. That was the last I heard from her so I figured she was just trying to get my attention and finally gave up—until she started calling again months later. By then Dahl had seen the e-mail and I knew better than to even talk to her. I wasn't taking any chances.

I still, to this day, can't believe I strayed from my girl. I'd like to blame it on being young and immature because, really, of all the things that I was—I wasn't a cheater. Or at least I wasn't until that one night. Hell, I was used to being pursued. I shouldn't have let her break me. Women have chased me my whole life— some relentlessly, but I never cared, not once before her and not once after her. Shit, back then I lived in a frat house and there was never a shortage of girls offering to have a good time. I always refused. I loved my girl and wasn't taking the chance of losing her.

CHAPTER 7
Your Call

It's still early in the morning when I find myself at the beach. I park a few miles from the house I used to share with Ben and remove my Converses so I can feel the grainy sand that usually comforts me, but once again it doesn't. As I walk along the shore, the tide rolls in and splashes of cold water prickle my skin. So many thoughts are running through my head. First and foremost: *What the hell just happened?*

I'm drawn to the water and wade in further and further until I am almost knee-deep. The salty air blows on my face and I take deep calming breaths, wishing away the pain and turmoil I can't seem to handle. As tears trickle down my cheeks, the salty scent of the sea air seeps into my nose. I stop and sit down in the cold water, now barely below my chin. Then I dive under and never want to surface. Life seems so tranquil down here.

When I come back up I make my way to the sand and just lie there. The beach is very quiet. Birds chirp peacefully as they soar overhead.

I close my eyes, willing myself to stop crying. I can't even figure out who I'm crying for—Ben, River, myself?

I must have drifted off because suddenly I can hear small children playing nearby and feel the hot sun beating down on me. I get up and wipe as much sand off me as I can and then make my way back to the car. Looking behind me, I see the footprints I left vanishing as people jog by without a care in the world, and I wish I had that same carefree feeling, the feeling I had just last week.

I grab my sneakers and sweater at the beach entrance—the only dry things I have. I take my keys out of my Converse and shove them in my jeans pocket. I pull my sweater around me with shaky hands, try to shake the sand from my hair, and hurry to the car, my head swimming with the unknown. I break into a sprint to get there, my bare feet crushing against the stones beneath me, but I don't even care. I'm almost gasping when I reach for my keys. Leaning my head against the steering wheel, I try to figure out what to do, where to go. Glancing over at my phone, I just want to hear his voice, so I turn it on and check my messages.

There are four—Grace, Serena, Aerie, and an unknown caller, but none from River. I'm not surprised. I'm mad as hell at him for not telling me what he knew, for making me doubt his trust, but he was just as mad at me for going to see Ben. I've never seen him like that. I've never seen me like that. I listen to the messages—Grace telling me to turn around and talk this out, Serena asking if I'm all right and telling me she's here for me if I need to talk, Aerie yelling into the phone to call her now, and the unknown caller, Ben, begging me to come back. Ben—the voice I hadn't heard in so long until yesterday, the voice of the man I loved unconditionally, the voice of the man whom I had always trusted.

My eyes are stinging and my thoughts are even more of a jumbled mess than they were before I got to the beach. I stare blankly at the traffic as it rushes by on the now-busy Pacific Coast Highway. My heart thumps out of my chest as I turn the engine on and jerk into the lane of traffic almost haphazardly. I skid to a quick stop at the first traffic light. I am driving way too fast, but my head is swimming with memories. Cars are honking for me to move as the light turns green. I accelerate as fast as I can and head to the only place that comes to mind right now.

When I pull up in front of the yellow house with the white picket fence, the FOR SALE sign still occupies the front yard. The place is neglected, in need of some tender loving care, but still, right now, it is my refuge.

Needing dry clothes, I call the only person I can. She answers immediately and forsakes the niceties. "Where the hell are you and what's going on?" she yells into the phone. In a much calmer tone she quickly adds, "Are you okay, Dahlia?"

She obviously already knows Ben is back, and I take one deep breath and contemplate what to say. "Aerie, I need some help. I'm at my house here in Laguna. Can you please bring me some dry clothes?"

I'm surprised when all she says is, "Sure, I can. I can be there in less than twenty minutes. Will you be okay until I get there? Grace called me this morning and told me everything. Dahlia, she told me Ben's alive."

"Aerie, let's talk when you get here, okay?"

"Okay, Dahlia, I'll be there as soon as I can. I love you."

I hang up the phone without another word and toss it into the console, open my door, and walk up the path to the house. A house I lived in with Ben, a house I mourned him in, and a house where I was close to giving up when life was breathed back into me by River. Now everything seems distorted, confused. When you trust someone and they break that trust—what does it mean? That's what I have to figure out, that's why I'm here—so I can think.

As I unlock the front door I hear the wind chimes that used to welcome me home and I enter the almost-empty house. I see the few pieces of furniture left—our oversize sofa where it always has been, the coffee table, and the two chairs. The rug is gone, the lamps were broken during the break-in that destroyed nearly everything, and anything left was moved into Grace's attic or to River's house.

Shivering, I pull my knees up on one of the chairs and just sit there, trying not to think about Ben, but that's all I can focus on. Remembering my life with him.

Before I know it, I hear pounding on the front door and Aerie is yelling, "Dahlia, are you okay? Why is the door locked?"

I hop off the chair, not even remembering locking the door. As I walk I glance at the old key-shaped holder Caleb rehung after the break-in, and Ben's keys are still hanging there. For some reason they make me feel uneasy. As soon as I unlock the door, Aerie swings it open, hurrying past the threshold with coffees and a bag in one hand. She looks almost as disheveled as me, in sweatpants, a T-shirt, her hair in a ponytail, and yoga shoes. I'm surprised because she never goes out looking so un-put-together.

Grabbing the coffee tray from her hand, I blurt, "What the hell happened to you?"

"Me?" She eyes me up and down once before continuing. "What happened to me?" She drops the bag to the ground and seems unable to talk for a few seconds. "What happened to you? Where have you been? Why are you soaking wet and covered in sand?" Her questions continue but I tune them out, really wanting to sip the hot coffee and strip off these wet clothes. Realizing I don't want to talk about any of it, I almost wish I hadn't called her. She takes the tray from my hand and sets it on the floor, then immediately pulls me to her and hugs me as hard as she can. We both stand there, me almost a head taller than her, and I can't help but cry.

She pulls back and looks at me. "I have been worried sick about you. Grace called me at six this morning, assuming you were headed to my house. Then as the hours ticked by and you didn't show up we all started to worry." She wipes the tears from my face before wiping her own. When she brushes the sand from her clothes, I can't help but laugh.

"Sorry, I didn't mean to get you dirty."

We both laugh and the Aerie I know is back, the take-charge Aerie. "Where have you—You know what? Let's get you changed first. You're shivering, and we can talk after."

She starts leading me down the hall to my bathroom like I don't know where I'm going, and I follow her like I need to be led. Once we reach the bathroom she pulls out some sweatpants and a sweatshirt from the bag and lays them on the counter as she starts to unbutton the shirt I have on—River's shirt.

Gently placing my hands over hers, I tell her, "I can do it. I don't need help."

Pushing my hands away she says, "Just let me do it, let me help you." I move my hands and she continues to unbutton the wet shirt. A moment of comfortable silence passes. Then she says in a soft, concerned tone, "I'm sorry, Dahlia. I really am." I know she isn't apologizing for helping me get undressed.

Suddenly it hits me—the last time she did this was when she came to see me the night Ben was killed. I remember now: she removed my black cocktail dress that night because I couldn't. Then she tossed it on the corner chair, where it stayed for a long time. "Aerie, this isn't like then." I pause and motion to where the chair in my bedroom used to sit. "I'm not going to fall apart like I did before. Sure I'm confused, but I know the situation is completely different."

Pulling my arms out of the shirt, I point to the two items on the counter and ask, "Is that all you brought? No underwear?"

Staring at me a little too long, she says, "Dahlia, I had no idea why I was bringing you clothes. I didn't think to grab a bra or a pair of panties. Why are you soaking wet, anyway?"

"I needed to escape all the chaos so I decided to go for a swim. You know swimming always clears my mind."

"In your clothes, Dahlia? Really?"

"Yes, in my clothes."

"You know that is not normal, right?"

I shrug.

She shakes her head and takes the shirt from me that I just stripped off. I unhook my bra and throw it in the sink. She stares wide-eyed at the huge purple bruise that seems to have morphed from my side to the front and back of my torso.

"I'm okay, Aerie—really I am. I'm not going to fall off the deep end."

I slip my arms into her USC sweatshirt and pull it over my head. She grabs the hem and pulls it down for me and I let her. Then she pulls my hair out of the hood.

"I think we need to get those tangles out. I'm going to grab a brush out of my purse. I left it in the car. I'll be right back. Will you be okay?"

"Yeah, of course." And then as she leaves the room I call after her, "Hey, you don't have any toilet paper in your car, do you?"

She laughs a little and says, "No, but I have Starbucks napkins. I'll bring you some." And with that she leaves me in the bathroom to change out of my now partially dried and stiffened jeans. Her sweatpants are way too short on me and soon I'm just staring at myself in the mirror. Memories of the girl who lost her fiancé are reflected back to me. I clutch the counter and close my eyes . . . I am not that same girl. I am much stronger. I will not fall back into a depressed state. What happened this morning cannot happen again—this I know. Jumping into the ocean to escape all the madness was simply a momentary lapse in judgment. Right?

Opening my eyes I take a deep breath and exit the bathroom. I glance over at the bed in the room I never wanted to be in after Ben died and try not to think of the pain and suffering his death caused me—and for what?

Back in the entryway, I grab the drinks and go sit in one of the chairs, blocking out all thoughts of Ben. Aerie comes in a few minutes later.

"Thank you so much for this." I raise my large paper cup in the air.

"Yeah, well, I thought you might need some and I grabbed myself a tea while I was at it."

When she says the word *tea*, I think about River and the first morning we spent together . . . when I wasn't sure if he was a coffee or tea drinker. How relieved I was that he drank coffee.

She comes over to me and the memory dissipates as she tries to brush the knots out of my hair but can't, so just ends up twirling it into a messy bun and securing it with the elastic she removed from her wrist.

"Always prepared."

"I try to be," she says, grabbing her cup and sitting in the chair next to me. She looks me up and down. "You know, we can go to my place and you can take a shower."

"No, I really just want to stay here."

She nods her head and we both sit quietly, sipping our drinks until I break the silence. "What else did Grace tell you about Ben, other than he's alive . . ." I start to speak the truth but the words sound strange, not real, and I can't even complete the sentence.

"All she told me was that Ben was involved in something dangerous and had to leave for his safety and . . . ," she pauses before adding, ". . . and for yours, Dahlia. But she didn't feel comfortable discussing anything else and I didn't push her."

Frowning, I say, "I can see why. It's a crazy story and honestly really hard to believe."

"Why? Do you think he's lying to you?"

"No. I don't. It was just a lot to process and then he said something that set me off and I kind of exploded."

"What did he say?"

"He told me he made the choice to leave."

"What do you mean he had a choice?"

"He got himself into a bad situation and instead of talking about it, and us facing it together, he left."

"Dahlia, did you stay to let him finish?"

"I tried, Aerie, I did. But I couldn't listen to him anymore. You know what I went through when he died and to hear he made a choice . . ."

"Can you at least try to forgive him, so you can move past this and get some closure?"

"No! No! I'm not going to forgive him for what he did. I can't!"

I'm unable to distinguish whether what I just said annoys her or saddens her, but from the slight downward curl of her lip, I'd have to go with saddens. We stare at each other for a long while and I know she's being cautious with her words.

"Do you think you should sit down and listen to everything? I don't know what he did, but I know he loved you and I'm sure the choice wasn't easy."

Not able to hide my irritation I tell her, "Don't you get it, Aerie? That's just it—talking to him again won't change anything."

We share silence for a few more moments.

She raises an eyebrow. "I know it won't, but I think it will help you better understand why he did what he did."

Wow. She understands more than I thought she did.

I pause for a minute, trying to understand why she's pleading Ben's case. When I think I've figured it out my face flames with skepticism and disbelief. "You don't think I'm going to just jump out of my relationship with River and back into Ben's arms? Do you, Aerie? Because it doesn't work that way."

Her eyes flash to mine. She sets her tea down and walks over and kneels in front of me, grabbing my hands. In a low voice she says, "Of course not. I know it doesn't work that way and no one expects that at all." Then she squeezes my hands tightly. "I know you love River. I even set you up to meet him to begin with because I knew how you felt about him. We've talked about that. This isn't about choosing one guy over the other. It's about listening to and maybe even forgiving a man you've known your whole life. Not ruling it out. That's all. I'm not saying this for him, but for you, for your own peace of mind. I know you, Dahlia—this will drive you crazy."

That wasn't at all what I'd expected to hear. And although I understand her intentions, I know forgiveness isn't in me right now.

She sighs and then shrugs. "Maybe try looking at the situation from his point of view, that's all. Just think about it."

I nod. "I'll try but that doesn't mean I'm going to forgive him."

With that, she stands up and goes to sit back in her chair.

Looking down at the coffee cup still in my hand, I swirl it around. "River and I got into a fight after I saw Ben this morning."

She says nothing. Fuck me, she knows that, too. I can tell immediately because she stands back up and paces the room, avoiding my intent stare at all costs.

"Aerie. What do you know?"

She doesn't answer and I stand up and walk over to her. "Aerie. Tell me now."

"Dahlia, I think I should let River explain."

"Well, River isn't here right now and he isn't talking to me anyway. So how about you explain."

"Fuck!" she says, and she never says fuck so I know it's bad.

She walks to the window and pulls her phone out of her pocket, then dials a number. "Serena, are you almost here?" she says, and after a few moments she hangs up.

I gape at her. "What's going on here? You called Serena already. Why?"

"Dahlia, please calm down. We didn't want to tell you right away about the attack because . . ."

I cut her off. "Did you always know Ben was alive? Did you know this whole time?"

"Jesus, Dahlia. No! No! I knew nothing about that, I swear. God, I would never have let you go through that if I had known, none of us would have. What I meant was we knew who attacked you, but that's all."

I study her face, trying to understand. "We? You mean all of you knew? Not just River?"

"Dahlia, please let River explain this."

"No Aerie, I want you to explain the 'we' to me now."

She sighs as if resigning herself to a fate worse than death as she slumps back in the chair and picks up her cup. She takes a few drawn-out sips before talking. "The night before you were attacked, Grace was notified that Ben's shooter was released. Caleb found him and chased him out of your house. He was worried that the guy would come after you. Grace tried to call you, Serena tried to call you, and Caleb tried to call you. They all left you messages but you never called them back. Serena tried again in the morning and River answered. They told him everything that had been going on, but it was too late by then." She stops for a few seconds as I continue to glare at her in total and complete shock.

"Go on. So why not tell me? I don't understand."

"Dahlia, we remember how you were when Ben died, and none of us wanted to bring that pain back on you. Grace wanted to tell you in person so she asked River to wait before saying anything. Then you two decided to go get married and not tell anyone. I questioned River's decision to not tell you first, but in the end I decided I'd rather see you happy than risk what might happen if we dredged up those sad memories." She stands back up and walks over to me.

I try to absorb all this information. Is there anyone I can trust? Wanting to put the pieces together, I run out the door to my car and grab my phone from the console. Back in the house I glance at the screen and see three missed calls. I immediately scroll through my voice messages. There are none from five days ago. River must have deleted them. I shake my head and throw my phone across the room. I can hear the sound of destruction as the screen shatters, but I don't care. I don't need it. He hasn't even called me, but Unknown Caller has called another three times.

I sink to the ground and pull my knees to my chest. "I can't believe he hasn't even called me since our argument this morning."

Aerie comes to sit next to me and looks at me questioningly. "Who? Ben?"

"No! Not Ben. I told you I don't want to fucking talk to him. River. River hasn't called me."

As I'm speaking, I hear the door open and look over to the foyer. Serena stands there with a bag of Chinese takeout in one hand and a bottle of vodka in the other.

"Maybe you should call him? You're the one who slapped him and left him at Mom's," she says when she walks into the room and sets down the bag on the coffee table.

"How do you know that?" I know I'm staring at her, but I can't help it.

"Dahlia, Mom saw the whole thing. She saw you and River at your car and saw you drive away. She called you to come back home, but you wouldn't answer."

"Serena, so much has happened in the last day. I'm doing the best I can. I'm just not ready to talk about it yet."

"I get it, Dahlia, but what you don't understand is that by avoiding the issues you're just causing a bigger rift between everybody. You need to stop running away and face what's right in front of you. You might actually be surprised by the outcome."

I drop my head into my hands. I don't even know how to respond because there are so many issues. It's not that I'm running; it's that my faith in Ben is shattered and talking to River seemed pointless at the time—we were both just too mad. Serena takes my hand and pulls me over to the sofa to sit next to her. We're facing each other as she says, "Dahlia, I know you don't want to talk about this, but you need to know what happened this morning."

"I have enough to think about. I don't need to hear more."

I start to stand up and Serena reaches for me. "Wait, you need to hear this. After you left this morning, Ben and River were yelling at each other in the driveway. River lunged at Ben and they started fighting. It took Mom screaming at them for them to stop."

"Oh my God. I never thought— I just never even thought about them seeing each other, let alone what would happen if they did."

Serena gives me a look and scolds me. "You would have known if you'd have answered your goddamn phone."

"I'm sorry but I just don't know what to do here—with Grace, River, Ben, I'm so angry, so upset, and confused. I really don't want to talk about them right now."

Aerie walks over to where my phone lies broken on the floor and picks it up. "Well, you don't have to worry about them calling you because you no longer have a phone."

To avoid tears, I mumble, "Well at least I won't be checking for calls that never come."

I stand up and head for the table. Serena jumps up, grabs my arm, and shouts so I can't ignore her, "Dahlia, grow up. You slapped him and left him standing there."

I turn to her in shock and scream back, "I know I did!"

"Well, what did you expect?" Then taking a breath, she says in exasperation, "Dahlia, you need to get your shit together."

"I know I shouldn't have left him there, I get it, but I also know we both needed time to calm down."

Serena rolls her eyes at me and says, "Your decision."

"Well, my decision right now is to eat this Chinese food and have a drink. Then I'll worry about what to do next."

Serena stands there shaking her head and Aerie just looks at me, not knowing what to do with me at this point. And I get it because frankly, I don't know what to do with myself, either.

So I do the only thing I can right now—I grab the bottle of vodka. Ripping the plastic off, I unscrew the top and take a long chug. Then I wipe my mouth with my hand as I endure the burning sensation traveling down my throat. Serena stands there with her hands on her hips. She's completely no-nonsense, just like her brother, but I try to set that thought aside.

"Fuck, Dahlia, I have cranberry juice and limes in the car, could you wait a minute?"

"No I can't. I don't care about mixers right now. I just want to stop thinking about all this madness." Lifting the bottle in the air I make a toast. "Here's to making dumb decisions and not always being able to own up to them." With that, I burst out laughing and then start crying. I take one more sip from the bottle.

Both of my best friends come over. Aerie grabs the bottle and says, "Here's to never being able to keep a boyfriend because you're just too damn picky."

I raise my hand as if holding a glass and say, "Here's to not being picky, but to waiting for Mr. Right."

After she downs a healthy dose of vodka, she hands the bottle to Serena. Serena takes it and holds it in front of her. "Here's to being a shitty parent. May your sons never get into the kind of trouble that you can't help them out of."

What? I look at Serena and know this isn't the time to ask but I wonder what's going on with Trent. I need to comfort her so I raise my imaginary glass again and say, "Here's to moms who do everything they can to help their children."

It's now that I realize these women have their own issues. And I should have been there to help them like they've helped me. How do I not even know what's bothering them?

I grab the bottle and make another toast. "Here's to always listening to your friends and understanding their issues."

Once all of our feelings are out there, we spend the rest of the afternoon eating Chinese and drinking what's left of the 750 ml bottle of vodka before we all pass out. The three of us are careful only to talk about Serena and Aeries's lives and never say the name Ben or River.

CHAPTER 8
Into the Nothing

Ben's Journal

I spent the morning pressing a bag of ice to my lip—nursing my wound and my pride, too. I didn't expect that pussy to go all Rambo on me. Maybe I should have taken him more seriously. Either way, he got a few good ones in, but so did I. I'm confident that pretty boy is at least sporting one black eye.

I knew Dahl wouldn't go straight to him after the argument I witnessed them have. That's not her MO. Whenever we argued we both always needed space to calm down before discussing issues. I thought she would be at the beach, so I wasn't surprised when I drove by our house and saw her car there. She must have been thinking of me, and all the years we shared together. That's evident just by where she ended up.

I stood on the front porch for at least fifteen minutes, trying to figure out if I should go in. Instead, I decided to revert to the way I won her back the only time we ever broke up. I grabbed a piece of paper from Mom's car and left her a note. I know she'll know it's from me the minute she sees it. Hopefully, it will be enough to convince her to call me. I don't care if I have to leave a million notes—if that's what it takes, I will. She has to spend time with me—it's the only way I can get her to see I'm the only one for her.

CHAPTER 9
Blurry

Hours later I awaken, sore, aching, and sprawled out on the over-size sofa with Aerie as my pillow and Serena as my blanket. The over-head lights are on, but do nothing to help me focus. It's pitch-black outside and the streetlights are on so it has to be late. I try to lift my head but the thudding sensation that kicks up at the movement makes my pulse race and my stomach turn. I gag down the bile inching its way up my throat, but all that does is make the taste in my mouth even worse.

Looking around at the Chinese takeout containers, I find an opened water bottle. As I sit up to drink it, I try not to disturb Aerie or Serena and scoot carefully off the couch. My head is pounding, but my heart feels like it has lost its beat. The rage I felt toward River has dis-sipated and I'm left with the awareness that we need to talk about what happened this morning. Yes, I was mad at him for not telling me what he knew, but Grace asked him not to. I get it, and I'm ready to talk now. I just hope he is.

When I walk through the house I can't help picturing how I was in the years after Ben died—all alone. It breaks my heart to think about how isolated and alone I felt. How my grief overpowered any feelings of hope. I wish I could go back and wipe away those years and the toll they took on me, but I can't.

Opening the front door to leave, I notice Ben's keys hanging on the hook. Why had I never gotten rid of them? I shake my head and walk out into the coolness of the night. When I approach my car I see there's a folded piece of paper on the windshield and I know instantly it's from Ben. The note is folded the same way as all the other notes he has ever left me—and he left me an abundance of them during our short three-month breakup when I thought he might be cheating.

I open the note and read the short but to-the-point message.

I'm sorry. I miss you. I love you. Let me talk to you.

Ben

Bitterness rushes through me. Is he kidding me? I am not going to forgive him. He made his choice, he left me alone, and now that I'm happy he thinks we can just go back to the way we were. Well we can't. And even if we could . . . I don't want to. I love River and that's something I would never change.

In fact, I know what I have to do—I have to cut my ties with him. I rip the bottom half of his note and shove the other half inside the kangaroo pocket of my sweatshirt. Opening the car door, I search for a pen, and then write a brief note to Serena, telling her to make sure Ben knows this house is now his. It hasn't been ours since he chose to leave. He can't have me, but he can have our house.

I walk back into the house and lay the note on the entryway floor and anchor Ben's keys on it. As I leave, I hear the wind chimes and I know this is the last time I will be walking out the door of this house. It's not my home anymore, it's not our home anymore, it's simply Ben's. My home is in LA and that is where I'm heading.

I spend the drive home trying to figure out the semantics of not telling versus lying, of trust versus forgiveness. I know River's lie of omission wasn't out of malice or spite but out of his overwhelming need to protect me. Ben's lie wrecked me, changed me, and left me alone. River's omission did none of those things. So maybe I can look past this. I think I can, actually, and I just hope I can still trust him. Why is facing our issues so much harder than escaping?

Xander's Mercedes is parked close to the steps leading to the front door when I pull into the driveway. It's one in the morning and I'm surprised he's still here; he's usually so uptight about getting up early for work.

After parking the car in the garage, I walk up the stairs and notice a huge hole in the wall next to the door. When I see the key we keep above the doorframe lying on the ground, I wonder what happened. The door is unlocked and as I enter the kitchen, I can see Xander passed out on the couch, his shoes still on, his arm slung over his head, and a half-empty bottle of Patrón on the side table. His shirt is untucked and his skin is exposed. Grabbing my concert T-shirt quilt from the hall closet, I pull it close to me for a moment, and then head back to the living room. Covering him with the blanket, I notice a hint of a tattoo down the side of his torso I never knew he had. I set the liquor bottle on the counter and turn the lights off before heading to the bedroom.

I'm a little apprehensive about seeing River. We haven't talked all day. Since we got together we've never gone this long without talking.

I'm not even sure anymore who was actually angrier. Me at him for not telling me he knew it was Ben's shooter that attacked me, or him at me for having gone to see Ben.

When I see that he's not in the bedroom, I'm a little surprised. Everything is how I left it, just messier. My wedding dress lies flat on my hope chest, with the garter and pearl earrings nestled on top of it. I put everything there so I could easily slip back into the dress and get ready again. Originally, I thought we'd be returning from Grace's later that afternoon. I hang it in my closet, having no idea when we will be getting married. The thought makes me a bit uneasy, so I seek solace by walking over to the glass doors. I look out into the night, at the beautiful view of the Hollywood sign that I love so much. I'm not sure why; maybe because it represents hope.

As I stand here looking out, a fleck of light catches my eye and I see him immediately. He's sitting in a chair down by the pool, just staring into the darkness. Opening the door, I pause to admire him; his long lean body, his always-messy hair, and I wonder if I really want to address our issues right now.

Taking a deep breath I walk the many steps down to where he's sitting and I know he must hear my approach. He sits there, one leg propped over his knee, leaning back, and sipping a beer.

"You decided to come home. I wasn't sure you were going to," he says without even a glance in my direction.

"River, of course I came home. Of course I did. I just needed time to calm down and figure things out. Get my head together."

"Hmm . . . funny, I'm not sure 'of course' can be assumed in any conversation we have from now on."

Taking another sip of his beer he adds, "And what do you mean you needed to figure things out? You needed to get your head together? I thought we did those things together, but I guess I was wrong."

"River, I was mad and . . . ," I start to explain but stop. He won't even look at me and I know I need to get his attention before we continue talking.

"You can't finish your thoughts. You could earlier. Should I help you? You're mad at me for not telling you, but I'm not going to apologize for that, Dahlia. I had my reasons. But the next time you decide to slap me after meeting with your ex-fiancé, maybe you could at least stick around to listen to what I have to say."

"I'm sorry that I slapped you. I shouldn't have done that. But I trusted you and you kept something important from me. How can I trust you won't mislead me again?"

Shaking his head he hisses, "Come on, Dahlia, you know you can trust me. I've never lied to you."

"I didn't say you lied. I said you didn't tell me. But you also allowed me to believe I was attacked by some random stranger. I know Grace asked you not to tell me who he was, but you really should have."

His stare is almost unbearable. He shakes his head and it infuriates me, but he says nothing so I keep talking. "Come on, River, you even hired extra security because you were worried that he would still come after me. I guess you went through all that trouble for nothing since they caught him. I'm safe now."

"Maybe you're right, but I'm not sure it even matters anymore."

"Of course it matters. Why would you say that?"

"Stop saying of course. I'm done with this conversation."

Since I've never really experienced him being angry at me, I'm unsure of how to proceed. Should I force him to talk about it? What will happen if I do? Am I ready to find out? I'm not sure about any of that. But what I do know is that River needs to understand that I love him. He needs to know that even though we haven't worked out our issues, he matters to me.

As tension fills the air between us, I watch him, still unsure about what to do. After a few more seconds of unbearable silence, I close the distance separating us and stand directly in front of him. Avoiding eye contact he leans forward, setting all four legs of the chair down. It kills me to be standing here like this, unable to touch him. I want him to talk to me. I have to break the silence. So I ask, "Do you know your brother's passed out on the couch?"

"Yeah, well, he did his best to keep up with me," he says, setting his beer bottle down next to at least a dozen others. Cocking his head to the side, he just barely glances at me. "So where does all this leave us?"

I answer in complete honesty. "The same place we were yesterday. I know we both have issues to work out, but I'm not sure talking about them anymore tonight is a good idea." Then I grab his hand and pull him out of the chair. He comes willingly. A bag of ice falls to the ground and I notice his other hand is wrapped in a kitchen towel. I swipe his hair from his forehead and try to look at him, into his eyes, but they are unfocused and the skin around one is slightly discolored. I cup his face and he closes his eyes. I run my fingers around the outline of his swollen bruise. "Does it hurt?"

"Nah, not anymore," he shrugs.

I lift his hand and can see that it's also swollen and bruised. "God, River, is it broken?"

He laughs slightly before saying, "You know, I have no fucking idea, but it hurts like hell. Xander had me move my fingers and when I did, he told me to suck it up."

I carefully caress his hand and bring it to my mouth, softly kissing it. "You can't go after Ben every time you see him. Fighting with him isn't going to change anything."

"Might not change anything, but makes me feel a hell of a lot better."

His body tenses and I know this still isn't the time to discuss Ben, but it is the right time to tell him how I feel. I run my fingertips along his cheek, silently apologizing for slapping him before saying it. "I really am so sorry." I hope he knows I mean it for more than just the slap. Leaning into him, I take his other hand and bring both to my mouth as I tell him what I've wanted him to know since I drove away this morning. "River, I love you. Ben being alive doesn't change that. You know that—right?"

Exhaling, he grabs my face and looks directly into my eyes. Despite his drunken state, his eyes seem more focused and his words are clear. "I want to believe your love is only for me. That your lips are mine. That your kisses are meant for me. That your body belongs to me." His arms move to my waist and tighten around me and he presses his hard body against mine. "But when you leave me to see him, it's hard to know for sure."

My breath quickens in anticipation because I know if my words can't put his mind at ease, erase his worries, or ease his fears—my body can. It always responds to him. It's not forced. It's natural. No one can ever make me feel the way he does. He knows this . . . I just need to remind him.

He shuts his eyes tightly as if he's trying to read my mind, but he doesn't have to. I know if he tries hard enough, he can feel my love. Opening his eyes, he stares back at me, as if waiting for me to respond to him, but I need to show him. So I crush my lips against his. And I'm surprised when he opens his mouth hungrily and allows me complete access. I wrap my arms around his neck and rub flush against him. I want to be one with him and I know he wants the same. His kisses start off hesitant, but when I push my hips into his, they become more aggressive. He runs his mouth down my neck to the bare spot that Aerie's sweatshirt doesn't cover.

Gasping, I push him back slightly, feeling guilty for using my body to explain my feelings when I know we should discuss what happened. "Maybe we should finish talking."

His lips find my neck again and at first he merely growls in response. "I don't think talking is what we need to do right now."

I drop my head back and let him find his way. How can I not? My body responds on its own. It's his. My anger completely evaporates at his touch. Leaving no bare place on my body where his mouth hasn't touched, he looks at me in a way that leaves me breathless, wanting him, wanting more.

He steps back and strips his shirt off before bunching the bottom of mine and doing the same. Not wanting to lose his touch, I lean into him. I need to feel his bare skin against mine before the sweatshirt is even over my head. He swiftly tosses it to the ground and snakes his arms around my waist, pulling me to him, thrusting his hips into me.

He moves his mouth to my chest and when I run my hands down the front of his jeans I hear his sharp intake of breath. We are both much more aggressive than we have ever been. I moan as he pulls and tugs on first one nipple, then the other. I hastily unzip his pants and shove a hand into them. His head drops back, but he hastily brings it back to mine and kisses me again.

Taking my hair down, he tries to run his fingers through my tangled strands and I know he can feel the sand in it. He stops immediately and looks at me questioningly.

"Did you go to the beach again today after I saw you?"

I nod and swallow, wondering why he's asking, but I answer truthfully. "Yes. That's where I went when I left Grace's."

"Why would you go back there? Did you see him again?" he hisses.

"No—of course I didn't go see Ben again. I went to the beach because it brings me peace. I needed to figure things out. If you would've called or texted me you would've known." I swallow back my hurt.

"Like I said, 'of course' is no longer assumed. And what exactly were you figuring out?"

"Nothing. Everything. You. Me. Ben. I don't even know." I notice he doesn't address not calling me, but let it go.

"I didn't realize we needed figuring out," he seethes.

"We don't. That's not what I meant."

He goes back to sit in his chair. He scrubs his face with his hands before picking up his nearly empty beer bottle and swallowing the rest of it down, but he never breaks his unnerving eye contact with me.

As he continues to stare at me in a way I haven't seen before, I decide I need my old River back before we can keep talking. I don't want to let him slip away, but don't know what to do. Averting his intense stare, my eyes dart to the stillness of the water and I know that is where I can find peace. So I strip off my pants and dive into the pool, wanting to wash my body of the sand and bottled-up emotion. Tranquility shoots through me as my skin meets the coolness of the water. Surfacing, I swim to the side and gesture to him to join me. He sits there, his pants unzipped, and shakes his head no.

Splashing water in his direction, I goad him, "What? Are you too drunk to swim? Because there sure as shit are a lot of empty beer bottles next to you."

He crosses his arms and smirks at me and I can tell he's trying not to laugh. A few more seconds pass. When I splash him again his expression changes and this time he smiles. "I could swim laps around you with all these bottles tied around my waist."

"Prove it. Come on. Don't be chickenshit. I bet you tomorrow's coffee run you can't beat me in your condition. In fact, I'll even throw in a hold-your-breath contest." I figure even though he always swims faster and can hold his breath longer, I doubt he can best me at either now. And honestly, I don't care if I win or lose—I just want him back.

"I'll take that bet and I'll have a double espresso, but it doesn't mean I'm not still mad as hell at you."

Without another word he stumbles slightly as he removes his

jeans and boxers, then dives in. He swims to the opposite end of the pool and grabs the ledge. I stay where I am, giving him his distance.

"So how's this contest going to go?" I ask.

He shrugs his shoulders. "Hold your breath first works for me."

"Okay, why not. Let's do it. On the count of three. One. Two. Three," I say and then I plunge underwater.

When I come up, I'm not even sure he went under.

"Guess I win," I say, gasping a little for air.

He nods but says nothing, his stare more intense with every passing second.

"Okay, what's next? Laps? First one to the end wins."

"Sure," he answers.

And with that, I say go and just take off. I feel him swimming near me as we pass each other somewhere in the middle of the pool.

When I finish my laps, I look for him but he's not swimming, he's standing next to me, watching me. He does his best to keep a straight face, but my exhaustion must be apparent. Through the glow of the moonlight I catch his expression.

"Stop smirking. It's not funny."

"It kind of is," he says as he hoists himself up and out of the pool.

I study his perfect naked body and he catches me when he turns to extend his hand. As he helps me up, his grip doesn't falter. I eye him as he watches me steadily, a slight hint of amusement in his face. Once I have both feet back on the ground he takes a step back. He drops his head and I can tell he's trying to contain his laughter.

Looking up, he grins and with a hint of smugness says, "You look tired."

I frown. "You cheated."

"That's a matter of opinion. I was the first one to your end of the pool. I finished my lap. You didn't say we had to return."

"Whatever." I silently dare him to go on, but he doesn't.

He just stands there and his closeness makes my pulse race. He's taking me in and I can tell. I take a step closer to him. I see his chest rising and falling a little more rapidly. I brace my hands on his shoulders.

"What do you want?" he whispers.

"You. I want your lips on mine. I want you to kiss me."

Maybe it was the touch, maybe it was my answer, but whatever the reason he swiftly picks me up. I wrap my legs around his waist and pull him closer to me. I tilt my head back and his lips attach to my neck. They are warm and soft. When they meet my mouth, it falls open to let him in. As water drips from our naked bodies, he carries me toward the stairs heading to our bedroom. With my arms draped around his neck, I rake my fingernails along his shoulder blades and he shivers. He hastily sets me down on one of the steps and hovering over me he asks, "What else do you want?"

Gasping, I manage to answer, "You. Just you."

He grabs me, yanking me forward, and I know we're not going to make it up the stairs. He takes my hands, raising them above my head, and locks our fingers together. He traces my mouth with his tongue and tugs on my lower lip. Freeing one hand, he runs it past my stomach down to my slick flesh. His touch sends an instant feeling of exhilaration through my body. My breathing speeds up and I work my tongue up his neck, wanting to taste every inch of him.

He inhales sharply and releases my other hand. Moving his hands to my waist, he then slides his hand to my lower back, forcefully pulling me to him. I am shaking with need as I shift my hands down to grab him. When my fingers stroke his thick shaft and I circle his tip, he groans.

He lifts his head and stares at me. "I need to be inside of you."

"I'm yours. Take me."

Forgoing any foreplay, his hands push my legs further apart. He runs his tongue over his bottom lip before crushing his mouth to mine.

I close my eyes as fire explodes through my body. Then he grabs both of my hands and raises them back over my head, holding my hands in place with one of his. I watch him as he takes himself in his hand, readying himself for me, and I gasp at the pure eroticism of it all. He plunges into me and I scream out as he takes what's his. The pace he sets is hard and fast. Watching him and feeling the weight of his body on mine makes me tremble. I can't touch him and somehow that only makes my need for him more intense. I know what he's doing—he's marking me, but I don't care. He already owns every piece of me. If he needs this to remind him, I'll give it to him.

When he grinds himself deep inside me, my head falls back and my legs tighten around him without any conscious thought. He urges me to follow his pace as he moves hard and fast and I follow. He seems to get lost in the moment, like he can't get enough of me. I close my eyes and just absorb every ounce of him.

We touch each other everywhere. Our hands, our lips, our bodies, they never leave each other. Running, pressing, skimming, and gliding over every ounce of flesh, we continue to move at a pace we never have before. I open my eyes in time to see his close. My moans turn into his groans and before I know it I am screaming, "Oh God, yes!" over and over again. Pausing before taking one final thrust, he does the same.

Shuddering, he pulls out of me and lifts my arms over my head again with one hand while the other moves down my body. I'm taken aback as to what he's doing but when his hot breath hits my neck and his hand cups my sex, I know. I moan. I can't help it. I'm already so wet from the combination of him and me that when he inserts two fingers inside me they easily slide in. His thumb presses against me as his fingers move in and out, over and over. I can feel him harden against my thigh and the need to have him inside me is stronger than ever. He moves his mouth to my breast and circles the nipple with his tongue before sucking on it, and, although I just came, I can feel it building again. The warm hardness resting on my thigh, his hand on my sex, his mouth on my nipple—it's sensory overload and I scream out as pleasure tears through me.

I'm still panting a minute later when, without a word, he picks me up and carries me the rest of the way up the stairs and into the house. After kicking the door shut, he sets me on the bed and lies next to me, urging me to move on top of him. Of course I do. I tuck my arms under his neck and lay my head on his chest. Once my breathing calms, I kiss his neck and then nuzzle into it. He kisses my head and rests his cheek there. We both know we have to talk, but neither of us wants to and that's okay for now.

After a few minutes, I peek up at him and his eyes are fixed on me. I raise one eyebrow and smirk at him.

He grins back. "What?"

I try to make light of a situation that I know is nothing but heavy. "You skipped all the romance, lover boy."

Laughing, he says, "You know it can't always be rainbows and butterflies."

I grin at him, remembering the first weekend we spent together and how I asked him if he was dreaming of rainbows and butterflies. Then, inching myself up next to him on the pillow so that we are nose to nose, I say, "I think you got the butterflies part down pretty well."

We lie together for a long while, but neither one of us falls asleep. Leaning over him, I push the hair from his eyes and kiss his nose. "I missed you today."

"I missed you, too."

"Don't ever not call me again."

"Dahlia, you're the one who wouldn't talk to me at Grace's and then took off. Calling you wouldn't change what happened, and, honestly, I was pissed at you and didn't want to talk to you."

Tears well in my eyes, and he pulls me back down to him. "Besides, how could I call you when you smashed your phone?"

I look at him, dumbfounded. "How do you know that?"

"I called Aerie this morning and she told me she was on her way to see you. Later on she texted me that you got mad and threw your phone. Care to tell me why?"

"I think you already know why, smart-ass."

"Yeah, but I want to hear you say it."

I give him a shut-up-now-before-you-get-in-any-more-trouble look and say, "Please promise to always call, no matter how mad we are."

"First you have to promise you won't hang up on me."

"I promise to never hang up."

Making a crossing motion over his heart, he says, "I promise to call."

"River, I'm sorry we never made it to Las Vegas." We haven't discussed our postponed elopement and I want him to know getting married to him is something I still plan to do.

He stares at me for a long time, maybe searching for answers to his own questions, questions he should already know the answers to. "There's a lot going on right now. We'll make it there when the time's right."

With that, I know we have done enough talking for one night. So when he wraps his arms around me, rolling us over, I close my eyes and get lost in him again.

This time we don't take it slow, either, but River pours his heart into every touch and I show my love for him with every single kiss. I don't know what time it is when we finish, but I lie back on top of him, ready to drift off to sleep. Tonight I don't need to pick a side of the bed. I will stay where I am, where I want to be.

CHAPTER 10
Rebel Beat

"*River,* get your ass out of bed! We have to meet with Ellie in thirty minutes." Those are the first words I hear, right as our bedroom door swings open. I grab for the blanket and pull it up as far as I can.

Rolling to his side, he pulls me behind him, shielding me. "What the fuck, Xander, did you forget how to knock?"

Xander stands there, looking very hungover. Leaning against the doorframe he says, "Shit. I thought you were alone. Didn't know the Muse came home. Well, we have a meeting, so get your ass up."

"I'm not going to any more meetings. Go without me."

"This one is with the label."

"Xander, I'm not going."

Xander shakes his head and mumbles something under his breath that sounds like "asshole" but then he says, "Whatever, lover boy! I'll call you later with the details."

As River pulls me tighter to him, I nestle my head contentedly on his shoulder.

"I'm sure you will," he says to Xander.

"I'm outta here. Glad to see you worked it out."

I wave goodbye to him and River says, "Xander, thanks for last night."

Xander rubs his hand against the back of his head. "Whatever, no problem, but maybe next time we could stick to vodka."

River and I both get a laugh out of that. Xander really does look like a mess. Funny, I thought he could hold his liquor.

"Yeah, man, but I'm not planning on there being a next time," River says, and I tighten my hold on him and kiss his shoulder.

Xander smirks as he leaves. Closing the door behind him he yells back, "By the way—nice shiner."

I lean around to kiss River; my fingers dance up his bare back. "You should go to those meetings, you know. It's not good for the lead singer of the band to look disinterested."

Turning his head to meet my kiss, he rolls over. Hovering over me, his lips almost touching mine, he answers me. "I'm *not* interested so I guess the way it looks is the way it is."

I shove him a little.

"What? It's the truth."

"Well, since the tour is really happening, I think . . ."

He doesn't let me finish before he rolls us over so that I'm once again lying on top of him. "There. Let's start the morning over."

I laugh and let him do what he's so very good at—changing the subject.

One hand moves the hair off my face as he asks, "What do you want to do today, beautiful girl?"

"I think we should probably work. Don't you?"

He shakes his head. "I just want a few hours alone with you."

Circling my fingers around his now very black eye, I grin slyly and say, "That can be arranged."

"So any ideas?"

"I don't know. Nothing, everything."

"Well, that narrows it down," he says as he continues to stroke my hair.

"Does it hurt?" I'm staring at his eye.

He raises his arm over his head and shakes it before saying, "Nope, just a little sore. I'll be able to lift the Starbucks coffee you're going to get with no problem."

I burst into a fit of giggles before I can respond. "First of all I meant your eye, but I'm glad your hand is better, and, second of all, I did not lose, you did! You couldn't have stayed underwater even if I would have held you there."

"Yeah, I might have been a little buoyant."

I can only laugh. He was more than a little buoyant, but talking about why he drank so much is not what I want to do right now. "How about we stop for coffee on the way to do something I have always wanted to do?"

He slides his body along the length of mine, then slips his arms under my back and presses his lips to my ear. "Hmmm . . . that sounds fun."

I sigh deeply. With his body so close and his warm breath on me, it's hard to concentrate. I think a day away from all the chaos will help us both find the courage to have the conversation neither one of us wants to initiate. With determination I place my hands on his chest and push him off me slightly.

"What?" he asks, glancing down at me.

"Not sex!"

He pauses, then kisses me. "I know," he laughs, "but I can't help it if my mind wanders when you throw words around like 'something I've never done.'"

Careful not to grab his sore hand, I scoot out from under him and pull him by his other hand. "Come on, lover boy, we're headed to Keanu Reeves territory."

He looks at me questioningly and shakes his head no.

"*Point Break*. Keanu Reeves. Johnny Utah. Latigo Beach," I say so he knows where I'm talking about.

All signs of playfulness and laughter disappear. "I know the movie, Dahlia. But I'm not going to the beach with you."

I gently clutch both of his hands and mold my naked body to his. Staring right into his emerald green eyes, I beg, "Please. Let's go to Malibu. I've never been and I think it will be a good place for us to spend the day together."

Resting his forehead against mine, he slowly shakes his head. "I don't know."

"You have to go to the beach with me eventually. Let's just get in the car and hop on the 101. Once we get there, if you're still not feeling it, we can just hit up Neptune's Net for breakfast."

He looks straight at me when he says, "God, why can't I ever just say no to you?"

Once I'm showered and dressed in my bathing suit, shorts, and my concert T-shirt of The Who, I pull my hair back and head downstairs. I'm in my office typing out a few e-mails when he enters. He had to take a call from Xander so I decided to get a little work done.

He comes in wearing jeans, a white short-sleeve T-shirt, and his Wayfarer sunglasses. It looks more than hot on him but it's not exactly beach apparel, so I have to laugh. Especially when I look down and see his Adidas—at least he traded his work boots for sneakers.

"You can't wear jeans to the beach."

There's a flash of the smirk I love before he slides the waistband of his jeans down so I can see his board shorts. Come to think of it I don't think I've ever seen him in shorts and I know he would never own a pair of flip-flops. I have to draw in a deep breath to compose myself because he looks amazing no matter what he wears, and showing me his bare skin does amazing things to me. But if I act on them we'll never make it to the beach.

"You're not going to make me wear a Ronald Reagan mask, are you?" he jokes, turning around and lacing his fingers in mine before pulling me out the door. We head back upstairs and grab some water bottles, towels, and my camera. As we exit through the kitchen, he stops to pick up the key lying on the landing and puts it back on top of the doorframe. I point to the hole in the wall. "Did you do that?"

"Yeah, I guess I did."

"River, why . . . ," I start to ask, but I know why so I stop.

He responds anyway. "Well, let's just say I was in a piss-ass mood and the key wouldn't cooperate."

I look away in avoidance. I'm not ready to talk more about Ben, and I know he isn't, either, so I step by him and head down the stairs. I really just want to spend the day together and enjoy each other's company.

We cruise down to Malibu in his vintage black Porsche, managing to somehow keep the mood light.

"Did I tell you Jack talked to me about helping him produce MC Hammer's *Too Tight* album?"

I snap my head in his direction; my jaw drops. "Shut up. You're shitting me. How did he get that? I thought it was buried along with his career."

He laughs. "No, I'm not. Jack picked up some small production company that years ago had acquired Death Row Records' vault, and it's just sitting in there, waiting for someone to show it some love. Jack just has to see if he can get MC to sign off on it."

"Isn't gangster rap a little passé?"

River shakes his head. "Maybe, who knows? But the cameo by Tupac will have everyone listening."

I nod my head, trying not to think about the sadness of Tupac Shakur's murder. River rolls his window down and I follow suit. Then he starts singing "U Can't Touch This," and I laugh hysterically. Soon I'm grabbing my camera and shooting pictures of him. He turns and mouths, "You can't touch this" as well as some of the other best lines, and I capture them all.

To get in beach mode, I pick up his phone and scroll through the iTunes store, downloading every song I can find with the word *beach* or *fun* in it. I want him to be excited to go to the beach, but most of the songs I select just make him roll his eyes—until I download "California Girls" by the Beach Boys. As it plays his smile widens. He sings along with me and we unknowingly have a contest for who can sing the words "wish they all could be California girls" the loudest. He smiles so brightly I can see his dimples. He even splays his hand out in the wind, thumping to his own beat. When the song finishes I turn the volume down and just watch him.

He glances my way and lifts his sunglasses. "Yesss . . ."

"Nothing, I'm just surprised that you like the Beach Boys."

"Well . . . not that I want to ruin my cool rocker image or anything, but I'll tell you a secret," he says, winking at me. "My dad made us listen to them every time we ever went to the beach, and after a while they started to grow on me."

"That's actually really cool. And your rocker image is still intact, no worries. I won't tell anyone." River falls silent for the rest of the drive. I wonder if it was the song, the conversation, or the fact that we are quickly approaching the beach.

A part of me knows River feels the beach was a place for me and Ben, but that simply isn't true. True, we both loved the beach, but that doesn't mean I can't love it with River. I want to be able to experience the beauty of one of the most magical places with him, and this feels like the time to bridge one of the last barriers between us.

We pull into the public parking lot and he swings the car into a spot. When he turns the ignition off, I can see his reluctance. "Hey, are you okay?"

Removing his sunglasses, he looks at me—I mean really looks at me—before speaking. Then, pointing to the beautiful Pacific Ocean that stands before us, he says, "I'm not sure we should be doing this."

I don't hesitate in the slightest before saying, "Well, I am."

Then I reach over and push the hair from his eyes. "I love you. Only you. Okay? And I want to share one of my favorite places with you. I want us to experience this together. We need to do this, River—for you and for me. For us."

He sits quietly, like he's weighing the pros and cons of what I just said. He stays like that for the longest time. I try to hasten his decision by opening my door. But when he doesn't do the same, I move back in my seat and decide to resort to enticement. Pulling off my T-shirt, I sit there with the hot sun beating through the window in my black bikini top, then lean back and wiggle out of my shorts.

While he watches me, his lips part and his chest moves a little more rapidly. A wicked grin appears on his face as he runs his finger up one of the strings of my top. "If you'd have taken your clothes off when we first got in the car, we probably would never have made it to the beach, you know." With that, he opens his door, takes his shoes off, and stands to strip off his jeans. I watch him and think he's right.

"*Come* with me," he says, quirking a finger and leading me up the mound of rocks. I stop halfway to snap photos of him climbing. His strong muscular legs easily carry him up the rocks. When he sits on one of the boulders, I crouch down and snap. The wind blows through his light brown hair and with his sunglasses on he not only looks content and carefree, but sexy as hell. Every muscle in his chest and abs is on display as I click, zooming in to capture one or two close shots. "Sing something for me." I have to raise my voice to be heard around the camera and the sound of the ocean splashing against the rocks.

He reaches his hand to pull me next to him but I stay right where I am. Standing, I steady myself and flip my camera to video mode. "Come on, one song."

His eyes move across my face, then drift down my body. He smiles a small sneaky grin. "Do I look like a jukebox?" he says, stifling a laugh.

Feeling the familiar heat of his gaze, I answer, "No, of course not. Why do you ask?" I already know his question has a purpose, and I'm extremely curious to discover what it is.

"You asked for a song. If I were a jukebox you'd have to insert coins to get me to play. Right?"

"Yes, I suppose if you were but since you're not . . ." I stand there admiring the glow of his hair in the sunlight.

He extends his hand again. "Then come here and give me a kiss, and I'll play something for you."

Slipping my hand in his, he pulls me to his lap. I wrap my arms around him and his lips find mine. His kiss is soft, warm, and full of promise. His hands move everywhere . . . up my back, over my arms, on my hips. His kisses become harder and deeper until we both break for air, both feeling that familiar desire surfacing. Placing kisses up and down my neck, his lips slide along my collarbone and up my chin to my ear. He starts singing "Beach Side" in my ear, and, in the exhilaration of the moment, I forget all about recording him. Next to kissing him, hearing River sing to me is the most romantic thing I've ever known.

For hours afterward we walk the beach and make sand castles, with River even using shells to carve out moats around them. We chase each other through the surf, and when he catches me he picks me up and twirls me around before throwing me in the waves. After lunch we even buy a kite and keep it flying in the air for at least fifteen minutes. Now that evening is rapidly approaching and our perfect day is just about over, he begins to sing to me again. He has seemed more like himself today, still a little sad, still a little on edge, but all in all his demeanor is far improved.

As I sit between his legs on top of a massive boulder, his song ends and he rests his forehead against mine. Then he pulls away with one lone groan. I can't help my grin. Knowing we've gone as far as we can on the public beach, we turn to the west to watch the magnificent sunset. Sunrises and sunsets are among my favorite things, especially to photograph. I lean back into his chest and continue to snap pictures as he wraps his arms around me, kissing my head. I don't want this perfect moment to end, and I know when we get home we have to talk. The fact that Ben is alive means that whether or not I want him in my life, we have to talk it through, figure out what it means that he's not dead. Ben and I share more than a past, we share more than possessions, we share a family—Grace, Serena, and Trent. And even though I'm a little upset with Grace right now, they are just as big a part of my life as his.

He jostles me out of my thoughts when he whispers, "I'm going to miss days like these."

"What do you mean?" I have to peer over my shoulder to see him.

"Us alone. No one else around. Days when it's just you and me against the world."

"We'll still have that, River. Maybe not as often or for as long, but we will."

Unsure where this conversation is headed, I wait for him to say more.

He kisses my temple and shifts his head down to my neck. "You know I don't want to do this. Don't you," he murmurs into my ear . . . and it's not a question.

I need to look at him for this, so I rise up from between his legs and move to sit beside him. Resting my head on his shoulder, I stay silent a long while. I know he's talking about the tour, but I feel helpless to assist him in any way. He made his decision and I don't want to add any stress to the already large emotional load he carries. Looking up at him, I stroke his cheek with my fingers and say the only thing I can. "I know, River, I know. Why don't you just tell Xander? Explain to him how you feel."

There's a haunted look in his eyes. "I can't do that. I promised I would do this, and I'm not going to break my promise."

I hesitate a minute, then ask, "Who did you promise?"

His body tenses and he inhales deeply. "Dahlia. I've never really explained how my dad died. Not that I haven't wanted to, but more because the memory isn't one I ever want to relive."

One look at his somber expression, and compassion and pain swirl inside me as I fight to keep my own face expressionless. Beyond sympathy for him, for losing his father, I also feel my own remorse. For never having pushed him to tell me how his father died, other than the fact that he died from a gunshot wound when River was sixteen. I'm not sure why I never did; I could just tell it was something he didn't want to discuss—and that was a feeling I knew well. My eyes lock on his and I give him a look that lets him know it's okay to go on, that I'm here for him.

Letting out a long cleansing breath, he starts to open up. "Xander and I promised our dad that we would do everything we could to be successful."

Cupping his cheeks I say, "Every parent wants that for their child, and, River, you are successful."

Sighing, he shakes his head. "No, Dahlia, he was always pretty specific. He wanted us to hit it big in the music industry. It was his dream for himself but no matter how hard he tried to achieve it, he never could. He teetered close twice. The first time he cut an album and toured, but low sales and low attendance had him starting at square one. When I was fourteen he got a second chance, but by then he was too far gone. After that he never performed again. Our family life changed forever the day he killed himself and willed his dream on us."

A wall of silence forms between us for a moment as my eyes widen in disbelief. Tears sting my eyes, and I want to hold him, to comfort him. But I can tell he wants to continue, so I refrain. "I'm so sorry, River, I never knew. But I'm here. You can talk to me about it."

Sniffing and looking toward the water he says, "Like I said, my dad was a dreamer—he always wanted to hit it big but never could catch a break. I never even knew how unhappy he was for the longest time. He made us his life. Taught us everything he could. He tried to provide for us as best he could by teaching guitar lessons out of our house during the day and performing on the weekends. When I was about ten, he started playing local joints at night and not coming home until late. It was about that time Grandpa started showing up secretly to slide my mom an envelope full of cash to buy groceries and whatever we needed. She took the money so my dad wouldn't feel like what he was providing wasn't enough. Xander used to get so mad at her for that. He thought she should just tell him, make him stop, but she never would. She wanted to believe he'd see his dream come true."

My heart breaks a little more with every word he says and I comfort him in the best way I can. "Well, your mom loved him—she wanted to be supportive and didn't want to hurt him. That's understandable."

"Dahlia, that's just it. That's the ironic part. He was hurting all of us, and Xander was the only one who saw it. My dad didn't live in the real world, and my mom didn't make him. He lived in his dream world, a world where he was a star. He started drinking to forget the reality of his situation. His drinking had gotten so bad that once my mom went back to work, Xander and I would try to sober him up before she got home. One day we came home after school and found him drunk and in bed with another woman. We cleaned him up and got the woman out of the house before our mom came home. My mom loved him, and that would have killed her. He always said how much he loved her, too. But that was a funny way of showing it. Xander hated him after that. I loved him, I hated him, but most of all I pitied him."

I caress River's cheek and push down my sadness. "What you felt was only natural. You love your mother and didn't want to see her hurt." Not sure I want to hear the answer, but knowing I have to ask the question. I whisper, "What happened to him?"

Framing my face with his gentle hands, he looks deeply into my eyes. "Promise me that after I tell you, we never have to talk about it again."

"River, I promise," I tell him, turning my head to kiss his hand.

My heart sinks as I prepare to listen to the rest of his story. His eyes sadden and his voice cracks as he tells it. "One day, Xander and I came home from basketball practice and dad was completely tanked. He had picked Bell up from school instead of having her go to her after-school program because he thought she needed more practice on the guitar. As soon as we walked in we could hear him. He was yelling at her, telling her she wasn't playing the right chords and to do it again. She was crying and her fingers were bleeding, actually *bleeding*. As soon as Xander saw that, he lost it. He attacked my dad, punching him over and over, and my dad didn't return a single one, but Xander didn't stop. He yelled for me to get Bell out of there and I did. I brought her to the neighbor's, called my grandpa, and by the time I went back, my dad was dead."

There is so much pain in his voice already I don't want to ask him to continue. Tears roll down my cheeks and my pulse is racing, but I know he wants to tell me the rest—I can see it in his eyes. So, taking a deep breath, I take both his hands in mine and urge him to go on. "What happened?"

His voice hitches, and he tells me something he has never openly talked about with anyone. "My mom had come home just after I left, and she had pulled Xander off him. My dad told her what happened, and she told him he had to leave, to get out. He went in the bedroom, and she and Xander thought he was packing his stuff . . . until they heard the gunshot."

Shivering, I hug him as tight as I can. "I'm so sorry, River. I'm so sorry."

He straightens his shoulders and pulls away, taking my hands in his. His voice tightens in anger as he talks. "That's not all. He left a note. It didn't say he was sorry, or why he did it. Instead it said, 'I love you all. Boys, take care of Mom, and, Bell, and don't ever settle for not being at the top, because I know you can do what I couldn't.' Xander and Bell never sang or played again after that day. But I never stopped. I don't know if I kept on for him or for me, but I loved it and was happy doing it until the day Xander came home from seeing my grandfather and told me he wanted to manage my career—to put me on top. I never asked why, but since then he's been determined to make the band succeed. Dahlia, I can't let him down."

"You owe it to yourself to do what's right for you now, River. Please think about that."

"My father always told us that scars are the road maps to one's soul. It took me forever to figure out what he meant, but I did when I met you."

Touched by his words but heartbroken by what happened to him, and to his family, I tip his chin up so I meet his eyes when I speak. "I love you so much."

He sags against me, touching his nose to mine. Then he buries his head in my neck and sighs. After a few minutes he brings his lips to mine and kisses me with a need I know I can fill. His kiss is deep, powerful, and unstrained. His strong frame hovers over me. The raw, desperate need I feel from him makes me surrender to him, and I let the conversation drop without further discussion even though I think we should talk about the upcoming tour. He wraps his arms around my back and dips my body down onto the rock.

We stay like that, devouring each other, until the sun slips through the sky. But once the sun has set on the horizon, it's time for us to head home. We have dinner plans with River's family, and we're going to be late. With his arm slung around me and my hand tucked in the waistband of his board shorts, he carries the bucket of shells we found along the shore and I carry my camera and our towels as we head back to the parking lot.

When we get to the car, he reaches to open my door and I grab his arm to stop him. I push myself up against his smooth bare chest so that our sunburns blend into one. "I had an amazing day," I tell him as I softly brush against the lips I just spent an hour kissing and still didn't get enough of. And then I feel the need to tell him something else. I'm not sure why. I run the back of my hand along his cheek, caressing it gently. "Everything you and I did today, Ben and I never did as adults. We never took the time to just enjoy the beach—so thank you for taking the time with me." I notice him flinch at Ben's name, but the tension quickly passes.

And even though we are both barely dressed and our bodies are pressed up against each other, he refrains from making a move. Instead he circles his arms around me and just holds me tight. Resting his mouth on my ear, he whispers, "Thank you for that and everything else."

Then he opens my door and ushers me into the car. We don't discuss anything we talked about today on the car ride back to LA. In fact, we hardly talk at all. Instead we listen to a new band that River really likes called Atlas Genius. He wanted his stepfather to sign them but he didn't. I love their single "Through the Glass"; he prefers their song "Electric." Both have strong lyrics, and as we listen I can't help but think we are both taking this time to reflect on all that has happened and everything we discussed.

We are so late that we don't even take the extra ten minutes to go home and change before going to Charlotte and Jack's. I've been over to River's mother and stepfather's house for dinner at least once a week since moving to LA, but tonight feels different now that I know what happened between Charlotte and River's father. I feel like I understand her more—not that I didn't before. Maybe I feel sympathy for her more now, but I know I shouldn't. She's a strong, caring woman who loves her family; and she's happy now, which makes me happy.

Before entering the house, I reach for his arm. "Did you tell Charlotte and Jack about Ben?"

He flinches. Then, lacing his hand in mine, he kisses my forehead. "No. I thought you should tell them when you're ready."

"Do you think Xander told them?"

"No, Dahlia, he wouldn't do that."

"So Bell doesn't know, either?"

"Hey, nobody knows anything. Okay?" he says, slightly agitated.

River walks in without ringing the doorbell and we find them all in the kitchen. Charlotte's kitchen is unlike any I have ever seen. It's huge and has an old-world feel. The double-stacked ovens are encased in a brick wall, and two sinks sit in one island. There's another sink along the wall next to the refrigerator, and there are even two dishwashers. A large wooden table seats twelve at one end of the kitchen while the cooking island planks the other end. Bell and Xander are sitting at the middle island in the center of the room. There's a gorgeous chandelier above it and five barstools.

The smell of garlic immediately assaults me, and I know the family's favorite garlic mashed potatoes are on the menu. When Brigitte, the housekeeper, didn't immediately greet us, I know she isn't here and Charlotte must be the one cooking tonight.

River spots his mother at the stove and heads over to her. I follow behind him, waving to Xander and Bell on the way.

He kisses his mother on the cheek. "Hey, Mom. Sorry we're late; we lost track of time."

"Oh, River, your eye," she says, brushing his hair from his face.

"Xander told me you two were playing around and he accidentally hit you, but I had no idea it was that bad." She turns to scowl at Xander, and I have to admire how the boys always want to protect their mother.

River walks toward Xander and Bell, and I kiss Charlotte as well. "Hi, Charlotte. It's my fault we're late. I insisted on going to the beach today."

She tucks my windblown hair behind my ear. "Stop it. You're not late. And it looks like the two of you got way too much sun today. Xander, grab them each a water, please, will you, honey?"

Looking at his watch, then at each of us, Xander says, "Since lover boy is late, I think he can manage his own water."

I look over to Bell, whose sense of style never falters. She's wearing an orange, off-the-shoulder shirt with army green skinny jeans and her always-present high heels. She rolls her eyes and punches Xander in the arm. "They aren't that late, just forty-five minutes. I'll grab them each a water," she says, smirking at Xander.

We walk toward them and she hands each of us a bottle and hugs us. She seems gleeful and I ask, "What's going on?"

Biting her bottom lip, then smiling a huge smile, she says, "I stopped by Jack's office today, and not only did I meet Zane Perry and hear his dad's record, I got an internship with Tate Wyatt."

River's mouth drops open and excitement lights up his eyes. "Zane Perry was in the studio today? Was he cutting a new album?"

Looks like I'm not the only one jealous that she got to watch Zane. He's a musical genius. His music just commands your attention.

Bell shrugs her shoulders. "I have no idea. But his agent, Damon Wolf, was there, too."

Everyone grows silent and River's gaze darts to Xander in a manner so blatant I can't help but notice. Then I see that Charlotte's normally vibrantly glowing face has paled, and she excuses herself. I don't ask why, and simply let it pass. I know Damon has a reputation for being a bit of a hothead agent, so who knows whose path he's crossed? His father is also the head of Sheep Industries, which owns *Sound Music Magazine*. Hmmm . . . that must be who Aerie was talking about. Strange that Damon's interested in the magazine. Maybe he's trying to settle down and get off the road. I know that after he proposed to Ivy Taylor, she severely cut her performance schedule and actually hadn't done anything in months. Her music career was on the fast track but she had put out only one album and really hadn't marketed it, which was a shame because she has the most unique style—I once dreamed of photographing her. I even had an idea worked up in my mind for an album design; she has the perfect face for it. We'll see. . . .

Bell puts her hands on her hips and pulls me from my fan-girl thoughts. "All I know is Jack signed him last week. Did you hear what I said about my job with Tate Wyatt?"

Xander seems distracted when he speaks—his voice is gruff and he avoids looking at anyone. "Who is Tate Wyatt?"

Bell sighs and throws herself back on the barstool. "Only the top event planner in LA. He has a waiting list a mile long."

River looks at her skeptically. "I thought you worked for the band."

"You guys are leaving soon and I'm not coming. I need something to do and Jack had the connection."

Xander chimes in, sounding annoyed. "Just because we're not here doesn't mean there isn't work to do."

Bell sticks her tongue out at him and says, "The internship is only twelve weeks unless I get a permanent position. Let's worry about that if it happens."

Xander rolls his eyes and Charlotte says, "Xander, this is a wonderful opportunity for your sister. You should be more supportive. If need be, I can help you."

Xander nods at his mother, River snickers, and I smile at her, mouthing, "Congratulations."

The door opens and Jack comes in from the backyard with a platter of steaks in hand. "Oh, good, you guys made it just in time." Motioning to the oversize refrigerator in the butler's pantry, he says, "River, grab yourself a beer and one for me, too, if you don't mind."

River obliges and we all sit down for dinner. I really love his family. I never had a big family so I marvel at their interactions as we eat our way through dinner. I haven't been hungry and my stomach is in knots knowing that River and I still have to have the Ben conversation, but I do my best to eat and socialize.

River, on the other hand, hardly touches his food and his relaxed attitude from the beach is gone. He's bad-tempered with Xander and even short with Bell. Honestly, he's just moody all the way around during dinner.

Jack does most of the talking, but then again, he usually does. I love to hear him talk about his record label and what new albums are coming out. He tells us about a few smaller companies he has acquired and winks at River when he does, adding, "whenever you're ready to pick one up," and then casually moves on. When he mentions that Denny Harris contacted him about the possibility of the D-Bags moving over to Tyler Records, I get a little excited. I love that band.

I nudge River and whisper, "Jack might actually sign Kellan Kyle. Did you hear him?"

River shakes his head and I swear I see the hint of a smirk, but, before he can comment, Bell chimes in, "Oh, he's my ex-boyfriend. That would be so cool."

Everyone at the table laughs and looks at her.

"What?" Bell asks.

Xander being Xander just says it like it is. "Bell, just because you meet up with a guy once doesn't mean he was ever your boyfriend."

I'm surprised he uses the term *meet up*, but I guess he doesn't want Charlotte yelling at him for swearing at the table.

Bell pouts her lips. "Shut up, Xander, you're just jealous because I actually have friends."

"Sure, 'friends,' Bell. That's what they are."

I really have to stifle my laughter when Bell sticks her tongue out at him. But I'm quickly reminded of River's despondency when he doesn't join in their banter like he usually does.

Charlotte clears her throat. "That's enough." It's all she has to say and the conversation comes to an end.

We spend the rest of the night talking music, and, whenever the Wilde Ones' tour is mentioned, River withdraws into himself even more. I can see Charlotte notice, and I'm surprised she doesn't say anything.

Once we've all helped clean up, River turns to me. "You ready to go?"

I nod my head and we say our goodbyes. Xander is right behind us as we leave and Bell has already run up to her room to get ready for a date with another "boyfriend."

Once River closes my door, I hear Xander call him over. I watch the two brothers and they appear to be arguing. I'm not sure what's driving River's moodiness—reluctance over the impending tour, Ben's return, or just simply exhaustion. I am determined that tonight we will finally sit down to talk and work through everything together.

CHAPTER 11
High for This

It's after eleven when we finally pull in the driveway, and I'm so tired. We hardly talked on the short drive home—the only conversation we had was when I asked him why his family reacted strangely to Damon Wolf's name and River told me Xander dated Ivy years ago. I didn't ask any more questions because he seemed to close the door to that conversation quickly with his abrupt answer. He opens my door and quickly leads me to the stairs. I know it's now or never, so I tug his hand in the opposite direction.

"What?" he asks.

"Let's go sit outside. I think we should talk."

Jaw clenched, he says, "You sure you want to do this now?"

Staring at him, I sigh, "River . . . I think we've avoided too many conversations in the last few days. So, yeah, I think we should do this now." I know it probably isn't the perfect time, especially since he just told me about his father, but even at dinner I could feel the strain between us and I don't want it to continue. We can talk about anything and everything—so why can't we talk about Ben?

He nods his head and leads me out the door to the lower pool deck. He pulls another chair over to where he sat last night and tries to avoid knocking over the beer bottles still there. We sit in silence for a long while, both of us facing the pool and the Hollywood sign. When I kick my shoes off, he does the same and catches my eye. I can see he's unsure about how to proceed, so I just start the conversation by blurting out what's on my mind. "We talked a little bit last night about this, and even though Grace asked you not to tell me who attacked me, I wish you had. It's not that I don't get why you didn't—I just don't like you keeping things from me. Actually, I really, really dislike it."

He leans over with his head down and his hands behind his neck. When he looks up at me his eyes seem clouded with indecision. "Dahlia, it's not just about keeping things from you. It's more complicated than that."

Starting to get angry, I try to control myself. "What do you mean? In what way? What's complicated about not keeping things from me?"

He closes his eyes. "I didn't see it as keeping anything from you. I intended to tell you. Just not right away. You don't understand how I felt."

Through clenched teeth, I respond, "What do you mean how *you* felt? You haven't told me how you felt or anything else, so how about you start with that?"

He cringes and sits back up. "Grace's phone call that morning was a shock. I was never expecting that. But the guilt I felt for not going running with you, the sick feeling I got when they wouldn't let me see you in the hospital, and then the regret that overwhelmed me when I finally saw you and you were lying there in the hospital bed, it was all just too much. The last thing I wanted to do was explain who had done that to you. I knew all it would do was open an old wound and cause you more pain, and you were hurt enough."

My anger fades in the face of his loving confession. He was trying to protect me in the only way he knew how, and, after hearing about his father, I understand his actions so much better. He's rubbing his palms over his jeans with his eyes focused on me. I have to let him know I get it, that I understand. So I scoot my chair as close to his as I can and taking his hand in mine, kiss it, then place it over my heart. No words can express my feelings right now. My head drops as I think about the amount of love I have for this man. And for me to be so upset over him not telling me, when he thought it was the right thing to do, doesn't seem right anymore. I don't want to argue with him or cause him pain, so I have to let this go.

He lifts my chin. "Hey, I didn't tell you that to make you sad. I just want you to understand it wasn't a simple decision. It's not like I consciously made a choice. I just felt in my heart that Grace was right. A couple of days for you to heal before telling you the news wouldn't matter either way. So although I'm sorry you got upset, I'm not sorry I didn't tell you right away. I did what I thought was best for you. I'll always do what I think is best for you."

A cool breeze rushes by and I shiver. I have to apologize, so I sit up and inhale a deep breath. But when I cross my arms and rub them with my hands, he immediately notices and walks over to get my sweatshirt that's been lying on the ground since last night. As he picks it up, the note from Ben falls out of the pocket. Immediately my heart starts pounding and I bolt out of the chair, trying to retrieve the paper before he reads it. But he's too fast. He snatches it first and quickly scans it.

I search his eyes, trying to get a glimpse of what's going through his mind. "River, it's not what you think."

Anger flashes across his face and it doesn't take me long to figure out what he's thinking as his body goes instantly rigid. With a look of betrayal, he stands there, just feet from me on the pool deck with his hands fisting at his sides, not saying anything—just staring at the note.

Stepping closer to him, I reach for the piece of paper. "Let me explain. Ben . . ."

He cuts me off as suspicion washes over his face. His voice is harsh, almost commanding. "Yeah, I think you should explain why you have a love note from your ex-fiancé in your pocket. You told me you didn't see him again. Did you lie to me?"

My jaw drops. I've never thought of Ben as my ex-fiancé and his words paralyze me for a moment. But as the silence becomes deafening and the tension turns unbearable, I finally manage to say, "No, I didn't lie."

Taking a step back, his green eyes alternate between looking at me and looking at the note he's waving in the air. "Then how did you get this?"

Flinching at his accusation, I start trembling as nerves overtake me. I know I didn't do anything wrong, but the way he's looking at me makes me feel guilty and it terrifies me. Not in a physical way, more in a he's-done-with-this kind of way. With that thought, I inhale a deep breath and say, "When I left my house yesterday it was on the windshield of my car. I needed to leave a note for Serena so I tore off the bottom half and shoved the rest in my pocket. It doesn't mean anything."

He closes his eyes and I can see his body start to shake as well. When he opens them again they're unfocused—looking everywhere but at me. "Let me get this straight. So not only did you spend the day at the house you shared with him, but he was there with you."

His observation is so blatantly false I don't falter in my response. "I told you he left it on my car. He never came in the house. I never saw him after I left Grace's. Like I said, the note doesn't mean anything to me."

"Fuck, Dahlia, how can you say it doesn't mean anything? He wrote you a love note and you kept it in your pocket. That means something to me."

I move forward. When I step into him and try to cup his cheeks, try to get him to look at me, he steps back. Crumbling the note in his hand, he shakes his head and tosses it into the pool. Without even looking at me, he walks over to where we were sitting, picks up a beer bottle and smashes it against the stairs. I watch it break into a million tiny pieces. The sound deafens me as he throws another and another.

I rush over to him and grab his arm. "River, stop it."

He bats my arm away and continues until every bottle lies broken on the ground. Looking down I hope I'm not looking at a reflection of the despair I swear I see on his face. . . . Is his faith in me shattered? Touching him, talking to him, I need to figure out how to make him understand. Grabbing his arm with one hand, I clutch his face with the other. "River, please talk to me."

Jerking his head back, he glares at my hand and then yells louder than I have ever heard him yell before. "Do you have any idea how it makes me feel to know that you're still a part of his life? Dead was one thing, but now he's alive."

"He's not in my life."

He stops me with one look, clenching his jaw as he walks away. Near the railing, he stops and leans back, crossing his arms. Glaring at me he seethes in anger and spits out, "Do you have any idea how I felt when I woke up yesterday and you were gone? Do you?"

Tears sting my eyes. I don't want to fight with him anymore. I just want all of this to go away and for us to go back to us, not these two angry people who don't know how to calmly discuss their issues. Trying my best to remain calm I quietly start to explain, "River, I left you a note—"

But again he cuts me off. His eyes cut to mine as rage clearly defines every inch of his body. "You left me a fucking *note* that you were going to see the man you spent your whole life with. The man you left me for the first time we met. The man whose ghost I have had to compete with every day of our lives together."

My eyes widen in disbelief that he felt that way, maybe still feels this way, and sorrow washes through me. My lip trembles as I try to explain. "River, why didn't you ever tell me how you felt? I had no idea. We could have talked about it. You know how I feel—that part of my life is over."

Clearly frustrated, he runs his hands through his hair. Then he quickly moves toward me, and, grabbing my arm, he points to my wrist. "Then why do you still wear this? Why haven't you taken it off? You know what? Let me answer that for you—because you can't let him go. Do you still love him?"

Irritated now, I raise my hand and contemplate slapping him. Having decided against it, I hastily drop it. But really, how dare he accuse me of that?

His eyes narrow. "If it makes you feel better to slap me again, go ahead."

My irritation returns, but I don't hit him. I'm really not a violent person. So instead I twist away, pause briefly, then head for the door. Fuck him. He isn't the only one who gets to be mad.

He's behind me in an instant, grabbing my hand and pulling me back. I turn around on my heels. "I am not going to talk to you when you're like this," I snap.

"That's it? You're just going to walk away?" he yells. Then letting me go, he turns around and walks back to the chairs.

Muttering under my breath I whisper, "This is getting us nowhere. I'm going inside."

My words set something off inside of him and he's quickly beside me again. For a few short seconds, we stand there, face-to-face, glaring at each other. He takes me in, every inch of me. There is a sense of urgency between us I've never felt before. My heart is racing. He walks me backward until my legs are flush against the stone railing surrounding our patio. With his eyes still burning into mine, he lifts me so that I am sitting on top of the wall. He fits his body between my legs. I run my hands down his chest and around to his back, my fingers digging into it.

Enunciating his words so that his message is crystal clear he tells me, "You're not going anywhere. Dahlia. I'm done with you walking away every time we have an argument. You got it?"

Nodding my head yes, I'm a little stunned by his aggressiveness but for some reason I'm also incredibly turned on.

"River . . . the note means nothing. Those are Ben's words, not mine. He's just stuck in the past. And you know the reason I wear the bracelet isn't about Ben. I told you why—to remind myself to live life to the fullest, to have no regrets. But River, you mean everything to me and I don't think I can get you to see that right now. I'm not sure you're in any state of mind to hear what I have to say. That's why I was leaving."

He forces me to look at him. "Dahlia, you're wrong. We *can* talk about this now; we are talking about this now. What it comes down to is that unless you tell me you still love him, there is nothing we can't work out."

Staring at his bleak expression, I break. "I love you. I want you. It's simply only you. I promise." My hands fist the hem of his shirt, wanting to pull it off. My hands clench and unclench in the fabric as my heart beats even faster.

His lips part and his eyes grow dark with desire. He lets his fingers drift down to my shoulders and I shudder. When he places his hands on my thighs, spreading them wider, I crave his touch everywhere. My blood races as his eyes hold mine captive.

When I'm finally able to break free of this trance, I lick the outline of his lips, tasting the salty seawater from the beach still on his skin.

Pulling back, he studies me and his green eyes gleam under the halo of lights from the Hollywood sign. I press my palms to his chest and run them up under his shirt. He groans, and then slips his tongue in my mouth. I gasp when he forcefully thrusts his hips into mine and lose my connection to his lips.

His hands move from my hips to my chest. He presses his fingers into my skin as he traces the small curves of my breasts, and then grazes each rib before stopping at the waistband of my shorts. When his hands reach my hips again he cups my backside and lifts me up. Leaning my head against his, I run my fingers through his hair, tugging it ever so lightly and cinch my legs around his waist.

Closing my eyes, I feel our mouths meet again. We're frantic for each other and our breathing becomes erratic. After a beat, he turns us around and starts walking toward the staircase. When I mold my body to his, he stops and presses my back against the wall, grinding into me. Again it's more aggressive than we've ever been, even more so than last night. Hastily setting me down, his hands are at my waist in an instant and I whimper with longing when he tears the button off my shorts and I hear it clink on the patio. He yanks my shorts, along with my bathing suit bottom, down and they fall to the ground.

The more he touches me . . . the more I want to touch him, love him, satisfy him. I reach for his jeans, unbuttoning and unzipping them as fast as I can. He groans when I slide my hand into his board shorts. His lips find mine again and when he bites down on my lower lip, I want his pants all the way off. His are not as easy to maneuver as mine so he does it for me. I lift his shirt up and pull it over his head. Looking at his smooth chest sends a rush of adrenaline through me.

Standing there completely naked, looking at me in anticipation of what's to come, he practically tears my shirt off. He hastily tugs at the string behind my neck and the triangles of my bikini top fall to my stomach. When he pushes against me I can feel how much he wants me. His breathing hitches and his eyes blaze as he stares at me intently, like he wants to devour me.

"Mine always," he whispers, nipping my earlobe with his teeth.

"Yours forever," I breathe, burying my head in his neck.

He's cupping my chin as we stare into each other's eyes, reassuring the other that the words we've just spoken are the truth. He surprises me when he turns me around and urges my legs apart. But when his head comes around me for a kiss and I twist to meet him, I don't care which direction I'm facing. Our tongues find the warmth of each other. With one hand he grabs my hip while the other one travels down to my slick flesh. His skin is warm and feels so good against mine. He plunges a finger inside of me and I gasp. Hissing in a breath, I prop myself up with my hands to the wall, telling him, "River, I want you. Now."

When he inserts another finger I moan out in pleasure and my moans grow louder when he circles his thumb around me. Not able to stand it much longer, I reach behind to grab him and slide my grip up and down his hard length.

He's nearly panting in my ear when I place him right where I want him. His hands go around my hips and he slams into me fast and hard. I'm bracing my palms against the wall for support as his thickness fills me. Each retreat is followed by another glorious penetration. As his pace quickens, he reaches one hand down and starts to circle my most sensitive spot. "Don't move," he says and pushes deeper into me at an increasing rate. When he lets out a low, almost primal groan, I know I have to experience him fully, so I push myself back and into him as hard as I can. Feeling him inside me is the single most fulfilling sensation in the world. When I hear that low groan from him again I know he feels the same.

I start moving up and down on my toes, pushing him as deep as possible into me. When his fingers dig into my flesh, I know his pleasure is building at the same pace as mine. He's no longer kissing my lips, no longer able to—I can tell from the sounds he's making and the way my body feels. As he continues to rock himself into me, my body responds rapidly. Closing my eyes, I inhale a deep breath and scream into the night, "Oh God, River, yes!" My body shudders and pulsates from its core as I come hard and fast, experiencing a feeling that makes everything that was wrong between us feel right.

His thrusts slow as my cries continue and a low groan escapes his mouth as he pours himself into me. It makes my muscles clench and my toes curl. He cocoons me against the wall, his arms on each side of me, his chest flat against my back, and his cheek resting on mine. We are both breathless and spent, but neither one of us wants to move—I don't want this feeling of utter pleasure to ever end.

When he tugs on the string around my back, my bikini top falls to the ground. I twist my head around and joke, "What? You want more?"

His lips meet mine and he kisses me with so much love that when he stops my lips are tingling. I smile at him and a devilish grin crosses his face as he says, "I always want more."

CHAPTER 12
Catch My Breath

The next morning we're back outside in the yard and I love how River's green eyes sparkle in the sunlight as I watch him from the lounge chair. I have my coffee in one hand and my Kindle in the other.

He turns to me and shoots me his full-blown smile. His dimples always make my heart flutter. Even with a black eye, he still takes my breath away.

"You're really not going to help me, are you?"

I shake my head from side to side. "Nope. You have to learn your lesson."

"What lesson would that be?" He walks over to me with the broom still in his hand.

Setting my book down, I hold my hand over my eyes to block out the sun and say, "The 'you break it, you clean it up' lesson, of course."

He lets the broom fall to the patio and pushes my knees up toward me as he straddles the lounge chair.

"Hey, watch my coffee!"

Taking my coffee from my hand, he sets it on the side table. His mouth is on mine before I can say another word. Then pulling away, he runs his hands up the inside of my thighs and says, "I have a few lessons I wouldn't mind teaching you. And I bet mine are much more fun."

I wrap my arms around his neck and pull him back to me. He presses his mouth to mine and with the taste of his lips, the feel of his breath, everything seems perfect. Suddenly he sits up and his hand comes to my cheek, where he cups my face for a long moment and then just stands up.

"Where are you going?" I protest.

With a sexy grin he says, "I have to finish cleaning up."

I pout my lips. I wasn't done kissing him.

He laughs. "I'm getting too turned on with you sitting here like this, but if you want to help me, we could finish a hell of a lot faster and start on one of those lessons."

I giggle. "Nah, I'm good."

He slips his Rolling Stones T-shirt off and tosses it at me. "It's hot out here." He grabs the broom and walks back over to the shattered green glass.

My eyes scan his perfect back—the way his muscles flex and move with every sweep of the broom, the way his skin glistens in the sunlight. "I know exactly what you're up to, and it's not going to work."

He smiles darkly. "Oh you have no idea what I'm up to. Trust me." He winks before turning back around. Bending over, he attempts to push the glass into the dustpan with the broom. He manages to get about a quarter in each time and the more I watch the more I feel bad. He really could use some assistance. I finally stand up and walk over to help him.

When I'm standing next to him, I place my hands on my hips and let out a deep, exaggerated sigh. "Hand me the broom and I'll sweep the glass into the dustpan."

His eyes peer up at me as a smirk crosses his face. "You sure?"

I nod my head and his smirk grows wider.

But instead of handing me the broom he drops it to the ground and lunges forward to hoist me over his shoulder.

"Put me down! What are you doing?"

"Lesson number one, beautiful girl—never feel sorry for the person who looks incapable of cleaning up because more than likely it's just a big act." And with that, he tosses me into the pool.

Surfacing, I sputter water out of my mouth and yell, "You suck."

"No, I'm just good," he says smugly.

When I reach the side and look into his seemingly content eyes I have to agree. "Yeah, you are good."

He strides toward me, reaching his hand to help me out. "You mean you're finally admitting it?"

"I guess I am."

After stripping off my wet clothes, I threw his T-shirt on and left him to finish cleaning up. With wet hair, I'm sitting at the breakfast bar in nothing but his shirt, attempting to eat a bowlful of cereal. His mood swings since Ben's reappearance are getting to me. One minute he's happy and normal, like this morning. The next minute he's quiet and distant like dinner last night—or he's angrier than I've ever seen him, like our argument over Ben's note. Even though we've discussed Ben and I've made my feelings clear, I feel like there's something left unsaid between us, something still lingering between us. But I don't know how to figure out what it is.

Arms tighten around me and River's chest presses against my back. "I'm sorry."

I almost feel like he's apologizing for more than throwing me in the pool, but since I'm not sure where a deeper conversation would lead, I just want to keep the mood light and our tempers even-keeled.

I swivel around and run my fingertips up and down his bare chest. Hovering my lips over his ear I whisper, "Never apologize for winning, because paybacks are a bitch."

Kissing me on the lips, he shrugs as he walks into the kitchen. "Paybacks sound like fun to me."

I follow him and pour my cereal down the drain. I haven't had much of an appetite the last few days and the bowl of Wheat Chex did nothing to increase it.

He takes the box of Cheerios out and sets it on the counter. "Not hungry again?"

I sigh a little. "No, not really."

Turning around, I lean against the sink and catch him shooting me a concerned look. He opens the cabinet to get out a bowl. I can't keep all of this bottled up so I take a deep breath and grab on to the edge of the counter as I let it out. "Can I ask you something?"

Leaving the bowl on the counter, he twists to look at me. The intensity in his eyes makes me want to escape this conversation. "You know you can."

"Why did you fire Caleb?"

He doesn't hesitate to answer. "Do you want to know what I told myself was the reason then or the real reason?"

"Both."

He says, "We didn't need him anymore since—" He stops as if unable to say why.

I finish the sentence for him. "They caught the asshole who attacked me."

He lets out a long sigh. "Yeah, that's what I told myself when I fired him."

"And that's not the real reason?"

"I just couldn't stand that he was, can't stand that he *is*, Ben's friend."

Ben and Caleb have been friends for many years. Somehow I always knew that was the reason River acted like he did toward Caleb. The only thing I can think to do is just tell him what he already knows. "River, even though I don't want to ever talk to Ben again, we can't avoid everybody he knows. That's not fair to our friends or family."

River nods his head. Striding over to me, he lifts my chin and cradles it. "Dahlia, I did hire Caleb back, but there is something else . . ."

The sound of the twisting of the lock abruptly stops our conversation. We both snap our heads toward the front door when it swings open.

Xander enters the foyer with his key in hand and signals hello with a single nod. Nix struts in right behind him and heads over to the sofa. He gives us an obligatory wave, and then does a double take. "What the fuck?" Nix says, pointing to River's eye.

River shrugs his shoulders and responds, "Not now, man."

Stepping in after Nix, a woman I've never seen before comes through the door. She has long dark hair and olive skin. About average height, she has the shiniest hair, and the most flawless complexion. She would give Aerie a run for her money. She's truly stunning.

She smiles at us and Garrett comes in right on her heels, practically walking into her. His blond hair is tidier than I'm used to seeing it, and he apologizes to the woman before looking over to us. "Hey River, Dahlia. What's up?" He, too, does a double take and also points to River's eye. "Ouch, hope you did some damage to the opposite end of the fist that nailed you!"

River stiffens but just grins at him, and for the first time I wonder what the extent of Ben's injuries were.

Garrett nods, grins back, and heads into the living room to turn the stereo on. River promptly redirects his attention to his brother, who ushers the exotic beauty our way.

"Xander, just because you have a key doesn't mean you don't have to knock."

"Shut up, River. I've been calling you since seven this morning. If you'd answer your goddamn phone I wouldn't have had to bring everyone here."

Nix makes himself at home and flops his feet up on the table. "Got any coffee?"

Ignoring Nix, Xander says, "Ellie Bryce, meet my brother, River, in the flesh. At least now you can see he actually does exist."

She extends her finely manicured hand over the bar and River moves beside me to shake it. When she speaks, her voice is confident and strong, "Sorry for the intrusion, but I do need your input. And Xander insisted we come over."

River responds as he releases her hand, "Nice to meet you. I'm sorry I haven't made any of your meetings, but now actually isn't the best time."

Xander shoots River a look. "No time seems to be the best time for you, so let's say we do it now."

River tenses. I wrap my arm around his waist and look up at him. "Hey, I've got stuff I can do. We can finish talking later."

Ellie reaches over to me and her silver bangles jingle as we shake hands. "You must be Dahlia. It's a pleasure."

"Hi. Nice to meet you." Then I become aware as I look at her that I have no underwear on under River's T-shirt. River is also only half dressed, which is evident when her eyes seem to linger a little too long on him.

He leans over and whispers in my ear, "You sure?"

I nod and tuck my hand in the waistband of his jeans.

River looks at Ellie and says, "Since Xander is insisting, what's so urgent?"

"Everything has to be marked URGENT with you, otherwise we can't get your attention," Xander retorts.

"We need to firm up some details for each tour stop and make arrangements for the venues," Ellie responds cheerfully, ignoring Xander's comment.

Xander takes a step toward the bar and pulls a stool out for Ellie. His eyes flash toward us and hastily away when he notices my clothing, or lack thereof. Smirking, he mumbles, "Guess we caught you at a bad time."

Unresponsive, River moves to stand in front of me as Garrett walks into the kitchen behind us. River twists his head and shoots him a look.

Garrett averts his eyes immediately. "Oh, sorry man. I didn't realize . . ." Cutting himself off he points to the pot on the counter and says, "Nix wants coffee, but I can make it later. Right now I'll make like a busboy and get the fork out of here." With that he promptly turns and leaves the kitchen, and I start laughing at him.

Looking back toward Xander, River tries to control his laughter as he says, "Why don't you take everyone out back?"

"Yeah, sure. No problem," he says but he doesn't move, he just continues to stare.

Back in the living room, Garrett slaps Nix on the knee and tells Ellie to follow him as he walks toward the glass doors.

Xander stays put until everyone has left the room; then running his eyes over River's bare chest he says, "Bro, it's almost eleven on a workday. You two really need to get over the whole rabbits-and-honeymoon phase and join the real world."

"Fuck off."

Xander feigns offense and puts his palm on his chest. Then gesturing to me he quotes the line River used to say to the guys before he became comfortable swearing in front of me. "Language, man, language."

River reaches his arm back around me and pulls the hem of my shirt down.

Xander continues to laugh as he walks toward the doors and exits to the patio. "Hurry up and get dressed. It's rude to keep everyone waiting."

River and I head to the bedroom. He grabs a shirt and as he's slipping it on says, "Hopefully this won't take too long." When he kisses me and turns toward the door, I grab his arm. "Hey, what were you going to say before Xander came in?"

He pauses a brief second, then kisses me again. "That I love you."

"River, I know something else is going on. What is it? Just tell me."

"It's nothing, really. I just think all of this tour shit is getting to me." Both his voice and his eyes waver and I'm not convinced that's really what he was going to tell me.

"Do you want to talk about it?"

"Maybe later. Let me go take care of the latest issues before Xander loses it."

I offer him a reassuring smile before he turns back around and walks toward the door. As he disappears I can't help but hope that the actual tour goes better than the planning of it—for everyone's sake.

In the shower I decide I should probably get a new phone today. On the way out of the bathroom, I glance at all the pictures on my dresser and my eyes stop on the one of Grace and me at my graduation. I have to talk to her today. Using the house phone, I call her and make plans to meet her in Laguna for lunch.

Once I pull my jeans on, throw my Madonna T-shirt over my head, and grab my black sweater, I put my tall black boots on and head for the kitchen. Glancing outside, I can see everyone is deep in conversation, except River. He's hunched over, scrubbing the palms of his hands over his eyes. Even though I know he's going on tour out of obligation, agreeing to it may not have been the best choice for him or the band.

There's a knock at the front door and I am surprised to see Caleb standing there. "Hey, come on in."

He steps in. "Hi, how are you?"

I give him a small smile, but don't answer. I'm not really sure how I am. I feel like I have a million questions to ask him, but don't want to get into it yet. He knew all about Ben—no, he didn't only know about Ben, he *helped* Ben. I feel resentment toward him and a little bitterness as well. I think he senses it.

He drops his head and looks anywhere but at me. "I just have to check on one of the circuits for the security system. The motion sensors seem to be failing and I think I need to replace the board."

"Oh, okay, sure." Then pointing over my shoulder I say, "You know the way downstairs."

"It shouldn't take too long."

"Caleb, it's fine."

"Hey, Dahlia. I'm sorry about everything. I never wanted you to get hurt."

I hear the glass doors open and I turn around. River walks in the room and Caleb looks up, startled—but quickly composes himself. "Hey, River, sorry to intrude. I tried to call."

Walking over to us, River extends his hand and Caleb reciprocates. "Hey, man, it's fine. What's up?"

"I think I know why the alarm system keeps tripping. I need to check a board. I think it might be faulty."

"No problem." River nods his head toward the stairs that lead to the security hub downstairs. "You need help?"

"No, I got it. It'll just take a minute." Caleb heads downstairs.

Looking over at River I can see he's stressing out. "Everything okay?"

He runs his hands through my hair. "Yeah, everything is fine."

Fighting back the urge to kiss him, distract him to take away his stress, I take his face in my hands. "They didn't look fine."

"We're just going through a list of details for each stop. Boring shit, really. You can join us if you want?"

"Ummm . . . I'll pass on the boring conversations, but thanks anyway."

Laughing a little he says, "I don't blame you; I wish I would have passed."

I shake my head at him. "You sure about this?"

His arms frame either side of me and he presses me up against the wall. He drags his tongue over his bottom lip and drops his head to my neck. "Sure about going back out there? No."

I push him back. "I mean the tour."

"I really don't want to talk about the tour," he says before his tongue finds mine and we both momentarily forget what we were talking about.

I hear Caleb clear his throat before saying, "Sorry to interrupt."

We both turn our heads and River stands up straight. "What'd you find?"

"Like I thought, I have to order a new board. It should be here tomorrow," he tells us as he walks past us and reaches for the doorknob.

River nods and says, "Thanks, man."

"No problem. I'll call you when it comes in." Caleb closes the door behind him.

Feeling relieved that all went well, but sad that Caleb and I seemed so distant, I tell River my plans for the day. "I'm going to go get a new phone and meet Grace for lunch."

He looks at me intently. "Do you want me to come with you?"

"No, it's fine. And besides," I say, motioning outside, "you're in the middle of a meeting."

With a glance over to the group huddled around our patio table, he says, "That's not important. I can bag out if you need me."

Taking his face in my hands and looking into his eyes, I say, "I think I need to talk to Grace on my own." There's a long pause before I remind him, "But I always need you."

I arrive at Aestas's first and the hostess shows me to a table. Sipping my water, I wait nervously for Grace. The restaurant is busy and people are animatedly talking around me. Playing with my new phone, I assign River his old ringtone, "Sexy Back." Then I send him a quick text.

> Dahlia: *Just wanted to tell you I have my new phone in case you want to tell me how much you miss me :)*
>
> River: *I always miss you and I was just thinking about you.*
>
> Dahlia: *What were you thinking about?*
>
> River: *The way you looked walking out the door in those boots.*
>
> Dahlia: *You're in a meeting, why are you thinking about my boots?*
>
> River: *Because I'm bored as hell and trust me, it's not only the boots I'm thinking about.*

Just as I'm about to text River back, telling him that I'd be happy to entertain him during his boredom, I feel a hand on my shoulder. "Dahlia, honey," Grace says, standing over me, and I drop my phone in my purse before standing up to greet her.

Looking down into her face, I see she looks older, worn, even. Her natural glow seems to have dissipated. Her usually tidy blond hair is disheveled. Her blue eyes look dull and there are dark circles under them. The tranquility I usually feel when I see her just isn't there. When I hug her, her body is shaking.

Clinging to her, I hope to calm her trembling. "Oh, Grace," is all I can manage before she pulls back. Her voice is shaky and I can see that this has really taken a toll on her. "Let's sit down and talk."

We both settle in at the small table draped in white linen and place our napkins on our laps. I don't even know how to begin this conversation. But Grace, being true to form, leads the way.

"Dahlia, how are you holding up?"

I shrug my shoulders. "I'm okay."

"I'm glad you called me."

"I'm sorry I didn't call sooner. I just needed some time."

Grace looks at me for a few moments and then asks point-blank, "Aren't you glad Ben's alive?"

Taken aback, I stammer. That's the one question I had yet to even ask myself. "God, of course I am." Because it's true, of course I'm glad he's alive and not dead. Who wouldn't be?

Her next question comes rapidly and I try to remain calm. "Then is it because of the way we told you? I'm sorry for that. That was not how I wanted you to find out."

"Grace, I'm not upset about how I learned that Ben's really alive. I get that there was no easy way."

"Then is it because of the attack? I am so grateful that you're okay, but you have to know he had no idea you'd be in danger."

"No, I was only upset that all of you knew and none of you told me who attacked me."

"Dahlia, that was for your sake. I wanted to be there when flashes of Ben's death would inevitably come flooding back to you. Hearing the news that Ben's shooter was released was so upsetting, but then learning it was him that attacked you would have been overwhelming. I just wanted to be with you, to tell you myself."

"Grace, I'm stronger now. I'm not that same girl you gave the necklace to—the girl who needed to hold on to the past. I don't like things to be hidden from me; it wasn't your decision to make to withhold that information. But honestly, all of that has nothing to do with Ben."

"I thought I was doing what was best for you."

"I know that. And Grace, I'm not upset at you for it anymore."

"So I'm confused, Dahlia. Why won't you forgive him? Talk to him again?"

Before I can answer, the waiter approaches our table and I order an extra dirty martini and Grace orders a sparkling water. When he leaves I pick up where we left off. "The word *forgive* means something different to each of us and we each choose whether we can do it or not. I did hear him out and once he started to explain everything it only made me angrier. I just don't think talking to him again will change anything. It won't make me forget what I went through—or help me forgive him. It would be like saying I'm okay with what I went through because of him and I'm not okay with that. I don't know if I ever will be."

Leaning closer, she squeezes my hand. "I'm not sure about that, Dahlia. I think if you just calmly sit down with him and really listen, you could try to understand why he left. He left to protect you—and if you can understand that, you'd be able to forgive him."

"I'm sorry, but I've really had enough with everyone always wanting to protect me. And how is causing me so much pain and suffering protecting me? Grace, I'm not mad at the fact that he didn't actually die. I just can't forgive the act itself—pretending to die."

Grace reacts more dramatically than I would ever have expected. "Dahlia, you just have to get past this wall you've put up and let him in. Forgive him. He gave up a lot for you! Surfing, and now his life."

As I stare at her, trying to understand where this conversation is headed, the waiter brings us our drinks. Without even glancing at our menus, we both order a salad. Taking a large sip from my glass, I set it down and prepare to tell her what she doesn't want to hear.

"His reasons, what he did, why he did it—they don't change the impact his death had on not just me, but all of us. We all felt the pain and mourned for him in our own way for a long time. And it was his choice, his choice to leave, his choice to keep evidence. Don't you get it—he made a *choice*. You may have been able to forgive him for all that and that's fine, but that doesn't mean I can."

Rubbing her hands together she says, "I do get it, but choices aren't always that easy, Dahlia. Ben suffered, too. In fact, he's still suffering."

Suddenly, it's like all of the emotional turmoil I've experienced these last few days comes rushing back. Setting my glass down, I have to tell her, "Danger, protection, disappearing—Grace, it's just insane, the whole thing."

Our salads arrive and we both push our forks around, without really eating or talking.

Without warning, she drops her fork and focuses on me. "Dahlia, will you please forgive him? For me? He has a whole life to rebuild, and he really wants you in it."

Exasperation takes hold of me and I have to tell her, "I am not getting back together with him. You can't possibly think that."

"No, I'd never ask you to do that. I know you're happy. Just hear him out. He needs your forgiveness in order to be able to move on, move away from these sad past few years. And Dahlia, before anything else you were friends. Can't you get back to that?"

I shake my head no. "What he needs? What about what I needed? What about the life I led?"

She stares at me for a long while before standing up and coming to crouch beside me. She holds both my hands and when she finally speaks, it doesn't sound like her voice at all. It's small and full of pain.

"Dahlia, I think of you as my daughter. You know that. And it's for this reason I feel you need to take a step back and look at what you're doing. You need to face the situation. Not only have you been through a lot, but so has he. I think talking to him will help you move past your anger and maybe even help toward rebuilding your friendship."

Standing up, I toss my napkin on the table and grab my purse. "Grace, I'm not ready to forgive him. There is nothing he can do to take back what I went through because of his decisions. My anger is justified, and I don't know if I'll ever get past it."

She makes one last plea. "Dahlia, you owe him at least forgiveness."

"I don't owe him anything."

With that, I have to leave the restaurant before I lose my composure. I try to take deep calming breaths. I reach my car and want to scream when I see the folded piece of paper on my windshield. I take his remember-me item and without even opening it, rip it into pieces and let it fall to the ground. Finally, all the emotion and events of the past days paralyze me as I'm getting into the car. I put my hands on the roof, taking short quick breaths, trying to pump the air back into my lungs. I think about what Grace asked me—and even though I would do almost anything for her, I can't do it. I can't look at the situation through rose-colored glasses like she always does.

Chapter 13
Come Undone

Ben's Journal

When Mom told me she was meeting Dahlia for lunch, I figured it was a perfect opportunity to leave Dahlia one of my notes. But when Mom came home later clearly upset, I had to wonder if that was why. Since she didn't mention the note, I can only guess it wasn't, but that their lunch didn't go well. She and Dahlia have always had a great relationship and the last thing I want is for their connection to suffer because of me.

I've never had that kind of relationship until I went to New York City and I was lucky enough to make friends with the head of the English Department at NYU. George took me under his wing and we quickly became friends. We'd go out for a beer or two after swimming laps and we'd discuss life in general, sports, and even his divorce, but I never told him about my life here—I'm wondering if I should have. I could really use him right now.

I've decided to take Dahlia up on her offer and plan to move back into our house. I need to help relieve the stress Mom is feeling. When Serena gave me the note Dahlia left her that said, "Give these to Ben, the house is his," I was surprised. I thought she would respond to my note, but she ignored it and sent that instead.

Trying really hard to find a reason not to drown myself in a bottle of Jack, I started to move my things back into our house. Well, my house now.

What the fuck am I going to do? I have no life left here—no job and definitely not my girl. I've tried to call her numerous times and she won't answer my calls. I'm beginning to wonder if she'll ever talk to me again. I thought I would be able to break through to her, but she seems determined not to talk to me. I really just want some time alone with her, to explain further. No, I really just want her back.

Caleb is also pissed as hell at me right now. When I went back to our house, it was still there—the old key holder. I knew she'd never get rid of it. I took it off the wall and pulled the cap off the end. The data chip was still there. I didn't want any of that information anymore, so I called Caleb and gave it to him to take to the agency. He told me he just fucking knew I kept shit. He reamed me, asking me if I had any idea the danger I had put Dahlia in. Honestly, at the time, I really didn't. I wanted her to have it in case. In case of what?—I don't even know anymore.

CHAPTER 14
Madness

It was one of the most perfect fall days. The weather wasn't too hot or too cold and the breeze was just enough to keep me cool. I had my windows down on the drive from Laguna Beach to LA and hoped that the scene with Grace at the restaurant wasn't as bad as I thought.

I had sat in the parking lot for over an hour before I left. I wanted to make sure my judgment wasn't clouded from my one drink. But all I kept thinking was five minutes, just five minutes, was all it had taken to put a tear in an almost perfect relationship.

The whole drive home I listened to the song "Into the Nothing" on repeat and went over our conversation in my mind. I loved her and would never want to hurt her, but I just couldn't agree to her request that I forgive Ben for what he had done.

At six o'clock I finally pull into the driveway and I'm surprised everyone is still there. I tried to call River from the car, but it went straight to voice mail. The music playing as I open the door tells me immediately that Nix took control of the playlist because it's his favorite song, "Radioactive." The kitchen shows the remnants of a party—pizza boxes stacked on the stove, bags of chips on the table, and beer bottles lined up on the counter. River's at the kitchen table with his hands fisted through his hair and Ellie sits next to him as they both look over a stack of papers. Xander's outside pacing the deck while talking on the phone and the other band members are sacked out on the couch.

"Hey," I call out when I walk through the door and hang my keys on the hook.

River looks up with a smile and pushes his chair back. Ellie turns, setting her beer bottle down, and I notice immediately she's removed her suit jacket. Her very low-cut silk camisole displays her ample cleavage and I have to refrain from rolling my eyes.

"Cute boots," she says, sounding like she means it. "Gucci?"

Looking down at my chunky-heeled tall black boots, I shrug my shoulders. I have no idea what brand they are but I'm sure they're not Gucci. I've had them for years and don't even remember where I bought them. "I'm not sure but thanks."

"I have a similar pair but can never seem to get the outfit right when I try to wear them."

Setting down my purse, I smile at her. "Really, I just throw them on with everything."

Her phone rings and she motions toward the living room. "Excuse me a minute."

River nods and stands up, his gaze locking on mine as he strides toward me and mouths, "Missed you."

Smiling at him, I take a deep breath and try to push my argument with Grace from my thoughts.

His gaze travels up and down my body before settling on my face. Then his lips are on mine and his arms circle my waist and I feel better already. "You were gone a long time. Everything go okay?"

I can smell the alcohol on his breath and know he's been drinking. "Yeah, it was fine." I really don't want to discuss what happened with Grace in front of Ellie.

Pulling back, he outstretches his arms and leaves his hands on my hips. "You sure? Because you don't look like everything's fine."

I nod and lean against the counter.

"Want anything? There's plenty of pizza left."

"I think I'll just have a beer."

He grabs a glass for me and fills it with ice, then opens the refrigerator to retrieve a bottle. Twisting the cap off he takes a swig and I watch the way his throat moves as the cool liquid goes down.

"Hey, that's mine," I tease.

Grinning, he pours the beer into the glass and hands it to me. "What, you don't share?"

I smirk back and before I can answer his warm breath is on my skin. When his parted lips kiss my neck and his tongue teases my flesh, I grip my glass tighter and ask, "You're working late. Are you almost done?"

Ellie responds for him. "Well, you know, since he," she says, pointing to River in case I don't know who she means, "is so hard to pin down, I have to take advantage while I can."

For some reason her tone bothers me, but I still shoot her a *glad he could be of service* smile. Then I tell River, "I'm really tired. I'm going to take these boots off and lie down for a bit."

He presses a kiss to my cheek before sliding his tongue to my ear and whispering, "Wait for me and I'll do that for you, just let me wrap this up."

Ellie quickly interjects, "River, we're not finished yet," and I wonder how she could hear us over the music—and why she was even listening.

But I'm not going to stick around and argue with her. Kissing River one more time, I head to our bedroom.

Moments later, I'm chewing some ice and standing at the window in front of my hope chest, just blankly staring at the Hollywood sign, when I feel his hand at my waist. He swipes my hair to the side with his other hand. Closing my eyes, I lean into him. He moves his hands to my stomach and presses his body against mine. "What do you say we take off more than just the boots?"

I laugh. "Are you drunk?"

"Who, me? Why would I be drunk after I had to spend the day discussing the ins and outs of every stage at every stop? I still don't get why Xander couldn't have taken care of all that."

I stretch my arms around his neck and tilt my head to the side. "Well, I think that would be because Ellie wanted you to help take care of it."

He pulls me flush to him and I can feel his hard body against every part of me. "She doesn't bother you, does she?"

"No, not really. Why would you think she bothers me?"

His fingers are inching inside the waistband of my jeans and his mouth moves up and down my neck. "I don't know. Because she bothers me." He laughs and I join in.

His other hand untucks my shirt and then moves up to slip inside the lacy cup of my bra. His hand fits perfectly around my small breast. He murmurs against my ear, "Do you want to talk about your lunch with Grace now?"

"Not when you're drunk, I don't," I say, angling my head so that his lips can find mine.

"I'm not drunk, I only had two beers." I'm not really listening as his lips travel down my neck and place openmouthed kisses along my skin.

He gently bites down on my lower lip. A quiver of sensation washes through my body when his lips lock against mine. Turning around, I wrap my arms around his neck and look into his eyes, which are blurred with desire. "I thought we could talk later," I purr as I slide my hand down the front of his jeans.

With the stereo on, the only other sound in the room is his low but unmistakable growl as he pushes me toward the bed. Falling on it, he hovers over me as I crawl back on my elbows and he follows on his palms, his knees sliding up the sheets. My hands glide up his flexing back and I relish the feel of each and every muscle. His mouth covers mine and we drink each other in.

Suddenly, the door opens. "Hey man, let's make like Linda Lovelace and blow."

We both look over and Garrett stands there with a shocked look on his face. "Shit, man, I didn't know Dahlia was home."

River and I look at each other, laughing uncontrollably, and Garrett rushes to close the door, leaving it open a crack to say, "Nix is ready to go. How much longer do you need?"

River collapses next to me and throws his arm over his forehead. "Give me five minutes."

I roll onto my side and rest my head on my hand. "Where are you going?"

"We're going. Sorry, I got distracted and forgot to mention it. Ellie wants to introduce the band to some of the setup crew and wants us to play a few songs for them, to 'get them in the zone,' as she put it. She's arranged for all of us to meet at Smitten's tonight. I guess she has a limo coming to pick us up."

"Of course she does."

"She does bother you," he says, leaning over to kiss the bare spot on my stomach where my shirt has risen.

"Well, it's more like her giant boobs bother me."

He laughs and looks up at me. "Didn't really notice her boobs," he says, pulling my shirt up the rest of the way, exposing my bra. He runs his tongue up my stomach to my chest, and once he lifts my bra he says, "I only notice yours." He nips my shoulder before locking his mouth around my nipple. With a quick flick of his tongue, he licks me and it instantly hardens.

My fists clutch the sheets as my back arches. "I want you."

Just as his hands fly to the button of my jeans, there's a pounding on the door. "Come on, lover boy, get Muse and let's go," Xander shouts.

Sighing, River mutters, "Fuck," under his breath and then yells, "Go without me!"

"Not happening. I'm coming in, so you better be decent," Xander warns and I quickly pull my shirt down as he opens the door.

I'm sitting up on my elbows as River once again throws his arm over his forehead. He doesn't even look at Xander when he says, "Seriously, Xander, don't you have anywhere else to be than up my ass?"

Xander approaches the bed and jerks River's arm, making him sit up. They stare at each other and Xander narrows his eyes when he says, "I'll be more than up your ass if you don't get your head in the game, bro. I've had enough of your shit. Now let's go, the limo's waiting." He doesn't wait for a response; he just turns and walks away, slamming the door behind him.

Smitten's is packed when we walk in. I hear the song "Done" playing and look over to the band. I haven't seen them before, but everyone's mouthing the words and dancing. They really have the crowd entertained.

River laces his fingers in mine and weaves his way through the crowd. I immediately notice the archway in the back leading to the poolroom is covered in plastic. I tap him on the shoulder and point to the construction. "What's going on over there?"

Chuckling, he informs me, "Smitty is remodeling the old poolroom. Turning it into a state-of-the-art billiards room, I guess."

Once we reach the bar, he orders us two beers and one glass with ice. While we're waiting he leans against the bar and seems to stare off into space. I'm starting to get more concerned about the stress this tour is causing him. Once our drinks arrive, he pours my beer into the glass and hands it to me. Then he says into my ear, "Sorry about earlier. I promise to finish what I started later."

I can't resist tracing the letters on his Ramones T-shirt when I tell him, "Way to get a girl all hot and bothered and leave her hanging."

"Dahlia! There you are," Bell shouts from behind me.

When I turn in her direction I notice she's wearing the birthday present I gave her, a Love Quotes scarf. It complements her black jeans and white-lace top perfectly. I smile and tug on the scarf. "Hi, Bell. How was your date?"

"Amazing. It's work that's killing me. Xander has me jumping hoops for this tour now that he knows I have another job. With both jobs, I feel like I don't have enough time for a boyfriend right now."

"If you really like him, tell him that. I'm sure he'll understand."

River pulls me back against him and Bell appears to suddenly realize it's her brother behind me. "Nice cover-up you and Xander pulled on Mom about the eye, but she saw right through it, you know."

Xander approaches us, motioning for River to follow him.

"I better see what he wants," he says to both of us and kisses me before walking off. I watch what looks to be a heated conversation. Bell notices, too, and bites her bottom lip before saying, "What's going on with those two?"

"I think River is just stressed over the tour."

"I guess."

Xander leaves River standing there. River once again looks stressed as he runs his hands through his hair and follows Xander to the table full of young guys all staring at Ellie, who has once again removed her jacket.

"Have you met Ellie?" Bell asks me.

"Yeah, I have. She seems . . . competent."

"Yeah, competent is one way to describe her."

I look at her and laugh as she squeezes her way to the bar. She orders us two shots. Handing one over to me she says, "To women who think they're all that, may their boobs drop at a young age."

I laugh so hard I can barely down my shot. She orders another and this time I make the toast: "To women who see through the women who think they're all that."

Bell sucks in a breath to control her laughter and drinks her shot, then asks, "You're not worried about her, are you?"

"No."

"Well, good, because you have no reason to be. My brother loves you."

I smile at her. "I know."

"Speaking of my brother, what are you doing for his birthday?"

I look at her blankly. "Shit, Bell. It's this Saturday, isn't it? I have no idea. With everything . . ." I'm not sure if she knows about Ben yet, even though everyone seems to know everything before I do. "I've been so busy I haven't even thought about it."

"Lucky for you I'm an awesome party planner."

"I don't know about a party, though. There's so much going on with the tour right now . . ."

"Nonsense, that's the perfect reason to have a blowout party—to celebrate River's birthday and the band's departure. Let's make it a surprise."

I look at her questioningly.

"Dahlia, I'll take care of everything. You just get him out of the house for a few hours Saturday. Take him to dinner or something for his birthday."

As my eyes roam the bar, they fall on River's table, where Ellie is leaning over him, handing him a shot. Her chest is on full display and I roll my eyes. "Okay, Bell. If you're sure. Come on, my turn to buy a round."

Three shots and two beers later, I am feeling no pain. Bell has changed topics so many times I'm having a hard time keeping up. She went from talking about birth control and how she can never remember to take the pill at the same time every day to her recent shopping spree at Avery's, and now she's telling me her plans for the party. I'm trying to stay focused, listening and nodding, but my mind keeps going back to Grace. I can't stop thinking about how we left things.

But the sound of a familiar voice brings me to full attention. My eyes dart to the stage and I see him up there, looking at ease, relaxed, like the stage is his second home.

"Hello, everyone," his deep voice welcomes the crowd. When I see him up there like that I can't believe he's mine. He stands with a power that commands attention. His toned muscles flex under his T-shirt with every twist and turn he makes as he adjusts the microphone height with his guitar slung around him, hugging his back.

For some reason every time I see him like that onstage it steals my breath away. His smile is wide, his dimples always on full display, his eyes bright. He's so steady and sure and his passion for singing couldn't be clearer. When he's up there I know it's where he's meant to be. For a moment I wish it could always stay this simple for him—just write songs and bring them to life, no talk of touring and moving up to a grander scale. But the band is on the rise and he deserves the fame and all that goes with it. I just hope he learns to be happy with it.

"I'm going to sing a few songs tonight that I wrote for my girl," he says, his eyes shining on me. The way he looks at me sends prickles along my skin. He pulls his guitar around him. "One, two, one, two, three, four," he mouths before the opening music surges throughout the room.

You were my once in a lifetime.
This I knew from the moment your eyes met mine.
You were my once in a lifetime.
This I knew the first time I whispered into your ear and
    my heart stopped.

You were my once in a lifetime.
This I knew when your face touched my spirit.
You were my once in a lifetime.
This I knew when I kissed your lips and felt it in my soul.
So where did you go, where did you go?

My concerns about Grace flee for the moment in my excitement at watching him perform. Hearing him sing about us, his feelings for me, brings such peace. His evocative voice captures the audience's attention. Couples start dancing, people begin to sway, and everyone is singing along. But he's singing it to me as if we were alone, and that thrills me. He stops playing the guitar and lets it drop. Grabbing the mic with both hands, his eyes close. With his legs shoulder-width apart he taps his thigh to the beat. He owns the music—of that there is no doubt. As the song ends he sways back and forth, playing the last few notes on his guitar and ending with an ever-so-slight bow.

The band moves right into the next song, but this time he takes a seat on a barstool. His black boots find their place on the rung and he rests his guitar on his thigh. He beams before he breaks into song, strumming the beautiful melody of "Five." Again I'm completely mesmerized. When he begins to sing, his focus slips further into the music as if he's the song. During the chorus some of the girls start screaming and standing, and he gifts them with his sexy grin. Wild thoughts of us in bed together flood my mind and I feel myself flush as I stand there, watching him, wanting him. He drops his guitar again and raises both hands in the air. His shirt lifts and the glistening skin of his lower abdomen is bared for all to see. "Come on, everyone, sing along," he coos into the mic, and, of course, we all do.

5 years, 260 weeks, 1,825 days, 2.3 million minutes.
That was how long ago I met you.

If I did it all again. Would you come along for the ride?
If I did it all again. Could you play this game with me?

I'm not sure I've ever seen anything sexier than his bright smile backlit by the golden lights of the stage. Here, in this small familiar venue, River is in his element. When the last notes fade, the audience bursts into applause and the sound dances through me. "That's all for tonight. Till next time," he says as he lifts his guitar strap over his shoulder. He waves to the audience while they clap and yell for more. Some girls are even calling out their phone numbers while others make suggestive comments, but he doesn't seem to notice. The Wilde Ones talk for a few minutes and then each guy leaves the stage, going their own ways.

I lose sight of him in the crowd and turn back toward Bell, who is also grinning from ear to ear. Then I sense his presence behind me before I see him. "Hey, beautiful." His warm breath travels down my neck and sends a shiver through my eager body. I lean into him and he wraps an arm around me.

Bell puts a finger over her lips and winks at me. "See you two later. I have to find Reston before he hits the stage."

"Reston? Who's Reston?" River asks, then kisses my neck.

"Don't you ever pay attention? He's my boyfriend, the drummer for Scandalicious." When he looks at her quizzically she says, "Duh. They're the band onstage."

He lifts his eyes to check it out but keeps his lips on me. "Sorry, Bell, I just can't keep up with all your boyfriends. But the band is rocking it."

"I really like this one," she says as she flutters toward the stage.

"Good luck," I call to her, but I've already turned so I can really kiss him.

"You were amazing up there," I tell him, raking my fingers through his hair and holding on.

Leaning back he takes in every inch of me. Then he's got me flush against his body, desire consuming my every thought. His eyes are hooded and I can see a reflection of my desire in his gaze—the passion between us is about ready to erupt. "Amazing, yeah," he responds, but his breath catches on the words.

Skimming my hands down his chest, I circle his waist and tuck my hands inside his jeans. Pulling him closer, I softly brush my lips against his neck and his body quivers from our slight skin-on-skin contact.

His hands glide up my back as he closes the small distance I left between us. When he slips his tongue into my mouth, I gasp. But when he bites down on my bottom lip and sucks on it, I can't help but whimper.

I pull away before things escalate any further. "Take me home and finish what you started before we left."

He looks around and then over at the table where Ellie, Xander, and the other band members are all sitting, still doing shots and engaging in animated conversation.

"I can call us a cab."

My body is way too impatient to wait for a ride and I let him know it when I rock against him and say, "I want you now, not in an hour."

He steps back and surveys his options. Watching him, I lick my lips and run my hands down my body. "Fuck," he groans, hissing through his teeth. When he drags his tongue across his lip, he looks so freaking sexy I know I'd let him fuck me in the bathroom.

He motions to the left, ushering me into the crowd and I hope no one is watching us. As we're making our way through it, he wraps his arm around my waist and pulls me into him. Pointing to where he wants me to head, he leans in and whispers, "I'm so hard right now."

My brain is a bit hazy from the drinks I've had tonight but it's not in the least bit clouded when it comes to this—I know what I want. And I know he wants the same. At the covered archway with the sign

POOLROOM above it, he looks around, then lifts the sheet of plastic and motions to me to slip under it. He quickly follows.

Once we're on the other side he takes my hand and leads me down the hallway. It's pitch-black; he has to hold his phone up to guide the way. Once we enter the room, I look around, but the only thing in here is the pool table covered by a white sheet. He sets his phone on it, and quickly hoists me up onto the table.

"You sure about this?" he asks with his heavily lidded eyes studying me.

Pulling in a shaky breath at the smoldering look in his eyes, I lean in to kiss the corner of his mouth and purr, "Absolutely."

With a soft groan he slides between my legs and the feel of him pressed against me makes me tremble. My breath hitches and my pulse quickens. Cupping my face in one hand, he traces the seam of my lips with the other. Not wanting to wait another minute, I wrap my hands around his neck and our lips move against each other with fervent need, and a soft moan escapes my throat. I can hear the band playing "Feel This Moment" and I lose myself in the music.

Something almost primal overcomes me. I moan in his ear loud enough that he can hear me. Sliding my mouth back to his, we consume each other as our lips move faster, harder, deeper against each other's. I don't care if I fuck him on the floor, the pool table, or against the wall when he rocks against me. I squeeze my eyes shut, just needing to feel his skin against mine; trying not to dig my fingernails into him, I want him so badly.

Opening my eyes, I stare at him, then quickly stand, and we turn so he's leaning against the pool table. His eyes lock on mine, as my hands find their way down his chest to unbutton and unzip his jeans. Shoving his pants and boxers down, I see that he's fully ready for me and my hand strokes his length. I push him back slightly and as I kneel I can see his chest moving up and down at a rapid pace.

I start slow, swirling my tongue around his tip before sucking on it. At the taste, I realize how hungry I was for him. I lick every inch of him. When I seal my mouth over him, he groans and his hands go to my head but I don't need him to guide me. I want to give him this—to relieve the stress I've seen on his face all day. Each time I move, I take him as deep as I can and each time he hits the back of my throat, he groans even louder. My mouth sucks, my fingers stroke, and my lips move in all the ways I know he likes it. "Oh fuck. Just like that. Just like that," he mutters and it thrills me to hear the pleasure in his voice. His muscles start to shake when my tongue revisits his tip. As I trace a path around the moistness already beaded there, he shudders and slides his hands down beneath my arms, quickly pulling me up to him.

His mouth finds mine and I know he must taste himself on me. We kiss each other as if we can't get enough of one another. Then he picks me up and sets me on the pool table. Panting, he bends down and un-zips one boot, then the other, leaving me breathless and gasping with anticipation.

"I've been thinking about taking these boots off you all day," he says as he tosses my boot to the ground.

The slight glow of the phone is the only illumination in the pitch-black room. I smile at him and love the look I see on his face right now. He stands me up and quickly removes my pants and panties, then sets me back on the pool table.

"God, I want you," I tell him.

Grinning at me he says, "Not yet," as he drops down and spreads my legs further apart. His fingers trace patterns around my slick flesh and then his tongue follows the same path. I have wanted him all day and with just this simple touch, I begin to feel a soft rippling. He thrusts his tongue in and out and I arch my back and call out for more. When his tongue finds its way deep inside of me, I start to tremble. Screaming his name as the room goes blurry, I lose awareness of where I am as I experience the most amazing climax. Thank God the band's loud bass drowns out the sounds we're making.

He stands back up and my vision clears enough to see the face of the man I love. I lean back and he slides us up the pool table. And this time when he kisses me, I can taste myself. He smiles while kissing me and I know he's thinking the same thing. I wrap my fingers around him and guide him to me because I can't wait another minute to have him inside of me. He groans as he plunges deep inside me and I raise my hips to meet his.

We both move in harmony at a quick but rhythmic pace, enjoying every second of becoming one. As I'm meeting each thrust with my own, River increases the pace and I feel my muscles start to clench again. I kiss my way up his neck and back down, and, in turn, he bites my lip, my cheek, and my ear.

He pulls back slightly, closing his eyes, and I know he's close. When I know I can't hold back anymore, I pull his ear to my mouth and whisper, "Come with me." As the wave of euphoria washes through me again, he calls my name and takes one final thrust before he, too, loses all control.

He falls to my side and pulls me close. "I love you."

"I love you, too."

We lie here for a few minutes, both quiet, both clinging to each other with a desperation we haven't had before and it scares me. Have recent events taken a deeper toll than either of us is willing to admit? Lying here in this dark room, hearing his ragged breathing, I can't help but think back on our intense sexual encounters the past few days. Is this aggressive need for each other our way of trying to tear down the wall between us?

CHAPTER 15
Love Remains the Same

Ben's Journal

I've been busy moving and trying to get my girl back. I moved the boxes from Mom's attic to my and Dahl's house. I started to unpack them yesterday, but when I found a bin full of broken pictures of Dahlia and me, I had to stop. I thought going for a run and then working out would completely exhaust me. But when I woke up in the middle of the night with a raging hard-on from a dream about her, I wasn't sure working out was the best choice. The dream was so real, but unlike anything I had ever experienced with her. It took me taking my dick in my own hand right then and there and getting one in in the shower this morning to finish myself off from that dream.

Since I've gotten back I've done everything to get Dahl alone. When I saw her on the beach I didn't go for it. I wanted to play it straight and tell her everything. I wanted for her to come back to me because she got it. Well that didn't fucking work. Since then

I've called her and left messages just asking her to meet me or telling her I love her. Not much, just simple short messages to get my point across. She hasn't called me back. I've even gone as far as leaving another note on her car. How fucked up is that? I had to track her down to do it and it didn't even work. So next time I see her, I need to get her alone and forget about all the words. I need to make her remember what we had—the love we shared, the sex—if I do, it will come back to her then, and she'll come back to me. She just has to let her guard down and really let me touch her. I only want her back.

I talked Caleb into going out for a drink tomorrow night. Like a needy chick I had to ask him to pick me up, but I'll be getting my car back tomorrow night so that shit will stop. Serena took the car from Trent indefinitely. I'll give it to him when he's ready and get a new one, but for now it's best for all of us if he doesn't have it. He's in bad shape and doesn't need to be driving. I've spent as much time with him as he'll stick around for, but that's not much. I tried to talk him into going surfing with me over the weekend, but he said no. He's going to stay with his dad for a few nights.

I need to get out anyway. I'm going stir-crazy. I've thought about calling Kimberly, but I don't want to hurt her. Soon I need to come clean to her and explain everything, but I can't face that just yet.

CHAPTER 16
Never Say Never

As I stand here fastening the bow around my waist, I can't help but think how similar the past few days appear to all the ones that preceded them—and yet there's something fundamentally different. River has had to meet with Ellie every day and I've been trying to work, too, but I've passed most of the jobs that have come my way on to someone else. I'm just not up to styling and photographing upcoming album releases. When River comes home his stress level is always off the charts. We haven't talked much about anything important. Instead we've spent our time playing board games or in bed.

I haven't told him about what happened with Grace. She's tried to contact me every day but I've avoided her calls as well as Serena's. Ben has been calling, too. He keeps leaving short messages asking me to call him, to meet him, begging me to give him a chance. After the fifth one I stopped listening and now just delete them. Yesterday, when I met Aerie in Laguna to shop for River's surprise party, he even left another note on my car. The stress of avoiding everyone and not telling River everything is really starting to get to me, so planning his birthday present with Bell's help has been a welcome distraction.

I check out my reflection in the mirror; everything seems to be in place. I'm a little nervous about the present; I've never done anything like this before. Bell threw the idea out there and then actually helped me pick out the entire ensemble. She told me the key to doing a striptease was to select the last thing that comes off, first. So once I selected that, I chose a very sexy black bra, matching thong, and thigh-high stockings with garters. Bell wanted me to use the stay-up hose. But I remember how much River liked garters the last time I wore them, when we first reconnected in Vegas. My top layer was an easy choice: a very sheer short black dress with ankle-strap stilettos. God, I hope I don't fall over in them.

Feeling more confident, I put my robe on, push away all thoughts except those of him, and take a deep breath. I can do this. I wanted to give him a present he'd never forget and I'm sure he won't forget this, whether I'm able to complete the dance or not.

When he enters our bedroom, I turn and smile. He's dressed and ready for dinner. Game on. He looks incredibly hot in his gray button-up shirt and black jeans.

Trying not to laugh, I ask, "You're not wearing that, are you?"

He looks down. "What's wrong with what I'm wearing? It should be fine for the restaurant."

"Oh, it's okay for Swoonworthy's," I say as I untie my robe to give him a sneak peek, and then promptly tie it back up. "But we aren't going there just yet," I tease.

His mouth drops open. I point to the chair in the corner of our bedroom, the one near the window, and motion for him to sit down. Once he sits, I light the candles I scattered around the room earlier.

As I walk around the room getting things ready, I drop my robe when I'm standing in front of him. Moving behind him, I purposely get extremely close, but don't touch him; I shut the blackout curtains instead. He tries to pull me to him, but I swat his hand. When he protests I turn to him and say, "Shh . . . no talking," and then I wave my finger, saying, "And no touching. My rules." I stuck with the no-touching rule, even though I wanted to throw that rule away the minute I opened my robe and saw the look on his face.

He grins and folds his arms while outstretching his legs.

Turning on my preselected music, "For Your Entertainment" starts to play and I know I picked the right song because by the look on his face he's truly entertained.

The sensual rhythm of the song helps guide me through my dance. When I feel comfortable enough to move to its beat, I strut over to him and walk around the chair. From behind I run my hands up his chest and then drag my fingers through his hair. Unfolding his arms, he tries to take my hand, but I motion with a *no-no* wave of my finger. I watch him as I dance across the room. His eyes never leave mine—he's transfixed on my every move and I feel like he wants to devour me whole. His grin has disappeared and his face is now a picture of pure lust. I notice his every movement when he shifts in his seat and pulls his legs in.

Striding to the center of the room, I turn my back to him. Staring over my shoulder, I meet his eyes. Unzipping my dress, I make a show out of bending forward to step out of it. I'm actually doing this. A striptease. By the time the second song, "Little Bad Girl," starts playing, I've lost all my inhibitions and just let go.

Never dropping my gaze, I prance over to him and place one foot on his knee. His legs widen, he slouches down in the chair a bit, his mouth drops open, and his breath hitches. I motion for him to unbuckle my straps, and he takes full advantage of being allowed to touch me. He reaches behind my knee and glides his fingers slowly down my calf until he reaches my foot. As he undoes my strap, he bends down and kisses my ankle, letting the shoe fall to the ground. When I put my other foot on his knee, he slides it up his leg to pull me closer. Biting his lip, he stares into my eyes. Without looking he unbuckles the strap and tosses my shoe over his shoulder.

Once he has removed my shoes all the rules are back on. Wanting to tease him, I leave my toes between his legs and slowly roll my stockings down. When I wrap the hose around his neck, he grabs my leg. I take a step backward, shaking my head and waving my finger back and forth. He groans and I smile.

"Right, your rules. I have a bit of a problem with them," he says in a lower voice before he leans back in the chair. I shush him and can't help but smile again. I made the right choice with this gift.

To further tease, I walk over to my hope chest and place one foot on top of it. I keep my foot pointed as I slowly caress my hose down my leg. When he curses under his breath, my smile widens.

I'm almost done and his reaction is better than I ever imagined. His green eyes are mesmerizing; they're really the most beautiful shade of green I have ever seen. I unbuckle my bra and slowly slide first one, and then the other bra strap down my shoulder. Pulling the bra off, I hold it by the straps with my arms above my head and then drop it to the floor. I cross my arms and hands over my breasts, then slowly turn around. His lips part and his head falls back. When I slide my hands across my body to reveal myself he curses even louder.

Alternating between clutching the sides of the chair and tapping his fingers, it's obvious my rules are killing him—his body language and his piercing eyes tell me so. Prancing back over to him, I use my hands to push his knees further apart, then prepare to strip off my final layer. Tucking my thumbs inside the strings circling my hips, I begin to lower them, inch by inch, and once they pass my hips, I sit on his knee and slide them the rest of the way down. When they reach my ankles, he grabs them and brings them to his nose. Standing up I take a step back to finish my dance, but he stands up and grabs me. With his mouth over mine he growls, "Fuck, that was the hottest thing I've ever seen. You have no idea the things I want to do to you right now. I'm done following your rules." Then he crushes his lips to mine and thoroughly kisses me.

I pull back and smile at him, pointing to the one thing remaining on my body—the red ribbon around my waist, and say, "Happy Birthday, River, you can unwrap your present now."

As River zips his pants back up, he jokes that he would've been fine with me wearing the sheer black dress to dinner. But I'm already slipping into the new outfit Aerie helped me pick out—a short strapless silver beaded dress with matching strappy sandals. He also suggests we stay in for dinner, but I tell him I want to take him out to celebrate his birthday. I have to get him out of the house so Bell and Charlotte can set up for the party.

Our quiet dinner is a welcome distraction from all the chaos at home. It's nice to be able to just sit and talk. I finally tell him about my argument with Grace. He listens but refrains from judging her. We talk in detail about his reservations concerning the upcoming tour, mainly his lack of interest in being out on the road—but we know there is no real solution for that. Discussing it further is fruitless because it always comes back to the fact that he can't let his brother and the other band members down.

We also talk a little bit about Tyler Records. Jack has recently acquired some small production companies and is looking for someone to run them. River tells me Jack asked him if he knew of anyone and River had suggested me. Jack has been trying to get River to take one over for a while.

I'm shocked. "I can't run a production company! Besides, I haven't even managed to get the business I'm working on now off the ground."

He grabs my hand. "I'll help you. We can find unknown talent and help them kick-start their dreams."

I shake my head. "This isn't the time to start a new business, River. You have to get through this tour and then we can talk about next steps."

River nods and with his eyes fixed on mine he says, "Yeah, I know you're right. It's just something I wouldn't mind doing someday."

Once our food arrives we push the heavy conversations aside and just enjoy each other's company. He runs his hand up my thigh and I kick off a shoe, sliding a toe down the inside of his leg. By the time we leave the restaurant we are both ready to get home—too bad we aren't going to be alone for a long while.

Pulling into the driveway after our romantic dinner, he parks in the garage and we head up the stairs toward the kitchen door. I have to fend off his wandering hands. I don't want him to get too carried away when I know we are going to be opening the door to a house full of people who have parked their cars in River's mother's driveway. Charlotte helped Bell with all the details for the party, but she didn't want to hang around and invade her children's space. I laughed at this because all three of her children love having her around, and to be honest, so do I.

Opening the door first, I walk into the kitchen. He's behind me and his hands are on my hips. He's kissing my neck when everyone yells, "Surprise!" Judging by the look of shock on his face, he really is surprised, and that thrills me.

I grab my camera and start snapping pictures. As we greet everyone in the kitchen, Bell brings us both a drink. She looks amazing and sexy as hell in her red lace dress with nude underlay. The deep V-neck and red leather waistband make it unlike any dress I've ever seen before and her heels must be at least five inches. With stick-straight hair now more red than copper she looks like a movie star. I snap a photo of her with River and can't help but think that she really outdid herself. The house is packed. Party decorations stream across every room, and there is a fully stocked bar in the kitchen. She even has a stage set up on the pool patio and the band we heard at the bar the other night is supposed to be playing soon.

When we finally make our way into the living room, Garrett is busy serving drinks, Xander is sitting on the couch with some girl I've never seen before, and Nix is out back with the band. Aerie couldn't make it. At the last minute she got called to Las Vegas to conduct an interview because the employee who was scheduled to do it quit. Ellie, on the other hand, is here and lighting up the room in her wrap dress that's more unwrapped than wrapped. Hers is one picture I purposely don't take. She's talking to someone from the label I've met, but I can't recall his name. She sees us, deposits her gift on the coffee table, and heads our way. I can just barely see the gift through the designer wrapping paper—it's a baseball of some sort in a case. Hmmm . . . she doesn't even know River prefers basketball. In fact, for the rest of his gift, I got us courtside season tickets for the Lakers and I plan to put on my jersey and give them to him tonight.

Smiling as she approaches with her cleavage on full display she says, "Happy Birthday, River," and reaches up to kiss him. I'm not sure if she was aiming for his lips, but I notice him turn his head and she kisses him on the cheek. We chat with her for a bit until River excuses us to go greet the other guests.

As we mingle, I sip another glass of champagne and River is handed a birthday shot every time he starts a new conversation. I leave him chatting with Xander and join Bell in the kitchen, where she looks insanely mad as she chews on her bottom lip. "What's wrong?"

"Tom was supposed to be here thirty minutes ago!"

"Tom who?"

"Doesn't River tell you anything? Tom is the bassist for the Mighty Storm."

"He's coming here? Why?"

She puts her hands on her hips and says, "Because he's my boyfriend!"

"I thought the drummer from the band that played at Smitten's the other night was your boyfriend."

"Reston and I broke up ages ago. I met Tom last night," she says, completely exasperated.

"Isn't he here now?"

"Tom?"

"No, Reston, isn't he down there playing?"

"Yeah, why wouldn't he be?"

"Never mind. By the way, thank you so much for getting this all together on such short notice. You did a great job."

"No problem. Now enough with the compliments and the boy-friend talk. I'm dying to know if my pole-dancing classes paid off. . . . Was I a good teacher? Were you able to pull off the dance?"

I look at her and raise my eyebrow. "Of course I was. I'm not completely incompetent when it comes to seduction."

She puts her hands over her ears as she says, "La la la! Can't hear you!"

I start laughing. "You asked."

"All I wanted to know was if my teaching skills paid off, I didn't mean I wanted to hear about the seduction of my brother."

"Definitely paid off!" I wink. "I'm going to go find him now," I tell her as I leave the kitchen.

Looking for River, I run into a few people along the way. Spotting him, I head his way as Scandalicious plays "Some Nights." River's downing another shot at the pool table. He sees me and motions for me to dance with him just as the band moves into "TiK ToK." The female lead singer sounds similar to Ke$ha, but when Reston chimes in he sounds exactly like P. Diddy. As soon as Reston starts the song with "Hey, what up, girl?" River starts to rock his head from one shoulder to the other in an almost robotic movement and I laugh, knowing we're going to have a good time. I raise my hands above my head and move my hips to the beat. As they hit the chorus River presses his body flush against mine and grinds his hips into me while dropping a kiss on my neck.

"What the fuck? Don't tell me you're just as pussy-whipped as this asshole over here!" yells a guy about ten feet away. Twisting around to see who it is, I can only assume it's Tom since he has his arm slung over Bell's shoulder. He's good-looking and Bell certainly seems to be attracted to him. He's about my height, his hair is the same light-brown color as River's, but his face is rounder.

My head snaps to the right when I see a taller figure standing beside him. I can't believe it—and I have what I can only describe as a fan-girl moment. As my mouth drops, so do my hands. I take a step back and just stand in shock. River sees Jake and grins from ear to ear. It's Jake, Jake Wethers in the flesh! The ultimate bad boy of rock is at my house, wearing his trademark black jeans and black T-shirt.

Looking at me suspiciously, River grabs my hand and leads me over to them. I can see Jake's famous tattoos on his arms and his blue eyes really do look like the ocean in contrast to his black hair. As we approach them, River sticks his hand out to Jake. "Hey, man, how are you? Long time no see."

Jake clasps his hand and shakes it. "Too long, man. I heard you guys are hitting the road soon. Would have been nice to have joined up again. Who knows? The Mighty Storm might be opening for you one day."

River chuckles, then swings his arm over my shoulder and says, "This is my girl, Dahlia. Dahlia, you know Jake. I'm pretty sure you told me you follow his career."

I shoot River an I-just-might-kill-you look. I can't believe he essentially just introduced me as a groupie.

"Nice to meet you, Dahlia," Jake says and I can't help but smile.

"And this is my Tru," Jake says and continues draping his arm over the shoulder of the girl next to him.

River reaches out his hand and as she shakes it she says, "Nice to meet you. I've heard all about you and the band. Jake only has nice things to say about you."

River says hello and graciously accepts the compliment.

Tru and I then shake hands and exchange niceties. I can't help but notice how beautiful she is.

Tom sticks his hand out to River and says, "Hey, man, good to see you, but am I the only one with a dick around here?"

He nods to me and says, "Hello, gorgeous."

Jake punches him in the arm. "Paws to yourself."

Tom rolls his eyes and turns, grabbing Bell by the ass. I guess Bell knows everyone already and she's skipping the introductions since Tom now has his tongue down her throat.

"Don't mind Tom. He likes to think he's hot shit," Tru says, and I can't help but laugh.

Tru and I then start talking about life on the road. She has been on tour with Jake so I have a ton of questions for her.

At some point I notice Bell and Tom have disappeared, but the rest of the party is in full swing. Everyone is singing along with the band, drinking, dancing, and having a great time. When Scandalicious takes a break, all the guys gather around River and start pouring shots of tequila.

I drag Tru to the kitchen with me and leave River with the guys. We need to do the cake because if we don't sing "Happy Birthday" soon, I'm not sure River will be able to blow out the candles. After giving Tru a brief tour of the house, we walk into the kitchen and I see Bell.

"Bell, I think it's time . . ." I trail off when I see she's on the phone with her head down and her hand over her free ear. I turn back to Tru and see Jake in the kitchen doorway.

"Sweetheart, we have to go," he says to Tru.

"Baby, they haven't even had the cake yet."

"Fucking Tom's already in the car," he mutters to her.

She rolls her eyes. "Tell me again why we rode with him?"

"No fucking idea, baby."

We say our goodbyes and I walk them to the door. Looking outside I can see Tom sitting in his car on the phone and another car behind him, which I can only guess holds the security team.

After they leave, I make my way back to the kitchen and see Bell step into the other room, still on the phone and seemingly arguing. I'm sure she's talking to Tom and I wonder if they broke up already. As I'm putting the candles on the cake, Caleb walks in and looks around before waving me over.

I walk over as he heads my way and we meet in the living room. "Hey, Caleb, what's going on?"

"Sorry, Dahlia, didn't know you were having a party. I tried calling you and River, but neither one of you answered."

"Oh, sorry. I'm throwing a surprise party for River. It's his birthday."

"Again, sorry to intrude, but I got a call that your security system is down, and I thought I should check it out."

"I have no idea what's going on with the security system but it seems to be causing you a lot of trouble."

"Dahlia, it's no trouble. It's my job."

"I know, but it's still nice of you."

He drops his head. "I won't be long. I just want to check the main fuse box."

"Okay, you know where it is."

He heads downstairs and I'm wondering if I should talk to him about Ben or ask him to stay for a drink when the front door swings open, and Ben walks into my house. He closes the door behind him and I stand there, staring. When he starts to walk into the living room I hastily move to stop him. "What do you think you're doing here?"

His eyes flash down my body and back up as he fingers the flower of my pearl necklace. "You added a necklace to your collection? It's beautiful, just like you."

I lean back and he drops his hand. "Ben, what are you doing? You shouldn't be here."

"Dahl, I'm with Caleb. We were out together when he got the call about the house. I was waiting in the car for him and I heard a lot of noise so I wanted to make sure everything was okay."

I stare at him in disbelief. "Really, Ben. Well, you've made sure now and everything is fine. So you can leave."

"Since I'm here, I want to talk to you. I've been trying to talk to you. Why won't you answer my calls?"

Holding back my agitation, I try to keep calm. "Ben, this is not the time or the place."

"Dahl, you won't give me the time or the place."

"Because I have nothing else to say to you."

His eyes seem to have been taking in the room since he arrived and when they settle on the large black-and-white picture of River and his band hung over the sofa he asks, "Why him? Is it because he's famous?"

I narrow my eyes and look at him. "Fuck you, Ben Covington. Get the hell out of my house!"

Ignoring me, he motions around the house. "I need to know. Did you know him while we were together?"

"Dahlia, you wanted me," Bell says as she walks up and stands next to me.

Her eyes flash to Ben and she gasps. I turn to look at her—she stares wide-eyed with her hand over her mouth. All the color seems to have drained from her face.

"Bell, are you okay?" I ask.

"S'belle?" I hear Ben question as he, too, stares and I instantly make the connection. Their reaction to each other and their body lan-

guage tell me I'm right. My head starts to spin as a vivid memory
flashes through my mind—

The e-mail. The words Reply to: S'belle, later tonight, green eyes,
touch, copper, *and* your apartment *in an e-mail on Ben's computer.
Ben hitting the* DELETE *button before I could read the whole message.
Knowing he was making plans with another girl—plans that weren't
platonic. Our breakup and path to reconciliation. River's sister is
S'belle. Ben and Bell!*

The bile rises up my throat as I run to the bedroom and open the
door. I slam it and flatten my back against it. Another memory flashes
before my eyes—River taking the broken frame from my hand, his eyes
narrowing as he stared at the picture for a long while. Recognition
flashed across his face, maybe even pain, when he asked, "Is this
him?" Me turning to face him when I hoarsely answered, "Yes. That's
Ben." River *knew* about his sister and Ben. This whole time, he's been
keeping that from me.

At the sliding glass doors, I open the curtains and look for him on
the pool deck. He's sitting there with Ellie sitting next to him, laughing and drawing something with her finger on the table. Then I see her
lift his hand and do the same. I want to yell for him to come up here
now, but I'm not going to make a scene. So I stand frozen, anticipating
the words I'll hear next—the words I don't want to hear from him because that will only confirm he knew.

My bedroom door opens and I immediately turn. Ben's standing
there, his face pale. He looks around and then walks into the room,
closing the door behind him.

"Dahl, how do you know her?"

Confusion sets in as I try to figure out what he's asking me, but
then I realize he has no idea who she is. "Bell is River's sister."

"Bell?"

"S'belle," I hiss.

"His sister?" He, too, looks like he might be sick.

He walks across the room and stands in front of me.

"Who you had your inappropriate relationship with in college is irrelevant right now, Ben. You need to leave."

With a huge sigh he reaches and takes my chin in his hand, saying, "Dahl, what do I have to do so you'll forgive me? Talk to me. Tell me."

The adrenaline starts to pump through my body as I realize all he has brought me is more pain. I step back but he follows and I can't help but scream, "Get the fuck out, Ben—now!"

He reaches for me again and this time tries to pull me to him. Just then the door abruptly opens and bounces off the wall. River stands there—his eyes narrowed on me. "Am I interrupting?"

He walks closer and his eyes flash to Ben. My heart racing, I take a step back. I am seething mad and he's not going to turn this around on me. Pointing outside I say, "Funny, I thought I might be interrupting you. I'm so glad you managed to pull yourself away."

He ignores me. "What the fuck are you doing in my room with my girl?"

"Your girl? I've already told you a substitute is not a replacement—they're never as good as the real thing."

My head snaps to Ben and I warn him, "You need to leave. Get out now."

But he ignores me and continues his taunting. "Oh, and another thing—she may be in your bed now, but she was fucking me in my bed for a hell of a lot longer and I bet she's still thinking about it."

Willing down a wave of nausea I scream, "Shut up, Ben. Just shut the hell up!" I can't believe he could be so crude.

River storms over to Ben. His eyes filled with rage, his jaw tight, and his fists clenched, he throws a hard punch at Ben's head before Ben even sees it coming.

Ben stumbles back, yelling, "Is the truth hard to take?"

"Fuck you! You don't even know the truth," River yells back.

Ben grabs River's leg before scrambling to his feet and slamming a punch into his stomach. Still, Ben doesn't let up. "Dahl, come on. Tell him what we were like."

I'm motionless, suspended in time, watching like I'm somewhere else.

A fury like I've never seen crosses River's face as he lunges for Ben, grabbing his arm and jerking it behind his back. He slams Ben to the ground, shoving his knee against his spine, wrenching his arm back. River gives it another jerk and Ben grunts, "Son of a bitch."

"River, stop!" I scream.

Snatching his other wrist, he pulls it behind Ben's back and seethes, "By the time I'm done with you, you're gonna wish you would've stayed dead."

I can hear how high and thin my voice is when I scream out again, "Stop it!" He doesn't seem to hear me. He's lost in the fight. His normally gleaming green eyes are shadowed in a way I've never seen before.

When Ben winces in pain, River leans down and whispers something in his ear, but doesn't let him go. My hand flies to my mouth and my tears are running down my cheeks—I just want this to end.

In a blur of movement, Xander pulls River off Ben, and Caleb drags Ben from the room as Ben yells, "This isn't over!"

River frees himself from Xander's hold and heads for the door, but Xander blocks him and shoves him to the bed. "That's enough, River! Enough! You need to get a handle on this."

Xander attempts to calm River and I'm trying to contain my own rage. "Xander, can you tell everyone the party is over?"

He nods and then drops down to his brother's eye level. "River, look at me. You need to do what we talked about. Do you hear me?"

River looked up at him for a moment before dropping his head back down again. Xander pats him on the shoulder and says, "Now." Then his eyes land on me. "I'll clear everyone out so you two can talk."

He closes the door behind him and River and I are left alone. I stand there for a minute, thinking about what Xander's just said to River, and I know that it's about their sister. Relief and fear burst through me—I'm relieved Ben is gone and fearful of what we are about to discuss.

"I saw the two of you," he says as he rises to his feet and heads for the door.

I hastily navigate around the bed and dash there first. Standing in front of the door, literally blocking his way, I force him to stop right in front of me.

"Well, I don't know what you think you saw, but whatever it is, I can tell you, you're wrong."

He takes a step back, eyeing me, and then turns to walk toward the glass doors. "Why was he in here, Dahlia? In our bedroom?"

Once again, I dash in front of him. I am not going to allow any space between us and he's not going to walk out of this room until we talk. "Why was she holding your hand?"

"Come on, Dahl, you really want to talk about Ellie right now?"

I grab his face, knowing exactly what he's implying by calling me by that nickname. "River, listen to me. I'm going to say this again—I am not interested in being with Ben. I am not in love with Ben. Whatever you think you saw, he wanted to talk to me about your sister. And I know you know what I mean. I just heard Xander tell you to tell me."

I stare into his green eyes, searching for any sign of confusion. But when his mouth drops open and he says nothing, I know for sure that he knew about them. From there, my irritation only builds. I jab my finger into his chest. "Yeah, like I thought, you knew the whole time and again you didn't tell me something."

He tries to reach for my hands, but I jerk away. I stare at him, my irritation flaring as I cross to the other side of the room. My rage mixes with hurt as I'm once again left wondering if I can trust him.

Grabbing my wrist, he swings me around to face him. "Stop walking away from me. Let me explain."

Shaking my head, I try to free myself of his grasp. "Oh, now you want to talk. It was okay, though, when you were the one walking away!"

His lip turns into a sneer. "That was different."

I laugh a little, now completely enraged. "The only thing different is that I was doing nothing wrong." My voice cracks.

His eyes close, and when he reopens them all I see is pain. He leans closer to me, dropping his voice to a whisper. "I was only protecting you. Because I wanted to save you from a heartbreak you didn't need to experience."

"River, I already knew that he came close to cheating on me. You were saving yourself from having to deal with how Bell and I would take it. I saw her face tonight when she looked at him. She clearly didn't know, either."

He sighs deeply. "I don't care how any of this affects me, you know that. I didn't want to dredge up sad memories for you or for my sister."

I stare at him and his grip loosens and moves to catch my hand.

I yank my hand from his. "River!"

"What?" He looks genuinely sympathetic.

I move back, frowning, and cross my arms over my chest. "You don't have to pity me. That part of my life was long ago. Ben can't hurt me anymore. It really doesn't matter to me who the girl was. But what does matter is that I have to be able to trust you."

He shoots me a look I don't understand. "You can trust me—we've been through that."

"You're not making it easy on me. Is there anything else I should know about?"

River's stare is unwavering as he looks deep into my eyes, but says nothing.

I need to escape this small space. I feel like I'm being torn apart from indecision—believe, don't believe, trust, don't trust. My stomach twists over his silence. Not knowing if he doesn't want to talk about his sister anymore or if maybe he's too drunk to talk at all, I head toward the door. But this time he gets there first. He cups the back of my neck and pulls me to him. My mouth is already open to say something, to scream at him to just talk to me, but he stops me with his lips. He flattens his mouth hard against mine, and for a few moments I allow it— letting the physical sensations block everything else out.

But then I stop kissing him and step back. We stand there so close, but so far apart. When his gaze flickers down my body, I can feel the heat between us. He grabs my elbows and steps into me. Again I don't resist. But this time, as soon as his mouth is on mine, I know where this is leading.

I whisper, "Please don't. You need to talk to me."

He licks his lips and swallows. "No, what I need is you," he says as he drops his hands to my waist and yanks me to him.

I put both of my hands on his chest and shove him back. "Stop it!"

His face twists and his eyes narrow. He lets out a sound of frustration and the smell of alcohol is evident on his breath. He leans into me and through clenched teeth he whispers, "Why? Are you thinking about him?"

Understanding he's drunk and doesn't mean what he's saying, I calmly respond, "No, River, I'm not. You know that. It's just we can't avoid talking by using sex this time. You need to help me trust you— talk to me, tell me what's eating away at you. Is there something else you're not telling me?"

He shakes his head in disbelief, his anger flaring. "There's nothing we need to discuss right now."

"I think there is."

"Fine, Dahlia, have it your way," he mutters; then he opens the door and slams it behind him.

My heart is in my throat and I can't catch my breath. Looking down, I see the red ribbon lying on the floor and suddenly I can't feel my own legs. I fall against the door, using it for support to help me stand. I suck in a breath and try to will away the tears. But when I hear the smashing of glass from the kitchen, I fall to the ground and cover my ears as the tears finally fall and my sobs escape me.

CHAPTER 17
Everywhere

Relationships are made up of so many different emotions, but the one thing that keeps a relationship strong is love. Can doubt weaken such a strong bond? Not if two people don't let it—right?

I understand that River wants to protect me, but at what cost? I am trying so hard to keep my trust in him, even through all the hurt his secrets have caused me. But hiding things, keeping things from me, has strained our relationship. He didn't tell me about his sister getting in an accident the night we first met, then he didn't tell me that he knew who attacked me, and last night I found out he knew about his sister and Ben. For our relationship to work, I need to make him understand that he can't keep hiding things from me in this way. What's strange is I know I should doubt his intentions right now, but deep down in my soul, my faith in him is unwavering and to me, that means our love is still strong.

My relationship with Bell has been amazing. We instantly became friends after our very first introduction. Over the past year, we've grown so close, so finding out that she's the girl Ben was communicating with behind my back in college was shocking—not only for me but it had to have upset her as well. I know I have to talk to her, but I'm not quite ready.

And truth be told, I'm not even mad at Ben about this. After our breakup and reconciliation, I got over it. And besides, I agree with Ben that it's old news. But that's about the only thing we agree on. As far as I'm concerned, there is no relationship between us on any level. But Ben, fucking Ben, doesn't seem to want to accept that I'm with someone else. Why would he come into our house? What was he thinking? Why would he follow me into our bedroom? And then purposely push River's buttons with his crude remarks? What does he want from me? I've made my feelings clear to him.

Then there's Xander. He knew about Bell as well. When did he find out? Did he know the whole time or did River tell him?

There's also Grace. I feel really bad I haven't talked to her and I know I have to face her and talk through our issues.

And of course there's Ellie. I know River loves me, and he isn't interested in anyone else. Sure I do. But she's after him. I know it. Whether he sees it or not, she is. And it bothers me that she's always around lately, like she's waiting for the pieces to fall, so she can be there to pick them up.

As the darkness turns into dawn, I lie awake, thinking about what has happened between us. I'm not sure if I ever dozed off, but I did walk over to the door at least ten times and grab the knob, though I never turned it. I wanted to go out there, to see him, to be with him. But I couldn't. River's tendency to keep secrets from me is not something I know how to handle until he's in a more coherent state of mind.

My phone rings and I sit up to see who's calling so early in the morning. When I see it's Ben's nephew, Trent, I answer immediately.

"Hello?"

"Dahlia," he says in a trembling voice.

"Trent? What's wrong?" Instantly, concern washes through me.

"I need help. I'm in trouble. Can you come get me?"

"Trent, where are you?"

"Don't tell my mom, Dahlia."

"Okay, just tell me where you are." I am panicked and worried, ready to agree to anything just so he'll tell me where he is.

I have to strain to hear his voice as he sniffles and tells me where he is before hanging up.

Jumping out of bed, I dash into the bathroom and then into our closet to throw on some clothes. I don't stop to brush my hair; I just pull it back messily. When I get to the living room I see River facedown on the couch, a bottle of vodka on the floor next to him. I try to wake him up, to tell him where I'm going, but he doesn't respond. I have to go, so I grab my keys and hurry out the door. I shouldn't be that long, especially since as soon as I hit the freeway, I drive as fast as I can. I've talked myself into not calling Serena until I find Trent, but I wonder if I should call Grace. I reach for my phone. Shit! I left it at home. Despite the light rain, I manage to get to Newport Beach in less than fifty minutes. I hope it's fast enough.

My heart races as I park in the lot near the Ferris wheel. Walking past it, I head behind the concession stand. The smell hits me instantly. Rows of garbage cans and trash lead the way down to what must be the back alleyway of the fairway. I stop immediately when I see them among the stacked boxes and empty beer kegs. Ben is squatting down in front of Trent, who is sitting on the ground, supporting himself against the building. His legs are outstretched and his head is back. I'm not sure if he's awake or asleep. One of Ben's arms is in a sling. He's talking to Trent, but I can't hear what he's saying. Trent seems to be moving his lips, but his eyes are closed. He looks so different. The once muscular young surfer looks to have lost at least twenty pounds, he has bruises on his arms, and seems frail. What happened to the boy with the big smile and dimples, just like his uncle? The boy on the ground is not the Trent I know.

Ben leans in closer—why I'm not sure. But when Trent's head falls to the side and Ben lightly slaps his cheek, alarm seizes me. "Is he all right?" I yell.

Ben looks up at me, surprised. "Thank fuck. I need help. Help me get him out of here, will you?"

I rush over to them. Trent's body has gone limp. Ben props Trent's arm around his neck and does the best he can to lift him up to his feet. Trent's eyes open and he sees me. "Dahlia, you didn't tell my mom, did you?"

With tears in my eyes I look into his vacant face. "No, Trent. No, I didn't."

"Good," he mutters and he tries to stand on his own. "I can do it," he says to Ben.

"What's going on? What's wrong with him?"

Ben motions for me to grab Trent's other arm and I do, wrapping it over my shoulder. Once we have Trent secured between us he looks over to me. "Let's get him to the car first, and then I'll explain."

Trent shuffles his feet as we assist him and Ben leads the way to his BMW. I open the door and Ben manages to get Trent into the backseat. Once he's closed the door Ben looks at me. "Did you know about him?"

"Know what?"

"That he's a drug addict."

I bring my hand to my mouth and my stomach turns. All I can do is shake my head no. Why wouldn't Serena have said anything?

"I figured you didn't. Serena's in denial and my mom is so distraught over it, she's not seeing things clearly. Do you mind helping me get him to the house?"

"Of course I don't mind, but shouldn't we take him to the hospital?"

"No, he doesn't need that. He's high. He needs to detox. I'm going to help him do that."

"You are? Are you sure you shouldn't do that with Grace?"

"No, fuck, I don't want her to know. We'll take him to our house. Mom or Serena can't see him this bad. Will you help me?"

I blink my eyes, knowing there is no way I can say no. "Yes."

"How did you know?"

"Know what?" I ask.

"That he was here."

"He called me."

Ben nods his head. "Yeah, he left me a message and as soon as I heard it I came."

Rain makes tracks down my face as I look at Trent through the window, not wanting to believe this to be true.

"Did he tell you anything else?" he asks.

"No, just not to tell his mother."

"I think he's in some kind of trouble. He's an addict. He keeps mumbling about owing people money." He stops and stares ahead.

The wind rips through me as his words sink in. "Oh, God!" I cry, wrapping my arms around myself.

He kicks the tire of the car, then he turns and heads to the other side of the car. "You coming?" he says, pointing to the passenger door.

"Yeah, but I'll follow you."

He shrugs and gets in his car. I'm wet and cold, so I turn the heater in my car on full blast. Following Ben to our house, *his* house now, feels so strange. It's a short drive, but it feels like it takes forever. I'm facing a deluge of memories as we get closer to the house. Memories that haven't surfaced in a long time. Flashes of our life together. Him as a young five-year-old blond-haired boy—making friends with me and playing with me in the sand. Him as a rebel teenager—the strong, resilient adolescent who was with me when I heard the news about the plane crash that forever changed my life—the one that killed my parents and my aunt. Our first kiss and our first time together on the beach. Images flash through my mind of the church altar and the stained-glass window reflecting upon it when Ben came and found me and told me I would never be alone. He was always there for me. He was my rock.

Even though I've known that he's alive for a while now, seeing him interact with Trent makes me actually *feel* it. He's here, right now, taking care of his nephew. Being the rock he always was. Somehow it's enough for me to let go of my resentment. I'm able to forgive him for the choice he made, and tears slide down my cheeks. The man who was my friend through everything isn't gone and I suddenly feel relieved. As my negative feelings toward Ben dissipate and are replaced with happy memories of our unbreakable bond, I know what I have to do. I have to actually talk to him. Maybe accept his apology. Maybe even be his friend. I think I can do that. Grace was right—I owe him that much.

I know River won't be happy that I'm here, but he'll have to understand that I came for Trent, because of Trent. I also feel that letting go of my anger toward Ben may ease the stress on my relationship with River. To be honest, I don't think Ben is even the issue between River and me anymore; the issue is really our inability to communicate effectively.

Arriving at the yellow house with the white picket fence, I wipe away my remaining tears and take a deep breath. I can do this. I can do this for Trent. I can do this for Ben. With a newfound determination, I hurry out of my car and help Ben. We manage to get Trent into the house. Once we get him settled in bed, he mumbles something I can't understand, then he seems to lose consciousness again.

Alarmed, I grab Ben's arm. "Is he okay?"

Ben looks at my hand and then pulls the blanket over Trent. He nods his head before wistfully saying, "He will be, just give him some time."

Ben walks into the bathroom and I stare at the broken boy lying in the bed. A sixteen-year-old with his whole life ahead of him. A young boy who loved cats and dogs is now a teenager in need of help. As I leave the room, I'm hopeful he can overcome this because he has so many things to look forward to.

Closing the door behind me, I notice boxes everywhere. Ben must have decided to move back in. I walk out to the living room and I stand there shivering, soaked to the bone.

Following me out of the room, Ben hands me a towel and says, "Here, dry off."

I take it and wrap the towel around my shoulders. He walks over to the fireplace and stacks some Sterno logs. As he lights them, they easily catch fire and I can feel their warmth from where I stand.

"I'll be right back," Ben says as he leaves the room.

Walking over to the desk that Ben must have taken from Grace's attic, I use the house phone to call River, but there's no answer. I don't leave a message because I know telling him where I am on voice mail will only piss him off more.

Ben returns a few minutes later, having changed. He looks like he always did in khaki shorts and a white T-shirt. I have to remind myself that everything that has happened was not a dream. My trance is broken by the awkwardness of the moment as he hands me a T-shirt and a pair of sweatpants and says, "Here, put these on, so you're not sitting here in wet clothes."

Accepting the dry clothes, I go into the hall bathroom to change. I can't help but think how strange it is to be here with him, in the house I shared with him for so many years. It used to be such a place of comfort but now everything is so different, and it feels unnatural to be here.

When I come out, I head toward the living room and drop my wet clothes near the door.

I can see that Ben's reading something on his phone.

He looks up at me. "I have to find a facility to check Trent into immediately. Can you help me?"

"Sure, what can I do?"

He hands me his phone. "You could make a list of all the rehabil-itation centers in Orange County and I'll start calling them. I haven't bought a new computer yet, but you can search for the numbers on my phone. It's the one thing besides my journal I brought back with me from New York City. I think you even know the phone number," he says with a weak smile.

Thoughts of him having to establish an entirely new life and then having to leave that life trigger something I never expected to feel for him again—sympathy. I haven't really spent any time thinking about how all of this impacted him; I've been so focused on how his leaving affected me. Coming back here and starting over can't have been easy.

We spend the next few hours trying to secure a spot for Trent. Once I've compiled the list, I leave Ben to the phone calls and go to check on Trent. I move my hand to his forehead and he stirs, mum-bling something about money he owes. When I come back to the living room, Ben tells me he got Trent on six waiting lists at private centers.

Sitting on the couch, I throw my legs up, completely exhausted. Ben sits at the opposite end and stretches out his legs. Uncomfortable at the familiarity of the situation, I scramble to sit up. I pull my knees up to my chest and wrap my arms around my legs, resting my chin on them.

Smirking, he watches me as he absentmindedly rubs his arm.

"How bad is it? Did you go to the hospital?" I ask.

"Fuck no. Caleb just popped it back in place."

I roll my eyes. "Of course he did."

We sit in silence as I stare at the sling and then I have to ask, "When I checked on Trent he was mumbling that he owes people money again. Do you know who?"

Furrowing his brows he says, "I think he was selling and owes some dealers. When he's more coherent I'll find out who and how much and see what I can do to settle his debt."

I let out a long silent sigh because there is nothing I can say to that. Trent suddenly yells and Ben rolls off the couch and hurries to check on him. When he comes back I ask, "Are you sure he shouldn't be in the hospital?"

"Yeah, Dahl, I am. I can do everything for him they can."

"What do you mean?"

Sitting in one of the chairs he tells me, "When I was in New York I taught drug management and volunteered at a rehab center."

"Really? What made you get into that?"

He looks at me, his blue eyes sad. "I had to find something to do that made me feel useful. I was looking for purpose and those kids needed someone. It worked."

"Have you thought about what you're going to do here?"

He props one elbow on his knee and hangs his head between them. Then he turns his head toward me. "No, I haven't. I can't do anything right now. First, I have to get my finances in order, reestablish my identity, and get through the legal proceedings. The frenzy will start once the press gets wind of the case and it will be hard to stay out of the public eye. I'm sure reporters will be hounding me. So until the trial is over, I can't even think about what I'm going to do."

At the glimpse of his pain, my heart sinks as I think of the life he has to rebuild and the hurdles he will have to jump to do so. I feel another sudden wave of sympathy. "I'm sorry, Ben. I had no idea."

He takes in a deep breath and slowly blows it out. "This isn't how I ever imagined we'd end up."

"I know, Ben, neither did I, but . . ."

He stops me midsentence. "Stop, Dahl, don't say 'but' yet," he says with a frown.

Rising, he moves over to me. He sits on the coffee table and faces me. He grabs my hand. "I don't know what I was thinking back then.

Why I left you here. I want so much to take it all back. Do it differently. I know I handled everything wrong. But do you think you can forgive me?"

Pulling my hand away, I keep quiet, letting my silence answer for me. Just because I can have a conversation with Ben about his situation doesn't mean I can forgive his actions; I'm just not sure I am ready to do that.

"I know this is hard for you, but I feel empty without you . . . I want to go back to where we were. Do you think you could try?"

"Ben, I'm sorry, but no. I'm with someone else now. We can't change the events that led us to where we are."

He looks away. He doesn't say another word and neither do I. We both remain quiet for a few moments, and then when I stand up, he grabs my arm and bluntly asks, "Are you happy with him?"

I take a deep breath and answer his question honestly, knowing this is going to hurt him. "Yes, I'm happy. Really happy."

He grabs for me again, this time pulling me to his lap. "Give us a chance. Give me another chance. I need you."

At this point I'm staring at him openmouthed; then I jump up and shake my head back and forth. "Ben, don't do this. I just told you how I feel."

"Come on, Dahl, it's just the two of us here. Be honest. This is about us."

My eyes narrow on him. "'About us'? What do you mean 'us'?"

"Fuck, Dahl, you know what I mean. We can start over right now. You could be happy with me, too."

I look at him. He's the same man he always was, and even though I know I no longer feel for him what I once did, making him understand that is difficult. But my expression must be enough of a reply because he gets up and crosses the room to look out the window.

Knowing that the difficult part is over, I address something that's been on my mind. "Ben, can I ask you to do something for me?"

Turning around, he grins. "Sure, you know I'm always up for anything."

I have to fight the urge to roll my eyes. "Can you please stop antagonizing River every time you see him? I really don't appreciate you bringing up our past to my fiancé. It's just not appropriate."

A pained expression crosses his face. "That's one thing I'm really not up for."

I sigh, disappointed that Ben hasn't changed a bit. Completely exasperated, I start toward the door, knowing it's time for me to leave.

"Wait. Can I ask you something now?" Ben says.

When I turn back, it's with a forced smile. "Sure."

He stands up straighter. Subtle, but still noticeable. "When did you meet him?"

"Why do you keep asking me that?"

"Can you just answer my question?"

My voice comes out low. "I met River one night while we were in college and we talked, but that was it. It wasn't until last year that I saw him again. Aerie sent me to do an interview."

I glimpse disappointment on his face. "Makes sense," is all he says and I don't ask why. Feeling uncomfortable with this discussion, I look out the window and see that it's starting to get dark. "Shit, what time is it?"

He looks at his watch. "It's six. Why—do you have a curfew?"

Deciding it's best to ignore his sarcasm, I just say, "I need to leave. Are you going to be okay here with Trent?"

"Yeah, Dahl, I think I can handle it."

"You're going to call Serena tonight? Right?"

"Look, I told you, I'm not calling her until the drugs are out of his system."

"You can't keep this from her. She's his mother. She has a right to know. She'll be worried sick."

He cocks his hip as he leans against the doorway. "When the fever and chills set in, it will be the toughest part." Then he braces his one hand up high on the frame. "Dahl, telling the truth is not always black and white. Sometimes it's best to stay in the gray so you don't hurt the people you love. Telling her now, bringing her here, would only cause her pain. I don't want her to suffer. So why would I do that?"

What he said makes sense and I almost have to agree with him. I don't want Serena to see Trent like this, but I can't justify not telling her, either. "You have a good point but I still think she should know."

He sighs and moves toward me, stepping into me. "I don't doubt that's how you feel. It's just everyone handles things in different ways. You're an idealist. I'm a realist. Neither is right or wrong."

In the past I'd have smiled and complimented him on his keen observation. Now, though, it doesn't seem right so I simply nod and move away. "I'm leaving now. Call me if Trent needs anything."

With a smirk, he asks, "What if I need something?"

I grab my wet clothes and reach for the knob.

He steps around me and blocks my way. "Please, don't go."

I look at him. "Ben, please move. I really do have to go home now."

He stands unmoving. His brow creases and he drops his head. He runs his hand through his hair and then moves to the side.

I step forward to the door and yank it open, hurriedly leaving.

Walking to the car, I think about what Ben said—life isn't just black and white. With that in mind, I am going to give River the benefit of the doubt. I really want things between us to get back to normal because if they don't—I'm not sure we will make it. I hope our time apart has helped his anger because I really want to sit down with him and have a real conversation. To be honest, I just don't think anything good ever comes from heated confrontations. My parents used to have many violent disagreements, and I never wanted that kind of relationship for myself.

On the drive home, I think maybe I should stop at a store and buy something to wear. River isn't going to be happy that I'm wearing Ben's clothes. But I decide to just go home—he'll understand why after I tell him about Trent and what happened. He has no reason not to.

I scan the radio, searching for songs that will make me smile— music is the one thing that always makes me happy. I thump my hands against the steering wheel and just listen to the beat of the music throbbing in my ears. Listening to each song, the lyrics seem to play out in my head—they tell me a story. Every beat plays within me, as natural as the sound of the rain hitting the ground.

CHAPTER 18
What I've Done

Ben's Journal

Last night's turn of events was completely unexpected. Caleb picked me up and we went to Reality Bites to grab some food and talk. I ended up doing the drinking for both of us. He was on call and refused to even drink one beer. Good thing, since he got a message that an alarm was down. When he excused himself to make a call, I wondered why he couldn't do it in front of me. I was outright pissed when he came back and said he had to leave. I told him I'd ride along with him because I had nothing else to do. Now I know why he was so hesitant for me to come and why he said I had to stay in the car.

When he pulled through the gates of the Hills, it all made sense. I thought he had gotten fired so I had to ask if we were going where I thought we were going. He didn't answer me as he approached a cul-de-sac and parked his car in front of what I assumed to be the fucktard's house. I had no fucking idea that he was actually part of the irresponsibly rich and famous. It had an absurdly long upward sloping driveway, a large decorative front door that looked like he was waiting for royalty to visit, and what really got me was the modest landscaping. Doesn't he know she loves flowers?

I sat in the car for at least five minutes and couldn't take it anymore. I had to at least go look around. I walked up a million steps to get to the fucktard's door. When I spotted the wind chimes I knew for sure this was where she'd been staying. I heard loud music and people talking and could tell there was a party going on. Since the door was open, I thought I might be able to steal her away and talk to her without his eyes on me the whole time.

I spotted her right away. She looked fucking amazing. She was dressed up and I really wanted those long legs wrapped around me. When she saw me, the scowl on her face was anything but welcoming. I asked her about the pearl necklace she was wearing. She ignored my question so I knew rich boy must have given it to her. I'm surprised she's with someone who tries to buy her love. When I asked her the one thing that's been bugging the shit out of me, my fucking worst nightmare happened.

My dirty little secret was standing next to me and talking to my Dahl. Dahl ran off and I hadn't even noticed because my mind was engrossed in the vivid memories of all the different ways I had fucked that girl that one night. I only refocused when S'belle looked at me. I could have sworn she was looking at me like she got me, like she saw through my bullshit. But then she asked what the fuck I was doing there, and I knew I was just imagining it. Honestly, I'm really fucking tired of that question. Didn't matter anyway because she didn't stick around long enough for me to answer. She fled like fire out the front door.

I followed Dahl and when I opened the door she had slammed,

I was surprised to see her hope chest on the other side of the room. I looked at the unmade bed and when I saw the black thong on the floor, I nearly lost it. I was in their bedroom. Fuck me!

When she told me how she knew S'belle I nearly shit my pants. Of course she's the prick's sister. It wasn't until I knew she didn't know the entire story that I could finally breathe. Just as I thought I was finally getting somewhere with Dahl, the prick came in, looking like he wanted to kill me. All I could do was laugh, wishing I had at least been trying to kiss her when he walked in. I felt an overwhelming urge to remind him who had her first, and, shit, he threw a mean right hook. But I just kept on reminding him that she was mine first. I thought I could take him if I pushed a little hard. But when he pinned me up against the wall, I couldn't believe he got me again. Fuck, he's fast, but I knew I was faster. But before I could show him what I really had, Caleb pulled him off of me.

When Caleb threw me into his car, he really laid into me. I didn't say a word. I just really didn't give a shit anymore. We didn't talk the rest of the way home and when we exited at Laguna I told him to drop me at Ana's Attic. He pointed to the elbow I was rubbing and said he might need to pop that in place and that I needed to get a sling.

After the pharmacy stop, I headed toward the bar and Caleb followed. Pretty boy kicked my ass and I needed a drink. I don't remember much except that I drank until my mind was numb and Caleb brought me home.

I woke up to my phone ringing but it stopped before I could get to it. I checked my messages and instantly sobered up. My nephew was in trouble and all I knew was that I had to get to him. Serena had dropped the car off at my house so I left as soon as I could to find him.

I regret having left Laguna for many reasons but when I saw

Trent lying there among the garbage and beer bottles in the alley behind the concession stand in Newport Beach, I knew he was my biggest regret. Dahl and everything else aside, my nephew needed me. He was never close with his father and over the years I had assumed that role. Then when he probably needed me the most, I wasn't there. What had happened in the years I was gone to the boy who was such a great athlete, student, and all-around happy child? He's now so strung out he barely knew who I was. I was terrified as I sat him up and he muttered things to me a sixteen-year-old shouldn't have to worry about.

I knew, looking at him then, that if he could be the only good thing I'd done in my life against all the bad—I'd take it. My mind worked fast and I knew I was the one who could help him get clean. I didn't want to call Serena or Mom. All I had to do was get him to my house. I pulled him to a sitting position, but with only one fucking arm I couldn't get him to his feet. And then as if God had heard my confession of sins and was forgiving me, there she was. She was there to help me.

I was surprised Dahl didn't know about Trent, but then again the way my sister was acting, I shouldn't have been. She helped me get him home and settled in what used to be our room. I had wanted to get her home and alone, but not under those circumstances.

We were both soaking wet and although I really wanted to strip off her wet clothes, I knew better than to attempt that under the circumstances, and, honestly, I wasn't in the mood. So instead, I gave her a towel and some dry clothes. Once she changed she helped me try to secure a location for Trent and then we sat down and talked. My plan to skip talking backfired. It felt wrong. I just needed to let her know I wanted her back.

It was a relief to get it out, but her reaction was far from what I had expected. I thought she would run and wrap her arms around me, maybe even jump me. After all, I changed my whole life for her. But instead, when I put it out there, she shot me down. She rebuffed my every move. Then after I laid it out and told her that I wanted her, I could see in her eyes she didn't feel the same way.

I tried to keep my cool while she was still here. Once she left I checked on Trent. Then I went into the bathroom and splashed some water on my face. I knew I had to keep it together. I had to concentrate on helping Trent. I was fucking exhausted so I lay down on the couch to try to take a quick nap. I knew I had a long night ahead of me and needed to catch some z's, but I couldn't sleep because memories of our life together seemed to be everywhere in this fucking house. I replayed her asking me to leave that pretty boy of hers alone a million times. I wanted to say _fuck no, riling him up was too much fun_, but I didn't want to piss her off. But as soon as she called him her fiancé, I was the one who was pissed off. I felt like she had just punched me in the gut. _I_ was her fiancé. Why I even asked if she knew him while we were together, I have no fucking idea because I already knew the answer—he had made that clear. I know she would have never cheated, but it still bugs the shit out of me. I'm really starting to doubt that I'm going to be able to get her back. Fuck me.

CHAPTER 19
Pieces

I'm blaring "I Found You" by the Wanted and singing along to one of my favorite songs when my calmness fades and annoyance surfaces. Ellie's car is parked in our driveway directly in front of the garage. What's she doing here this late? Doesn't her workday end at five like most people's?

Jerking the wheel, I turn and park right in front of the steps. I rush out into the rain, and then hurry up to the landing. Turning the knob, I discover it's unlocked, and I open the door slowly. Why is she here alone with River? What am I going to walk into?

I expect to see them sitting at the kitchen table, so when I see River on the couch and her on the floor beside him, I'm more than a little surprised. I take in the whole scene. The gifts have been moved to the counter. He's leaning over the glass coffee table, looking at a stack of papers. Her red shirt is unbuttoned so far that her matching bra isn't the only thing showing. Her legs are bent to the side and her tight black pencil skirt is riding up pretty high. She's leaning against the sofa with her arm resting on the cushion, very close to River's thigh. Her other hand is holding a pen over the stack of papers that River is looking at. She's removed her leopard-print high-heel pumps, showing off her red-painted toenails. Her bare feet lie pressed against our wooden floor and she looks a bit too comfortable to be conducting a business meeting.

"Hi." It's all I say but it's enough to make River's head snap up, his eyes meeting mine.

"Hi," he says back and his face is unreadable, but I swear I see guilt in his eyes.

The next series of events seems to play out in slow motion. Ellie swings her head around and her mane of silky black hair follows. She looks up and gives me a fake smile and a slight wave. She flutters her unnaturally long eyelashes and glares at me like I'm intruding. I can't help but return the look. Then I avert my stare and look around. There's a pizza box and a few beer bottles on the coffee table and I have to wonder how long she's been here and how much they've had to drink. I feel my heart tear a little at the picture before me, but it rips my heart out when I see Stella, his guitar, propped against the couch on the other side of Ellie.

Water is dripping down from my wet hair and onto my face. I push the hair out of my eyes as she says, "Oh sorry, did I block you from getting in the garage? I never thought of it."

I can't help but sneer at her and say, "Of course you didn't." Afterward, I abruptly turn toward the bedroom and throw over my shoulder, "Sorry if I interrupted." My head is spinning as I move to escape the large room that suddenly seems claustrophobic. I slam the bedroom door, kick off my shoes, and throw myself onto the bed. I know I wanted to come home and talk calmly to River, but now I'm just annoyed.

Staring out the window, I try to see the Hollywood sign, but the rain is falling so hard that I can barely make the letters out. I'm not a jealous person, or least I never have been, but there's just something about that woman. I begin to wonder if I haven't picked up on what's clearly in front of my eyes. Have we been over and I just didn't realize it? Is the bond I thought we shared not as strong as I envisioned?

Flashes of our fairy-tale romance swim before my eyes—our fun drive from Vegas to LA, our games, his crazy made-up rules, the fountain and our wishes, waking up with him every morning—him always asking if I can "wait a bit" for my coffee because he's got better things in mind, sleeping on whichever side of the bed we happen to be on because being together is all that matters.

"What the hell, Dahlia!"

Without turning around I ask him, "Is there something going on between the two of you? Is that what you're not telling me?"

"No!" he snaps and then I feel the bed dip as he moves across it. He hovers over me and his hand slides along the curves of my waist before resting on my hip. I shudder at his touch. With his lips near my ear he more calmly says, "Why would you even think that?"

I turn around to face him. "You've been spending a lot of time together. Then I come home and she's here again."

He shakes his head. "She's here working."

"I'm afraid she's here just waiting to pick up our pieces."

"There are no pieces. We'll never be in pieces."

I whisper, "But I see the way she looks at you."

His eyes meet mine and he whispers back, "I don't care how she looks at me. You're the only one I see."

I know I shouldn't say this, but I have to, I have to know. "It didn't look like that tonight. What was she doing here? Did you play for her?" I can't bear the thought of him playing his guitar for her. When he plays for me, he bares his soul, and it feels like the most intimate moment two people can share without touching one another.

"Dahlia, I didn't play for her." But as he says this, his body stiffens and he throws himself back on the bed.

My heart lodges in my throat. "What's wrong? I know there's something you're not telling me."

He sighs, then announces, "I quit," before throwing his arm over his forehead.

"What? Just like that!" I scream, bolting upright and looking at him in complete shock. I know we are having some issues but I never thought he'd just end us like that. "Without even trying to work this out, you're just going to throw us away?"

He sits up and forcefully pulls me to him. "Fuck, Dahlia. No. Not us. I could never quit us, not ever. You're a part of who I am. I was talking about the tour. I'm done with it. I quit the band." He lets go of his hold on me and runs his hands through his hair.

I'm not entirely surprised, but I am a bit thrown. "Are you sure about this, River? You're weeks away from the tour. What did Xander and the other guys say?"

He throws himself back on the bed. "Yes, I'm sure. I haven't told them yet. I wanted to see what would happen to the guys first. Make sure my quitting doesn't have a financial impact on them. That's why Ellie was here; she was pointing out the penalties for breach of contract."

I want to say I bet she was, but I know this is not the time for jealousy. Right now he needs me. I lean down next to him and stroke his cheek with my thumb. "River, why are you doing this now?"

He squeezes his eyes shut for a few seconds. "I just can't do it. I never wanted it to begin with and now with everything else going on, my heart just isn't in it."

"River, you cannot quit because of us."

"That's just it, Dahlia. It's not because of you or us; it's because of me. You know I never wanted this. It won't be good for me and it won't be good for the band if I go through with it."

He pulls me closer and our mouths collide. His tongue lightly probes mine, and I realize I have missed his lips. I have missed him. He pulls me on top of him and his hands slide down to my backside, pushing me into him. I get caught up in the moment, and then suddenly remember we still need to talk about yesterday.

I murmur against his lips. "River, we need to talk."

He breathes back, "I need you right now."

"I need you, too, but I meant what I said yesterday—we can't keep trying to solve our issues with sex."

Pulling back, he looks at me. I move to sit beside him and he sits up, too. Sighing, he tucks a lock of hair behind my ear. "I know we can't, beautiful."

All I want to do is grab handfuls of his messy hair and pull him back to me. When I look into his eyes, I see the same look I saw when I walked in the door: guilt.

"River, we have so much we need to talk about."

He nods his head and looks resigned to the discussion. I notice his hands start to twitch when he says, "Dahlia, there are just some things that are harder to talk about than others."

"I know. But we need to have these difficult discussions."

"You have to know, I just never wanted to have to say anything that might hurt you. . . ."

When the house phone rings, I jump. I reach to answer it, but he stops me. "Let it ring."

"It might be about Trent," I tell him and grab the receiver. "Hello," I answer.

"Let me talk to River," Xander demands.

I cover the receiver and mouth, "It's Xander, and he wants to talk to you."

He exhales a heavy breath and takes the receiver. "What?" He's quiet for a few seconds and then frowns. "I don't want to talk about it now." Then he turns the phone off and tosses it to the floor. "What's going on with Trent?"

"He called me crying this morning. He sounded scared and alone. He said he needed me to come get him in Newport. I tried to wake you up to tell you."

He studies me. "You lost me. What was he doing in Newport and why did you have to go get him?"

"River, he's an addict."

"How do you know that?"

I know he's not going to like this. "When I got to Newport, Ben was already there. He needed help to take Trent back to the house."

His mouth sets in a firm line and his eyes narrow. "What house, Dahlia?"

"My house in Laguna."

"Are you fucking kidding me?" he says as he stands up. "You spent the day with him and you're worried about what Ellie was doing here?"

"It's not the same and you know it."

He heads for the door and just before he leaves the room he says, "You got that right!"

I follow him out into the living room. "River, we need to talk about this reasonably."

River's eyes snap to me. "Whose clothes are you wearing?"

There's a hard knock and the front door swings open. Xander stands there, scowling.

River ignores him. Pain contorts his features. "I asked whose clothes you're wearing."

"It was raining and I was wet so I had to change."

Xander isn't going to be ignored. He walks right over to River and says, "I want to talk to you now!"

"Fuck off, Xander." River's voice is low and filled with fury. I don't think he's even trying to control himself as his hands clench into fists.

I flinch when Xander grabs River by the shirt and gets right in his face. "Listen to me. I said I want to talk to you, and it isn't a choice," he seethes.

River shoves him away and looks back at me. "You're wearing his clothes! Did you let him fuck you?"

"Hey, bro, calm down," Xander says.

I gasp in shock that he would say something like that. My voice breaks but I manage, "River, no, of course not. You know there's nothing going on between Ben and me. Let's just sit down and talk about this." I tell him this, suppressing my own temper—trying to remain calm and pretending Xander isn't really here listening to all of this.

His voice sounds rough, broken even. He shakes his head just once. "I don't want to fucking deal with all this shit anymore!" Suddenly, his expression grows dark, almost dangerous. Then before I know what's happening, he kicks the glass table from underneath, the papers that were sitting on it scatter in the air, and the tabletop itself flips over and shatters. The sound is piercing. Without looking at me he storms out the kitchen door and stomps down the stairs. I can hear his engine rev and then his tires squeal.

From the front door I watch as he takes off. I call after him, but he can't hear me. I just stand there frozen. I shiver and I know it's not because of the chill in the air or lingering rain.

In the next moment Xander is standing behind me.

"Muse! Did you hear me?" he says in an incredulous tone.

I turn around and his eyes snap to mine. "What the fuck is going on?" he demands.

All I can do is shake my head. There is so much going on, I'm not even sure what he wants to know.

"He's smashing shit and running out. He's not acting like himself. Why?"

I swallow. "He's mad."

He takes a step forward, curling his lip into a sneer. "Ellie just called and told me he quit. How is it I didn't even fucking know he quit? Is it because of you?"

I lean back against the open door and try to open my mouth to speak but the words won't come out.

His jaw clenches and his fury seems to overcome him. He slams his fist against the wall. "You have nothing to say. He doesn't answer his phone. He won't talk to me. And you two are going at it . . . again. You're the reason he quit. Aren't you?"

"No. No, I'm not the reason. He just doesn't . . ."

He cuts me off. "Fuck it! I'm done."

With a disgusted look he brushes by me and walks out.

"Xander, let me explain," I call out but he just ignores me.

I watch him leave as well, then turn and close the door.

A memory suddenly flashes before my eyes—the first time I saw River's gorgeous silhouette across the bar, his intense gaze, our instant connection. Is it gone?

Walking into the living room I pick up his guitar and strum my fingers along the strings. When I look at the glass table now broken into a thousand tiny pieces, I think, *You were wrong, River, we are in pieces.*

CHAPTER 20
Everlong

Faint morning light streams through the window as I slip off our bed and try to call him again. Standing over the nightstand I clutch the portable phone. My call goes directly to his voice mail but I don't leave a message; I haven't left any messages because I'm not sure what to say, what will make any of it better. I just think if we could sit down and talk reasonably, we could work it out. Or at least I hope we can.

As I hang up the phone I have an urgent need to find something that will bring me some comfort. I peer out the window, looking for the sign that's blocked from my view by the heavy rain. I open the sliding doors and make my way down to the pool deck to get a little closer so I can catch a glimpse. Once I'm standing on the half wall that acts as our railing, I shade my eyes and I see a faint hint of the letter *H*. I spread my arms out and throw my head back. The rain pelts down on my face and I look into the heavens and ask—why are we falling apart?

I stay out in the rain until I'm shivering and my teeth are chattering.

Making my way back into the house, I take off my wet clothes and slip on my bathrobe. Ben's clothes are still lying in the same place I threw them last night when I stripped them off. Picking them up, I walk into the kitchen and throw them away. I can see why River hasn't answered his phone; it's sitting on the counter, its screen illuminated and beeping to indicate that he has messages. I feel some relief that at least he isn't ignoring my calls.

On my way back to our bedroom, I stop in the music room and sit at the piano that River bought me for Christmas last year. I had told him that my dad had been teaching me to play before he died. Since then, River has taken that role on and I have perfected many songs, but I am most proud that I've mastered the one my dad was teaching me before tragedy stuck—"Lullabye" by Billy Joel. I sit at the piano for a long while, drawing my fingers across the keys and thinking about our happy times in this room before finally deciding to take a shower.

Standing under the hot water, I try to rid myself of the chills that don't want to go away. When I finally get out, I start to get dressed and the phone rings. I dash for it, assuming it's River.

"Hello?"

"Dahl, it's me. I need some help."

"Ben? How did you get this number?"

"From Caleb. Why, are you not allowed to get calls?"

"What do you need, Ben?"

"I want to go check out one of the centers that have availability for Trent and make sure it's not a shithole, but I can't leave Trent alone."

"Sure, I'll be there as soon as I can," I say and hang up.

I throw on a pair of jeans, select one of my dad's concert T-shirts, and put my boots on because I know River likes them.

I can't find my phone. I have no idea where I left it yesterday morning in my haste to get to Trent. So I leave the house without a phone again, but this time I leave a note for River. I know he thinks I'm still upset with him and he's obviously upset with me, but I want him to know how I feel.

River,

*If I could have one wish, just one, then my wish would be you . . .
to wake up with the feel of your breath near my neck, the warmth
of your lips on mine, and the sound of your heart beating in sync
with my heart.*

*You're the one who turned my world around . . . made it
right. You brought me back to life. I can't imagine my life
without you. I know this past week has been tough for both of
us, but I love you more than words can say. I'd never do anything to hurt you and I know you'd never do anything to hurt
me. Reach down deep into your soul, remember who I am,
who we are, and I know you will have no doubts.*

*Just remember you're my everything. I know we need to talk.
I love you more. I love you always!*

I'm yours, Dahlia.

P.S. I hope you know which one is missing.

Once I finish and tuck it under his phone, I run to the bedroom
and pull out the six guitar picks I gave him for Valentine's Day. Placing
them on top of the note, I leave all but one and place the one I selected
inside my pocket.

I also need to tell him I'm going to Ben's to keep an eye on Trent,
so I take a Post-it from the drawer and write a quick note that I stick to
the refrigerator before leaving.

I arrive in Laguna much faster than usual, so I pick up a few items at
the grocery store that I know Trent likes and then go through the
Starbucks drive-thru and get coffees.

When I get to the house, I step on the front porch and can't help
but think it seems so strange to knock, not just walk into the house that

I lived in for so long. I lightly tap on the door, not wanting to wake Trent in case he's sleeping. When there's no answer, I open the door and peek my head inside. "Ben."

There's no response so I decide to step inside. I've just set the bags and coffees down in the kitchen and turned to open the refrigerator when he walks in. He's shirtless, his hair is wet, and he's trying to run a belt through the loops of his shorts. His other arm isn't in the sling, it's hanging limply by his side. He looks surprised. "Shit, you really did get here fast. I guess you were already awake." Then with an impish grin he says, "What, doesn't he have blackout shades?"

Quickly averting my eyes, I ignore his comment and push the coffee tray toward him. "I brought coffee."

He steps right into me. "Am I making you nervous? You've seen me naked a million times, Dahl."

I turn my back to him and start unloading the groceries.

"Hey, you okay?"

With irritation setting in, I sigh. "Ben, I'm fine."

I feel his hands on my hips and his mouth near my ear as he says, "No, you're not fine. I know you better than that."

I freeze, not expecting his touch. "Ben, don't."

Ignoring me, he rests his chin on my shoulder as he wraps his arms around my waist, pulling me into him. "I'm sorry, Dahl, I can't help it. I miss you."

For a split second I'm transported back to when we would go days without talking and this was always his way of apologizing. But when I feel his lips on my neck, I step away, and move to put the boxes of cereal in the cabinet.

"Come on, Dahlia—don't you miss us?"

"Ben, how many times do I have to say this? You can't put your hands on me anytime you want anymore."

"What we had was good. That doesn't just go away."

I turn to look at him. "It was good. But things are different now. I'm not in love with you anymore. I'm in love with River."

His discomfort at the sound of River's name is apparent, and his face contorts as he seems to ignore what I just said. He puts his palms out like he's surrendering. "Look, I'm sorry. Old habits die hard," he says as he takes one of the coffees from the trays.

I take a sip of my coffee and exhale the breath I didn't even realize I was holding as relief washes through me. I've been afraid to really let him touch me for fear of what his touch would do to me, but now I'm more certain than ever—I just don't have any romantic feelings left for him.

"I'm going to check on Trent. Could you put a shirt on?"

He nods his head as I walk past him and leave the kitchen. Needing a minute to myself, I stop in the hall bathroom. I close the door and look at myself in the mirror. I really look awful—my eyes are puffy with dark circles beneath them, my hair is a mess, and my face looks tearstained. I splash cold water on my cheeks and look back in the mirror—glad I finally told him.

When I come out, he's waiting for me. Leaning against the wall with one hand shoved in his pocket and the other now back in the sling, he says, "Okay, I'm outta here. I shouldn't be too long, but if you need anything you can call Caleb." Then he turns and leaves.

I check on Trent often, but he's sleeping soundly.

Sitting on the couch, I look over to Ben's desk and decide to call Aerie. I miss her and wonder how long she'll be gone.

"Hello?"

"Hey, Aerie."

"Dahlia? Why are you in Laguna again?"

"Long story. How are you?"

"Feeling like my head is going to spin off. I think I'm just about ready to start looking for a new job."

"What do you mean? You love your job."

"Hmmm . . . not so much anymore. There is always so much to do and management never listens. I really wish you were here with me. While I'm conducting this interview, I also have to write a story about my uncle's band's rise and fall before his death."

"Yeah, well, helping you probably would have been a better option."

"A better option than what, Dahlia girl?"

I tell her about the party and what happened—about finding out that Bell was the girl Ben e-mailed years ago and that River knew about it; then I tell her about the fight River and I had. I also tell her about Ellie. And finally I tell her about Trent and where I am now.

Aerie sounds shocked. First she tells me how sorry she is about Trent. Then she says she can't believe what I told her about Bell. We talk about how I feel, knowing River's sister is the girl he almost cheated on me with. Finally she tells me that River and I need to do a better job of communicating and once again I agree with her.

When I hang up, I walk over to the kitchen window looking out onto the flower garden. I fill a glass of water and stand there, just drinking it. I'm so lost in thought that I don't even hear Ben come in the door. I turn around and he's just standing there, leaning against the doorframe, staring at me. I jump and water splashes everywhere.

"Hi, I didn't know you were back." I'm trying to keep my edginess at bay by keeping my voice even.

He cocks his head to the side. Grinning at the water stains down the front of my shirt, he stares at my chest. "Did you miss me?" he asks.

I roll my eyes and cross my arms over my chest, leaning back against the counter.

"You ready to spill it?"

I have had enough of his comments but for some reason I still ask, "Spill what?"

"Come on, Dahl, I know you. I know something's going on. I can tell. Are you sure you don't want to talk about it?"

Pointing to his arm in the sling I say, "You know very well what's going on."

He furrows his brow, then grins. "Trouble in paradise?"

"Fuck you, Ben Covington!"

Standing up straighter he moves closer to me and cups my chin. "There's the girl I know."

I roll my eyes again; I'm not going to let him get to me. Walking past him, I start to head for the hallway, but he grabs me and pulls me back to him.

I jerk away, glaring at him. "Ben, touch me again and I'll make sure you have no arms left to use."

With that, I go to say goodbye to Trent—he's asleep, or trying to sleep. He's curled up in a ball, shivering. I only stay a minute because I can't look anymore—the little boy I watched grow up is gone. God, how did I miss this?

When I walk back into the kitchen to get my keys, Ben is making some toast. "Want some?" he asks, and I remember those words from a different time and a different context.

I shake my head no.

"Well, let me know if you change your mind," he says. Then he points to the hallway. "Sorry about that before. I really will try to keep my hands to myself, but I can't make any promises."

I nod and try not to laugh at his cockiness. Accepting that Ben will always be Ben, I get to the reason I came here to begin with. "What did you decide about Trent?"

"We'll check him into a center for a twenty-eight-day program. He'll learn the twelve steps, hate life, hate me and his mother, but hopefully come out with the ability to fight his addiction."

His bleak assessment takes me aback. "He's lucky he has you."

"I don't think he'll see it that way."

"He'll come around. Speaking of coming around, did you call Serena yet?"

His demeanor, his attitude, they all shift gears and he seems somber, maybe even uncertain. "I'm not going to call her until tomorrow morning. She thinks he's at his dad's so she's not worried. By then I hope the fevers and chills have subsided."

"Okay, Ben." He's right, Trent looks terrible and I'd hate for Serena to see him like that. Knowing there's nothing else I can do, I reach for my keys and head out the doorway. "All right, I'll check in with you later."

"See ya, Dahl, and thanks," he calls after me.

I turn to face him before I say, "Ben, I am really glad you're alive."

"Thanks, Dahl. That means a lot. And I really am glad you're happy," he calls.

I smile at him and our eyes meet, but he quickly averts his gaze. Then I leave the house, probably for the last time.

As I pull out of the driveway, I can't help but be sad for Trent, but for some reason I'm sad for Ben, too. There's so much sadness surrounding me right now; focusing on any one facet of it is difficult. Something Grace told me comes to mind as I drive down the street. "There is something beautiful about each and every scar we bear no matter where it comes from . . . I will always be here for you," and it hits me that she has been there for me, and I should be there for her. I've never stopped to think about how Ben actually being alive has impacted her—she had scars, too.

Regardless of the reasons I acted the way I did, I should never have walked away from her. I realize this as I drive by the beach and look at the families so effortlessly playing, swimming, and smiling, happy to be together. I have to talk to her and apologize for my behavior.

When I reach her house, I open the front door and call out her name.

She's sitting at a small desk in the corner of the living room, going through some papers with only the desk reading light on.

She looks up from under her reading glasses. "Dahlia, honey, is everything okay?"

In a haze of emotion, I run to her and hug her as tight as I can, blurting out, "I'm so sorry."

Glancing down, I notice documents with Ben's name on them—his death certificate, a life insurance policy, and the coroner's report.

Breaking our embrace, she clears her throat and in a small, almost raspy voice says, "Dahlia, you're not the one who needs to apologize. I'm the one who should be saying I'm sorry." She sets her glasses on the desk. "Come on, let's sit down over here and talk."

Walking over to the couch I can't help but think how much this room feels like home to me. How all I want to do is sit here and just be near this woman who has been like a mother to me for my whole adult life. My intention was to come here and apologize to her, but now all I want is the comfort she has always brought me.

I try to disagree, but as she tucks a piece of my hair behind my ear, she keeps talking. "Sweetheart, listen to me. All I wanted was for you to try to understand why he did what he did, see if you could forgive him."

I take a deep breath and start from the beginning. "Grace, I understand that now. And I have talked to him . . ."

I tell her everything that happened since his return—how I feel like walls keep going up between all of us and we are all being torn apart. We talk for over an hour. She interjects and gives me advice every now and then, but she mostly listens. She tells me that when people love each other, telling them things they know will hurt them isn't always easy. I can tell she's also talking about herself.

When I'm all talked out, she explains her feelings to me. "All I want is for Ben and you to be happy, but I know that doesn't mean together. I know you're happy with River. It's just that I'm concerned for Ben. He's lost and the life he knew is gone. I just thought the reason he hasn't made any decisions on what to do with his life is because he still thinks you may go back to him. That's the only reason I wanted you to forgive him. So he could see there was only friendship left." She pauses to catch my eye. "And, Dahlia, he called me a bit ago and he now understands."

She doesn't elaborate, but I know what she means. She smiles a small smile and releases my hand. My heart breaks a little for the love Ben and I once shared, but that love is gone. I can't bring it back, nor do I want to. I can only hope that someday Ben will find what I have found with River.

Standing up, Grace says, "You need to go home and talk to River now." As she ushers me toward the door she opens it and clutches my hand. "Be honest with him about everything—your feelings, how you feel toward him, your wariness concerning his behavior, all of it. Don't hold back. If you can open up to him, you will work it out because the love River and you share isn't a love that happens for everyone. I know this, Dahlia, because every time I see the way the two of you look at each other, I'm reminded of the way my husband and I used to look at each other. That's how I know what you two have is unbreakable. What I had with my husband was so strong that I will never forget it, even after all these years."

Hugging her goodbye, I can't help but think how right she is. I know how much she loved her husband and although I never met him, I saw her love for him every day. As we stand embracing at her door, I feel compelled to tell her something I never have before. "Grace, you know how much I love you. You're not just like a mother to me, you have been my mother."

Her chin trembles and with the smallest of nods, she hugs me even tighter. "Dahlia, I love you so much. And thank you for that."

When we pull away, I look more closely at her. She looks so worn out. I notice dark, bluish circles under her normally sparkling eyes. "Grace, please don't worry so much. Ben will work everything out. I know he will. He's tough and resilient. He will be fine."

"I hope so, Dahlia, I hope so. Now go home and talk to River," she says as she motions me down the steps and into the rain. Then she calls out, "Dahlia, honey, where's your umbrella?"

I have to laugh because she knows I can never find any of my umbrellas.

As I get in my car, I watch her standing in the doorway through my rearview mirror. I open my window and call out one last time, "Thank you, Grace. Love you."

She blows me a kiss and waves goodbye, then wraps her arms around herself and goes into the house. I'm so happy we talked and everything is back to how it's always been.

Serena pulls into the driveway as I'm pulling out and she honks her horn repeatedly at me.

Putting my car in park, I open the window.

She hurries over, the rain soaking her clothes. She looks furious. "Who the hell do you think you are, keeping something like that from me?" she says, trembling with anger.

I know she's talking about Trent, but don't know what to say. "Serena, I'm sorry . . ."

She leans down into the window, her fists clenched and her eyes flashing with anger. "How could you of all people not tell me? I thought you believed in telling the truth!" With that, she storms off toward the house.

I get out of the car and run after her. "Serena, I do, let me explain."

"No, Dahlia, you don't get to explain. Just remember I'm his mother," she says, slamming the front door in my face.

I stand there trying to figure out if I should go into the house or not. She's so mad, but I can't blame her. She had a right to know. I decide it's best to not try to talk to her right now. I'm sure she wants to talk to Grace about Trent and I'm not sure anything I say will make a difference in her state of mind.

Driving off, I once again find myself heading back to LA. So much has happened in the last twenty-four hours since I made this same trip home, yet it seems so little has changed. Well . . . Grace and I made up. It feels right that we were able to put our issues behind us. Ben and I seem to have come to an understanding—we may even eventually be able to be friends. He's back, but our lives will remain separate and I think he has accepted that. Then there's the bad . . . Serena is not talking to me, and neither is Xander. Then there's the unchanged . . . River and I haven't talked all day, he never came home last night, and I'm not sure what's going to happen when I get home.

As I think through all of this, I can't help but notice the damp chill in the air and the steel gray color of the sky.

CHAPTER 21
All In

As I pull into the driveway, I glare at Ellie's car parked in the same place it was yesterday. I take a deep breath and blow it out. I just can't deal with her right now, so I decide it's best not to go in. I want to talk to River and try to get past all this, but I know seeing her again will just enrage me. I just can't stop thinking about the look of betrayal on Serena's face—the same look I know I had a few times in the past week.

I decide I should probably go see Bell and make sure she knows I'm not upset with her. I haven't had a chance to call her, and, hopefully, by the time I come back, Ellie will be gone.

River's mom lives less than five miles from our house. When I arrive at the large two-story house, I ring the doorbell. As I wait, I keep my eyes fixed on the large metal doorknocker. I know Charlotte's at work, but I can't stop from wondering if she knows about Bell and

Ben. I'm sure she does. Bell tells her everything. I'm suddenly nervous and my heart starts pounding. When Brigitte answers the door, I jump, suddenly feeling more nervous as she greets me.

"Hi, Dahlia, come in. What a nice surprise." The longtime housekeeper is more like a part of their family. The short elegant Frenchwoman has her curly brown hair pinned up and is wearing a white shirt and black pants, looking the same way she does every time I see her.

"Hi, Brigitte. How are you?"

"Fantastique!" she says with a heavy French accent. Her enthusiasm makes me smile.

"Dahlia!" I hear and I look up the staircase to the balcony. There stands Bell—she could be River's twin, with her light copper-brown hair pulled back in a ponytail, wearing a USC sweatshirt that must be Xander's, a pair of jeans, and chewing her bottom lip.

She rushes down the stairs. "I've been calling you. I thought you were mad at me."

"Excuse me, ladies, I'll let you two talk," Brigitte says as she makes her way toward the kitchen. Then she turns around and looks at Bell. Shooting her a wink she says, "See, missy, I told you she wouldn't be mad at you."

Bell smiles and says, "You're always right, Brigitte."

"If you need anything, let me know, girls," Brigitte says and leaves the room.

"Bell, I'm not mad at you. It's just . . ." I shake my head. "I didn't even know your name was S'belle."

"It's not. I spent my freshman year in France with my aunt and everyone there called me S'belle. When I came back to the States I thought it would be fun to keep my French name, so I told everyone at USC to call me that."

"Okay, that makes sense, I guess . . ."

She cuts me off as she pulls me through the kitchen and into the large family room. Before we have a chance to sit down, Bell asks, "Why haven't you called me back, then?"

I can't help but notice her vibrant green eyes are teary.

"I'm sorry, Bell, I didn't know you called. I haven't been able to find my phone."

She rolls her eyes, and then shakes her head as she settles into the mirror image of the chair I am sitting in. "What a surprise."

"You could have called the house phone."

"Shit, I always forget about landlines. It's just I called you, I called River, I even called Xander, and none of you answered."

"I'm sorry, Bell," I say and shrug my shoulders, not wanting to be the one to explain the tour fiasco to her.

"Dahlia, I'm so sorry. I didn't know my Ben was your Ben. I was immature back then and I didn't respect other people's relationships. When I met Ben at the initiation party, I just had to have him. Nothing else mattered. I didn't know he had a girlfriend at first and even though he told me, that didn't stop me. I tried to get his attention at every party and finally one night when he was really drunk I got it."

I didn't miss the way she said his name. Like she knew him. I should have been more prepared for this moment, but what did she mean? Her Ben? Had to have him? Just went for it?

I avert my eyes from her and momentarily stare at the collage of family photos on the wall. Xander, River, and Bell in front of the Eiffel Tower with Charlotte and her sister on each end, the three kids sitting down for a picnic, and a young River onstage with his guitar. A million questions run through my head as she continues to talk.

"Dahlia! Hey, are you okay? You said you weren't mad."

I blink my eyes and try to refocus. "Wait a minute. I'm confused. You need to start from the beginning."

"Sorry, I assumed River told you everything."

I shake my head without speaking.

"I just thought . . . I don't know. Maybe not. Knowing River, I guess not."

"He didn't say much. Go on."

She blinks, watching me closely. "God, Dahlia, I'm sorry."

"Bell, just tell me," I manage. It feels like my throat is closing up and my voice comes out as a squeak.

She squirms a little in her chair and looks away. "I only knew Ben for the two-month period before I left school. After the accident, you know, I never went back. And even though my time with him was short-lived, it had a long-term impact."

"You mean long-term because of the accident?" It's all I can manage to ask. I say nothing more, not trusting my voice or its ability to fully convey my real question.

I can tell she's nervous as she rubs her feet together, then pulls them up to the chair. "No, Dahlia, that's not why I really left. I needed time to recover, but I didn't go back because of the baby."

My hand flies to my mouth. Baby? What baby? My heart's pounding, but I bring my eyes back to hers and nod, urging her to tell me the rest.

"Oh, God, Dahlia, that's not where I should have started."

She opens her mouth as if she wants to say more, but closes it abruptly. I take small shallow breaths, watching her, waiting for her to tell me the rest. When she doesn't I say very calmly, "Bell, go on, it's okay. Just start wherever you need to."

She turns to completely face me and places both of her feet firmly on the ground. Her face crumples. "I met Ben one night at the beginning of school at a frat party. We talked, but he ignored my advances and then disappeared. But that didn't sway me. I was determined—I had this strange feeling that even though he said no, he meant yes. I was a little self-absorbed back then. One night at an after-rush party for Kappa Sigma, I was assigned as Ben's little sister. Well, I begged the committee to let me be his little sister. That night, I took care of keeping the alcohol flowing for him and the new prospective pledges he was overseeing. We were all pretty drunk by the time he sent the pledges on a scavenger hunt to find a pair of pink lace panties." She pauses as if stopping again to assess my reaction.

I have none. I am weighing the cold bare facts of what she's saying and know what's coming. She adjusts her ponytail and I try to calm my stomach. It feels like it's leapt up into my throat. I'm feeling anxious and just want her to get it out.

"Please remember I was young and immature, and I'm not proud of how I acted," she says and once again all I can do is nod. "Once the pledges went off on their hunt, I came on to him again. And just like all the other times, he refused. I promise he did. But then I followed him into the bathroom and made sure he couldn't resist anymore. I locked the door, pulled my shirt off, and unzipped my skirt, letting it fall to the ground before asking him if black lace would do."

I put my hand up in a stopping motion. I don't need to know any more. I got it.

"Dahlia, it was all me—honestly, it was."

All me? What does that mean? He was in a relationship. He should have been able to walk away. God, he did actually cheat on me. Was he always a cheater?

My voice flat, emotionless, I ask, "Was it more than just the one time?"

I wait for her to meet my gaze. Not that it should matter, but for some reason it does. Did Ben have an ongoing affair and I never knew?

She nervously tugs on her bottom lip and shakes her head no. She puts her hands in the pockets of her sweatshirt. It doesn't really matter anyway. He still cheated. I start to feel dizzy.

With guilt evident in her voice she says, "Dahlia, I'm so sorry."

"Bell, what did you mean by 'baby'?" I manage to get out.

Her eyes fill with tears. "I got pregnant."

I swallow. "You have a child together?"

"No, Dahlia, we don't. I gave the baby up for adoption after it was born."

Freezing, I gasp. I can feel my eyes widen in disbelief at the magnitude of her words. Time stands still. Bell doesn't say another word, as if letting the shock wear off.

Finally, I manage to mutter, "Did Ben know?" I brace myself for the answer.

She pauses and with a sad expression says, "No, he never knew. I never told him. We were supposed to meet the night I got in the accident; I was going to tell him then. But after the accident, it took months for me to recover. Once I did, I tried to contact him, but he never returned my calls."

"Does your family know?"

She's crying now as she tells me, "Yes, they all knew, but I made them promise to never say anything to anyone. I told them I was pregnant after the accident. Xander and River demanded to know who the father was. I knew it was Ben because I hadn't slept with anyone since I had slept with him. I was still hoping he wanted more. They sought him out, wanted to know who he was, I think they even stalked him at some of the frat parties. But Mom demanded they leave him alone. In the end, when I decided to give the baby away, they were nothing but supportive. Honestly, without my family to help me through it, I don't know what I would have done."

And with those words it all falls into place—Xander's anger at me the night we met and River's reluctance to tell me anything.

I frantically search for something to say, but I have no words.

"Bell, I have to leave." Then I somehow manage to get on my feet and dash toward the door. I know I'm going to throw up and hope I make it outside first.

Brigitte is in the kitchen as I hurry through and says, "Dahlia, I just made coffee for you and the missy."

I don't answer her; I can't. Shock and anger pulse through me. Ben cheated on me. I always trusted him and believed him. He's nothing but a fucking liar!

CHAPTER 22
Six Degrees of Separation

Almost two hours later, I find myself heading north on the 101 and have no idea where I'm going or how I got here. All I know is that when the shock and anger consumed me, I had to get away. But now the numbness subsides, and pain takes over.

Completely exhausted, I get off at the Santa Barbara exit and pull into a gas station to ask directions to the nearest hotel. The clerk tells me if I'm looking for a nice place, the Four Seasons is due west. I'm not looking for anything in particular, but I follow his directions. Within fifteen minutes I'm pulling into the hotel. It looks more like a Mediterranean getaway than a place to be alone and not think about anything. But at this point I'm so tired, I don't really care where I stay.

Walking into the lobby, I immediately notice its grandeur. I go to check in without any luggage and the front desk assistant tells me they only have Premier rooms available. I hand her my credit card and tell her that's fine. When she asks me how many nights, all I can tell her is that I don't know. She smiles at me and says they can't guarantee availability any night other than tonight if I don't commit, so I tell her a week. She smiles and hands me a room key, asking if the valet can get my luggage. I just tell her I'm good but she still asks the doorman to show me to the elevator. He does so and pushes my floor number before sending me up to my room.

Opening the door, I head straight for the phone. The anger has been building inside me and I have to tell that son of a bitch what a fucking asshole he is. When I dial the number I haven't dialed in so long, my fingers are trembling.

"Hello?" he answers.

"You fucking son of a bitch. How could you lie to me for all those years?"

"Dahl, calm down. What are you talking about?"

"Don't tell me to calm down, you asshole. You cheated on me and said you didn't. How could you?"

"Dahl, it was a mistake. It didn't mean anything."

"Are you fucking kidding me?! A mistake is forgetting to pay the mortgage. You screwed someone else."

"I'm sorry, Dahl. Let me explain."

"No, Ben, not this time I won't. No more. I wish you never came back—then I wouldn't have had to know what we really were—nothing. You've only caused me more pain. Your death put me through hell, and just when I'm about to start my life over—you come back to hurt me some more? I wish you would have kept playing dead!"

"Please, Dahl, just come over. We can talk."

"Fuck you, Ben. I don't ever want to talk to you again," I scream and hang up.

After I slam the phone down, I try to calm down. I call room service and order a pot of coffee. I hope my queasy stomach can handle it. I move to the glass doors and close the wall of curtains. I briefly take notice of the beaches and mountains out the window before pulling the drapes closed and shiver as a sudden chill goes through me. I stop and scrutinize my own reflection in the glass. How was I so naive? I saw the e-mail! How clichéd were his attempts to get me back? And I fell for him then, never questioning his fidelity. I try to look into my own eyes, but see nothing but that young girl.

There's a knock on the door and I hear, "Room service." I wonder how long I've been standing here evaluating the merits of my stupidity. I close the curtains, open the door, and take the tray over to the fireplace. I sit in the large overstuffed chair and inhale the fresh coffee bean aroma wafting from my cup. Looking at the tray, I notice the sugar bowl. I take a deep breath and wonder if I should have ordered tea instead because all my thoughts suddenly drift to River. Would he do the same thing to me? Is he doing the same thing to me?

I can feel my heart beating faster than it should. I drop my spoon on the floor and when I bend down to pick it up, I start to cry when I see my boots—the boots River loves to see me in. I unzip them and toss them to the ground. Then I remember them hitting the floor at Smitten's and my stomach falls. What we have is different than what Ben and I had. I know it is. And I also know he would never do to me what Ben did.

I think about him asking me the first time we had coffee together if I used sugar, and every day since then making sure I always got my morning coffee—until this morning, and yesterday morning. I miss him and suddenly wonder if I should have just gone home.

As my thoughts continue to bounce all over the place, I try to focus on everything Bell told me. After a while it all comes together in an easy-to-understand picture. She was in an accident the night I met River. I left the bar early that night, fearful of what would happen with River if I stayed. Bell was going to tell Ben about the baby that same night. Bell and Ben were supposed to meet that night. And Xander fits into the picture somehow as well. As one of Ben's frat brothers, he knew Ben had a girlfriend. But I never talked about Ben to River's family or friends.

It all makes sense now—I went back early, so Ben couldn't leave the party. Bell didn't know this and got in that car so eager to tell him she was pregnant. River came to the frat house later that night to look for Bell because obviously she had been hanging out there. And since I hardly ever went to the parties, Ben knew I'd never find out.

As I sip the last of my coffee, the chills seem to subside. I mentally start building what-if scenarios. I start thinking about what path all of our lives would have taken if I had stayed that night and talked to River. Would he have brought Bell home if he didn't have to look for me? Would Bell have met up with Ben and would they be raising a child together? Would I have broken up with Ben and chosen River? Would Ben have not taken the *Los Angeles Times* job and gone to grad school instead? He took that job so he could buy us a house. If he never worked for the *Los Angeles Times*, would he have taken on that story? Without that story he never would have had to die. Would we all have had our happily ever afters?

My head is spinning, so I lie down on the bed and pull the comforter up, thinking I will just lie down for an hour and then . . . exhaustion takes hold and my mind finally finds peace as I fade away into sleep.

CHAPTER 23
The Change

Ben's Journal

Today wasn't just another shitty day in a long list of shitty days; it was probably the shittiest day yet. I spent hours on the phone yesterday trying to secure a place for Trent in a facility. One finally called back last night, but I needed to check it out before sending him there. I could have called Caleb to come over and stay with Trent, but I really needed to see her again so I called Dahl. That was my first mistake of the whole fucking day.

When she got to the house in record time, of course I thought she really wanted to see me. Maybe she'd thought about yesterday and decided she missed me like I missed her. I was so sure spending time together would evoke those feelings. Fuck, was I wrong. She not only rejected me but when I tried to pull her to me like I used to, she acted like I repulsed her.

For some reason I couldn't let her see that she got to me. Why? I wanted to explain my feelings, but, fuck, I've never been able to do that and even when it probably mattered the most I still couldn't. So instead I hightailed it out the door. When I got back she seemed even sadder than when she got here. I tried to talk to her, to comfort her, but she squashed my attempts once again. I'm seriously starting to wonder what kind of hold this guy has over her because when she left today, I got the feeling she wasn't coming back.

The day didn't get any fucking better when my sister showed up a few minutes later. She talked to her dirtbag ex-husband and he told her Trent was here. I had to explain everything to her but I wasn't in the right headspace to deal with her shit. She did agree to send Trent to rehab tomorrow. She stormed out pissed and said she'd be back to stay the night. She wanted to tell Mom in person.

Then as if the day wasn't already bad enough, the phone call came. The one I knew would come eventually after seeing S'belle at Dahlia's house. I hoped Dahl wouldn't find out. I tried to tell her yesterday to soften the blow, but just couldn't do it. Of course the college chick had to be the dick's sister. They look so much alike, no wonder I felt like I knew him. Fuck me.

That call ended any chance I had to get my Dahl back and now I'm left here, wondering why the fuck I ever came back.

CHAPTER 24
Beneath Your Beautiful

I wake up and look at the clock; it's 5:45 a.m. Shit, I've been asleep for more than twelve hours. For the first time in my life, I don't like being in the dark. I quickly get up and open the curtains, letting the faint light of dawn into my room. I turn the fireplace back on and get under the thick mass of blankets, once again feeling chilled to the bone. I grab the hotel phone and decide I should at least tell Aerie where I am. But when she doesn't answer, I leave her a message. I don't call River—we need to talk in person.

Blasting the radio of the hotel alarm clock, I lie there and just listen to whatever songs come on. Music tells so many stories. It's a world within itself. It calms me. Speaks to me. Gives me the guidance I sometimes need. So as I listen to "Clarity," I close my eyes and think about everything again. I think about it as a story that accompanies the words to the song. And when I do this, really listen and visualize myself as part of the song, everything seems clearer than it did yesterday. Taking a series of deep breaths, I feel a little better.

I doze off, and when I wake up again it's 7:15 a.m. I actually fell asleep with the light coming in the room. I've never done that before. "Broken" is playing when I wake up again and I say out loud, "I'm not broken." Because I'm not. I know I'm not. What Ben did is unforgivable but he hasn't been my future for a long time. I can't let his infidelity change what's right in front of me.

As the song ends and a new one begins I don't even hear the words, I just lie there, staring at the ceiling, and think about River and me—our fights, our love, our life. I have to believe everything will okay. His reluctance to tell me anything about Bell and her accident was done out of love, not deceit, and I not only accept this, I understand it. I can trust him—I do trust him. He didn't want to tell me that Ben had betrayed me. He didn't want to hurt me in that way. It would have been so easy for him to turn me against Ben from the day he figured out who Ben was, but his love for me stopped him. After everything, I still believe we will be okay. My only question: Has he forgiven me? I quickly jump out of bed—I need to get back to LA.

I'm sitting down to put my boots on when I hear the song "Sexy Back" playing outside my room. I stop what I'm doing and wonder if I'm imagining it. But when I hear a knock on the door, I know what it means. I drop my boots to the floor and run over to open the door without even looking through the peephole to see who it is, because I know. I have to grip the knob for support to keep my knees from buckling beneath me. I draw in a slow silent breath of relief because there he stands, leaning against the doorframe with his head down.

He looks up and his eyes are sparkling as he hands me my phone. "I did promise to always call," he says and his words make my stomach flutter. I reach for the phone. My breathing stops as I take him in. He's breathtaking. He's long, lean, and so alarmingly good-looking that I can't look away. It's not because of how attractive he is, though—it's because of his eyes. They tell me everything I need to know. This is the man I love. The man who loves me. The man I will be with forever. I feel like I'm being transported through time, back to the night I first met him. He's wearing his Foreigner *Double Vision* T-shirt and black beanie, his light brown hair sticking out underneath it. His guitar is strapped over his shoulder and he sets it down inside the room as he places his phone to his ear. Justin Timberlake's song is still playing on my phone. "And you promised to always answer."

I'm standing so close to him, but not near enough. I'm trembling as a sense of utter euphoria pulses through me. He came for me, he really came for me. Gripping the phone, I step closer to him and smile. "No, I promised to never hang up."

He, too, steps closer and we are now standing toe-to-toe. "You have to answer in order to not hang up so technically you promised to always answer."

I smile at him as he takes the phone from my hand and hits the END button. He does the same to his and tosses both phones inside the room. He removes his beanie, tossing that as well, and then combs his hands through his hair. Our eyes connect and it feels like minutes pass, but it's only seconds. That electric pull is still there, stronger than ever.

"I hope you don't think I'm a stalker. Aerie told me where you were."

I bite my lip nervously and gaze into his gleaming green eyes. "No, you're definitely not a stalker."

He smiles, not a full smile but that half-grin I love so much because it emphasizes his dimples. His lush lips are begging for me to kiss him and I don't want to waste another minute as I throw my arms around his neck and crash my mouth to his. He puts one hand behind my neck and the other on the small of my back. We both open our mouths wide as our lips connect, and I feel the connection between our souls. This kiss leaves me breathless.

He slowly pulls back and grabs my cheeks with the palms of his hands softly rubbing my skin. "I love you more."

"And I will love you more forever," I say back because it's the absolute truth.

He leans in and this time he softly puts his lips to mine, never taking his hands off my face. I can feel tears of joy streaming down my face.

After we finally come up for air, he lifts me in his arms and then carries me to the bed. He sits down with me in his lap and I curl my legs around him. Kissing my head repeatedly, he tries to ease my sobs, but they won't stop. I start to settle as he lightly rocks me. When his hands softly rub my back, I touch my head to his. I can feel his heartbeat as his chest rises and falls. It is the most beautiful feeling in the world.

"I'm sorry," I whisper.

He blows out a long breath, "No, Dahlia. I'm the one that's sorry. We should talk. We need to talk."

I know that's what we need but seeing him now, being in his arms when I wasn't sure I ever would be again, I don't want to talk. I just want to be with him. I feel the last of the walls come down between us as we sit here wrapped in each other's arms and all that is left is pure emotion, true love. I rest my head against his chest again and this time inhale his scent, having missed it, and relish being so close to him.

I look up at him and with a shaky breath I tell him, "We will. Just not yet. Please. I don't want to talk about what a mess we made out of everything right now."

"Okay, baby, okay. But a beautiful thing is never perfect," he whispers as he kisses the top of my head and clings to me as tightly as I cling to him.

Slipping my hands under his T-shirt, I trace the perfectly sculpted lines that outline each lean muscle. I feel his heart pounding above his ribs. When my tears keep falling, he continues to rock me. Then he puts his mouth to my ear and with a low, husky voice starts singing a song I've never heard before. It makes my skin tingle. I peek up at him and through muffled sobs ask, "What are you singing?"

"A song I wrote for you. It's called 'Never in Pieces.'"

He continues to sing and I sit here listening to his beautiful words. His voice wraps around me, bringing the comfort I know only from him—the amazing man singing to me. The words of the song push into me, making my heart expand with every word. He sings about never knowing what love was until he found me. His velvety voice sings in my ear with such intensity that I feel like I'm touching his soul with every lyric. I look at him and his eyes close as he sings about our relationship never being in pieces because nothing can break us. I absorb every single verse as my heart pounds and desire sweeps through me. I've never felt such an intimate connection to him. When he finishes I know exactly how he feels and I feel the same way. Nipping at his jaw, I press myself into him, then I tip his chin back and look into his tranquil green eyes. "River, make love to me."

He looks at me with his intense bedroom eyes and doesn't hesitate in saying, "There's nothing I want to do more right now than to touch you and taste you."

I feel him instantly harden beneath me as he reaches and pulls my T-shirt off. I pull his off in turn. His mouth is on mine, his tongue finding its way into mine, and I'm hoping to leave a little bit of myself inside of him.

As I sit on his lap enjoying every kiss, every lick, every touch, every breath we share, I know I will never take moments like these for granted. After a few minutes he lifts me off the bed, turns us around, and sets me on my feet. Kneeling in front of me, he undoes my button, pulls my jeans down, and I step out of them. Our eyes stay connected every second. When he very slowly slides my panties off, I kick them aside. He guides me to sit on the edge of the bed and places each of my legs over his shoulders and starts kissing the inside of my thighs. My body tightens with anticipation.

His eyes are still on mine. He runs his fingertips up and down the backs of my thighs and places his hands behind me, pulling me into him. His tongue is on me, but he's taking it slow this time. His face is in between my legs, right at my center. He starts by placing small kisses up and down my slick flesh. Then his fingers open me and his tongue strokes and licks perfectly. When he peeks up at me as I watch him he says, "Dahlia, I need to taste every inch of you." I lift myself against his mouth, urging him to move faster, and he does. Then his hands are on my hips, keeping me firmly in place as he plunges his tongue inside me over and over. I start convulsing; the feeling is so unbelievably euphoric. My body trembles. "Oh God, River," I call out, but he doesn't stop. He keeps sucking me even through my orgasm, pushing me further. Gripping my hips tightly he licks, kisses, and laps every inch of me. I don't even feel like my body is my own when another wave blasts through me. "Yes, oh God, yes," I scream and when I know I have nothing left, I gently push his shoulders back. He looks up at me and I drop to the ground to sit in front of him.

I kiss him and he smiles through our kiss. "I wasn't finished. I wanted to hear you scream my name again."

"Oh you will, I promise." I unbutton his pants and run my hand inside his boxers, just needing to feel him. He stands up and pulls me with him. I love the way it feels to be in his arms. Setting me on the bed, he quickly removes his boots, pants, and boxers and stands there looking so incredible—his taut muscles on full display. He takes my hand. "Dahlia, can I make love to you now?" he asks and I melt. Every move, every motion is done with an almost unbearable slowness.

I nod my head and pull him to me on the bed. But I want to feel every inch of him so I roll us over and hover over him. He groans and pulls me down to him. He traces his tongue around the shell of my ear and then whispers all the things he wants to do to me. Dragging my tongue down his neck, his chest, I take him in my hands, gently stroking him and he groans even louder. Placing a knee on either side of his legs, I glide my lips down his stomach. My hands continue to move up and down his length and when my lips meet his tip, he shudders. I lose myself in the moment. This is the intimacy that I've missed. But when my mouth covers him, he pulls me back up to him.

I lie against him, pressing my naked body into his, and look at him. "Why'd you stop me?"

He lets out a sigh and groans, "I want to be inside you when I come."

I move my mouth to his ear so I can whisper, "You can be."

"No, Dahlia, I won't be if you do that."

He molds my breasts with his palms and whispers things in my ear in that hot, raspy tone that makes me ache for him. Moving my hips he pulls me on top of him and he's right where I need him to be. Elation sweeps through me as he easily slips in. His hands move to my backside, pressing me into him. When I fold my knees beneath myself and sit up, he lets out a long groan. But when I try to control the pace by interlocking my fingers with his on either side of his head, he grins and shakes his head.

He leaves our hands there for a few moments and I rock into him over and over, rolling my hips. Before long, his hands are on my hips. But I got this. Leaning back, I rest my palms on his knees and move slowly, rising up just far enough so we both feel the thrill of him sliding back inside. With every passing moment, I sink faster and deeper but stay closer. My pulse pounds with excitement. Before I know it, he's clutching my legs, focusing on my every move. Our eyes meet and we are hypnotized by each other's expressions of pure pleasure. When I reach down between us and alternate stroking and squeezing whatever flesh I can get my hands on, he groans and curses so loud I lose myself.

Continuing with this rapid pace, I feel nothing but complete bliss.

The pressure builds swiftly and I am quickly on the brink of climaxing again. It's heavenly. He pulls me to him and seals his lips to mine, thrusting his hips up. Breathing heavily, I know he's close. He rolls us over, never breaking our connection. Pulling my hands over my head, he takes control and it's perfect.

I watch as his body flexes rhythmically with mine. He moves faster, kissing me furiously. I'm pushed over the edge the second his tongue hits the roof of my mouth. "Oh God, yes, River, yes," I scream once again and he stills, shouting my name as my waves of ecstasy bring on his own climax.

When we are both spent, we fall into each other's arms and cuddle close together. "I love you, River," I say and I'm going to tell him this over and over again.

"I love you, Dahlia, I love every single thing about you. You're perfect, really." I can't contain my smile. I haven't heard him say that in so long and hearing the familiar words sends shivers up my spine.

"I missed you," I whisper.

He smiles at me. "Tu m'as manqué."

I look at him questioningly. I know he's speaking French, but have no idea what he just said.

Tracing his finger around my lips he says, "Brigitte told me once that in France they don't say I missed you, they say you were missing from me, and you were."

I have to compose myself before placing a soft kiss on his lips and nuzzling his nose. That is the perfect way to say it. It's how I have felt, too—like he was missing from me.

As I settle back in his arms, I think about how when we were together, there was no need for instant gratification because there were no doubts between us. We both knew we had the rest of our lives together. I kiss him again and close my eyes, laying my head on his chest. He strokes his fingers up and down my bare back and I feel myself fade. His soft tender voice awakens me. "Hey, when was the last time you ate?"

I playfully start biting his chest. "Well, I was planning on having you, but you stopped me."

He laughs and it's the first time I've heard that sound in a while. "No really, I want you to eat something."

I look up at him with a wicked smile on my face.

"Food, Dahlia. Food." Then he smirks his devilish grin and says with a wink, "Then you can have me for dessert."

I sit up. "Do you think it's too early for a grilled cheese, a chocolate milkshake, and French fries?"

Without answering he sits up and grabs the hotel room phone to call room service. "I'd like to order two chocolate milkshakes, two grilled cheeses, and two orders of fries, please."

He slips his jeans on without boxers and I wrap myself in the hotel robe. The food arrives and we eat, dipping our fries in each other's shakes. We alternate feeding each other and licking the shake off each other's mouths. We laugh and have fun like we haven't in what seems like forever.

Once we've finished eating we sit down and finally talk, and I mean we actually talk—we don't yell, accuse, avoid, or blame.

He settles against the bed. "Okay, let's do this."

I nod in agreement as I sit at the foot of the bed.

Sighing, he drops his eyes. "Bell came over to see me as soon as you left Mom's house. I know she told you everything."

I wrap my arms around my knees in an effort to brace myself.

His eyes rise up to meet mine and he crawls down to me and lifts my chin. "First, you need to know how very sorry I am . . . how many times I tried to tell you . . . I just could never get the words out. I couldn't hurt you like that."

I close my eyes, his apology so sincere that pain pierces through my heart from the weight of the secret he kept, not just for me, but for him as well. The burden had to be almost unbearable. Taking a deep breath, I open my eyes and look at his gorgeous face for the longest time. Then I bring my lips to his and kiss him. It's not a burning-with-desire kiss—it's a kiss that lets him know he doesn't have to apologize anymore. I understand. When we break away we smile at each other and he lets out a long sigh before moving back to where he was sitting.

"Bell's pregnancy and decision to not keep the baby were really hard on all of us. Mom wanted her to keep it. Xander and I stayed out of it but we also knew she wasn't ready to be a mother. But her decision to give up the baby was her own. I never voiced my opinion either way. I just told her I would be there for her. The day she had the baby she didn't want to see it or to know if it was a boy or girl. Mom was in there with her and she saw the baby and held it just once. To this day, we never talk about it."

Wiping my fingers under my eyes I think about what he just said. Regardless of the fact that Ben fathered that child, the situation was heartrending and I could only imagine how torn Bell was. That could not have been an easy decision to make.

"River, I called Ben and confronted him about the affair, but I didn't tell him about the baby. I'll never tell him about the baby. It's not my place."

He nods somberly, agreeing with me. He rakes his fingers through his hair and I can tell he has more to say.

"What is it?"

"There's more. Bell is not the only reason I didn't tell you. When he was dead I didn't want to hurt you that way. It didn't make sense, so I didn't say anything. When he came back, when he was standing right there in front of us, I wasn't sure if you'd go back to him. So I didn't tell you, but this time it was because of me—I needed you to pick me because you wanted to be with me. Not because of how you'd feel about him when you found out."

I'm not mad or angry with him for his admission; I had already let that go. Getting off the bed, I go sit next to him. I need to tell him how I feel. How I've always felt about him. I need to tell him what I should have all along. I never did because it felt wrong when Ben was dead—like if I said the words out loud Ben would hear me.

Cupping his cheeks I speak from my heart and divulge something I've never once said out loud. "River, it's always been you. From the minute I saw you at the bar, I think it's always been you. I never even set a wedding date with Ben and maybe that was why. Because you were the one for me, you are the one for me."

After a moment passes, he sighs and brings me to his chest and just holds me, whispering, "Thank you."

We stay that way until he dips his head to mine. "By the way, Bell probably isn't speaking to me. I got really pissed when she told me she had talked to you."

I allow one small smile and tell him, "I'm sure she'll get over it. She's used to your moods."

He chuckles. "Yeah, I guess she is, and, besides, she's so happy right now with her new job I don't think she could stay mad at anybody for long."

I smile big at that. Then I sit back on my knees. "I talked to Grace yesterday."

He looks at me with concern. "How did it go?"

I smile. "Really well. We're fine, more than fine. And after I talked to her I only wanted to come home and talk to you, but Ellie was there and I couldn't face her. I was so upset to see her there again. I just knew it would piss me off to go inside and I wanted so much to talk to you without any anger. So that's why I decided to go see Bell first and make sure she knew I wasn't mad at her."

He nods. "Ellie dropped by and I was in no mood for her crap, but she tried making one last-ditch effort to get me back on the tour, and when she knew it was a lost cause, she left and I waited for you to come home. I drove out to Laguna, couldn't find you. Came home, found your phone in the closet, then stayed up all night. I called Aerie, even Caleb. Then I wrote a song to pass the time just not to go crazy."

I start crying again. "I'm so sorry I didn't call or come home. I wanted to. I have no idea why I didn't."

"Shh . . . don't cry. We're okay. We're together now and nothing like that is ever going to happen again."

Wiping my tears, I kiss him for a long while, then break free and decide it's time to talk about our jealousy. Ellie is easily put to rest and surprisingly so is Ben. He still half flinches when I say Ben's name, but I don't think that will ever pass and I'm okay with that.

River tells me, "Once I read the note you left me, I knew I had nothing to worry about, no reason to be jealous."

He believes me and I believe him; we both trust each other because, after all, isn't that what love is—knowing someone can crush you, but believing they never will, trusting them not to?

We talk about everything else that has happened between us over the last few weeks—our urgent sex needs, his tantrums, my running away, my avoidance, and his need to protect me. These are talks from the heart and they open up many old wounds for both of us, but it is okay. We even discuss his fervent need to protect the women he loves. He has a hard time explaining it, but I get it. I think it stems back to his father's selfishness. In the end we both decide we will work toward communicating better.

We also talk about the tour. He doesn't want that life, and I respect him for knowing when too much is just too much. He tells me Xander, Nix, and even Garrett aren't talking to him right now. He makes a joke that he's glad his mother is out of town or he's sure she would have organized a sit-down. We both laugh at the thought, but we're also laughing because the seriousness of this rift among the band is more than we can bear.

Finally, we talk about what happened the last two nights, and how that couldn't happen again. We both agreed. I regretted that I didn't go home and stayed the night here alone the same way he had the night he stormed out. He knew why I went to a hotel, but I needed to know why he didn't come home. He explained that he went to Smitten's and was pretty drunk by the time Xander, Nix, and Garrett found him there. They all went back to Garrett's house and spent the night arguing. Xander and Nix walked out and then Garrett and he drank until they both passed out. When he woke up Garrett took him back to get his car and then he came home, but by that time I was gone. All that was left was my note. He told me after he read my note he, too, found the strength to look past the chaos. So much had happened in such a short period of time and we just weren't prepared for it. Neither one of us ever doubted the true strength of our relationship, but we doubted each other's investment in it, and that was the scariest part.

After baring our souls to each other, we lie together, embracing as if we are one. We know our love is strong; we have withstood what we hope to be one of the biggest issues we will ever have to face—Ben's return. I know we are much stronger because of it.

Once the hard conversations are over we enjoy the peacefulness of just being alone together. I'm lying on my side, mindlessly twirling one of my diamond stud earrings and he's watching me intently.

"Did I ever tell you my parents had a thing for birthdays?"

He smirks. "Most parents do, Dahlia."

"No, I mean really. They had an obsession. They would start asking me what I wanted for my birthday months ahead of time. For my twelfth birthday I told them I wanted a carousel. Now I meant a toy one, but they rented out the merry-go-round at Griffith Park for an entire Saturday afternoon. It was amazing."

With a wicked grin he slides his fingers down my bare stomach. "I could rent it out for your next birthday and we could have some fun—if you're still into merry-go-rounds, that is?"

"Hey." I feign offense. "What can I say? I was twelve and liked riding the ponies!"

He laughs so hard he's almost crying. "You walked right into that one."

Laughing along with him, I say, "Yeah, I did."

Holding his stomach, he takes a deep breath and manages, "Okay, tell me about another outrageous birthday present."

"See these?" I say, pointing to my earrings. "Well, for my thirteenth birthday I told my parents I wanted something that sparkled, like Ariel's mermaid tale. And these are what I got."

He kisses my forehead. "They're beautiful. And Dahlia, I can understand why your parents wanted to always make you happy. They loved you."

Then, as if deep in thought, he starts caressing my back and humming the "Happy Birthday" song. I suddenly have a strong desire to hear him play. It's been so long since we've shared that intimacy and I'm craving it. "River, can I ask you to do something?"

He leans over and kisses me, then he whispers in my ear, "Sure. Are you ready for dessert?"

I almost forget what I wanted to ask him when his lips meet mine again, but I quickly remember. "Well, of course, but first will you play 'Never in Pieces' for me?"

He props up on his elbows. "Now?" he says as he leans back down and resumes kissing me, this time trailing feather-soft kisses up my neck.

"Yes, please," I beg.

He sits up and gets off the bed. "God, why can't I ever say no to you?"

"Because you love me so much?" I smile at him.

"Yes I do, my girl, that I do," he says while pulling up his boxers. And I notice what I didn't notice before, that he's wearing his Pac-Man boxers.

My breath quickens just watching him. I suck in a breath and happy tears form in my eyes. "You wore my favorite boxers."

He grins his familiar heart-stopping grin and winks at me as he tugs on the waistband and nods. Then he picks up his guitar and sits on the edge of the bed. The muscles in his back flex in a way that makes me want to lick a line around each one. He twists sideways, and his abs and pecs ripple with each movement. I bite down on my lower lip in anticipation as he sets himself up. His strong arm cradles the guitar as he rests it on his thigh. He looks over at me and pats his free hand on the bed, motioning for me to sit next to him. Closing the distance between us, I study him further as he begins to play. His nimble fingers pick the fret board and I am mesmerized as he moves with effortless ease. Watching him I can almost feel his fingers touching me with the same gentleness. My eyes travel from his fingers up his arm. I study the muscles in his forearm, how his leg bobs up and down as his shoulders rock back and forth.

I look at his face—even with his eyes closed he's beautiful. Strong jaw, sculpted nose, smooth skin . . . As I soak in the sight of him he's fully entranced in the music he's creating. And then he opens his eyes and smiles and I melt. His green eyes gleam and his dimples come to life. He's the epitome of sexiness and he's mine. He glances over at me as he sings the chorus and my smile couldn't be any bigger. And just as his body sways to the beat of the chorus, so does mine.

There are no pieces, I promise you
Glass can shatter and bones may break
But I will always call, I will always find you
Our love is strong
Let me ease your mind, let me in, I will always love you
I will always love you
We'll never be in pieces

River is my future. I love him, I trust him, I need him. I lay my head on his shoulder and peek up at him. I'm completely captivated by his adorable expression while he's so engrossed in the music. When he finishes playing, he sets the guitar down.

"I love that song."

Happily he says, "I love you." He laces his fingers in mine. "Are you tired?"

I look at the clock; it's only noon but feels like midnight. I yawn a little and he laughs. "I think that would be a yes," he says as he pulls me down to the bed.

"River, can we stay here tonight?" I just want to put my head on his chest and listen to his heartbeat . . . to shut out the rest of the world for just a little while longer.

He kisses my head. "Yeah, I was planning on it," he says as he yawns and stretches. I think he's asleep before I even close my eyes.

Hours pass while we both sleep soundly. When I wake, I can see the sun is just about to set. I turn toward the window, trying not to wake him. The view that I ignored when I first arrived is magnificent. The beach is so beautiful and the mountains are majestic. This sunset would make a beautiful photo.

"It's beautiful, isn't it?" he whispers in my ear.

I turn toward him and give him a soft kiss. "I thought you were still sleeping."

"No, I was just lying here thinking."

"What about?"

His body covers mine and he props himself up on his hands, one on either side of my face. "Our life together. What it will be like."

"What do you see for us?"

He collapses his full weight on me. "Besides this," he says, kissing me, tugging on my lower lip before rolling to his side and draping his arm around me. Pulling me close, he grins. "I see us together, married. Having kids. Doing fun family things that our kids will never forget."

I feel myself tremble as I imagine our perfect life—our children's lives being completely unlike either of ours were as children. "How many kids do you want?"

He shrugs his shoulders. "As many or as few as you want."

Smiling so hard, my face hurts, I run my fingers along his cheek. "Three, I think. Three. Yours is the perfect-size family."

Kissing my fingers he says, "Yeah, it is. Three is a good number."

His eyes smile with that light I love, and I ask, "What?"

He rubs his hand over my stomach. "I was just thinking about how beautiful you're going to look pregnant."

Tears of joy escape my eyes before I kiss him—kiss him with love, with adoration, and a happiness that makes my stomach flutter.

He nestles his head on my shoulder and we lie quietly for a while, listening to the rain and just enjoying being together.

After a while River looks up at me. "I love you," he whispers and his warm breath sends a shiver down my spine.

"Me, too."

"You love yourself?"

"No, silly. I love you."

I feel his mouth against my neck. "Can we promise to always use words to tell each other how we feel?"

"Of course," I say, because I can promise him that. I want to spend my life with him. I love him more than words can ever express.

Reaching his hand down between my legs, he smirks and coyly says, "I'll take 'of course' as a green light in any conversation we have from now on."

Giggling because it wasn't long ago that he said "of course" couldn't be assumed in any conversation and now he's laughing about it, I hop off the bed and go find my jeans. Reaching into my pocket I pull the guitar pick out and close it in my hand. Back in bed next to him, he just looks at me skeptically. Opening my palm I show him the pick that reads, "I love you."

Eyeing the pick he says, "I knew which one was missing immediately and I want that back, you know." Then he gently lifts my hand and kisses it and the pick together. "I love you, too."

God, I love everything about him and I don't want to wait another day to be his wife and have his babies. I prop my elbow on the pillow and rest my chin on my hand. Pressing into him so that our bodies are melded together, I ask, "River Wilde, will you marry me?"

"You can't ask me that. I've already asked you that question." His hand moves to my backside and pushes me further into him—solidifying us as a single unit.

"No, I mean marry me tomorrow. We can go home, grab a bag, and head to Vegas."

His hand slides down my thigh. "I don't know. My proposal was much more romantic. I'm the kind of guy who likes to be wined and dined, and besides, I'm not sure we can hop a flight to Vegas naked."

Hiding my smile I tell him, "All right, lover boy, no making fun of my proposal. It was impromptu."

He grabs my left hand, lifts it to his mouth, and kisses my ring. "I would love to marry you, Dahlia London. Tomorrow can't come soon enough."

I smile widely and lean in to kiss him.

He pulls away, and draws an X over his heart. "And I promise you'll never regret marrying me."

His words sear me, branding me to the core. I know I will never regret one single second with him, and suddenly I know what I have to do. I quickly stand and he sits up, staring at me in confusion. I walk over to the room-service tray, grab a butter knife, and return to the bed. Sitting in front of him, I hand him the knife and offer my wrist. He looks at me as if questioning what I'm asking him to do.

I nod my head. "I don't have to wear a no-regrets bracelet because I know I will never regret a single moment of my life with you."

He swallows and then loosens two of the screws on my bracelet. He stares intently at me as he removes the last thing connecting me to Ben. I'm now completely his, not that I haven't been since the day we met, but somehow this cements it.

He touches his forehead to mine and whispers, "Thank you."

I lean back and clutch his face in my hands. My eyes meet his and there are no words to describe the look on his face right now.

He pushes aside a piece of my hair and tucks it behind my ear. Slowly kissing his way down my neck, he tells me, "I want you forever."

I whisper back, "God, I love you so much."

His lips lift into a smirk. "Good, because now that we've both professed our undying love for each other, can I touch you everywhere?"

CHAPTER 25
All or Nothing

"Amazing Grace" starts ringing from the floor where River had tossed our phones. They rang on and off all day, but neither one of us paid attention to them. We needed time together, alone, to just shut out the world.

As I look sleepy-eyed at the clock, alarm overcomes me. It's only 4:23 a.m. Why would Grace be calling so early?

Jumping out of bed, I look for the illuminated phone on the carpet; the phone stops ringing before I get to it, but starts again immediately. I hit the ANSWER button.

"Hello?"

"Dahl, I'm sorry to call you like this," he says, and I tense at his wistful tone, anger surging through me. How dare he use Grace's phone to call me.

"Ben, I don't want to talk to you. Don't ever call me again." I seethe and move to hit the END button.

"It's Grace," he manages before I actually hang up.

My pulse races as I stagger to the bed.

River sits up. "Give me the phone. I'll take care of it."

I shake my head no and hold up one finger.

"Ben, what about her?"

Ben is quiet for the longest time.

River's mouth tightens and he tries to grab the phone from me, but I turn away.

"Ben, tell me what's wrong."

River reaches to turn the light on and wraps a blanket around me.

"Dahl, she's in the hospital."

My eyes fill with tears. "Hospital? What happened?"

"It's bad, Dahl. I'd rather tell you when you get here."

Seeing my pain, River senses the urgency. He stands up and pulls his boxers and jeans on.

"No, tell me now."

"We rushed her to the ER last night. She had a massive stroke."

"A stroke? What does 'massive' mean?" I am trembling as I reel from the news and try to understand what it means.

River is on the hotel phone calling the valet.

Ben is crying. "She's unresponsive. Her brain is hemorrhaging. I think you should come now."

"She's going to be all right, isn't she?"

"Just come now. We're at Mission," he says and then hangs up.

I can feel my face go slack, my mouth dropping open slightly, and all I can do is stare wide-eyed at River. He's looking over at me with concern. I open my mouth to speak, to reassure him, but snap it shut and gulp. Finally I manage, in a raspy, barely audible tone, "We have to get to the hospital in Laguna as soon as possible. It's Grace."

He squeezes me against his chest and I allow myself a minute to lean into him. His fingers find my chin and lift it up. "I'll be with you every minute. Okay?"

I nod. I blink. I've been broken and glued back together so many times already—not again. *Please not again.* I rest my face against his chest and cry out, "Please let Grace be all right."

Sirens wailing, lights cycling red, an ambulance pulls into the entrance where the bright blue letters read "Emergency Room." River follows the signs to visitor parking and we enter the dark underground garage. I stare silently ahead as he squeezes my hand and we head into the hospital; I'm suddenly petrified of what's going to happen. The sliding doors open and shut as we enter. Stopping at the information desk, River gives Grace's name. After a few clicks of her keyboard, the woman directs us to an area called Comfort Care and I'm not sure whether that is good or bad. I flinch as we walk through the hall and hear a snapping noise. Someone is raising a gurney and for some reason the noise is more than I can take right now.

Every step brings me closer to Grace. I look around as we walk and think how hospitals are strange places. People are always whispering everywhere. Why? Are they afraid that speaking out loud makes everything more real? I look into each room as we pass them; families sit with their loved ones, some old, some young, some looking well, and some looking very sick.

We cautiously approach the ICU and Serena is talking to one of the doctors who has a chart in his hand. He looks down at the papers and she nods her head, her face expressionless and unreadable.

River stops at the waiting area, but I keep walking. He squeezes my hand. I know he's here for me, but I have to go see Grace. I'm scared of what I will find, but I know I have to do this. I turn to look at him and he nods.

I travel what seems like miles. When the doctor goes in the room, Serena turns and sees me. "Dahlia!" she cries, her eyes filling with tears. I look into the room, see Ben by the side of the bed, and start to walk in. Serena grabs my arm. Ben's position is preventing me from getting a clear view.

"Serena, I want to see her. How is she?"

I look at her face, and I know it's bad. "Let's go over here and talk," she manages, taking deep breaths in between her words. She walks us back to where River is standing and motions us both to sit down. She sits next to me and grabs my hand. River holds the other.

Taking another deep breath she says, "They just did a CT scan and the swelling has moved to the other side of the brain."

I blurt out, "It will go down, right?"

She squeezes my hand even tighter. "No, Dahlia. There's nothing they can do. It's just a matter of time before her heart or lungs give out."

I shake my head. "But we're in a hospital. Of course there is something they can do."

"They're giving her morphine to ease any suffering and she's on oxygen to help with her breathing. But, Dahlia, she has no brain activity. She's already gone."

"No, Serena. I don't believe it." I can't accept what she's telling me, but I pull her to me and hug her as tight as I can. My heart shatters, but I struggle to pull myself together. Grace is Serena's mother and I know what it is like to lose your mother. I blink back my tears, trying to be strong for her.

"I want to see her."

She nods her head and stands. I look over to River and walk with Serena to see Grace.

As we walk back down the hall, I say a silent prayer. I haven't prayed to God since he took my parents from me, but I pray now. I pray for him to turn Grace's condition around and to give me the strength to make it through whatever happens.

My stomach is in knots as I take slow, cautious steps toward the bed. Red lights blink from various devices, and a white sheet covers most of her small body. The closer I get I can see that it's Grace lying there, but it doesn't really look like her. She's too pale, her hair unkempt. She looks asleep, like I might be able to wake her if I try. So I take her lifeless hand and squeeze it, mentally willing her to squeeze back, to wake up. But her hand is cold and unresponsive against my feverish skin. I clutch her hand harder, trying to warm it, and bend forward to place my forehead against hers, kissing her. "I love you, Grace," I whisper.

Through the metal bedrail I see so many wires, tubes, and cords leading from one machine to another and then to her. I'm surprised how noisy they all are for such a quiet place. Every *whoosh* pumps oxygen through a clear tube, each *bleep* indicates the rate at which her heart is beating, and the sound of air compressing monitors her blood pressure. An alarm goes off and I jump. When Grace's body twitches slightly and she gasps for air, I look at Ben in horror and scream, "Shouldn't someone be in here to monitor her?"

He looks at me somberly, withdrawn even as he answers, "It's okay, that's just a warning that her oxygen saturation level is low."

Quickly, a nurse comes in and turns the dial near the tank. She waits a few minutes to take Grace's pulse, and then she leaves. I hear whispering behind me and see Serena is talking to River outside the door.

When my eyes return to Grace, it strikes me anew how ashen and lifeless her complexion looks. How can this be happening to Grace? This woman has been my mother since the day mine died. She shared all my ups and downs and guided me through so much. My throat tightens and I suddenly feel dizzy. I can't stay in here. I run out of the room and go to River.

He sits me down and I pull my knees up to my chest. He crouches in front of me and strokes my cheek with his fingers, but doesn't say a word. When he tips my chin so that I'm looking into his eyes, he whispers, "You have to do this. You have to stay with her, baby. She needs you."

I unfold my arms and cup his cheeks, and simply nod. He pauses as if to gather his own strength before standing and pulling me up. His arms circle around me. "I'm so sorry."

I kiss him softly on the lips, my heart filled with so much love for him and so much sadness for Grace that I'm sure it's going to burst. I don't think I have room left for any other emotions.

I tell myself he's right. I am strong. I can be there for Grace, Serena, and even Ben. One more deep breath and then I make myself walk back into the room. I look at Serena, who seems paralyzed with fear. I look at Ben and his eyes are closed, but when he opens them they are ravaged with pain.

Moving next to Serena, I grab her hand and can feel how her body trembles.

Her voice breaks. "Are you okay?"

"No, I'm not okay," I say in complete honesty.

She turns to me. "I know. Neither am I."

Hugging her, I whisper, "I'm so sorry for not telling you about Trent."

She shakes her head. "No, I'm sorry. I should never have yelled at you that way. Ben explained everything."

My gaze moves to him, noticing his sad blue eyes, and I quickly look back to Serena. "Oh God, where is Trent? Is he alone?"

"We took him to the recovery center yesterday afternoon. She came with us," Ben says, his voice cracking and his eyes focused on his mother. "We went back to Laguna and brought her home. I walked her in and she had trouble getting up the stairs. She said she felt dizzy and then all of a sudden she complained of a severe headache. She hadn't been feeling well all day so I had her lie down. When I couldn't wake her up, we called nine-one-one and got her here as soon as we could. But it was too late."

Tears are streaming down his face as he tells me. I can't see him like this. I hate him, but my heart aches for him. For a while Serena, Ben, and I sit in silence by Grace's bed; then I step out into the corridor. River is in the waiting area, looking out the huge window. It's still raining and I have no idea how long we've been in the room. Walking over to him, I lean on him and he wraps his arm around my shoulder, kissing my head.

"You need anything?"

"No, just you."

I sit with him and neither of us talks at first.

He shifts slightly and whispers in my ear. "You know you're just like her—amazing."

Suddenly, I realize why people whisper in hospitals. It's not because they don't want to face what's before them, it's to ease the mind of those around them, to lessen the pain. Facing him, I swipe the hair from his forehead and stare into his green eyes. I can feel a single tear drip down my cheek, and he wipes it away. Brushing my lips softly to his I say, "Thank you," and hug him as tightly as I possibly can.

Glancing up, I see Ben behind us, just staring. He gives me an odd look and then heads back to the room. After a while, I get up and take River's hand. "Come on, come with me."

"I don't think I should, but if you need me I'm right here."

I smile at him and squeeze his hand. "I know."

When I walk back into the room, Serena wipes her tears away and stands. "I'm going to grab some coffee. Do you want some?"

Ben and I both decline.

When it's just him and me, the silence between us is deafening. He looks up from his chair beside Grace and says, "It's my fault, you know."

Looking at him, I feel anger and then a wave of sympathy. I don't say anything, but I slide my chair around the bed to sit next to him. I take hold of Grace's hand, and it's so cold. I just sit there, not sure if my touch offers her any comfort, but it feels like the right thing to do. Ben stays silent for the longest time, and the tension between us seems to say it all.

"Dahl, did you hear me?" he asks with sorrow in his voice.

I try to ease his pain. "It's not your fault, Ben. Strokes aren't caused by other people."

Placing his hand on Grace's arm, he looks over at me. "Maybe not, but I can't help but think she wouldn't be here if I never came back. Everything's a mess. I'm just so sorry. You know I never meant to hurt you. I've always loved you, even though my actions didn't always show it."

I can't believe he's using this time and place to atone for his mistakes. He hesitates only for a moment before edging closer to me. He runs his finger over my wrist, where his bracelet had adorned my arm until yesterday. I start to move away but something feels wrong. His eyes . . . they're filled with remorse, grief, and maybe even loneliness. That wave of sympathy I felt earlier now shatters me. My eyes close in a subconscious effort to block out the bad memories. He clutches my hand tight to his face, and, for a few heartbeats, I leave it that way until a high-pitched sound fogs my senses, and then quickly brings reality crashing down.

The steady beeping of the heart monitor changes to one long tone. It's a constant high-pitched whine, no breaks in between. Just a long, flat, piercing sound that penetrates my ears. Doctors and nurses flood the room. Time seems to slow while at the same time the room comes alive. Backing away, I watch the clock tick as they desperately try to bring her back, but she's already gone. I know she is. The nurses rotate through compressions and give nervous glances to each other as the seconds pass. The doctor grabs the paddles from the cart. "Clear," he yells and I twitch at the same time Grace's body does.

And then, just like that, all efforts stop as they let her go. But this can't be real. I'm here, she's here, but things will never be the same. I can't stop staring at her. Her lips are parted as if she's in midsentence and I wait for her to say, "Dahlia, honey, where's your umbrella?" But she doesn't.

Serena stands in the doorway, looking blankly at the bed. Ben rushes to his mother's side, and I hear him screaming, "No, Mom! No!" Serena goes over to him, and as I watch the two of them, I start to back away from the deafening sound. Its only purpose is to alert us to what we already know—Grace is gone.

Serena pulls Ben to her and everything in the room seems to cloud over. Sadness, anger, disbelief, guilt—they're all fighting for their place inside me and I just want out of this skin. All of the sounds, voices, movements, and bodies around me form a big blur and I feel like I'm suffocating. A sob rises in my throat, and I quickly turn to escape the room. I run down the long corridor and it suddenly seems stark white. The automatic doors open, allowing me to flee out into the safety of the rain. Finally, I can breathe. The rain falls down harder and harder as I let the tears flow at the same pace, the tears I've been holding in so I could be the stronger one.

I cry for time that won't stand still, for losses that should never have happened, for friendships broken, for mistakes made, for my pain, and most of all I cry for Grace. Especially for Grace.

I try to understand why death takes a person from you, but not the relationship. It leaves you to carry on with only half of what you need to make things whole.

Lifting my arms out to the side, I raise my head up toward the heavens and scream, "It's not fair! Do you hear me? It's just not fair!" My scream turns into a whimper before I finish and my anger transforms into sorrow as the reality hits me that no matter how mad I am or how sad I am, she's really gone.

Water drips from my hair, absorbs into my clothes, and soaks me to the bone. Grief besieges me as I feel another piece of my soul chipped away and I wonder how much more could possibly be left.

How much can one person take until there is nothing left—to take or to give?

"Dahl!" Ben yells, and my name sounds desperate on his lips.

"Dahlia!" River calls and this time my name sounds calm, tranquil.

I turn and see him standing in the doorway to the hospital entrance.

"River!" I cover my mouth and shake my head.

"I'm sorry," he calls out to me and I run to him, because I don't want to run any other way. I jump into his arms and hold him and I know that what's left of my soul is for him.

CHAPTER 26
Everybody's Changing

Since Grace died, I just can't shake the feeling of being a little lost. She taught me so much—she was always there for me. I loved her so deeply. Tears threaten to spill again, and I start to worry that I might not be able to keep it together. River's lying beside me in bed, rubbing circles along my back and asking me what he can do for me. I know he's unsure of what to do or say, and so am I.

All I want is not to have to think about her being gone, so I close my eyes and drift off again. When I wake up, I'm alone. It's dark and I take a moment to compose myself before making my way into the bathroom. But once the coolness of the tiled floor hits my feet, I want it to numb me all over. To take away the grief and help me get through the next few days. And most of all, I want it to help me say goodbye to Grace.

Dropping down onto the floor, I bow my head in my hands and let the tears fall yet again. Sitting there, I have to wonder how many tears a person can shed for loved ones lost before they're all dried up. Suddenly, the bright lights blind me and I squint at him, standing near the door.

"Dahlia, are you okay?"

I nod.

"What are you doing?"

He looks terrified. His hands reach under my arms, lifting me up. I can tell he's worried I'm sinking fast and won't be able to pull myself up. But as I stare into his eyes, I know I will be okay. I have to be. For him.

On his lap now, I push the hair from his eyes. "Hey, I'm okay."

He strokes my check. "You sure?"

I nod and stand up. Reaching for his hand, I lead him back into the bedroom. "Can I show you something?" I ask as I open the curtains and see it's a beautiful sunny day. It finally stopped raining.

He sits in the chair and just looks at me as if uncertain of how to answer. It's a look that makes me smile. "It has nothing to do with sex, if that's what you're thinking."

Almost horrified, he tells me, "No, that's not what I'm thinking at all."

"I know. I'm just kidding, silly." I want to reassure him and let him know that even though I'm sad, I will be okay.

My mother's hope chest is old, and the creamy-white paint is almost completely peeled off. Bending down to reach it, I open the lid and realize I haven't looked in here in a long time, not since the break-in when I had to put everything back in it that wasn't destroyed.

I smile when I see my dolls, yearbooks, diplomas, and various mementos. As I'm digging through the contents, I feel his arms wrap around my waist as he hugs me tightly. I clutch his arms and squeeze him back for a few seconds before moving to sift through the items for what I want to show him.

When I find it, I have to hold it close to my heart first. Then I turn to hand it to him. Smiling, I point to the small, blond-haired girl in the photo, surrounded by seven adults. "For my tenth birthday, when my parents asked what I wanted, it was an easy choice—I wanted to meet Elton John. My mom started to say no, but my dad just beamed at me and told me of course he could arrange that. And he did."

I look at River and he's studying the picture as I move across it with my finger. "That's Grammy, Auntie, Uncle Scott, Mom, Dad, Grace, and that is Sir Elton John himself. My dad even managed a private show before the concert where Elton John sang 'Believe' and then 'Happy Birthday' to me."

River leans over and kisses my cheek. "Wow, what an awesome birthday present, especially for a ten-year-old."

I grin because I remember that day so vividly.

He looks at me and in complete seriousness asks, "Why Elton John and not Hootie and the Blowfish or someone a ten-year-old might gush over?"

"Because of Grace. Elton John was her favorite. Every day after school I stayed with her until my parents came home. We would sing 'Crocodile Rock' and 'Bennie and the Jets' so many times, Serena threatened to throw the CD away and Ben would run and hide in his room. Neither of them liked Elton. But Grace and I loved him, and she always said meeting him was one of the best days of her life." I notice he didn't even flinch this time at the sound of Ben's name.

River takes the picture and walks it over to the dresser, standing it on display next to the one of my parents and me. "How about we leave it out so we can both enjoy that memory?"

I nod and as I start to close the chest, I notice the screwdriver that Ben had put in there so long ago and know what I have to do to stay close with Grace. But the doorbell breaks me out of my thoughts as I take the screwdriver and close the chest.

Before either of us moves to answer the door, Xander is yelling, "Lover boy, Muse, we're coming in so you better be decent."

I look over to River and I can see he's somewhat unsure about this, but the light in his eyes tells me he's happy. Just hearing Xander's smart-ass voice like everything is okay between them warms my heart. I hold out my hand and he grabs it. Leading the way, I squeeze it tightly and he does the same. Odd that I'm the one reassuring him right now. It makes me feel a little more whole.

The front door is still open as we enter the foyer. Looking into the family room I can see that Xander is standing near Bell, who has a shopping bag in one hand and is pointing with the other. She's giving orders to Garrett about where to set the tinfoil-covered pans of food, Nix is lugging in a cooler, and Xander is just standing there, his arms crossed, watching the scene unfold.

We stand in the foyer and River clears his throat. "Hey, what's going on?"

Xander's eyes shift to River. "Talk to your sister. She insisted we bring dinner over."

River looks at him. "Thank you for that."

He looks back. "No problem. Actually, we all wanted to be here for the both of you."

My eyes move to Bell, who looks a little apprehensive as she shrugs her shoulders and I give her a warm smile, assuring her that our relationship is intact. Then I shift my gaze to Xander. "Thank you, Xander."

"Anything for you, Muse," he says.

River nods in appreciation to both his brother and sister. Everyone looks over at us and it's quiet for a split second until Garrett says, "Why is everyone acting like someone just died?"

Bell gives him a swift kick and he turns pale and freezes. His eyes dart to mine. "Shit. Oh my God, Dahlia. I'm so sorry. I wasn't thinking. I was only trying to lighten the mood."

Nix smacks Garrett across the back of his head and says, "Man, you always talk out of your ass. It's a good thing no one ever listens."

We all laugh to break the tension, and the flurry of activity continues.

I rest my head on River's shoulder as we watch them set up the meal they've brought over for us. He kisses my hair and then whispers to me, "Are you okay with this?"

I nod and let go of his hand, turning to cup his cheek. Motioning with my eyes to Xander, I quietly urge, "Go talk to him."

With a determined nod, he gives me a swift kiss and heads toward the kitchen. I watch him walk with that same gait I've seen a thousand times. But it's thrilling each time—how lucky am I to have a caring, compassionate, and loving man like him in my life?

He cautiously approaches Xander, who pats him on the shoulder, then motions him outside to the deck. Xander looks back before exiting through the sliding glass door to give me a nod and a quick smile.

"Hey, Dahlia, you doing okay?" Nix asks and I have to blink because I never saw him approach me. I have to swallow repeatedly to hold back the tears. I wasn't expecting condolences from any of these guys. As I try to find the words to answer, Garrett is at my side, giving me a one-armed hug. "I'm sorry for your loss, Dahlia."

I take a deep breath and return his hug. "Thank you," I manage and step back before turning to Nix and answering his question. "I'm doing better than I expected."

It's true. I am. I'm actually interacting with people, rather than withdrawing into my own world like I have so many times before—a world where I can't focus on what people are saying to me, where my responses are nothing but mindless nods, and my hugs are nothing but stiff embraces. I'm stronger than that now.

"Hey, you guys are suffocating her. Move away and let her breathe," Bell says.

She takes my hand, pulling me to the sofa. Once we sit she looks anywhere but at me. I want to be the first to say something, to reassure her that I'm not upset at her in the least bit, but she beats me to it.

"I'm so sorry all this has happened. I don't even know what to say. Do you think of me differently?" she asks, hesitating as she tucks her foot under her leg.

Taking her hand, I cover it with mine. "Bell, look at me." Her sad green eyes dart to mine and I say, "Of course not. I don't blame you for anything that happened. I don't. So please don't think that. I know the situation is awkward, but let's not let it change things between us. Okay?"

Nodding, she bites her lip. "You know I never knew he was the same person."

"Let's just not discuss him. Please?"

"I'm sorry, Dahlia," she says. Then, just like her brother, she has the uncanny ability to change topics seamlessly. "How are you doing?"

"Much better than I ever thought I would. How about we see what's in all those trays in the kitchen? I'm hungry."

She smiles at me and pulls me in for a big hug. "I love you, Dahlia."

"I love you, too, Bell."

We head toward the kitchen and I look outside. Nix and Garrett have joined River and Xander and they're all sitting around the table, talking calmly. I hope they can come to terms with River's decision because they're so important to him. It wasn't easy for him to quit, but I've come to believe it was the right thing for him to do. He loves to sing and play guitar, but he never wanted to be famous; he couldn't live his father's dream. He loves music, but it needs to be on his own terms.

I'm staring out the window, watching as he runs his hands through his hair, when I blurt out, "Do you think everything happens for a reason?"

Bell grabs a stack of plates and sets them on the counter. "Yeah, I hope so. I'd like to think it does, anyway."

Shoving the pans in the oven, I close the door and turn it on. My next words catch in my throat but I push them out. "What made you decide to give up the baby?"

She stares at me for a long moment before she answers. "After everything that happened, I just knew the baby would be better off with two parents who loved it."

There's another stretch of silence, but I think it's understood that we both accept the strange situation. We will be okay. Neither one of us will let anything harm our friendship. Opening the refrigerator, I grab two bottles of water and hand her one.

Bell laughs and takes a sip. "And come on, Dahlia, let's be real. Could you see me with a five-year-old right now?"

"I think you'd be surprised at what you could do."

Snorting, she says, "What? Isn't it normal that a twenty-five-year-old lives with her mom?"

"Bell, you can change that anytime you want. You're doing great—you're managing to juggle two jobs and, from what I hear, doing fantastic in both of them."

"Actually, I am moving. Xander found me an apartment in West Hollywood after I told him how much I really love my job with Tate. Xander is replacing me as soon as possible so I can start working full-time there."

"That's great, Bell. See, you can do whatever you want!"

The front door opens, and, in a whirlwind, Aerie rushes to the kitchen. She throws her purse on the counter and hurries over to me. We hug each other for a long time. "Dahlia, I am so sorry," she says.

When we break apart I look into her saddened eyes as she looks at me with affection and I manage to say, "I've missed you so much," before breaking down completely.

Bell leaves us alone and joins everyone else on the back deck. I have so much to tell Aerie but now doesn't feel like the right time. She puts her arm around my shoulder and leads me through the front door where we sit on the steps and talk about Grace.

About fifteen minutes later, the door opens and Bell stands there with the portable phone in her hand. "Dahlia, it's Serena. She says she really needs to talk to you." Handing it to me she whispers, "I'm going to go get dinner ready."

I nod and give her a warm smile.

A million horrible thoughts about Trent drift through my mind as I put the phone to my ear and cautiously say, "Hello."

"Dahlia, please come over. I need your help. I just can't do it."

"It's okay, Serena, calm down. What can't you do?"

"Pick out her clothes," she cries into the phone.

"Her clothes?" I swallow.

"I have to bring them to the funeral home by six. Could you come over and help me pick something out?"

Sadly, I know exactly what she's talking about. "Let me just change and I'll be there as soon as I can."

My stomach knotting, I look at Aerie. "I have to go. Serena needs help with some of the arrangements."

Before I even get to the door, River opens it. His arms circle me and hold me tight. He kisses my head and whispers, "What's going on?"

I am not sure how he's going to take this, but at the same time I have to go and he can't come with me. Even before I can tell him anything Aerie says, "I'll drive you to Grace's."

I nod okay.

River and Aerie say hello to each other and she steps inside.

"Do you want me to take you?" River asks me, reaching his hands to cradle my face.

My determination falters as I contemplate letting him drive me. But I know I can't because if Ben is there they'll just go at it again. And I can't do that to Serena. "I think I should go alone. Please understand."

His body stiffens, but relaxes when I lean into his touch and slide my mouth to kiss his hand. He then presses his forehead against mine, silently acknowledging his acceptance.

As we enter the house the rest of the guys are just walking inside. Bell is in the kitchen taking the trays out of the oven and Nix and Garrett start shoving each other to get the first plate. Xander is helping to set the rest of the food out as Aerie instructs him how to do it. He snaps at her and she doesn't hesitate to give it right back to him. Everything looks back to normal.

I grab River's hand. "Come with me. I'm going to change my clothes before I go." Then pulling him down the hall with me I ask, "Will you be okay here?"

A small chuckle escapes him. "Yeah, I'll be fine, Dahlia. I'm a big boy."

He flops himself on the bed, kicks his feet up, and leans back against the headboard.

"That's not what I mean. How did your conversation with Xander go?"

He smiles and pulls me onto the bed with him. "It went much better than the last time. We didn't yell or argue. It started out rough but Xander surprised me. It was like it somehow clicked, like he finally understood that that life wasn't for me."

Staring into his tranquil green eyes, I'm relieved that he and his brother are talking again. "What about the other guys?"

His smile grows even wider. "We talked and they aren't happy that I won't be with them, but they've accepted my decision. They told me our friendship is more important than anything else."

I close my eyes in gratitude for a second, so happy his brother finally understood and he has his friends back.

"Ellie agreed to Jack's suggestion for a potential new lead singer. They're going to meet tomorrow."

I sit up and glare at him. Rolling my eyes I mutter, "Yeah, I bet she did."

Reaching for my hands, he sits up, too, and pulls me onto his lap. Cradling his face in my hands, I examine his expression before kissing him hard, making sure to suck on his bottom lip before stopping. Shrugging, I joke, "Sorry, I just needed to get her name off your lips."

Shaking his head, he grabs my T-shirt and pulls me back to him. Our mouths meet with such intensity that I almost forget for a moment about everything that has happened. He pulls back and both of us are breathless. He takes my face between his palms, his eyes beaming with the same emotion I feel when I'm with him—pure happiness. And I know what we have will never be torn apart.

The light at the intersection turns green and cars drive past us as horns behind us relentlessly honk. Aerie sits in the driver's seat, gripping the steering wheel in utter shock. "That f-ing son of a bitch."

As she's never one to really swear, I'm used to hearing her curse in abbreviations.

I wasn't going to say anything to her, but one thing led to the next when I thanked her for driving me since my car was still in Santa Barbara, and the whole story about Ben and Bell came tumbling out.

"That f-ing son of a bitch. Wait until I see him," she repeats as she swings the steering wheel to head down the street leading to Grace's house. Silence fills the air and I can see the gears turning in her head.

"Aerie, not now, not today. Please," I tell her as she parks the car.

Looking around, I don't see Ben's car anywhere. Serena must be alone and I know she needs me—only me. "Do you think I can call you when I'm ready to head back?"

She nods her head and draws me in for a hug. When she lets go she says, "Make sure you call me if you need anything at all."

"You know it. And thanks again for the ride." Then I'm opening the car door and walking slowly toward the house. "Serena, I'm here," I call as I enter the family room. Sadness hits me as I look around the room that still feels like it's filled with Grace's presence. Climbing the stairs, I head to Grace's room. I knock and slowly walk in. All of

Grace's clothes are thrown on the bed and Serena's pulling shoes off the rack in the closet and tossing them to the ground. "Serena," I call but she doesn't answer. I reach her and pull her to me in a hug that I hope will offer some comfort. My heart aches for her as words pour out of my mouth. "Serena, look at me. I know how hard this is. But I'm here. Let me help you."

She turns around and hugs me back while she cries and I am so thankful that I get to be the one to comfort her, to help her through this.

Together we sort through Grace's dresses, which are all spread out on the bed, and when I see it, I know it's the one—the navy sheath dress with a matching belt, the one that always made her eyes light up. Serena agrees and then frantically turns to what's left of the rack filled with shoes. She finds a match immediately. Lifting up a pair of blue pumps she says, "I remember buying these with her at Avery's. We were in LA for the day at a luncheon. She had worn some strappy sandals that were killing her feet, so after the event was over we decided to hit up Beverly Hills." She smiles at the memory and then abruptly says, "We need some underwear."

"Right," I say, trying to keep up.

"And what earrings should she wear? Her gold or silver ones?"

I grab her arm. "Hey, Serena. Slow down. It's okay. Let me get the jewelry."

Inside her large wooden jewelry box I see my engagement ring from Ben. It's still on the chain, sitting on a velvet square all by itself. I pick it up for just a moment and as if it scorches me, I immediately put it back down.

"He told me, Dahlia, and I'm so sorry," I hear Serena whisper as I pull a pair of small silver hoops from the jewelry box.

I take a deep breath but say nothing because neither she nor Ben really knows the whole truth. I turn to face her and hold my hand out with the pair of earrings in it. "Here, I think that should do it."

"Will you come with me to the funeral home? Ben seems to be a no-show. He was supposed to be here by noon. I've called him and left messages, but he hasn't returned any of my calls."

I take another deep breath. "Of course, Serena."

We head downstairs and as I open the door to leave, Caleb pulls in the driveway. Serena yells she'll be out in a minute and I stand on the porch as Caleb rolls down his window. "Dahlia, is Ben here?"

I shake my head. "I haven't seen him. Serena and I are just headed to the funeral home to drop some things off. Serena said Ben was supposed to be here but she hasn't heard from him."

He frowns. "Thanks." Then he adds, "Dahlia, I am so sorry about everything. I never meant for any of this to impact you."

"Caleb, it's not your fault, really it isn't."

He sighs. "I'm leaving town for a new job. I called River and told him who his new security contact is earlier today."

I nod. "Caleb, good luck."

He nods back and closes his window as I head to Serena's car. I call River from the car and ask him to come pick me up at the funeral home. It's getting late and I don't want Aerie to have to drive to LA and back tonight. I also call Aerie to let her know that I'm all set with a ride.

We drive to the funeral home in silence. Walking in, I immediately feel uneasy. I subconsciously hold my breath, but the funeral home smell still hits me immediately.

Serena has the bag of Grace's things in one hand and my hand in the other as we walk down the hall, passing the viewing room first. The office is an open area at the end and an older man comes to meet us. He introduces himself and motions for us to sit at the table. Serena seems to have switched into business mode as she discusses the details with him.

I excuse myself to use the restroom but am somehow drawn into the showroom. Caskets of all colors and sizes are on display. I walk over to the white casket with a beautiful light-blue lining and I think that color would be perfect for Grace.

Running my fingers over the smooth satin, a familiar hand covers mine. "I'm really sorry, Dahl. I just want you to know that. Please forgive me. I need you."

I look up. He's unshaven, he's wearing the same clothes he had on yesterday, and he looks like he hasn't slept. Irritation flares through me as I step back and quietly say, "Please, Ben. Not now. This isn't the time."

As he steps forward a wave of women's perfume permeates the air and fills my nose. "Dahl, I know it's not. But I'm so alone."

My voice falters as I try to keep my resolve. I can't be the one for him to lean on. I just can't. "Ben, I'm here to support you and Serena for Grace. But I can't forgive you right now and I don't know if I ever will."

He drops his eyes and pulls something out of his pocket. It's a small journal. His hand is shaking as he hands it to me. His voice is soft. "While I was away I kept this for you. It was how I communicated with you when I thought I'd never see you again." I'm caught by surprise and he must sense it because he says, "Please take it. I want you to have it. Do whatever you want with it." I take it from his hands because even after everything I can't inflict any more pain on him.

But I refuse to give him a chance to say anything else, and turn around to leave. My heart skips a beat when I see River leaning against the doorway. His eyes are narrowed on Ben, but as they meet mine they immediately soften. Even here I can't help but admire his appeal. His lean body is clothed in a black T-shirt and jeans that hang low on his hips. That strong natural stance. He holds his hand out to me and without giving Ben a second glance he asks, "Ready to go, beautiful?"

Smiling at him, I take River's hand and we go to find Serena before he leads us home.

CHAPTER 27
All I Want

Ben's Journal

A bottle of Jack later, and here I am. My life is a mess. I don't even know how to get my life together anymore. How fucking pathetic. One minute Mom was concerned about Trent and the next she was gone. There's no one to blame but me. I can't help but wonder if she'd still be here today if I would have stayed buried. Was the stress of my return too much for her body to take? I can't believe she's gone.

And now Caleb is leaving. He took a job with the FBI, so I have no one. Plus, my sister is pissed as hell at me. And Dahl—I've really lost her. I even tried to call Kimberly, but she shot me down. Before she hung up she told me to call her when I wasn't drunk and could tell her where I was. She never used to be so demanding.

My life is full of epic mistakes, one bad decision after the other. I don't even know which one came first anymore or which one was worse—chasing notoriety and paying the consequences, coming back and thinking I could pick up where I left off, or cheating on a girl who loved me unconditionally, a girl who didn't deserve it, and then watching her choose someone else over me.

After Mom died and I watched Dahl turn to him for support, I needed to get out . . . to forget everything. So I did. I don't remember much except that I drank until the pain felt like it belonged to someone else and then I went home with some girl. And just like it once used to—the sex helped me forget. Even for a little while.

I was so drunk that I passed out in her bed. Fuck, I never stayed the night with a chick that was only a fast lay. Then there was no need for the awkward morning conversation. But this time I woke up to my phone ringing. Still feeling drunk, I checked my messages. Listening to them, I instantly sobered up. My sister had left six messages. I was supposed to meet her to make funeral arrangements. I had no idea what the girl's name was, but I told her she had to drive me back to my car. I had to get there. My mom would want me to be strong. I couldn't disappoint her again—I had enough guilt.

Just as I thought she'd be, Dahlia was there. I apologized again but I no longer believe she will forgive me. I gave her the journal and I hope one day she'll read it and at least know I really did love her.

CHAPTER 28
Tears in Heaven

As the sunlight streams through the windows and the Hollywood sign is clearly visible, I move to slip on my pearls. Clasping the strands around my neck, I look at the image in the mirror and I know who I see . . . I don't have to look twice. I see a woman in control of her own life. A woman whose life has been guided by strong role models. And she's found true love and knows loneliness is far behind her. I stand tall and know I will make it through today and tomorrow and every day after that.

Grace was the one I wanted to be like—the one who always saw the world through rose-colored glasses, and who rarely let anything get her down. She was strong and independent, fun and loving, caring and nurturing, and I was lucky enough to have had her in my life. I owe her the comfort of knowing I will be all right—no, not just all right, I will be more than all right. I have learned to face the truth and because of it I will never have any regrets.

Today we have to say goodbye to her. Her body may be gone, but I know that her spirit will live on through me. I tuck the diary that Ben gave me in my mother's chest. Then I put my no-regrets bracelet in my purse with the screwdriver, muster up my courage, and make my way down the hallway to find River. He's sitting at the breakfast bar, waiting for me. The very sight of him makes me smile . . . strong, resilient, soulful, loving—and all mine.

Taking a shaky breath, I tuck a piece of hair behind my ear. He stands and holds his arms out to me. His lips set in a soft smile as I approach him and hug him tightly. For a minute I rest my head against his neck, breathing him in. Whispering in my ear, he tells me I'm strong and I can do this. Then he leads me to the car and we make the long drive to Laguna Beach and to the church where I will say my goodbyes to Grace.

My movements feel mechanical as we walk through the entrance. I've done this so many times I think I know how many steps it takes to get to the vestibule. River's grip on my hand tightens. The church is filled with all kinds of flowers and so many people. As we make our way to the front, I can see Ben and Serena are already there, sitting in the first pew.

We sit in the row behind them. I lean forward and place my hand on Serena's shoulder; she turns, wiping her tears with a white hankie that used to be Grace's. Xander, Nix, Garrett, Bell, and Charlotte soon follow and sit next to River. Aerie makes her way in and sits on the other side of me. I'm overwhelmed that despite all our issues we've gotten through them and everyone I love is here. Caleb is the last to enter the church and he takes a seat beside Ben. He glances at us and nods hello.

"Blessed are those who mourn, for they will be comforted." Those familiar words start the service and Grace begins the first part of her journey toward her final resting place. Ben turns to look at me and although the pain he has inflicted on me is still raw, I can't help but feel conflicted—torn between the compassion I feel for the son who lost his mother, the sympathy I feel for the teen who comforted me when my parents died, and the contempt I feel for the man who betrayed me. Despite his flaws, Ben was always there for me.

I can feel my gaze softening as I look at him and there's a growing feeling of closure. As he turns back, I know he must feel lost without Grace, and I wish I could be the one to help him but I can't. Ben will have to find his own way. He's on the road he paved, the one I followed for so long, but it's not my road any longer. My heart aches for the family we once were—Grace, Serena, Ben, Trent, and me. Grace is gone, Trent's not here, and Ben—there's just nothing else to say.

"Friends, as we gather here . . ." The service continues and I focus on the words. I've heard them before but the beauty of them moves me and I think about the woman I knew and loved. When the music starts we all stand. When it stops, we all sit. I know what's coming, so I just close my eyes.

When the priest begins reciting the Final Commendation and Farewell, my eyes snap open. It's too soon—I'm not ready. I squeeze River's hand so tightly my knuckles turn white. He lifts my hand to his mouth and kisses it; then he places his other hand on top of mine. The music starts to play and we all stand again. Now it's time for each of us to make our way to the front to say our own private goodbyes.

My hands clench and unclench and I take a deep breath. Approaching the angelic white casket, I see her there in her navy dress, but her eyes aren't sparkling. The normal glow of her skin is gone and replaced by white chalky powder. Her lips are pressed together and I notice right away she has lipstick on. She never wore lipstick. I want to wipe it off her. My tears fall to the satin interior, leaving their mark. I want to kiss her, to hold my hand over hers, but I can't. I've never been able to touch someone lying there like that. They seem so close and you just want them to open their eyes and give you a reassuring smile, but you know they aren't able to.

Voices murmur behind me as I open my purse and place my no-regrets bracelet on top of her folded hands so it sits right next to her diamond ring. I tuck the screwdriver inside the satin lining of the casket and then whisper, "Grace, I'm giving you this to hold forever. Please know I will always say what needs to be said and will live my life with no regrets." I turn, but twist to look back one last time. Her ring shines so bright it catches my eye. It's the same ring she wore on her finger for so many years even though her husband had died so long ago and I think, *That's the kind of love I have now.*

Making my way back to the pew, I wait for everyone else to say his or her goodbyes. I squeeze River's hand and look over to him. He catches my gaze and looks at me with so much love. I know with him by my side I can make it through anything. The music starts and we move to exit the pew. With one last glance, I look up to the same altar I have looked on many times before. But this time, as the stained-glass window reflects on the statue at the altar, I don't have to wish for it to bring me peace because I am at peace.

CHAPTER 29
Run

River

Three weeks later

I yell over the crowd, pumping my fist in the air. I can't help but grin at her. I just knew she could do it. I'm completely mesmerized as I watch her move around. When she motions for me to join her, I put my hands out in protest—no way am I doing that. But she's relentless and since I can never say no to her, I quickly cave and move to join her.

It's karaoke night and the words are flashing across the screen, but it feels bigger than that. My girl is up onstage, living out a small part of a childhood dream that had long been forgotten.

Rihanna's "Umbrella" ends before I even get onstage. Thank God, because if I had to sing that song I would never have heard the end of it from the guys. Just when I think I'm in the clear, my smart-ass brother cues up Maroon 5's song "Moves Like Jagger." Of course he'd pick that song. Asshole.

I jump onstage and Garrett hands me a mic. I have to say, I don't mind sharing the spotlight with her. In fact, I kind of like it. I decide I'm going to seize the moment and play it up. I've seen the music video, and I can move like Jagger. The music starts and I jump into it, pointing to Dahlia.

I stop mid-sway and harden on the spot when her part cues up and she curls her finger toward me, shoots me a wink, then runs her hand down the side of her body. Fuck, that was hot. Upping my game to match hers, I pull my T-shirt off. Tossing it at her, I run my hands down the front of my jeans. She likes the lead singer of Maroon 5; I know she does, so if I have to sing his song I might as well really get into the role.

When the song ends everyone starts clapping. We continue to sing the chorus without the music and the applause escalates. When I hear catcalls from the audience, I grab her and pull a Marlon Brando. I kiss her hard in front of everyone, just in case some guy gets the wrong idea. When she pulls away, she wipes her hand across her mouth and makes a disgusted face, whispering in my ear, "Adam, I have a fiancé and he won't be very happy with you."

I know she's anything but disgusted, and, in fact, I'm hoping she'll let me take her to the poolroom again, but then I notice it's reopened. *Shit.*

After we bow and she tosses me my shirt, she kisses me again. When she slips her tongue in my mouth, I wonder how much she's had to drink because the bathroom is looking really good right now. As we start to walk away, people are laughing and she stops to take another bow. The crowd likes her. No, they *love* her. God, do I know how that feels.

I hop offstage first and extend my arms. As she leaps into them she lands squarely in front of me—she did that on purpose. Of course I want to take her home immediately, but tonight is the first night we've all gone out together since I quit the band. Even Zane Perry, the new lead singer of the Wilde Ones, is here. My stepfather actually suggested him for the job. I'm not sure about the name, but since his father makes musical history with every album he puts out, I can't imagine any better choice. I've met him a few times and he's pretty cool, seems to fit right in. He wants to ask me some questions so we have to hang around for a little bit longer.

The band is up after the karaoke opener is over. I haven't heard the band all play together and you'd think it would be strange for me to watch the Wilde Ones jam without me, but I know it won't be. I am loving my life right now. I'm where I'm supposed to be. I'm working on cutting a few singles of my own and will slowly work toward an album. But, more importantly, Dahlia and I have decided to start our own production company. We've named it Amazing Grace and we are going to cater to small independent bands.

Xander told me everyone is happy with the way rehearsals are going with the new lead so it looks like there will only be a slight delay before they hit the road. He also told me Zane's been hooking up with Ellie pretty regularly. Dahlia will be happy to hear that, not that she ever had anything to worry about. I was never interested in that chick or any other chick; I haven't even looked at another girl that way since the day I found her again.

Dahlia puts her hands into my back pockets and pulls me closer to her. Slipping my arms around her waist, I inhale her scent and whisper in her ear, "You're killing me—you know that, right?"

I can feel her smile. When she starts nipping at the skin behind my ear, I really think I might lose it. We've been here almost three hours and the whole time she's been torturing me like this. I somehow stupidly agreed to a game of Who Can Hold Out the Longest on the way over here. We were discussing the last time we partied at Smitten's and our poolroom experience, which led to the so-called game.

Then she offered a wager: If I could go the whole night without trying to get her alone, she'd concede that she was the one who had instigated the hot pool-table sex. Then she added two more rules—I wasn't even allowed to say "sex" or "I want you."

"I'll take that bet and throw in coffee runs for the whole week if I lose," I replied.

She laughed. "I highly doubt I'll lose."

"Game on," I told her.

But now my cockiness is starting to wane and I'm not sure I'm going to make it much longer. I keep thinking about the bathroom; maybe she's drunk enough that she won't remember the bet?

The thought of taking her someplace private is driving me insane. I pull back and grab her hand. "Come with me, beautiful girl."

She smiles wickedly and I lead her to the back of the bar. We're only halfway there when my sister taps me on the shoulder. "Hey, there you are."

"Hi, Bell. What's up?"

Dahlia rests her chin on my shoulder and wraps her arms around my waist. "Hi, Bell."

Bell's eyes shift to Dahlia. "Dahlia, I need some advice. Can we talk?"

"Sure. I'll see what I can do." Dahlia steps around me to stand next to my sister.

Bell motions her head over to one of the couches. "In private."

I shoot her an amused look. "Is that a hint? Should I get lost?"

Dahlia tries not to laugh but giggles anyway. "Why don't you grab us some drinks?" Bell starts over to the seating area. Dahlia rubs her nose on mine, moves to kiss me, but bites down on my lower lip instead, and then whispers in my ear, "I think I just won."

Her beautiful eyes are boring into mine and there's a huge grin on her face. I hate to disappoint her, but I have to disagree. "Ummm . . .

that would be a giant negative. I haven't said anything I'm not supposed to and as far as I can see, we're still dressed," I whisper to her.

"Okay lover boy, you want to play it that way? I know where you were headed and so do you, but since you didn't actually say anything I'll let it slide. How about you grab a few rounds of shots?" she says and then turns around to follow Bell.

I have to laugh because I know she thinks if I have another drink, I won't be able to control myself and she'll win. Funny, since I'm not drinking tonight and she hasn't even noticed. I have to stay on my game, plus I want to drive home and not cab it, and lastly and most importantly I want to make sure she has a blast. Tomorrow is the anniversary of her parents' death so I've made it my mission to make tonight as bright as it can be for her.

I'm heading to the bar when I hear the band doing a sound check. Okay, so maybe it will be a little weird to hear them. When I stop to watch them onstage, I see that Garrett is already sitting behind the drums, sticks in hand. Nix is in the corner, throwing the finger at someone. I missed who it was, but I can only guess it was Xander since Nix is now walking onstage with his bass guitar and not his Fender Stratocaster. I know I'm right when Zane hits the stage, holding his twelve-string in the air. Fuck, Nix is going to be hating life if he plays that at every gig.

I look around the bar as the audience migrates toward the stage. When Zane slings his guitar over his shoulder and picks up the microphone, some of the girls start screaming. "Hello, everyone. Nice to meet you!" he says and the girls go crazy. He walks to the edge of the stage and grabs some of the girls' hands. I grin because he seems to really be enjoying the attention.

"I'm not sure if all of you know this yet, but I am the lucky—or maybe it's unlucky—son of a bitch who took the spot for the irreplaceable River Wilde." I'm a little shocked that he mentions me.

"Hey, you okay?" I feel Dahlia's arms go around my waist and she rests her chin on my shoulder in a familiar stance that makes me smile.

I nod to her as the crowd cheers and Zane moves back from the edge of the stage. "We're going to start with a few covers tonight, if that's okay with you?" he asks the audience. They yell and he smiles. He flicks his wrist behind him and Nix starts to play. I know the song immediately and understand why he chose the twelve-string. "So I picked this song because I think this is how I am going to be feeling by the time the upcoming tour is over." Bon Jovi's "Wanted Dead or Alive" blasts through the speakers as the band starts to play together. I'm actually impressed with his performance.

Everyone sings along, including my girl, and as the song ends the crowd rushes toward the stage, waving their hands in the air. He's a hit. I look around for Xander but don't see him. Dahlia hugs me tighter.

Zane raises his hand over his eyes and scans the audience as Garrett and Nix start playing another song I know well. His eyes land on me and he points his finger. "There he is! Hey man, this is for you! And we want you up here now." Xander appears out of nowhere and Dahlia releases me from her embrace. I put my hands out in a *no-thank-you* motion, but Dahlia whispers in my ear, "One last time, baby—do it one last time for them, and for me." *Shit.*

I turn to look at her and her face is so bright there is no way I can say no. She gives me a quick kiss and Xander shoves me forward.

"Enough, lover boy." Then winking at Dahlia he says, "Good one, Muse."

"You knew about this?" She shrugs her shoulders and then puts her hand over her heart and blows me a kiss. God, I love her.

People clap me on the shoulder as I approach the stage. I hop up and Bell hands me my guitar, my simple acoustic—Stella, the guitar named after my dad's favorite singer's daughter, the guitar my dad gave me.

I give her a look and she shrugs her shoulders. "I may have swiped it this morning when I stopped by."

I smile at her. "Thanks, Bell."

Zane approaches me, taking his guitar off his shoulder, and hands me the mic. He goes over to stand behind the keyboard. Nix starts warming up and just like that, I'm on.

"Hey, everyone! Let's do this one last time," I say as I clip the microphone back on the stand and start playing the first eight bars in D. I scan the crowd, looking for my girl, and grin when I spot her. "One, two, one, two, three, four," I say into the mic as I start to sing "Come Together."

Zane joins in before the end of the first verse and during the refrain I watch Dahlia approach the front of the stage. My eyes move over her body and meet hers at the same time hers meet mine. Her smile is so wide that even if I screw up John Lennon's masterpiece, being up here for her is all that matters. She runs her fingers through her hair as I sing the second verse. Every time I sing "shoop" I wish I was hugging her. She starts singing along and I can see her singing "me."

When I start the guitar solo she closes her eyes as if absorbing every single note and I do the same. I open my eyes and she's staring at me. I can feel her love. As I sing the next verse, she runs her tongue over her bottom lip and I have to bite mine to keep it together.

The second half of the song begins and I look over to the side of the stage at Xander. He gives me a nod and smiles, signaling that he accepts my decision to quit the band. I turn around to catch Garrett's eye and then do the same to Nix. They both smile at me and I know we are all cool. I grab the mic off the stand and walk it over to Zane. "You're on, man."

I jam out the rest of the song on my guitar as the crowd cheers us on. When we finish, I sling it around my back, knowing this is the last time I'll be singing with these guys. We've spent our lives practicing and rehearsing together as we moved from garage to garage to this stage and I know that the bond we formed will always remain whether I am part of the band or not. They all gather around me and before I know it we are huddled together; even Xander is up here. The moment we break apart, Zane has a tray of shots in his hands. I'll let myself have one drink. Garrett makes a toast and we all drink to get the lumps out of our throats. Bell and Ena, Xander's new assistant, join in as well. Ena is doing well and Xander doesn't seem quite so grumpy.

I hop off the stage and Dahlia runs over to me and wraps her arms around my neck so I can lift her off the ground and swing her in a circle. When I put her back down she crashes her lips to mine and threads her fingers through my hair. I want to run my hands down every inch of her body, but she pulls away too fast and places her hands on my cheeks. Her eyes flicker over my face as she examines me, like she's looking for something.

"Dahlia, I'm good. Really, I am," I assure her because I know she's concerned I may be regretting my decision.

Once she's satisfied that I'm fine, she leans in and whispers in my ear, "River Wilde, take me home now. I want you."

I know I must be wearing the biggest shit-eating grin. "Dahlia London, I would love to take you home. I want you, too." And I try, I really try not to gloat, but I can't resist. I lean back in and trace the seam of her lips with my tongue before kissing her ear. "Looks like I won and you're on coffee duty for the week." I laugh.

Then she laughs and says, "And don't think I didn't notice you were drinking water all night to stay on your game."

I just shake my head. She knows me so well.

Holding hands, we say good night to everyone. I sling my arm around Dahlia and she tucks her thumb in my back pocket. As we walk out the door together I am more than 100 percent certain that I made the right decision.

We approach my car and she says, "Mr. Lennon, my fiancé won't like me going home with you."

I lean over and whisper to her in my best British accent, "I bet I could kick his ass." She laughs so hard she's hiccupping by the time we get in the car. On the ride home we sing along to Beatles songs, neither of us faltering on the lyrics because we are both avid fans. By the time we get home I'm pretty proud of myself. I managed to stay in control and wait to have her in our bed. I actually have a surprise for her first, though.

When I send her to our room and tell her I'll be right behind her, she looks at me like I have three heads.

"What?" I ask.

She narrows her eyes at me, then heads down the hallway, throwing over her shoulder, "River, I know you're up to something."

I just shake my head. She knows me. I am up to something, but nothing big. Tomorrow is going to be a tough day for her so I want to shower her with my love and just be with her, letting her know she's everything to me. We went through a rough spot. For a long time I was never sure if I would have been her first choice, and doubt shadowed me. When Ben came back, that doubt no longer shadowed me—it loomed large, almost haunted me. My guilt over the things I knew—what I couldn't tell her, what I should have told her the first time I figured it out—sent me over the edge. Every time she saw him it tore me to shreds. I wanted her to choose me but not because of what he did. When I got home that morning after I'd stormed out and read her note, I knew she'd always been mine.

The last few weeks were just as tough but for a different reason—she lost someone again and her pain rips through me. I want to make it go away, make everything right for her, but I know all I can do is be here. So I am. I've kept her busy, mostly delving into our new business. We've got the wheels in motion and I'm hoping before the end of the year to bring on our first client. Of course, my stepfather's knowledge of the business has helped tremendously. Dahlia and I have spent a lot of time over there seeking advice and developing our strategies.

It's amazing how well Dahlia and my mom get along, and although I know she's not looking for someone to take Grace's place, I think she finds comfort in their friendship and honestly so do I. She seems to need a mother figure in her life, and I get it. I've had Xander to help me with what was missing from my life when my father died; my mom had her sister to take care of her when their parents died, but Dahlia only had him . . . Ben. I can say his name now. I no longer view Ben as anything more than someone from Dahlia's past and I can live with that.

Thinking about the two women who mean everything to me, I can't help but notice how very much alike they actually are. It's not just the tragedies they have endured, but the unconditional love they both give to those around them.

Smiling, I open the refrigerator and grab the bottle of champagne and the huge bowl of strawberries I snuck in there earlier. Then I take two glasses out of the cupboard and manage to bring it all to our room. I can hear music playing as I approach the door. It's partially closed and when I open it my jaw drops as I step inside. She's wearing a lacey white number slit up the front and she looks like an angel. "God, you look incredible," I tell her, biting my lip to stop from smiling the biggest grin ever. She's the sexiest thing I've ever seen in or out of clothes and what she's wearing now makes me want to skip everything I have planned.

She cocks her head to the side and she breaks into a grin that takes my breath away. "Come here, so I can love you."

Grinning back at her, she doesn't have to ask me twice. I set my stuff down on the dresser and stride over to her. Embracing her, I run my hands down her silhouette and tell her, "You're the most beautiful creature I have ever seen."

She looks at me. "Creature?"

I shake my head.

"That doesn't sound beautiful," she mumbles.

"It is," I whisper against her lips. I can't even explain to her what I see when I look at her. I must look at her a hundred times a day and each time I find something else, something more beautiful, than the last time I looked. It's not just her physical beauty that captivates me. Honestly, I don't care if she's wearing a ball gown or sweatpants; her beauty is all of her—it's who she is. And I want to spend the rest of my life looking at her, pulling her to me, loving her. I will spend the rest of my life doing all of those things—of that, I have no doubt.

Sliding my hands around the small piece of fabric she's wearing, I nip at her lip. She smiles and tries to catch my mouth with hers, but with each passing minute my body throbs with anticipation. She lifts the hem of my T-shirt, pulling it over my head and I don't waste a second before pressing my bare skin to her. I can never get enough of her. I want her in every way. I don't even know if she realizes how much I want her—no, not want, how much I need her.

My hands skim the lace on her backside and I press her closer to me. We're both breathing pretty heavily by the time she steps back and bats her eyelashes. "Maybe you could offer a girl a drink before trying to seduce her."

Joining in the fun, I say, "Why, of course. Where are my manners?"

Turning toward the dresser, I glance back and take a moment to appreciate the way her eyes watch me, the smile that lights up her face when she sees I'm watching her. I have to bite down on my bottom lip hard to remind myself I have a plan. When I pull the cork, champagne fizzes everywhere. It's like I shook the bottle or something. Shrugging, I let it drip down my bare chest. I look over at Dahlia and her hand is over her mouth like she's trying to stifle her laughter, which makes me laugh. As I pour the first glass, she looks at me with fire in her eyes and my insides blaze. When I pour the second glass, she bites her lip in a way that turns me on even more.

My eyes are fixed on her and before I know it the champagne overflows and spills out of the top of the glass. "I told you, bartending isn't my thing." We both laugh and I wipe up what I can with the T-shirt from the floor. Then after I've dropped a strawberry in each drink, she circles her lips with her tongue and I really think I might explode. I wedge another strawberry on the rim of each glass, because I know she likes two. Her grin widens as I do so and then she says, "Adam or John, whatever your name is, it's not for your bartending skills that I brought you back to my place."

With both glasses in hand, I head back her way. I thought I'd be cool with role-playing, but I have to say, I'm not. The only name I want screamed from my girl's lips is mine. Getting as close as I can without spilling our drinks, I wedge my knee in between her legs and hand her a glass. She gasps at the contact and all I know is that we have way too many layers of clothing between us. I stroke my thumb along her cheek before softly kissing her there. "Have I told you today how much I love you?"

She murmurs, "You have, but don't ever stop. I want to hear it again and again."

We're standing so close that the sound of my pounding heart can only be matched by her quickening breath. She stares at me, her hazel eyes now the darkest brown, with a look that makes me crazy with desire. Taking the strawberry off the rim of my glass, she dips it in the champagne. When she offers it to me, I take a bite, then watch as she does the same. Her tongue licks the berry and then her teeth bite down in a way I think I've felt before. She walks over to set our glasses down on the night table and when she turns around I can't help but stare. My pulse speeds up with every step she takes toward me. She strides from her hips—it's the sexiest walk I've ever seen. When she chews on her lower lip, I want to be the one chewing on it.

When she's close enough I try to scoop her up but she pushes me down on the bed. She doesn't say a word as she hurriedly pulls off my boots and removes my jeans. I sit up and reach for her but she pushes me back down on the bed. I love when she thinks she's in control.

She takes a sip of champagne and when she kisses me I can taste the champagne from her lips. Before I know what's happening, her cold tongue traces the lines of my lower abs. I look down as her lips brush across my stomach and I suck in a breath. When she peeks up at me through her long lashes, my muscles clench.

"I." Another kiss on my stomach and I can feel her smile against my skin. Her hands run over me and I know she's aware of how much I want her. I think she likes making me wait until I'm overcome with need for her.

"Love," she says as she drags her tongue up my chest until I feel like I might explode.

"You," she whispers, nipping at my jaw.

"More," she teases before finally touching her lips to mine, sending a shiver through my core.

More—we say that to each other all the time, but it's not about who loves the other more, it's simply that we love each other more than words can possibly express. And nothing or no one can ever change that.

Her kiss tastes like strawberries, but most of all she tastes like Dahlia and I know I will never get enough of her.

She rises up and I take hold of her. Looking at her, I know what we have will last a lifetime. She's everything I have ever wanted and more. To think I almost lost her still scares the shit out of me. We've both learned a lot over the past month about our relationship and ourselves. I've learned that protecting someone I love by withholding information isn't really protecting them at all. I made her doubt us, made her doubt my trust. I will never do that again. This amazing girl can trust me for a lifetime. She was made for me. And right now I want nothing more than to show her exactly how I feel—to connect our bodies and our souls.

With that thought in mind, I roll us over and rest my forehead against hers. My breathing is so ragged that I have to take a deep breath. Letting it out, I dip my head and graze my lips across her chest. With every soft touch and every warm breath that passes between us I feel our connection more strongly. Kissing her neck, I work my way up to her mouth. She parts her lips slowly and eagerly accepts my tongue's invitation. I'm working on control, on taking it slow, and tonight of all nights I really want to succeed. But I already know that's going to be challenging, if not impossible.

Her hands take fistfuls of my hair. She's tugging on it as if she needs something to hold onto—like she's also looking for a way to pull us closer and make us one. Stroking my fingers along her silky lace panties, I stop and apply pressure in the spots I know she likes. When she moans, I know she's as eager as I am to make love. She wants it bad. I swear I hear her whimper when I stop to lean over the night table and grab a strawberry, then dip it in a glass of champagne. Twisting back to face her I notice how intently she's watching me. Her breathing is much heavier and she's got a huge smile on her face.

I slide the tip of the strawberry from the edge of her panties up between her perfect breasts all the way to her mouth. Placing it between her teeth, I bite down on it and she does the same. I kiss her, licking the excess juice from her lips before tracing my tongue down the champagne trail I left behind.

Unhooking the front of her lingerie, I peel it off her. Her nipples are so hard and tempting and I can't resist quickly circling my mouth over one, licking away the champagne that has dripped there. Her chest rises and falls rapidly and I can tell she wants more. Not wanting to break my momentum, I continue my journey down to what I know she wants.

At her belly button I stop for only a quick second to dip my tongue in and swirl it around. Her body hums with my every touch. Her eyes remain closed and her lips slightly parted. She's fisting her hands in my hair again, and when I slide my tongue into the waistband of her panties her body writhes beneath me. With gentle teasing fingers I pull the lace down until my tongue reaches her soft flesh.

Looking up, she's chewing on her lip again. Her eyes are open and she's watching me. I can see the love and want on her face. Suddenly, I am overcome with the need to have every inch of her all at once. I really want to keep taking it slow and stay in control but it's just so damn hard when she looks at me like that. With a huge grin, I stand up and take my boxers off and then pull her to the center of the bed. Kneeling before her, I rip her panties off and throw them to the ground. Slow can only last so long.

When I press my palms into her soft curves and run them down her naked body, my desire is nearly uncontrollable. I trail kisses along her inner thigh until I reach her slick core. I teasingly blow on her center and watch a shiver run through her body. Spreading her thighs wider, I cover her sex with my mouth and dart my tongue inside her. She tastes like pure heaven; the strawberries and champagne have nothing on this girl. She's amazing. I lick and suck, letting her body react and guide my rhythm. She's panting as she tangles her hands in my hair. Her breathing quickens and watching her body respond to my every touch, taste, and movement intoxicates me. There's nothing that makes me feel the way she does.

"Please don't stop," she begs.

"I'm not stopping. I'm going to leave you breathless, unable to think of anything but me," I growl.

Completely turned on by the signs of her impending climax, I grab her thighs and pull her closer to me. I slide my tongue one last time through her slick opening up to her clit. She's moaning and arching her back. When her hands move to tightly grip the bedsheets and her legs start trembling, I cover it with my mouth and suck greedily, then watch as she falls apart . . . breathing in short bursts, eyes closing, head tilting back, and mouth opening slightly. And finally her thighs turn to steel as her body clenches and waves of pleasure overtake her. She comes hard, screaming my name over and over and I love every minute of it.

Seeing her come takes away any self-control I had left. I'd say I did pretty well. But now I need to be inside her, to feel her warmth, her tightness gripping around me. Once her body calms, I crawl on top of her and look down at her flushed, but still perfect, face. She smiles up at me with hooded eyes.

"That was amazing," she whispers, still trying to catch her breath. "But now I want you deep inside me, I want us to come together."

"Oh, I think that can be arranged, beautiful girl." If only she knew how badly I want to grant her that request. I am rock-hard and I'm not going to last much longer. Reaching down, I slip a finger inside her. She's soaked and when she lets out a small moan, I know she's more than ready for me. I playfully twirl my finger around before I pull it out and easily slide into her, plunging as deep as I can. I groan at the sensation. "You feel so good," I whisper in her ear and then I bury myself deep inside her, the magnitude of my pleasure increasing with even the slightest of movements.

She wraps her arms around me and I kiss her. Now I can taste her and I know she can taste herself—a combination that does more than just turn me on. We move together as one, the intensity building with every thrust. It's a feeling I wish would last forever. In fact, I wish I could stay buried inside of her—there is no place in this world I'd rather be.

Breaking our kiss, I hungrily nip at her jaw and press my mouth down her neck. Thrusting in and out, I give her everything I can and she willingly takes it. I'm trying to hold on, not wanting this feeling to end. But when her head falls back and she arches her body, I tell her, "Come with me."

Her muscles clench and her inner walls tighten around me as she whispers breathlessly, "I'm right here with you."

And that is all I need to hear. Burying my face in her neck, I thrust a few more times and just as I still and start to explode, her body shudders with an intense orgasm that can only be matched by my own. "I love you, Dahlia!" I manage as we come together, sharing the most intimate connection two people can ever know. We're truly one right now—one body, one soul. She's not only mine, she's mine forever.

CHAPTER 30
I Belong to You

River

October 31

The white light creeps in through the window. We left the curtains open last night so we could stare out into the night, admiring the view, and feeling absolutely content—content knowing we will always be there for each other. I know today is the hardest day of the year for her and I want to do everything I can to guarantee she has a smile on her face.

I've been watching her sleep, waiting for her to wake up. I'm lying on my back and she's draped across my chest with her cheek pressed against me and her golden strands pulled back just enough so I can see her beautiful face. With her next to me naked in bed, I can't stop myself from sliding my hands over her smooth skin.

She opens her eyes only the tiniest fraction and kisses my chest. She skims her fingertips down my stomach, stopping to trace lines over each muscle, stoking the heat between us that never dies.

"Good morning," I tell her, kissing her head and smelling the sweet scent of her hair.

"Morning." She nips my skin and sends me over the edge.

Rolling her over, I hover above her and bury my elbows into the pillow. My mouth trails down her neck and she giggles, "You're tickling me."

"Giggling and tickling aren't what I'm going for," I murmur back as I continue to lick and nip her skin.

She pulls my head to hers and when our lips meet I want to devour her, but when I brush my tongue against hers, she laughs. Ignoring the sound, I suck on her bottom lip because I know how much she likes it. When I do, she smirks and stifles any noise that would accompany it. I plop down beside her and rest my head on my elbow. Lifting her chin to look into her eyes I ask, "What are you doing?"

She flutters her eyes. "Why, whatever do you mean?" she answers in her cute fake Southern accent.

Grinning, I say, "I'm trying to make love to you but you seem to be finding it funny."

She pouts her lips and drops her eyes.

"What's wrong, baby?" I ask, grabbing her hand and lacing my fingers in hers, not sure what I did.

She smiles and I swear I feel my heart stop from her beauty. "Nothing's wrong. I'm just waiting to see how long it takes you."

"Well, if you'd let me get started, you'd be able to see." Then raising an eyebrow I ask, "Wait, what exactly are you waiting to see how long it takes for?"

Now she's laughing hysterically and I start to question my manhood. When she settles down she gives me an impish grin. "To say happy anniversary, silly. Not what you're thinking!"

A bright smile spreads across my face. "I guess it's an anniversary of sorts—six years ago today, you stared at me across a bar and look where I am now," I say, trailing my fingers down her bare arm.

She tells me, "Well, I think it went more like this . . . six years ago today you stalked me and look where I am now—in the arms of Jack the Ripper."

Grinning, I remember that first night we met at the USC campus bar and the conversation we had. Then I decide if I'm ever going to concede, this is the time. "Okay, I'll give you that one."

She keeps my hands laced in hers and moves closer to me. She kisses me and then says, "I love you—I thought I loved you from the first moment I saw you in the bar. And I knew I loved you five years later when I saw you in that conference room. But it wasn't until you said that you weren't just kissing me—you were whispering in my mouth—that I fell madly in love with you."

"Did I say that? I'm pretty smooth."

She nods and smirks. Fixing her gaze on me, she seems very serious all of a sudden. She holds my eyes captive. Clearing her throat she says, "You know today has always been the saddest day of the year for me and I was wondering if you would do something to help me change that?"

There's a lead-in that that I would normally pounce on, but I know she's being serious, so of course I don't. Instead, I kiss her hands. "You know I'd do anything for you, Dahlia. You don't even have to ask. Just tell me and it's done."

She looks at me for the longest time before speaking. "Will you marry me today? Make this my happiest day of the year instead of my saddest day of the year?"

Like she really has to ask. I can't even answer her right away because I'm so full of emotion I have to compose myself before saying, "Dahlia, I would have married you at the campus bar that night if you would have asked. You're the only one I have ever really loved; the only one I *will* ever love. You, beautiful girl, are every breath I take. So of course I'll marry you today."

In all honesty there is nothing more I want to do. I'm not the kind of guy to cry but I swear I feel tears in my eyes when I look at the glow on her face. All I wanted to do was make her happy today and all she needs to be happy is for me to marry her—of course I can do that.

She closes her eyes for a moment and when she reopens them she says, "So Vegas it is."

My heart thuds in my chest as I fall to my back and pull her on top of me. "No, I'm done with Vegas. We're getting married nearby and I am taking care of it all."

With her palms flat on my chest, she lifts herself up. She's biting her lip and has a contemplative look on her face.

"What?"

She raises an eyebrow and a small giggle of disbelief escapes her mouth. "You're going to take care of everything?"

I prop myself up on my elbows and meet her gaze. "That's what I said."

"Okay, then." She grins at me and it's decided—today is finally the day and it's mine to plan.

Rolling on top of her so our bodies are perfectly aligned, I lean down to taste her skin. When she rocks her hips into mine I let out a low groan. She feels so good and my urge to be inside her becomes a frenzied need. I lock my lips around her earlobe and whisper, "You can see how long it takes me now, if you want."

She combs her hands in my hair and tugs at my scalp in that way that drives me crazy. When she runs her nose up my neck so I can feel her warm breath against my skin, her lips find mine and she murmurs, "Yes, I want."

It's a little while later and I head downstairs to plan the day—our wedding day. I promise myself that this time we will be married by the end of the day. The wedding may not be traditional in every sense of the word, but I want to make sure we hit the most important parts—the ceremony and of course an unbelievable wedding night. With that in mind, I quickly call my sister and tell her about the wedding. She says she'll be right over but I know if I want something done a certain way I have to stress it over and over, so I repeat myself, "Bell, remember these two words—sunset and simple." But I know she's not even listening as she hangs up the phone.

I'm surprised when she gets here and has already secured the location. And all of her ideas are perfect—except one. As she leaves, I beg her to skip the monkey suit, but she only rolls her eyes and says, "Be at Grandpa's store at noon. Xander will meet you there."

As she's leaving, she yells over her shoulder, "Don't forget to tell Dahlia to meet me at Avery's at one!" I actually haven't been to Grandpa's store since his death. About a year before he died, he had asked all three of us if we were interested in taking over the store, but we were young and that responsibility seemed too daunting so we all declined. Now someone else owns it.

Feeling good about Bell's involvement, I decide to search for my girl to reassure her that it's all under control. She doesn't have to worry about a thing. When I find her ending a call with Aerie, I tell her only a handful of minor wedding details. I want the location to be a surprise. When she looks at me skeptically, I feign offense and then promptly send her off to do whatever it is a woman has to do before getting married. I also have things to do myself. First on my list, write my vows; second, select the most perfect song to dance to; and finally, come up with a plan to make tonight unlike any other night.

My monkey suit shoes are in the closet, and as I look at the laces, I know I will be switching them out for my Adidas. Bell's going to kill me, but those shiny shoes are just not for me. Dahlia's still out and I'm making sure I have everything ready. I jump in the shower and start singing "You Make Loving Fun" because for some reason thinking about last night makes me think about that song. Everything about her amazes me and the simple fact that we can go out and have a great time together no matter what we do just makes me appreciate her even more.

As I'm shaving, I'm humming and singing along. When I look up I see her in the mirror. She's leaning up against the doorframe with the biggest smile on her face. Seeing her carefree and happy like that makes it hard for me to see straight. Twisting around to catch an even better glimpse, she's already walking my way. I meet her in the middle because I can't wait to get my arms around her and feel her body against mine. She slings her arms over my shoulders and I lace mine around her waist. When she runs her fingers through my wet hair, I groan and cup her backside. She rests her head in the crook of my neck and I pull her into me as close as I can and fight back the urge to devour her.

Even our bodies fit together. It's perfection. We're two people meant to be together.

As she nips at the skin on my neck, my resolve to wait to have her is beginning to wane. I had decided earlier that we should not have sex again before tonight. I've booked a room at the Beverly Wilshire and Bell is going to make sure it's filled with everything to make the night special—flowers, champagne, my guitar, and "a few other things," she said. I rolled my eyes at the "a few other things" comment, but thanked her anyway.

Her soft lips touch my shoulder and I breathe her in. She slides her fingers down my bare chest to my towel and I squeeze her tight to me. She tugs at the knot and unfastens it, letting it fall to the ground. When she purrs, "You didn't wait for me to take a shower," a raw heat starts to consume me.

I lean back and try to control the fire raging through my body. "That's because I knew I wouldn't be able to restrain myself if I did that."

She walks me backward until I'm leaning against the counter. When she reaches down her fingers quickly wrap around me and it feels so good. Of course, I was already hard before she even touched me; I was hard the minute I saw her.

"Why would you have to restrain yourself?" she asks while stroking me.

Fighting the urge to rip her clothes off I manage to say through gritted teeth, "Because I thought we should wait until after we're married to have sex."

A deep throaty laugh escapes her lips as her thumb lightly circles my tip and I feel myself swell even more inside her hand. At this point there's no going back.

"Okay, that's sweet and I like traditions, but that tradition only applies if the two people have never had sex."

I grip the counter with one hand and her with the other. She continues to stroke me and I throw my head back. "It's not tradition," I manage to say. "It's one of my rules."

She laughs again. "Okay, I don't get it, but since I always love your rules, I'll be happy to follow your lead." Then she twists her palm over the head of my cock in the way she knows I like. "So I can't do this?"

My voice comes out low and strained as I answer, "No, I mean yes—you can do that."

When she drops to her knees and wraps her mouth around me, she sucks so hard, I can no longer control myself. I close my eyes and just let go. Before I know it, I'm thrusting my hips, clutching her hair with my hands, deciding technically this isn't sex.

For all the complaining I've done about my sister's party planning in the past, I take it all back today. She really outdid herself. She managed to secure the ideal location, compliments of pulling the "my grandfather was a major benefactor" card, she arranged limo transportation, compliments of an old boyfriend and she even had Garrett become ordained so that he could marry us.

Glancing out the window, I see dark clouds are rolling in and I'm hoping it doesn't rain. Dahlia and I are riding together, but I want the location to be a surprise so I have her blindfolded. Getting it on took a little bit of coercing. Of course, she had some smart-ass comments to make about not knowing how kinky I was and then asking what I planned on doing to her once I got the blindfold on. I had all kinds of ideas of what I could do to her, but it was neither the time nor the place.

Although she made fun of me for traditions, she wanted to keep one herself—she didn't want me to see her in her wedding dress until the actual ceremony. So she's wearing the dress Aerie got her the day we were originally going to elope to Vegas. She'll change at the location of the ceremony. And even though I know this isn't her wedding dress, I can't take my eyes off her. She looks so beautiful. But in truth, as gorgeous as she looks right now, I just know that when I see her walking down the aisle, this moment won't compare.

Glancing at her, I notice something on her leg. I run my hand up between her legs, and, even blindfolded, she's a fast catch. She has my hand in hers in a flash. "No, no. You don't get to see that until after we're married."

"Dahlia, I can see it now. I'm not the one with a blindfold on, remember?"

"Oh, I remember. You might be able to see, but no touching."

I creep my fingers back up her leg and she slaps my hand. "No, not now. Remember your rules. I don't want to tempt you into something, so no touching, got it?"

"I got it, beautiful," I say and lean over to kiss her, beyond happy that she's mine. Her lips, her legs, her body, her humor, her everything—she's all mine. "Whatever you say."

Everyone else went ahead of us, but I had a stop I wanted to make first. When the limo comes to a halt, I take her hand and help her out of the car. As I guide her up and we step onto the wooden platform, I already feel the magic of this location. I completely understand why as a child she'd have asked her parents for this as a present. I was uncertain if I should bring her here or not. I didn't want to make her sad by bringing back memories of her parents, but I wanted them to be a part of our special day.

I brace her hands on one of the poles and signal to the operator. When it starts to move, I remove her blindfold. I'm standing right in front of her, but her face is unreadable.

"Are you okay?" I ask.

She lifts her head, staring into my eyes. "I'm more than okay."

And I know it's true. Her eyes dart around, taking in her surroundings, and I get to see this magical fantasy world come to life through her eyes. As the organ music begins and the merry-go-round turns, the prancing wooden horses move up and down and even I feel like they are inviting us to join them.

"May I?" I ask softly as my hands grip her waist and lift her to sit sideways on the colorful moving horse.

She traces her fingertips over my cheek and then motions for me to join her. I quickly hop on behind her and reach around to hold onto her hands on the pole. The mirror plates reflect both of our smiling faces and allow me a glimpse of the twelve-year-old girl who requested this birthday present. We ride in a circle over and over, and occasionally I kiss her neck or press my cheek to hers and every once in a while she leans back into me or rests her head on my shoulder.

As the ride ends, the horses and music stop. But I know the enchantment in our life together never will.

I hop off and see that her eyes are squeezed closed. When she opens them, her smile brightens. She mouths, "Thank you." Then she wraps her arms around my neck and leans into me, softly and tenderly kissing me.

I want to give her a present before we go. Leaning back, I open my jacket and reach inside for the black velvet pouch. "Give me your wrist." When she does I take out the stack of gold and silver bracelets and pull them over her hand to her wrist. She looks at me questioningly. "These were the bracelets Janis Joplin wore at Woodstock. My grandfather was her drummer and she overheard a conversation he was having with someone that his wife was so mad at him because it was their anniversary and he wasn't home. That night Janis sent my grandfather a letter with this pouch telling him these bracelets were made of love from all around the world and she was sure if he gifted my grandmother with them she'd forgive him."

Dahlia looks at me intently. "Did she?"

I laugh. "Of course she did."

She looks at the bangles for a long while and throws her arms around me, the metal jingling. "God, I love you. Thank you so much. They're beautiful."

I hold her. "No, you're beautiful. Are you ready to finally do this?"

"I'm ready to finally do this!" she says as she reaches in my front pocket and snatches the blindfold I stashed there.

"Hey!"

"Hey yourself. It's my turn later," she says with a wink.

I laugh as I take her in my arms and kiss her. Then, hand in hand, we walk back to the limo.

As we pull up to the Griffith Park Observatory, I know Bell made the right choice. Dahlia clasps her hand over her mouth and turns to me to say, "It's perfect."

Xander's new Porsche is parked right in front. I asked him if I could borrow it to drive off in at the end of the night. I just wanted to see if he'd let me take it because since I learned to drive he had a thing about me taking his car. Needless to say I was surprised he said yes—guess he's more of a romantic than I thought.

Aerie and Serena come rushing over and take my girl from me. As she turns and blows me a kiss, her pearls swing from side to side and I can't believe we're actually doing this, it's actually going to happen. Dahlia is finally going to be my wife—Mr. and Mrs. River Wilde. I like the sound of that. I feel like we've waited a long time for this day and I want it to be absolutely perfect, just like my girl.

Breaking my trance, Xander's in my face, shoving me forward, "Bell's on me because you're late, lover boy. So get your ass in gear and stop gawking like a schoolboy."

I just shake my head, glad things are back to normal. Upstairs, I'm floored by what Bell has done to the place. The observation deck, which I have been on a million times, has been transformed into the most beautiful place on earth. White twinkling lights stream from the open window arches, wildflowers cover almost every inch of the room, the makeshift white carpet ends at the center arch with a perfect view of the Hollywood sign, and everyone we care about is here—my mom, Jack, Serena, Aerie, Garrett, Nix, Xander, Bell, and even Zane.

Garrett moves to stand at the end of the carpet and I have to chuckle because he's trying to be so professional. Looking at his watch, he clears his throat and opens his book. My chuckle turns into a laugh when I see the title of the book he's holding is *War and Peace*. But really I'm touched that he has put so much effort into things.

Just as the sun begins to meet the horizon, and the Hollywood sign lights up the sky, Zane starts to play Wagner's "Here Comes the Bride" on the keyboard that Bell set up on the back of the deck with the other band instruments. The Wilde Ones will be playing tonight after the ceremony.

Xander taps me on the shoulder and motions for me to stand near Garrett. As I do, everyone takes a seat. When the song stops, Dahlia comes around the corner and Aerie swiftly joins the others. Dahlia has never looked more beautiful. Her dress is long with a scooped neck and thin straps, exposing her shoulders. She looks sexy as hell in it. Her hair is loose and flowing with a small simple braid keeping her hair out of her eyes and tucked behind her ear. My heart skips a beat as I look at her angelic face. Her expression is a mixture of love and wonder, her eyes are more hazel than I have ever seen them, and her gleaming smile overwhelms me. That one tear that's been welling in my eye finally falls. And I know that I was able to turn her saddest day into her happiest day.

As she stands there waiting for the music to cue again, her mouth drops open when Ryan Ogden starts to sing "I Can't Wait." Jack is a friend of the lead singer from Runner Runner and his song couldn't be more perfect for me to dedicate to my girl. With just his guitar in hand, he starts to sing and she slowly walks down the aisle with the handful of wildflowers I picked for her from her flower garden this morning. A wave of sadness suddenly overcomes me. For one small moment of watching her walk alone, I wish her father were here to walk her down the aisle . . . and then I wish my father were here, too. But I shove those thoughts aside as I move to meet her halfway.

"Hi," I whisper.

"Hi," she whispers back.

My eyes drink her in. She looks absolutely beautiful in her silky long white dress. It hugs her body perfectly, showing off her amazing figure, and I can't help but think she looks like Grace Kelly. But it's the look on her face that sets my soul on fire.

I manage to say, "You look absolutely beautiful."

Her glossy eyes look at me and then she, too, trails her eyes up and down my body. "You look amazing, and I love your shoes," she says with a wink.

Then Garrett clears his throat and we both laugh. As I start to tell her how much I love her, she raises her hand and touches her index finger to my lips and mouths, "Shh."

I kiss her finger and then grab her hand, moving to stand beside her. With our fingers laced together we walk the rest of the way down the aisle.

The ceremony is short. Our vows are a mixture of traditional lines mixed with our own words. Dahlia is surprised when it's time for the ring exchange and I actually have matching wedding bands.

"Where did you get them?" she whispers, a look of utter happiness on her face.

I whisper that I got them on the day we were supposed to first get married. Tears roll down her cheeks and when I show her the inscription on the inside of hers, her hand flies to her mouth. I'll take the happy tears over the sad tears any day. I kiss them away, knowing my life was never really complete until I met her.

Looking into her eyes, they tell me everything I need to know as I slide the ring on her finger and say the words that now touch her skin—"I love you more."

The mood quickly changes from deeply emotional to hysterically funny when Garrett asks, "If anyone here knows why these two should not be wed, speak now or forever hold your peace." I can only assume he printed an old-fashioned copy of a wedding ceremony script off the Internet. He looks around in question and then shakes his head, muttering something I can't make out. Then taking a deep breath, it's finally time. I look into her shining eyes as she says, "I do," and I say the same.

When Garrett announces us as husband and wife, she's finally mine and I get to kiss her for the first time as my wife. I wipe her tears, and while everyone claps, I take her face in my hands. I study her, moving my fingertips gently over her soft lips, etching every detail of how beautiful she looks today into my mind. But I know I don't have to because her beauty is permanently etched into my soul.

So with the sun setting in the west, I kiss her. I pour all my love into this single, most important kiss—the kiss that ties us together forever. I brush my lips against hers, smelling the scent of the wildflowers all around us, and move my hands to pull her closer to me. Her back is bare and I find the soft spot in the middle and press my palms against it. She wraps her arms around my neck and kisses me back with the exact same intensity. When Garrett clears his throat for the third time, we break away, both breathless. I lean my forehead against hers.

"We did it," I whisper.

"We did it!" She smiles and I pick her up and swing her around as she giggles. God, I love that sound.

We spend the next hour taking pictures around the grounds. When we return to the observation deck, other guests have arrived and Nix and Garrett start popping champagne corks. Glasses are being filled and once served, Xander surprises me by clinking his glass with a spoon and making a toast.

Holding his glass up and looking at both of us he says, "If any two people in the world deserve happiness, it's you two. The love you have for each other is something I can only hope I will experience a small piece of one day. To my brother, I want you to know that I admire you for always going after what you want, and although I may not always show it, I really do love you. And to my new sister-in-law, it wasn't long ago that you said to me you'd keep hoping and wishing for the day I'd say I love you. Well, that day came a long time ago; I just didn't tell you so I'm telling you now. Muse, thank you for making my brother so happy. I love you."

We all clink our glasses and my eyes lock on Xander's, silently thanking him. He's with a date. Her name is Amy and he's dated her off and on for years but I know he doesn't love her. I hope he's lucky enough to find a girl like mine someday—because he deserves this kind of love. I know he had it once.

Looking around at the rest of my family, I don't see a dry eye among them. Looking sophisticated in her party dress, Bell comes over with Mom and I motion to Xander to join us. Jack follows and as we clink our glasses again my mom says, "To our family . . . may it grow and change, but never break apart."

"My turn, my turn," Bell insists and she makes the next toast. "To River and Dahlia, I love you both. And thank you so much for letting me plan your dream wedding with less than a day's notice. No, but really, thank you. It did get me a full-time job with Tate Wyatt . . . my new boyfriend, and an assistant to boot," she says, pointing over to a girl I hadn't noticed, directing some waiters where to put their trays of food. Raising our glasses, we laugh and congratulate her on her new job and her new boyfriend. The music starts to play and the family moment is broken. But I'm so appreciative of how easily Dahlia was welcomed by all of them and so thankful to have them. I watch Xander head back over to Amy and think how funny it is that he admires me. He was the strong one, the one who took the road that was right for him from the start, not the road that our father wanted him to take.

Looking around, Zane approaches Aerie and she seems to be asking him to do something with the cake because he picks it up and moves it. But she doesn't seem to be happy with its location—she's shaking her head no and pointing to a different table. Zane, looking fed up, picks it back up and sets it down where it was to begin with— who knows what's going on? Even the cake itself makes me laugh because it has big purple flowers all over it—thanks to my sister still insisting that dahlias only come in the color purple.

With the party in full swing, I can finally get Dahlia alone. I pull her aside and lead her down the stairs. Most people come to the Griffith Park Observatory to look up at the stars and planets and to gaze at the picture-perfect view of the Hollywood sign. But tonight I only have eyes for my wife, my soul mate.

When we get to the bottom of the stairs, I open the door and lead her to the large white fountain in front of the building. Looking into her eyes and then at the fountain, I reach into my pocket and pull out two pennies.

Handing one to my wife, I grin before asking her, "Do you remember the rules?"

In her cute Southern accent she says, "You know what, kind sir, I think I do but maybe you'd better remind me."

"I'd be happy to. First, we both turn around. Then, on the count of three, we both throw the coins over our shoulders into the fountain while making a wish."

She pulls me closer to her and says, "You look so adorable when you explain your rules, I just wanted to watch you explain them again."

I shake my head. "Again, adorable isn't what I'm going for."

She pulls me to her and drags her tongue along the inside of my lower lip. "Adorable turns me on."

"Adorable works, then," I groan and just then the sky opens up and it starts to rain.

"Come on, let's do this before the rain really starts to come down."

Quickly, we both turn around and holding my fingers up, I say, "One, two, three," and then yell, "Go," and we toss our coins over our shoulders and into the fountain.

I grab her hand. "Let's make a run for it."

But she lets my hand go and bends down to take her shoes off.

"Dahlia, what are you doing? You're going to get soaked."

"Taking my shoes off."

"I can see that. Why?" But I already know why. God, I fucking love her.

"Because, silly, I want to jump in the puddles," I say, right along with her. I clearly remember the day I watched her do this very same thing and just as I did then, I watch her with amazement and wonder.

And as the raindrops turn into tiny wishing wells gathering all around her, the same overwhelming urge to grant this girl her every wish doesn't terrify me anymore. I now know the connection we share can never be broken—I know without a doubt that I will be her happily ever after.

After she jumps from puddle to puddle, she closes her eyes and raises her arms out to the side. She tips her head back and spins in circles as I join her. When I hear the band cue up the song I selected for our dance, I draw her in close to me and rest my fingers on her hips. Taking her face in my hands, I kiss her hard. She wraps her arms around my neck and I feel lost in her, lost in her touch, her soul, her love. But it's not a kind of lost where you want to be found.

Slowing down, I never break our kiss as I concentrate on making sure it conveys how much I truly love her. When she starts to quiver I lean back and just stare at her—she's everything I have ever wanted, everything I need. Pulling her body close enough to mine so that our hips are cradled together, I start swaying to the music and ask, "Beautiful girl, will you dance with me?"

She smiles at me, nodding her head. Looking at her now, I know I will always give her a reason to smile. She deserves that. As the song "Waiting for a Girl Like You" starts to play, we surround each other. We rock back and forth and I sing the lyrics to my wife, the words that are so perfectly fitting for the way I feel about her.

When the song ends, I slide my nose to her ear and whisper, "A long time ago, I wished for you and now I have you. See . . . wishes really do come true even if you tell someone your wish."

Standing in the pouring rain, I place my hand behind her neck and gather her in close to me. When her lips meet mine, we kiss with a passion that only she has ever made me feel and it's exhilarating and mind-blowing at the same time. Sliding my hands down her bare back, I look into her eyes and this time I ask, "What did you wish for just now?"

With her hands tangled in my hair she says, "Only for you, always. You're the only thing I want to wish for. From the day I met you my life changed . . . the way you make me feel can't be put into words. You make me smile in a special kind of way . . . you brighten my world . . . you make me fall more in love with you every day. I love you forever, I love you more, River Wilde. You turned my life into a fairy tale and I don't need to wish for anything else as long as I have you."

Her words sear me; just knowing she feels like that makes me shiver. With my hands pressed against the bare spot on her back I tell her, "That's one wish I guarantee is granted. I love you, Dahlia Wilde. You turned my life from ordinary to extraordinary. You're perfect, really."

ACKNOWLEDGMENTS

"Where words fail, music speaks."

—Hans Christian Andersen

My thanks to the artists and musicians who inspired me through every chapter. Music is a world within itself. It is a language we all understand. And although I hope the words in this book do not fail you, I also hope the music helps to enhance them. Music speaks to me, tells me a story, and when I listen to songs, I listen to that story. . . . I hope I have succeeded in telling you a story that was brought to life through both words and music.

This section is by far the most difficult to write because it is so very important to acknowledge all of those who have never wavered in their support of not only myself, but of the Connections Series as well.

First and foremost, I have to thank Kimberly Brower of Book Reader Chronicles. She not only beta-read *Torn*, she did so much more. Her willingness to motivate me and talk me through every difficult scene contributed tremendously to me being able to complete this book. Thank you so very much. You've become a lifelong friend.

I would also like to thank my other beta readers:

Christine Bezdenejnih Estevez of Shh Mom's Reading for taking the time to read and reread, always making suggestions on what could be improved.

Becky Nicklus of Reality Bites! Let's Get Lost! beta-read *Torn* and messaged me this while reading: "I keep thinking of the saying 'after the wedding the marriage begins' and it kind of holds true for falling in love as well, because that is the easy part. It is after that the relationship begins and all the work that comes with it. And that is definitely what *Torn* is about for me. I don't know if that made any sense at all but it did in my head! LOL." Becky, it made perfect sense! Thank you.

Mary Tarter of Mary Elizabeth's Crazy Book Obsessions for your overwhelming support from day one. Thank you for all your help and for your friendship—both of which I truly value.

In addition, I would also like to thank my test readers: Jennie Wurtz, Kristina Amit, Liis McKinney, America Matthew, Trisha Rai, Jody O. Fraleigh, Laura Hansen, Nikki Groom, Deb Tierney, and Ellie Lovenbooks.

To Aestas—thank you for reading and pointing out what I didn't clearly see. I truly appreciate it and with your feedback I hope I was able to make it better.

To Aerie again for spending countless hours on my visuals helping me promote both *Connected* and *Torn*.

To B&X for agreeing to appear on the cover of my book again. You are an amazing couple and I am so glad I've had the opportunity to get to know you.

To Amy Tannenbaum of the Jane Rotrosen Agency, who believed in *Connected* enough to sign me and then dedicated the time to help me throughout the writing of *Torn*. You are such an amazing person and I couldn't be more grateful to have you as my literary agent.

To Penguin. When I began this journey with *Connected*, I never imagined I would land a publishing deal. So thank you, Kerry Donovan and the team at NAL, for so eagerly and enthusiastically taking me on and helping get book two of the Connections series published.

To all of the bloggers who have become my friends—you're all so amazing and I cannot possibly put into words the amount of gratitude I have for each and every one of you!

And finally, my love and gratitude to my family—to my husband of twenty years who became Mr. Mom while continuing to go to work every day, to my children who not only took on roles that I for many years had always done—laundry, grocery shopping, cleaning—but always asked how the book was coming and actually beamed to their friends when telling them their mom wrote a book.

Without the help of those mentioned above, plus all of the support from my readers who have contacted me daily since *Connected*'s release, the writing of *Torn* wouldn't have been possible—a giant thank-you to all of you.

Kim Karr lives in Florida with her husband and four kids. She's always had a love for books and recently decided to embrace one of her biggest passions—writing.

CONNECT ONLINE
www.authorkimkarr.com
facebook.com/authorkimkarr
twitter.com/authorkimkarr

$\mathscr{The}$ magic of rock and roll—it casts a spell on you. I'm no exception. I'm a band manager and I'm living the dream, touring with the Wilde Ones, helping them secure their well-deserved place in the music industry. I love being a part of it all, especially watching the band perform live—the crowds, the cheers, the music. It's a high and a low all at once, and I wouldn't trade it for anything. Every step of the way with this band has been fun, exciting, stressful—every possible emotion. Obviously we've had some breaks, but mostly we all put in a lot of hard work—myself, Garrett Flynn, Phoenix Harper, River Wilde, and now Zane Perry.

"Can you hear me now?" he bellows.

I nod my head as my heart pounds in my chest. My hands feel cold and clammy, and a nervousness that makes me weak and shaky takes over. Doubts race through my head, and I'm questioning if he's going to make it through this. A vague awareness that something bad could happen kicks around in my mind, and I can't shake it. The Wilde Ones are doing a sound check on stage, and Zane's not on his game.

It's July and the weather has been brutally hot. But today it seems cooler. Maybe it's the California weather; maybe it's the excitement of being home. The Beautiful Lies tour bus finally rolled back into our home state of California after six months away. When we pulled into the amphitheater, we could see tanned kids in board shorts and bikini tops already lined up at the will-call window. Security guards in polo shirts directed us to the artists' parking lot, and we were officially home. Tonight, we'll be headlining our biggest show to date. We're on tour without River, and still more than half of the shows are sold out, including tonight's. The album is on its way to gold, maybe even platinum, status. The songs on the album were written and sung by River, but are performed in concert by Zane. Having him as my brother's replacement has been the key to our successful transition in a world where replacing leads is normally unsuccessful—simply put, we're lucky as hell to have him.

River promised to make a surprise appearance at our next stop. It's going to be epic.

But tonight is all about Mountain View and the Shoreline. "That's enough," I yell to the band, and call rehearsal. This place is the biggest outdoor venue we've played, and I couldn't be more stoked—or more nervous. A sold-out show and a rocking opening band—what a combination. But a lead singer with another cold, and a weakened voice that can't be heard throughout an amphitheater, scares the shit out of me.

I head straight for the bus and spend the next few hours with Nix, hashing out a song, which he calls a jumbled mess of muscular sense and big-riff sunshine—whatever the hell that means. All I know is that it needs help, and that's why he's turning to me. I hadn't played guitar since I was eighteen, but for some reason, over the course of this tour, I've picked it back up. At first I used whatever was lying around, but last month, I had my mother mail my old one to me and it feels like home. It's a light-blue-and-brown Gibson, and I had to have it because it was the guitar that Slash played on. Playing again seems to help pass the time and brings a calm over me that I haven't felt in a while.

Hours pass, and before I know it, it's almost showtime. We make our way over to the amphitheater, do the typical festival schmooze fest, and then settle back to wait. Waiting for them to take the stage is always the most nerve-racking time. I'm sitting in the practically vacant makeshift meet-and-greet area backstage and sipping a beer in a worthless effort to calm my nerves, when a voice travels through the sound system. It's a powerful and emotive mezzo-soprano range that is nothing short of explosive. She sounds unlike any singer I've ever heard before—with only one exception: Ivy Taylor. I can't see her on-stage, but I know that the voice belongs to Jane Mommsen. Her band, Breathless, is playing right before the Wilde Ones.

A hand on my shoulder startles me. I twist and glance up as Amy sits down beside me, crossing her legs. "Hi, Xander. I thought I saw you earlier at the hotel."

She's a beautiful woman—long, wavy dark hair, petite figure, very natural looking. She's wearing jeans, a blue shirt with some kind of foil design, and silver sandals. Grinning at her I say, "Finally, we can catch up. Can I get you a drink?"

"I'd love that. How's life on the road been?"

"You know, it has its ups and downs, but it's actually not bad. You?"

"Jane's been going full-force for a while now. But the tour ends with the summer. I'll be glad to be back in LA."

Standing up, I laugh. "I know the feeling. I'll be right back. Let me grab us that drink." Tossing my empty bottle, I make my way to the coolers lined up under the tent and grab two beers. I know she'd rather have a glass of Chardonnay, but beer it is. Amy is Jane's assistant and I've taken her out more than a few times. We went to high school together, and Amy and I know most of the same people, so whenever I need a date, I ask her. Last time I saw her was almost nine months ago, when I took her to River and Dahlia's wedding.

Heading back to the table, I hear Jane yell out to the crowd, "Are you ready for three of the hottest guys in music?" The audience starts screaming and the stage lights dim, cuing the guys that it's the fifteen-minute countdown until they take the stage. The band huddles together in their typical preperformance stance. I'll have a quick drink with Amy and then join them. As I hand her the bottle, my fingers touch hers and we both grin, knowing that we will end up alone by the end of the night.

"You sticking around for the whole show?"

"I think I might." She smiles.

"How about we ride back to the hotel together and grab a real drink at the bar?"

"Sounds like a plan."

"Great. Time for me to get back to work."

She rises from the table. I do the same. She stands up on her toes and kisses me quickly on the lips. "See you tonight." She smiles.

"Catch you later," I say, and then cross the room to join the band.

"You're late," Nix snickers. "What's with you two anyway?"

I shrug my shoulders. "Nothing. We casually see each other once in a while."

Garrett raises an eyebrow. "Chicks are never cool with casual."

Shaking my head at him, I don't bother to disagree. Amy and I have been doing this for years. It works for her and for me. We like each other's company, but we only see each other sporadically. I'll call her once in a while and we'll go out, but we are in no way exclusive. I don't ask her about other men, and she doesn't ask me about other women.

I grab the bottle and pour the amber liquid into the shot glasses stacked on the cap. It's our preshow routine. A shot and a prayer, so to say. It's Garrett's turn tonight to "pray," so this should be good.

He raises his glass. "Here's to hoping Xander gets laid so he'll get off our backs."

Tipping my glass back, I quickly down the amber liquid. It burns as it makes its way down my throat. Once we've all drunk our two-shot maximum before a show, Garrett follows his toast up with "Seriously, man, you need to get laid."

The guys laugh and I actually join in. Jerking off in the small bathroom on the bus is definitely one of the downsides of touring. I've slept with a few girls at some of our stops, but screwing groupies isn't really my thing. I'm not one to have time for a girlfriend, but I'm also not about to pull my dick out backstage, so it's been a long six months.

Zane coughs after he slings back the shot, and I look at him with concern. "You're going to a doctor tomorrow."

He shakes his head. "Yes, Mom, if you say so."

"I'm not kidding. Your voice sounds like shit."

"It's a fucking cold. I took some medicine. I'll be fine."

"Doctor. Tomorrow. I mean it. I'll have Ena set it up."

"I can always sing," Garrett chimes in, and I smack the back of his head.

"Hey. I can."

The lights start to flicker, and I look at Zane with that feeling of uneasiness again. Second time this tour he's coughing and hacking. We're screwed if he really gets sick. He nods at me as I pat him on the back. Slinging his guitar over his shoulder, he heads out first, raising his arm in the air. The crowd goes crazy. The six-foot guy is a chick magnet, and no one misses my brother tonight. Garrett heads out next, yelling, "Great to be here, Mountain View!" and Nix follows with his trademark nod. Zane skips his normal charming banter, and I know he must be saving his voice. Again, I think about how we're fucked if he gets sick.

I stand at the edge of the stage all night, until they finally come to their last song. "It Wasn't Days Ago" is a simple but crowd-affecting ballad, and Zane belts it out. Shouts from nearly thirty thousand fans call for an encore. Turning away from the microphone, Zane coughs again. Biting his thumbnail, he looks over at me, and I slice my finger across my neck.

"One more song for tonight," he tells the screaming fans, and my blood pressure rises. "This one is a cover, an 'ode to' I'll call it. It's for Xander Wilde, the band's manager, and it's his favorite song. Everyone ready?" As he starts to sing Linkin Park's "Iridescent," I close my eyes and listen. When he hits the chorus, his voice gets so low my eyes snap open. Zane turns to grab a bottle of water while the guys continue to play, but I can tell something isn't right.

Last night definitely didn't go as planned—a visit to the ER, then sleeping in a chair next to Zane all night on the bus because the steroids he was given freaked him out. It's noon, and Amy and I are just arriving at the Pelican Hill Resort. Breathless was leaving right after the show last night, so Amy had already planned to ride with us and meet up with them in Irvine. She invited me to some party being thrown by her band's label, which I would rather not go to, but Ellie, the tour manager, insisted we all go for the good PR.

I'm exhausted and really need some sleep before dealing with the press and tomorrow night's show. The paparazzi have been everywhere—by the bus as we exited to the waiting car in LA, outside the doctor's office, at the gates of Zane's father's house, and now they're here, in Irvine at the hotel.

To avoid the chaos awaiting us in the lobby, I call Ellie, who is already here, and ask her to check me in and meet me at the pool bar with the key. Draping my arm around Amy, we head that way. I've been here a few times, so I know my way around. Cutting through the grotto and over to the pool and the cabanas, I steer Amy to the right and stop in my tracks as all the air rushes from my lungs.

My body floods with adrenaline and my gut twists. I don't even have to do a double take because I'd know her anywhere. There's no mistaking her. She's just so beautiful—the elegant planes of her face, those high cheekbones, the red lipstick, her platinum blond hair shorter than it used to be and tucked behind her ear, that face of an angel. She looks the same. No, she looks better. Her skin glistens in the sun, and my gaze automatically follows the shape of her long legs. They look smooth and tan against her white bathing suit. An ache forms in my chest as I think about running my fingers up them. She's still that eighteen-year-old girl I once knew, but now she has the body of a woman—lean and toned and full of curves. When she moves, it's so familiar, it doesn't seem like a day has passed—and everything I ever felt for her, it's all still inside me.

My pulse races at the mere sight of her. She's lounging in the cushioned chair, reading a magazine, just outside a cabana. My heart slams harder in my chest when she sticks her earphones in her ears like she always used to do, and it transports me back to the last time I saw her do the very same thing. We'd skipped school and were at my grandparents' house—their pool. She was lying on the lounge chair, listening to music and singing along—her voice so full of soul. I'd moved to sit with her under the guise of putting lotion on her back. She sat up and smiled that shy smile she didn't need to have when she was with me. I squeezed the lotion into my hand, and after rubbing my hands together, I slowly applied it to her back, kneading my way up and down, touching every inch of her that I could.

It brings me back to the here and now, when she suddenly sits up and looks over at me. Her eyes pin me in place. She looks at me as if she remembers me for who I was, what we were, not what I did to her. With my chest pounding, memories of us keep flashing through my mind. Fighting a smile, I wonder if she's thinking the same thing—remembering what we were, what we shared, how we loved.

She quickly breaks our connection when she averts her eyes over to the man handing her a drink. I suck in a deep breath, trying not to feel sick at the sight. He's nearing fifty, wearing a terry-cloth robe. He's about my height, dark brown hair, meticulously groomed facial hair, and not exactly ripped but fit. He's Damon Wolf, a man I've never actually met but hate all the same. I've seen their picture on TV and in magazines. He's her agent, her fiancé, and I'm sure he's the reason she's not singing anymore.

She looks up at him with that same forced smile she used to give people she just wanted to appease and mouths, "Thank you." I have a sudden urge to go over and deck him when her gaze shifts back to mine and he pulls her chin back to look at him. I can sense a discomfort between them. We could sense each other's feelings even when we weren't near each other.

Amy's hand slides down my face, and I have to blink a few times before I can hear what she's saying. Glancing one last time at Ivy, I see that she's staring at me again. Then suddenly, her mouth forms a scowl and she flicks her attention toward Damon. Hooking her arm around his neck, she pulls him down for a kiss, and I think I might throw up.

"Are you okay?"

I nod. Not able to say a word.

"Isn't that Ivy Taylor over there? The girl you used to date in high school?" Amy asks. There's an irritated tone to her voice that I'm not used to hearing, and it makes me agitated.

"Yeah, it is." That's all I say. She's not just a girl I used to date; she's the only girl I've really loved, a girl I've never forgotten. She's the girl whose heart I broke—and she's the girl I'd do anything to have back in my life.

"I think that's Damon Wolf with her. We should go say hi."

My body goes cold and my face blank at the thought. I straighten, and just as I'm about to say, "No fucking way," my phone vibrates in my pocket. Squinting at the screen, I see that it's my brother. I look over to Amy and motion toward the bar. "Hey, this is River. I need to take it. I'll meet you over there in a minute."

"That's fine. We can catch up with them later. I'll go order us a drink." She smiles and starts toward the bar.

Turning around to avoid staring at Ivy, I answer the phone. "It took you long enough to call me back."

"I was in a meeting and stepped out as soon as I could, so don't start. What did the doctor say about Zane?"

"He's out for the rest of the tour and we're fucked."

"You sure? You're back in LA for almost two weeks after tomorrow night, right? Isn't that enough time for him to heal?"

"Technically, yes. But his old man wants him out. The doctor said that he couldn't be sure how long the blood that accumulated under his vocal cords had been there, but obviously last night, the amount of ruptured vessels was enough to cause his voice to change. He advised at least two weeks of rest before another evaluation to see if surgery is necessary. Zeak wants his son to take a longer period of time off. He's just afraid that if Zane keeps singing and it keeps happening, scar tissue will build up and cause his voice to change forever."

"Do you blame him?"

"No, I don't," I tell River, and I feel like shit that I have to put him in a position to do what he didn't want to do in the first place. But I also know that if I don't, the band won't survive. If I have to cancel this tour, the Wilde Ones are done. So I ask, "Did you talk to Dahlia?"

He sighs. "Yeah, I did. She's cool with it, Xander. I'm just trying to figure it all out."

"You know I'll do whatever you need me to do, right?"

"Shit. Why can't you just be an ass and make it easy for me to say no?"

"Because you have no idea what this means to me."

"Actually, I do, and that's why I'm going to make it happen. But, Xander, remember I can't play a twelve string."

Laughter and relief take hold of me. I feel a huge weight lift off my shoulders. "Right now, I wouldn't care if you only played the violin," I joke.

He laughs and I add, "You'll be here tonight?"

Now he sounds slightly annoyed. "I said I would. We might be a little late, so don't get your panties in a wad."

"That's cool. Thanks for everything. Hey, one more thing."

"What?"

"Ivy Taylor's here."

"No way. Have you talked to her?"

"Fuck no. You know she won't talk to me. And besides, she's with that asshole."

"You should talk to her. Tell her the truth."

"What's that going to do now? She'll just think I'm lying."

"You want me to talk to her? I can explain everything."

"No. I don't need my little brother to fight my battles. I'll talk to her if I feel the time is right. Do you hear me?"

"Whatever you say. Look, I have to run but I want to discuss this later. And, Xander . . . you don't know he's an asshole. Just because Dad said his name once doesn't mean shit."

"Right. Okay, see you tonight," I say, and end the call. My head is spinning, knowing that after all these years, I'm actually in the same place she is. I want to talk to her, tell her everything, but what would it matter now anyway? Glancing behind me, I catch another glimpse of her with him that turns my stomach. He's such a slimeball. Since his father was hospitalized and he took over the business, he's been scooping up labels, tearing them apart, and rebuilding them with bands he thinks are better fits. My guess is that he picked up Jane's label—that's why he's here. I heard they were having some financial difficulty, and he's just the kind of bottom-feeder who would want to capitalize on not only being her agent, but now also her producer. The sight of him touching Ivy makes my skin crawl.

Damon Wolf—two of the last words my father ever spoke to me before killing himself, and I never knew why. Of all the guys in the world Ivy had to end up with—why him? I look up and they're gone. But I'm anything but relieved. Rubbing my chin, I'm antsy, agitated, pissed as hell, but feeling more alive than I have in years.